Praise for L

'Gives Harlan Coben and [...] their money'

MARK BILLINGHAM

'A psychological thriller of superior style and plotting. Riveting!'

LIZ NUGENT, ON *TRUST IN ME*

'Breathes new life into the psychological thriller genre with a captivating and gripping storyline . . . Everything I look for in an action thriller. I couldn't put it down'

C.L. TAYLOR, ON *YOU NEVER SAID GOODBYE*

'A barnstorming, rocket-paced thriller about an ordinary man thrown into an extraordinary situation. Fans of John Connolly and Linwood Barclay will love it'

MARK EDWARDS, ON *YOU NEVER SAID GOODBYE*

'I've been a fan of Luca Veste's books since the beginning . . . Totally gripping!'

C.M. EWAN

Luca Veste is the author of several police procedurals and standalone crime novels including *You Never Said Goodbye*, *The Bone Keeper* and *The Six*. He is the host of the *Two Crime Writers and a Microphone* podcast and the co-founder of the Locked Up festival. He plays bass guitar in the band The Fun Lovin' Crime Writers. He lives in Liverpool, with his wife and two daughters.

Also by Luca Veste

Trust in Me
You Never Said Goodbye
The Six
The Bone Keeper

LUCA VESTE

The Stranger in the Room

HODDER &
STOUGHTON

First published in Great Britain in 2025 by Hodder & Stoughton Limited
An Hachette UK company

The authorised representative in the EEA is Hachette Ireland, 8 Castlecourt Centre, Dublin 15, D15 XTP3, Ireland (email: info@hbgi.ie)

This paperback edition published in 2025

1

Copyright © Luca Veste 2025

The right of Luca Veste to be identified as the Author of the Work has been asserted by him in accordance with the Copyright, Designs and Patents Act 1988.

All rights reserved. No part of this publication may be reproduced, stored in a retrieval system, or transmitted, in any form or by any means without the prior written permission of the publisher, nor be otherwise circulated in any form of binding or cover other than that in which it is published and without a similar condition being imposed on the subsequent purchaser.

All characters in this publication are fictitious and any resemblance to real persons, living or dead, is purely coincidental.

A CIP catalogue record for this title is available from the British Library

Paperback ISBN 978 1 529 35744 8
ebook ISBN 978 1 529 35741 7

Typeset in Plantin Light by Manipal Technologies Limited

Printed and bound in Great Britain by Clays Ltd, Elcograf S.p.A.

Hodder & Stoughton policy is to use papers that are natural, renewable and recyclable products and made from wood grown in sustainable forests. The logging and manufacturing processes are expected to conform to the environmental regulations of the country of origin.

Hodder & Stoughton Limited
Carmelite House
50 Victoria Embankment
London EC4Y 0DZ

www.hodder.co.uk

In memory of two of the best people I will ever know . . .

Nick Johnson – 03.06.1961 - 14.12.2023

*Thank you for all the laughs, the pantos, and the cheesecakes.
You will be forever missed.*

Cath Hale – 18.08.1958 - 11.02.2024

Thank you for being so kind, so welcoming, and so generous.

The Night He Died

There was nothing wrong with Ben Lennon's life.

Not after he'd finally broke up with her. He was free. Heading to university, without anything tying him down.

No worries, no strife. It was easy.

Life was good.

He was smiling as he walked home. Only a bit buzzed, not properly pissed. He'd spent the previous few hours with a bunch of his mates, drinking a few cans down on the dips. People had come and gone – drifting in and out, as always happened.

There had been one bad moment, when *she* turned up, but he wasn't worried about that now. It was over. And she knew that. It had been fun while it lasted, but it was never going to be forever. She should have known that.

Besides, he should never have got involved with her in the first place. Everyone had told him that. Didn't matter that she was one of the nicest-looking girls in sixth form – she came with too much baggage.

He'd been walking alone for a few minutes – breaking away from everyone else, as they headed home. Only a few streets to navigate and 25% battery left on his phone. Enough to get him back. He popped in his Buds and fired up Spotify.

It was two a.m., but that was okay. His parents wouldn't notice him coming home that late. And probably wouldn't be too pissed off about him blowing off some steam anyway.

School was done for summer. He was eighteen. An adult. He'd slip inside without them knowing a thing.

It was all good.

The street was black. Houses closed up, people fast asleep behind closed blinds and curtained windows. A Tuesday night in suburbia. The only sound, his feet against the pavement, his keys jangling in his jacket pocket.

Inside his head, it was loud. Music blaring into his ear canals, too loud to notice anything around him. Only Drake, morphing into J. Cole. The bass and rapid-fire lyrics the only soundtrack to the short walk home.

He had his phone in his hand, as his Spotify playlist filled his ears. Instagram notifications being ignored, Snapchat messages disappearing.

Ben felt something in the air change. He ignored it. The hairs on the back of his neck raised, his senses trying to tell him something, but he wasn't interested.

He was five hundred yards from home. He couldn't see the house yet, but he wouldn't have been looking for it anyway.

This was a walk he'd done a thousand times.

A breeze picked up, but he barely felt it. His jacket rippled in the wind, but he didn't pull it tighter around him.

He was humming softly along with the music in his head.

A few hundred yards from home now. Down the alleyway, that separated this road from his own. Away from the houses for a few seconds. A cut-through he'd taken a million times in the past.

Back to his bedroom, his PS5 still on pause, waiting for him to pick up the controller. A bottle of orange juice waiting in the fridge, waiting for him to grab and drink straight from. A bag of crisps, half-full on the kitchen island nearby, waiting for him to dip his hand into.

Life was good.

Until it wasn't.

The breath on his neck wasn't enough for him to turn around. The shift of weight, the raise of the hammer.

He didn't hear the sounds of anyone behind him. Only the rhythmic beat of music, destroying his hearing little by little.

No.

The first moment of realisation came to Ben when the ground was suddenly rushing towards him. When one of his Galaxy Buds popped out of his ear and clattered to the ground.

When he hit the tarmac and his phone flew from his hand and disappeared into the darkness.

He couldn't breathe – his chest bearing the brunt of the impact and knocking the wind out of him.

Ben didn't feel the pain in his skull at first. The hammer that had crashed into the back of his head an unknown quantity.

He would never know what it was that hit him.

He couldn't focus, the world blurred around him. As Kanye spoke-sang in his left ear, he made a sound. It wasn't words. It wasn't screams.

It was a moan.

An athletic young guy, six foot two in height, and in good shape. Young.

He should have been able to fight back.

He should have been able to quickly get back to his feet and at least put some distance between himself and whoever had attacked him.

Ben tried to right himself, just as the next blow came. A thud of impact into the side of his face.

This shouldn't be happening, was all he could think. He had to move.

Only, his mind wouldn't cooperate. His body even less willing.

He could only lie there, as blow after blow landed. Not a sound to be heard. Not a face to recognize in the darkness.

Not a reason why this was being done to him.

Life had been good to Ben for so long.

His death was the complete opposite.

It took a long time for Ben to stop trying to move. To stop trying to get any words out.

To stop trying.

His phone was taken from the ground where it had fallen. His watch lifted from around his wrist.

He was left with his music, slowly fading away, as the Bluetooth connection became weaker and weaker.

Ben died listening to Kid Cudi.

Ben died for the worth of a Samsung Galaxy S24 and a Breitling watch his grandparents had bought him for getting into university.

Only, it wasn't those things he had been killed for, of course.

He would never know that.

Ben died not knowing why he hadn't seen it coming.

1

There's no roadmap for being told your child has died. No guidebook, no list of dos and don'ts.

They don't hand you a manual when your kid is born, with a small section near the back in case they don't come home one night.

That's the bit that's not supposed to happen.

I knew something was wrong the moment the doorbell rang. Granted, it was four in the morning, so that was enough to push the idea that something was wrong, of course.

For a brief second, my mind had tried to trick me into believing it was just Ben, having forgotten his key. He'd been going out later and later in the previous few weeks, now the school year was over. Pushing the boundaries that didn't really exist anymore. He was eighteen, about to go off to uni. An adult, I guessed. A man.

I opened my eyes carefully, Greg not having moved an inch as the Ring doorbell chimed around the house. His light snoring didn't skip a beat.

I blinked a few times, but was already awake. Being a light sleeper was both a blessing and a curse. It meant that I was always ready for action, but most of the time that action was the stairs creaking and not a home invasion.

The clock on my bedside table said 5:04 a.m., which didn't make sense for a moment. Then, those thought processes kicked in. Ben had forgotten his key. He couldn't remember the four-digit code to unlock the safe ornament for the spare. Typical teenager.

Only, I knew, somehow, deep down in my gut, that it wasn't that. It wasn't something that I could tut and shake my head about. That I could get quietly annoyed about. Intuition, some would call it. I didn't believe in any of that.

There was just that foreboding knowledge as a parent that something bad could happen at any time. An underlying anxiety that never really leaves you.

This was one of those times.

I was out of bed, pulling a thin dressing gown across my shoulders to cover the bare skin. It barely covered anything, but I was already out of the room just as Greg said my name.

'Alison? What's going on?'

Down the stairs and peering through the glass before he'd even got out of bed.

Opening the door to two police officers in uniform standing on my front porch as he called my name again.

'Mrs Lennon?'

And I knew. Right at that moment. It was written on their faces, in big black permanent marker.

For a moment, I wondered if it was Ellie. Only, she was asleep upstairs. Fifteen years old going on thirty. Every conversation with her the precursor to an argument. Had she sneaked out and got herself into trouble?

No.

Of course not.

There was only one of my children they were here for.

And it was one of my children. They weren't there at four in the morning about one of her parents. An aunt or uncle. Someone else would be here for that.

It was Ben.

'Can we come in?'

I led them into the house, suddenly aware of how little I was wearing. I looked for something to wrap around me – a blanket, or something – but they were already standing in my living room. I felt exposed. Vulnerable.

Thoughts ran through my mind like crosstown traffic.

'We're sorry to wake you,' one of the policemen said. He was at least twenty years older than the other one. Two guys, both with short beards masking their faces. The older one had taken off his cap, but the younger one left his on.

'What's happened?' I said, shrugging off the apology. I wanted to hear him say it. Tell me why they were there.

He cleared his throat, his eyes boring into mine. 'There's been an incident with your son Ben.'

There were a few seconds when I began thinking of all the things it could be. An incident sounded benign in that moment. Had he been caught drinking? Driving while drunk? Maybe it was drugs. Some light vandalism. A fight that had got out of control.

Anything other than a reason for them to be there at that time, looking the way they did. The older one, still staring at me, his eyes glassy in the lamplight of the room. The younger one, shifting uncomfortably on his feet.

Waiting for his partner to deliver the killer blow.

'I'm afraid he was found with severe injuries. He was discovered a few streets away. Paramedics were called, but I'm afraid there was nothing they could do.'

I didn't move.

'He didn't survive, Mrs Lennon. Ben is . . .'

I didn't hear him say dead. Blood was already rushing in my ears, blocking sound.

Greg heard him say it, because his voice broke through the silence.

'No.'

A simple, two letter word, that couldn't have been less impactful. It changed nothing.

'Sorry, sir, are you Mr Lennon?'

'What are you saying?' Greg said, coming to my side, as I tried to make sense of what was happening in my home. I turned slowly to him, as he faced the officer. 'There must be some kind of mistake.'

'If you could maybe take a seat, we'll talk you through what we know so far.'

Greg was shaking. Shivering. I wanted to find him something to put over his bare chest. His body.

I couldn't move.

I had to be led to the sofa, where the older policeman sat down next to me and directed the younger cop to get me some water.

Greg was still arguing with reality, but the policeman was well-versed in this, it seemed. I wondered how many times he'd done this. How many lives he'd changed forever with a single visit. I couldn't comprehend the sheer number of lives this man may have been responsible for shattering.

The young policeman came back in holding a glass of water like he was a priest bringing the blood of Christ. He handed it over and I took it out of absentminded politeness.

I didn't drink from it.

'We haven't even identified him yet and you're already coming here and telling us he's dead? It could be anyone. Someone might have stolen his wallet, or his jacket, or something. Left it somewhere and picked it up. You can't just come round and say these things . . .'

Greg might have been able to sleep through an earthquake, but the moment he was awake he was able to instantly speak a thousand words a minute. And be argumentative without even trying.

I hated that about him. I hated many things, secretly of course, but that was near the top of the list.

'Mr Lennon, if you would give me a moment, I can answer your questions—'

'Where is he?'

I had asked the question quietly, but the men stopped talking to turn to me as I spoke.

'Alison...'

'Greg, I swear, I don't need to hear your voice right now. Tell me, where is he?'

'He's at the hospital in the city,' the policeman replied, his stare returning to me. 'We can take you there now.'

'Thank you.'

I bet he went home after his shift, to his own family, and forgot about what came before. He would have to. There was no way you could live with the weight of that responsibility crushing you every single moment of your life.

'We'll get dressed,' I said, placing a hand on Greg's and pulling him away. He was still talking, but I wasn't listening. Wishing I had the ability to do that at any moment, rather than just when I'd been given the worst news I would ever hear.

The next hour was a blur. Putting clothes on silently, as Greg finally lost his voice. Deciding to wake up Ellie, so she didn't wake up to an empty house and no clue as to what was happening. Sitting in the back of a police car, as it drove endlessly on a Green Mile towards the end of normality.

Then, we were in the depths of the local hospital. Clean white walls, clean white floor. The smell of antiseptic and grief hanging in the air like an unwanted passenger.

And I could only wait for the inevitable.

Greg was still shifting on his feet. A coiled spring with no release in sight. I knew him too well. He wouldn't be able to handle this. This moment, what was coming at us. The days and weeks that would come after that. He would shut down.

Let grief and guilt swallow him whole. Walk about in pity for himself.

The thought of that disgusted me.

I knew what was going to happen next.

They were going to show them our son's body. We would know he was gone. That there was no turning back.

I knew Greg would roar with anger, with hurt.

I knew I would slip away. I could already feel it coming on. The feeling of a million butterflies taking flight in my stomach.

I knew it would break us. The final nail in the coffin.

All the time, Ellie was sitting with a young police officer who couldn't even bring a glass of water to a mother hearing the worst news she would ever receive.

I held my breath, waiting for the inevitable.

Then, minutes passed again in a blur, until I was suddenly looking down at my son's body.

I blinked and remembered him as a baby. As a toddler. As a child.

His first Christmas. His first words. His first steps. His first day of reception class. His first day in high school. His first football match. His first exams.

His first, his first, his first.

His first . . .

His last.

That's all his life would be now. His last everything. The last time I felt his arms around me. The last time I felt his kiss on my head. The last time he smiled at me. The last time he said,

'Love you, Mum.'

The last time I would ever see his face.

And I was right. Greg roared with anger.

And I slipped away into darkness.

2

Mia Johnstone was seventeen years old when she realised people around her tended to die.

Only, that wasn't quite right. It wasn't just family members, or those old people who were ready for death anyway.

This was people who had wronged her in some way.

One day, there. The next . . .

Gone.

Younger, older. It didn't matter.

It took a while for her to catch on.

That she was the reason it happened.

That she was responsible for them being dead.

And that was a lot to take for someone so young.

A lot to take, when you weren't sure if you were to blame for it.

There's always that moment when she wakes up where she doesn't quite understand anything that is happening. Where she was, when it was, who she was.

She always needed just a little more sleep. A half hour, hour tops.

No matter that it was already midday, at least. Light was winning the battle against the curtains across her window.

'Only seeing if you're awake, Mia?'

Her mum's voice. The reason why she wasn't fast asleep still. Getting that extra hour, hour and a half tops.

'Yeah,' Mia answered, only it came out through a fog of confusion and dry throat and sounded like someone other than herself. She swallowed and reached for the empty glass on her bedside table, coming away disappointed. Flopped her head back on her pillow and screwed her eyes shut.

'It's almost lunchtime,' her mum continued, sounding like her usual self – disappointed and exasperated with Mia. 'I don't want to nag you . . .'

'It's fine, I'm up now,' Mia said, wanting the conversation over. She slowly opened her left eye, then her right when nothing bad happened.

The glass may have been empty, but when she reached over again and picked up her mobile, that was less disappointedly devoid. Numerous notifications. Not unusual, but even so, there was always a pang of regret that she hadn't been around and awake to receive each of them.

She unlocked her phone, sitting up in bed as she moved her pillow behind her head.

WhatsApp messages – too many to count. Conversations within groups, that were in triple figures.

Snapchat, over twenty. A few DMs on Insta.

Even a couple of text messages.

No missed calls.

No one called anyone, even if someone had died.

And someone had.

It took a while for Mia to realise, of course. There was too much all in one go to make sense of what had happened. She scrolled back in the group texts, until that got frustrating and she switched to Insta.

Are you okay?

Do you know what happened?

No. She *really* didn't.

It was only by the time that she read her actual text messages that she realised what people were talking about. What people had found out, since she'd last looked at her phone the night before.

A noise escaped the back of her throat. A moan, or something approximating it.

I'm really sorry, but Ben was found dead on the corner of his street last night.

Sorry.

Really sorry.

It was from Grace – someone in her friendship group who Mia wasn't exactly close with.

The clarion of death had begun.

Everyone wanted to be the one who told her, it seemed, because the other text was from Liv. Pretty much the same message as Grace.

WhatsApp was similar. Private messages from Maddie, Harper, and Riley. All in the same vein.

Snapchat was where the guys got in touch. Jack, Elijah, Ryan.

She read them all in silence. Scanning through the death messages with an unclear mind.

It wasn't real. Couldn't be.

One of those rumours that spread through the town, with no evidence and whispers alone. Started by some offhand comment and by the time it reached her, Ben was dead and almost buried.

Only, he couldn't be dead. She'd seen him the previous night and it couldn't be real. He couldn't be dead. It felt impossible. Like a dream.

Only, on some level, she knew it was true. And she was already working out what she was going to do.

How she was going to act. What part she was going to play in this whole thing.

Because she knew what was going to happen next.

She wanted it to be a dream. That she was still asleep, having a nightmare that her boyfriend – *ex-boyfriend* – was gone.

No such luck.

Another knock at the door.

'Mia?'

'Mum, I know, I've seen,' Mia said, her voice sounding more normal now. 'I'll be down soon.'

She could hear her mum's low sigh through the bedroom door. Could almost see the dip of her shoulders, the shuffling feet, as she tried to work out what to do. What to say.

'I'll be waiting,' her mum said, finally.

Mia listened for her mum to go back downstairs, before going back to the phone in her hand. She looked on Twitter, seeing that a few people she followed were already talking about it publicly. She searched for one word and it began.

Baycliff.

The name of her town, in the news again. The first time had barely got further than a few social media posts and a couple of pieces in the failing local paper. The second – that was a bit heavier. Only, someone famous had died and the news had moved on quickly. Mia knew the family had tried over the past year or so to keep the story going, but without much luck. It had quietened down now, but Mia knew people still had it in the back of their minds when talking to her.

She didn't think it would be like that this time around.

She wasn't thinking properly. She could tell that already.

She was already worrying about what was going to happen next. To her, to her friends, to her family. What she would have to do, have to say.

She thought about Ben's parents. His younger sister who never liked her. Her circle of friends at the same school.

They wouldn't let her forget him. Ever.

She was going to be linked with him now. She knew that. The doting girlfriend.

Mia could already hear the words Ben's family would say in public. The plans he had for the future. The university he'd been accepted to. The career he wanted.

The girl he wanted to eventually make his wife.

That would be her.

Only, Mia knew that wasn't the case. She knew a different Ben to them.

Her phone buzzed in her hand and she realised it was an incoming video call. She ended it without answering. It started up a few seconds later and this time she looked to see who was calling.

Anna.

She closed her eyes and breathed in slowly.

Then, answered.

'I wasn't going to just send a message,' Anna said, without preamble. 'I know everyone else will have.'

'Not even gonna ask if I know?'

Mia watched as Anna rolled her eyes theatrically. 'If you're on your phone, you already know.'

'I don't know what to think—'

'Don't say too much,' Anna said, cutting her off before she had a chance to finish her thought. 'Not until you've processed this. It's . . . it's huge, this kind of thing. I couldn't believe it.'

'I know,' Mia replied, checking herself in the small video in the corner of the screen. She could see dark circles under her eyes, but if she lifted the phone up a little, the light from outside made them fade a little. 'Me neither.'

'When did you last see him?'

Mia knew Anna wasn't trying to interrogate her – question her story. Still, she felt the ball of anxiety in her stomach grow a little. 'Last night.'

Anna shook her head. 'Listen, just make sure you get things straight in your head before you talk to anyone, okay?

This isn't the first time something like this has happened, remember? They'll be looking for patterns where none exist, right?'

'Right,' Mia echoed, switching the phone from one hand to the other as she massaged her forehead. She could feel the beginning of a headache beginning to form behind her eyes. 'I need to go. My mum will be waiting for me to go down and talk to her.'

'Okay,' Anna replied, leaning forwards to the camera lens closer. 'I'm here any time, Mia. You know that. Just let me know when you need me.'

'Thanks,' Mia said, ending the call and taking a deep breath in. She let it go, her eyes closed now. Tried to imagine the weight of the world leaving her body as she did so. It didn't work.

Her mum was waiting in the kitchen when she finally made it down. Sitting at the breakfast bar, a cup of tea cradled in her hands. Mia didn't say anything, crossing to the fridge and taking out a carton of orange juice. Opened the dishwasher and removed a glass, all in silence. Poured herself a glass and sipped it slowly.

'Mia—'

'Mum, I know,' Mia said, cutting her off before she could start with the platitudes. The inanity of comforting words. 'You don't have to say anything.'

'Where were you last night?'

Mia turned sharply, surprised by the question. 'I . . . I was out with friends.'

'What time did you get back?'

Mia shook her head. 'I don't know. Late, I guess.'

'Your dad said he didn't hear you come home and you know how late he stays up. And then, we hear about this horrible thing happening last night and . . .'

'And what?'

'And I was worried about you. That's all. I know you don't think we care, but we really do. When you have kids—'

Mia sighed, drained the last of her orange juice and slammed the glass down on the kitchen counter. It stopped her mum's usual monologue about being a parent. For a second, she thought it was going to shatter, the glass shards splintering and piercing her hand. She could almost see it happen, see the blood blossom from her veins and drip over her skin. Pooling on the surface below. She stared down for a few seconds, envisioning the sight. Feeling the sharpness of the pain. Enjoying the sensation.

Finally, she turned to her mother. 'I'm just in shock,' she said, wrapping her arms around herself, in case they betrayed her and went for the glass again. To slam it down harder. 'Nothing else. I need time to work out what the hell has happened, okay? So, leave me alone.'

Mia walked out of the kitchen before her mum could say anything else – her breathing hard and fast. Stomped up the stairs and slammed her bedroom door behind her, causing a picture hanging on the wall beside it to crash to the ground.

A few minutes later, Mia would pick up the picture and realise it was the one she'd had framed of her and Ben – only a few weeks ago. Taken on her phone and printed off in Asda and hung up on her wall. Like she was from the nineties or something old like that.

She would pick it up and slump to the floor. Tears springing to her eyes, as she let the grief and guilt swallow her whole.

3

What do you do in the hours after you identify your dead son's body?

I didn't know. And it didn't seem like anyone wanted to tell me. You could hardly just go about your day as normal. There were things to do. People to speak to. Arrangements to be made.

Police to deal with.

A murder inquiry. That's how they'd put it. Some kind of liaison officer would be at the house for the foreseeable future. Other things had been said, in the few minutes since we'd seen Ben, but I'd stopped listening.

I was thinking about what the first thing we had to do would be.

First, we had to tell Ellie.

How do you tell a child that someone they loved is dead?

The words could never be right. Maybe because there are no words that you can use that would make any difference to the substance of what you were telling them.

Someone you thought would always be in your life has gone. And won't be coming back. Now . . . you have to keep living like it didn't really happen.

I felt Greg's arm snake around my shoulders, as if it were a scarf made of iron, impossible to shift.

Ellie only had to look at our faces and she knew that there hadn't been a mistake. That it hadn't been someone else's brother lying motionless in the bowels of the hospital.

Greg took the lead anyhow. 'Darling, I'm sorry.'

'It's really him?'

I could barely stand, never mind comfort my daughter. It was taking everything in me to stay conscious. Standing upright. Walking. I wanted to melt away into nothingness.

'I'm sorry,' Greg said again, as if that was enough. As if that was the best thing that could be said in the circumstances. His arm had shifted from my shoulders and to my waist. Somehow that was worse. I wanted to shake it away, start running down the corridor. I wanted nothing more than to have it away from me. To have *him* away from me. Everyone.

I couldn't look at Ellie.

'Mum? What happened?'

Finally, I lifted my head slowly and met my daughter's eyes.

Her scream would haunt me forever.

That much pain. That much sorrow.

One child gone. One in unimaginable hurt.

It was at that moment that I felt like the worst parent in the world. I had failed.

We both had.

Greg's arm finally left my body and I felt relief for a split-second, before I saw Ellie crumple to the ground, as he reached out for her.

I couldn't move.

We were led into a car outside. There was no reason to stay there. Identification had taken place and now all that could be done for Ben would be carried out by other people. Not his parents. Not his mum.

It felt like I was being told I was done now. It was over.

He wasn't my responsibility anymore.

'We had one job,' I said, as we pulled up outside our home. It was morning now, the street coming to life, just as mine as I'd known it had ended. 'That's it.'

Greg shifted uncomfortably next to me, his eyes hollow and body shivering from a cold I couldn't see. 'What do you mean?'

'As parents,' I replied, hearing the hollowness in my voice. The words coming from somewhere I couldn't identify. They certainly didn't feel like they were coming from myself. I didn't feel any kind of control of anything at that moment. 'We only had one job. Keep them safe. And we've failed.'

Greg shaped to say something, but then thought better of it.

I knew he agreed with me.

'They're going to be asking us some questions,' Greg said, changing the subject as quickly as he could. 'About where he goes, what time he usually comes home. Who he's usually with when he's out, things like that.'

I turned to my husband and met his eyes for the first time since we had left the house a few hours earlier. Since we'd been told to identify our dead son. 'How do we get through this? How can it be real?'

Greg let my eyes bore into his for a few seconds, but then he scrunched them closed using his fingers to massage his forehead. I could see new lines there that I couldn't be sure had been there the day before.

'We have to do what we can,' he said, but I knew he didn't feel it. Didn't believe we could do anything. 'Just . . . just keep moving forwards. I don't know. I don't have any answers for this.'

I was surprised by that admission. Greg usually had an answer for everything. A way out of any situation. A solution to any problem.

This was so far away from normal life that he didn't have anything to give me. A sliver of hope. A whisper of a way out.

He had nothing for me.

★★★

The detective in my living room didn't seem to be in any hurry to leave. Despite my attempts to convey my distaste in them being there. Still. Hours after we'd finally made it home.

Greg had been doing all the talking. Thankfully. I wasn't sure I had anything left. I couldn't make sense of the situation. It felt like a dream. A nightmare. Only, there was too much reality around me. I could hear, I could smell, I could touch. Everything may have been reaching me on a slight delay, but I knew I was awake.

'Are there any other names we should add to the list?'

I realised the detective was talking to me. I turned my head slowly from where I'd been staring at the wall above the mantelpiece. Looked at her as if she'd appeared without warning. 'Sorry?' I said, my voice sounding like it didn't belong to me.

'So this is the list of names of people who Ben may have been with last night, but I was wondering if there might be any that may have been missed?'

I took the notebook from her outstretched hand, the weight of it feeling too heavy to handle at first. I glanced through the list, scanning the names and not taking them in. I had to read the first line more than a few times before I began to take it in.

I couldn't even remember giving her some of the names now. It was people I'd known of for years. All through primary school, high school. Ben's group of friends, kids I'd seen grow from childhood until the cusp of adulthood.

They would continue on. They would be going off to university. Their parents wouldn't be making lists of people's names who may have seen them last. Their parents wouldn't be thinking about funeral services, what to dress their child in for his last journey. Their parents wouldn't be thinking about the last thing they may have said to them.

Their parents wouldn't be stuck, forever, in a single moment. A single image.

Their child, lying dead, not being able to even touch them.

'Alison?'

The words had blurred on the pad below and I tried to focus again. Words stuck at the back of my throat, as I handed it back soundlessly.

Then, at the last second, I held onto it. Looked at it again.

'It's missing Mia.'

Greg let out a sigh. 'I thought they'd broken up?'

'They're kids, Greg,' I said, tired of having to explain everything I ever said. Ever thought. I couldn't have that happening now. Not after what had happened. 'They break up, they get back together, that's how the world turns when you're a teenager.'

'I hope not,' Greg replied, unable to keep the disdain out of his voice. 'I never liked her.'

'She was okay . . .'

'No, she wasn't right for him,' Greg said, his voice raising and making me shrink back a little, before I checked myself. He seemed to notice it and realise how it might have looked to the detectives sitting in the room with us. 'Sorry, I'm just saying she was a distraction he didn't need.'

'It doesn't matter now, does it?'

'Right, okay,' the detective said, cutting us off before the argument became worse. She finally took her oh so important list back from me. 'What's her surname?'

I couldn't remember at first. Simply stared back at the detective, as my mind tried to whir into action. Everything slowed down. Had been slowing down since the moment I'd been woken in the early hours of the morning.

'I . . . I'm not sure,' Greg said, and I could feel his eyes on me. Waiting for me to fill in the gaps of his knowledge.

And when that came to the kids, it was the Grand Canyon of emptiness. He barely knew a thing about them, other than surface-level things.

He wasn't the one who had actual conversations with them. Learned their likes and dislikes. What they thought of the world they'd been forced into. He was content to just let the days and nights play out and wait for the next one. He provided for them, that was how he saw his job. He didn't need to know them all that much until they were older, is what he'd told me once.

I knew Ben and Ellie. Who they were, what they wanted, what they liked, what they hated. Who they were friends with, who they didn't get along with. Greg never had time for anything like that. The kids had never said as much, but I knew they didn't even bother trying to tell him anything now.

Finally, the name came. 'Johnstone. Mia Johnstone. She lives over on Debrayer Street.'

'Thanks, Alison,' the detective said, making a note and then closing her notepad over. 'I'll pass all this information out and we'll speak to everyone who might have seen Ben last night. Some have already come forwards, but we won't leave any stone unturned. I promise you, we'll do everything in our power to find out what happened to your son and bring you the answers.'

Greg thanked her, but I could barely tear my eyes from the wall above the mantelpiece.

I knew why.

Surrounding them, on walls, on end tables and multiple surfaces, that's where the photographs could be. Would be. Waiting for me – smiling visages of a former life.

My son. Happy, alive, breathing.

Something that would never be again.

And just the thought of it made me want to run. To jump up and burst out of the house. To run and just keep running forever.

So I would never have to face the facts.

He was gone and would never be coming home.

4

It was after lunchtime, but it didn't matter anyway. Natalie Williams wasn't about to be going out to lunch. She wasn't even sure if she would get to eat, never mind leave the office.

A nice café. Some sourdough bread. Goats cheese and red onion chutney. That'd be nice. Her mouth watered at the thought of it.

A dead eighteen-year-old kid was spoiling the dream.

She knew this was the life she had chosen, but it didn't mean she had to enjoy it.

It had been four months since she'd relocated. A smaller town, more affordable houses, nicer schools. All good reasons to have made the move, but it didn't mean that the job got any easier.

She wasn't even sure there was a nice café she could get what she wanted from anyway.

Not for the first time, she regretted deciding to move to the area. It may have seemed like a good idea at the time, but the bigger cities had something going for them at least – nobody knew anyone there. Sure, you had those little communities that would know each other a little, but it wasn't on the scale of a small town. A village.

Social media didn't help. Now, there are all those community pages that spring up. A thousand or so residents of each small town, all on Facebook to ask inane questions or inform others about situations no one ever needed to know about.

How long is the queue to the tip?

Anyone know why there's a helicopter out?

What's that noise on Egerton Street?

Anyone know if the tip is open today?

To the person who beeped at me coming out of the Asda car park – I was just trying to decide if I needed to go back in or not for cat food. Hope you're happy with yourself.

Is the queue for the tip worth joining today?

Natalie actively avoided it all. It was becoming more difficult to do so. Mainly because that was a good place to find out information if say, someone is murdered at two in the morning on a quiet street in that town.

Not for the first time, she dreaded leaving her little home on the water and going off to work. She might have got lucky in having a husband who worked from an office slash dining room, so there was always someone to send the kids off to school in the morning and welcome them home hours later.

It was still a wrench to go off alone.

Especially when you get a call at seven in the morning telling you that there had been a teenager killed overnight and you were suddenly part of the investigation.

It wasn't a job she could see herself doing for very much longer. She wasn't interested in promotion. She didn't see it as a calling. It was, for all intents and purposes, an accident that she was even in that position.

One day, maybe she would do something else entirely. Maybe write, like a fair few ex-coppers seemed to do now. Usually crime fiction. Usually meticulously researched. Usually loosely based on the way they saw themselves.

She hadn't read any of it.

Everyone was supposed to have a book in them. She didn't think that was true. When she looked inside herself, all she saw was a desire to go unnoticed.

'His phone hasn't pinged off a tower since just before we think he was killed.'

Natalie focused back on Carter, who was leaning his hip against her desk. She picked up a ruler and slid it between the wood and his body. He jumped back, as if she had bitten him.

'So, it's probably been destroyed by now, I guess,' Natalie said, shaking her head. 'It follows the route from the . . . the dips, did you say?'

Carter nodded, a little too enthusiastically. 'Yeah, that's what we've got. Our killer probably took it, but destroyed the SIM card or something. Could be anywhere now.'

'We have people canvassing neighbours for CCTV, so hopefully we can track from that. We don't have anything other than the victim on his own walking, though, so far?'

'Unfortunately not, no. A bunch of them will have doorbell cameras, which should hopefully pick up something, but he was killed just as he was entering a cut-through, so there's no houses there. And no cameras.'

'What was the result of talking to the immediate neighbours?'

'No one heard anything,' Carter said, a grimace appearing across his face. 'They didn't even know anything had happened until he was found. And even that was by chance. A random old guy, walking his dog. He was going to keep walking, only he saw the blood.'

'Walking his dog at three in the morning?'

Carter shrugged. 'His story seems to stand up. He was quick to tell us that was normal – he works shifts and that's the time he takes the dog for a walk. I think he showed the uniform who took the statement Ring camera footage of him leaving at the same time every day. We're asking neighbours just in case.'

Natalie leaned back in her chair, shuffling the pieces into a correct order. That's how she liked to work – logically.

It made sense most of the time. 'So, could it just be random then? Just a street robbery gone wrong?'

She didn't wait for Carter to answer, before she thought of the correct response in her mind.

No.

'Too violent,' she said, almost to herself. 'No sign of him fighting back, as far as we can see. No scrapes on his hands, no defensive wounds. This was someone coming up behind him and striking to kill. He was already gone by the time he hit the ground.'

'I was going to say that,' Carter said, not sounding as sure as the words he was using. 'He was targeted.'

'That's my guess,' Natalie replied, giving the younger guy a pass. He seemed like the type that worked better with praise and soft guidance. She didn't mind that. 'So, why would someone want to kill an eighteen-year-old lad?'

'The usual reasons I guess. Money, drugs . . . sex.'

Carter drew out the last word on his list, his cheeks flushing red. Natalie ignored it. She considered the list of names Greg and Alison had given them an hour earlier. 'Then we start by going through this list – talking to his friends, his family, and find out which of those fit best.'

'Okay boss.'

'Dish them out – get statements that can be followed up on. We'll talk to the possible girlfriend . . . Mia Johnstone? Get her details up and we'll head there shortly. If she's the closest to our victim, then we should do the initial interview.'

Carter seemed to agree and then left Natalie, sitting at her desk, wondering about the list. The three things. Rule of three. They might have been the usual reasons, but there were always more.

It had only been a few hours since she'd been informed of the death, but already she was thinking about when it would be over. When the next one would land. And the next one, and the next one . . .

On and on. Always reasons to kill. Always reasons for someone to lose their life.

Never-ending.

5

Once the two detectives left, there was silence in the house. Some bored-looking officer in uniform was sitting in the kitchen, which meant that I stayed in the living room.

Out of sight, out of mind.

I wanted to sleep, but I didn't think that would look right. Who to, I wasn't sure. It would look like I didn't care, but I was exhausted.

Greg was the opposite – wired like I'd never seen him before. He kept wringing his hands, as if he was washing them in an invisible sink. Trying to get rid of some dirt only he could see.

'What time did you come to bed last night?' I asked, breaking the silence that had been the only 'sound' for the previous fifteen minutes.

Greg shrugged. 'I don't know.'

'Well, try to remember,' I said, unable to keep the exasperation out of my voice. 'Don't you think they'll be asking you questions like that? They will think we might be responsible. If you start "forgetting" things, they'll jump on that.'

'It'll be fine,' Greg mumbled, which was the way he became when he realised I was right about something, but didn't want to admit it. 'It doesn't look like they're about to start accusing us of anything.'

I couldn't be bothered worrying about it. In any other circumstance, I would have been weirdly pleased that he was under the spotlight. Only, that would mean the police wouldn't be out there trying to find the actual murderer.

Murderer . . .

My son had been murdered.

It didn't make any sense.

I was like everyone else – I'd watched enough of those true crime documentaries to have a working knowledge of how this type of thing could play out. I also knew from them that it could happen to anyone.

It didn't make me feel any better.

It also didn't help that nothing felt real. I wasn't sure what we were meant to do. I already felt like we were being watched – that everything we said and did would be examined. That was before the detectives did what I knew they would do next, if they didn't have an outside suspect within a few hours.

They'd start looking at us. Greg, probably, in particular.

'We should eat something.'

I didn't even bother responding to Greg. I just shook my head. The idea of putting anything in my stomach made me feel sick.

It was the last thing I was thinking about.

Greg sighed and flopped down on the sofa opposite. Pulled out his phone and began scrolling.

I didn't even know where mine was. Which was an alien thing to me – usually I had it in my hand or nearby at all times. Usually watching endless reels of short videos, while watching TV silently with Greg.

He didn't like me talking during that time. And I didn't tend to enjoy what he wanted to watch. Which meant we ended up on opposite sides of the sofa, while he ignored the fact that I wasn't happy.

'It's on the news,' Greg said, almost as an aside. 'My God . . .'

'What are you talking about?'

'Look,' Greg said, turning his phone to face me. I couldn't really see, other than some kind of news app open on his screen. 'On Sky News. Just says teenager killed in Baycliff. Unless there's something they're not telling us, I'm going to say that they're talking about . . . about Ben. No details on there – just says police are investigating, yada, yada, yada.'

I closed my eyes, wondering at what point it had been that Greg had forgotten how to be a human being. A husband. A father.

I ignored him, as I did more often than ever. Drew my knees up to my chest and hugged them closer to me.

The tears that had dried on my cheeks were wet again within seconds. I thought about what would happen next. How I would handle it.

The feeling was overwhelming.

I could feel the familiar ball of anxiety grow in my stomach. I opened my mouth to say as much to Greg, but stopped myself.

He wouldn't understand.

He never had.

'Have you checked on Ellie?' I heard Greg say, as I scrunched my eyes shut and tried to stop the tears again.

I shook my head.

He sighed again, quieter this time, as if he was trying to hide it from me, but still wanting me to hear it. 'I'll go up and speak to her.'

I wanted to tell him not to. To take the lead. Only, he was already on his feet and I knew it would be pointless.

I knew he'd try to talk to her in his condescending, logical way. Not emotionally – just seeing the problem and telling her how she was going to get through it.

It wouldn't work. It never did.

I should have got up and stopped him, but I didn't have the energy. Not for any of it. I wanted to curl up into a ball and close my eyes. Wait for the nightmare to be over. Wait for the feeling in the pit of my stomach to disappear.

I wanted to be anywhere else than there.

Greg stopped in the doorway and I could feel his eyes on me. I didn't look up. Waited for him to say his piece.

'We have to be together right now,' he said, his hand on the door, closing it over so he couldn't be heard elsewhere in the house. 'We can't let this break us. I know things have been difficult – you know, with what you've been going through – but we need to stick together more than ever.'

He said it like he was doing me a favour. Like he was throwing me a bone and could stop me from doing something stupid.

I couldn't look at him.

'What I've been going through?' I said, the usual thought process that stopped me from answering back nowhere to be found. 'What do you mean by that?'

I heard him sigh, yet again. Honestly, the man seemed to only breathe through heavy exhalations.

'You know, the change and that.'

I could feel myself slipping – letting the anger bubble up and over. Something I'd been more aware of lately than ever – it was why I had become so numb in recent months. Years, in fact. Scared of letting myself be real, in case it made everyone leave me.

He was standing there, waiting for me to answer him.

I wanted to make him disappear.

I wanted him away from me.

I could already see he was going to make this all about him. How he was dealing with what happened, how he was going to be the saviour in the situation.

Without actually doing anything.

I wanted him to fight. I wanted him to do something that would actually matter.

I remembered the growing number of arguments in the previous eighteen months and wondered if it was our fault Ben had died.

Wondered if we hadn't been so focused on each other and the silences that had grown between us, whether that had led to us taking our eye off the ball when it came to being parents.

I felt the guilt grow inside me. Rivalling the ball of anxiety for size.

Greg was still standing there. Waiting for me to agree with him, which was the only language he understood. In his head, everything he said was logical and right.

I remembered him saying once during an argument that the reason he felt he was always right was because he saw no logical reason why he would argue if he wasn't. He could never accept the idea that he could be wrong.

And now, Ben was dead. Our son.

I looked up finally, searching his face to see if the reflection of hurt and loss would be there.

I couldn't see it.

Another memory from the past year or so came to me then. Of Greg arguing with Ben.

Greg dismissing his son, when he wouldn't just agree with him. The way he did it, so cold and detached. Frustration building and building, until it suddenly stopped dead.

Was that the moment we'd lost him?

Greg stared back at me and it was like I was looking at a stranger.

I shook my head and turned away. 'Do whatever you think is right,' I said, my voice barely above a whisper.

I'd let him take control of everything. The house, the parenting, even what we watched on TV. Let him control how we acted around each other. Let him control the level of affection he allowed us to have towards each other.

All in small increments.

Without me even noticing.

I wasn't going to let him control how we dealt with our son being killed.

I wasn't going to let him control what happened next.

If I couldn't help Ben the night before, I could help him now. I could help him by finally being what I'd always wanted to be.

6

It didn't take long.

It was early afternoon when they turned up. Two of them. A pair. That's what she expected, if she'd been made to guess. She'd seen enough TV to know they usually came in pairs. None of that good cop, bad cop, routine, though. That was a myth. She knew that was just something that had been made up.

One usually took the lead. Asked the questions, while the other noted the responses.

There was a TV show she watched whenever it was on. Everyone did. One of those Channel Four documentaries, that tapped into a certain subsection of society.

24 Hours in Police Custody. Mia and her friends had been obsessed with it – complaining that previous series weren't available easily enough. Sharing links to dodgy websites that had poor quality versions of years-old investigations.

'Why would anyone say anything other than "no comment" in an interview? Just asking for trouble.'

That had been the popular refrain. Unless it was a particularly juicy crime, in which case group chats would explode with fury that they weren't hearing from the person who'd killed someone, or the like. Then, they all wanted to hear directly from that person, no comment be damned.

Now, she had two cops in front of her and all of that was forgotten. The idea of saying no comment in her own living room, when her boyfriend – *ex-boyfriend* – had only been dead a few hours, was ridiculous.

It would only make her look guilty. Like she had something to hide.

Which she did, of course.

'We're really sorry to meet under these circumstances,' the one taking the lead said. She was older, significantly, than the man who was with her. 'I'm sure this is a difficult time for you, Mia.'

Her dad sighed as he leaned against the wall near the door. His arms folded across his chest.

Mum was sitting next to her, having at first put her hands in Mia's before removing them when she didn't get any reciprocation.

'Have you found the person who did this yet?'

The female cop didn't take her eyes from Mia and towards her mum who'd spoken. 'Jennifer, is it?'

She felt her mum stiffen beside her. Mia knew she didn't like her full name being spoken in the house. She didn't know why that was.

'I think it's a reasonable question,' her mum said, but her voice was lower now.

'Of course, but I'm afraid I can't divulge any information at the moment about the investigation. Please be sure that we're working hard to find out what happened to Ben.'

The last part had been for Mia, she knew. It was almost as if the spotlight was on her and everyone in the room knew it. That she was the star of the show.

She didn't like it.

They'd introduced themselves to her twice. She didn't know why. In the hallway, it had been Detectives Williams and Carter. No first names. Not until they had been sat down in the living room and it had become Natalie and Robert.

Nice and informal.

She didn't like either of them. Natalie looked as if she would make a really annoying headteacher and Robert reminded her of a guy who worked in the local Asda, who always perved at her and her friends when they went through the self-service checkout.

They used to make sure he was working when they bought alcohol, because he would always let them through without checking ID. That had been before a few of the group had turned eighteen and didn't need to worry about that kind of thing anymore.

'Tell me, Mia, when was the last time you saw Ben?'

Mia glanced up, saw Detective Natalie staring back at her and averted her gaze quickly. 'Yesterday.'

They waited for more, but that was all she was giving them.

Detective Robert cleared his throat and made a note of something in his notepad. Mia could see him stealing glances around the room. Taking everything in, she guessed. Making assumptions. Both of the detectives were ignoring her dad, who was trying to make his presence known. She could sense him wanting to jump in. Wanting to take control of the situation. She knew they wouldn't let him.

'Okay, what time would that be?'

Detective Natalie had this way of making a question sound like an accusation. Mia knew she was imagining it, but she couldn't help but feel like she was waiting for her to slip up and say something wrong. Something that would make them ask her to come down to the station for further questions.

There wouldn't be any reason for it, she knew. They didn't suspect her of anything. Not right then. They couldn't.

'About nine p.m., I think.'

'Alone?'

Mia shook her head. 'No, there was a group of us.'

'And who was in this group?'

Mia shook her head. 'Groups. I was with one group, Ben was with another. We were down on the dips.'

'The dips?'

'Yeah, the dips.'

Detective Robert leaned forwards towards Detective Natalie. 'It's the sand dunes down on the front by the river.'

'I see,' Detective Natalie said, nodding to herself.

Mia realised she was new to the area. It was a little nugget of information she noted and stored away.

'So, you were with a group of friends, down at these dips, and you saw Ben?'

'Yes,' Mia said, still keeping with her monosyllabism. It seemed to be working – in the sense that she was annoying the detective and not giving anything away. Probably making her look guilty too, she suddenly realised. 'It happens a lot. There's not many places to go around here and you end up bumping into people you know all the time.'

There, Mia thought. Nothing but empty words, but at least it was better than a one-word answer.

'I understand you had been seeing each other until recently?'

'That's right.'

'And how had the break-up been affecting you both?'

Mia heard her dad sigh again. This time he couldn't help himself. 'What does this have to do with anything? They're teenagers – they get together and break up all the time. From what I've heard, it seems like this was a mugging gone wrong?'

'We're not making any assumptions about what happened at this stage,' Detective Natalie said, finally turning to give her dad a look she couldn't see. 'I'm just building a picture of the entire situation. We're not ruling anything in or out at this time. It's important that we speak to everyone who saw Ben in the hours before he died and your daughter – someone who was close to him – was one of them. Let me assure you, we're talking to everyone who saw him last night. Which is why we're here right now.'

Mia waited for another interruption from her dad, but none came. She knew he could be argumentative when he wanted to be. One of those people who have opinions about everything and didn't mind sharing them. Often and loudly.

She knew it annoyed her mum a lot that every argument they had between them wasn't like other married people arguments. Dad would analyse everything that was said, looking for ways to trip her up and win.

It was probably why they slept in separate rooms these days. Not just about dad's snoring, as they liked to pretend. It was late at night when dad would like to go on and on when mum just wanted to sleep.

Every little imagined slight he'd received that day – whether that was some bloke at B&Q, a woman in the car park at Tesco, Mia or her brother Harry. Or her mum.

Those were the worst discussions. Dad very calm. Mum's voice penetrating the walls, as she tried to explain herself, her feelings.

Sometimes, her and Harry would talk about it. Most times, they ignored it.

'Mia?'

'It was . . .' Mia began the sentence then didn't know how to end it. What was she supposed to say that wouldn't make her look bad, mad, or sad? She had been all of those things. 'It was fine. We'd started talking again.'

That had been true, at least. Although what they had been talking about wasn't something she was going to divulge.

'You were talking about getting back together?'

'Something like that,' Mia replied, trying to sound non-committal. 'We both loved each other, but it had become hard in the past few weeks.'

'Why had that been?'

'He cheated on me,' Mia said, unable to stop the words coming out before they did. 'I mean, he had been talking to another girl, in our friendship group, and couldn't explain a few things. They both denied it, but I had my doubts.'

'Doubts?'

Mia breathed in, thinking of the right thing to say. 'They would message each other all the time. She'd be the first to like anything he did on Instagram and I saw Snapchat stuff pop up on his phone from her. He would tell me it was nothing, but . . .'

'Sometimes you just get a feeling, right?'

Detective Natalie was looking at her more softly now. As if she knew exactly what she'd been going through. Probably she did. It wasn't as if it was out of the ordinary for a man to check the grass on the other side of the fence every once in a while. Mia glanced over at Detective Robert, who shifted uncomfortably on his seat and she knew he was thinking of something similar he'd done himself, no doubt.

Mia was almost eighteen and she could already see what was in her future.

'But you'd been talking about getting back together?'

Mia nodded slowly. 'They were both so adamant that nothing had been going on that I started to doubt myself.'

She could feel her dad tensing over by the door. She couldn't look at him. She knew he wasn't happy about the idea of her going back to Ben, but it didn't matter now.

It was never going to happen.

'So, how was he when you saw him last night?'

Mia shrugged. 'Seemed normal. Nothing wrong at all.'

Detective Natalie was staring at her. She could feel her eyes boring a hole into her skull. It was making her feel two things – nervous and angry.

She wanted to stare right back. To push her shoulders back and dare her to say what she was really thinking.

'I know this is a difficult time for you, Mia,' Detective Natalie said, an edge to her tone that Mia didn't like. 'But it's really important that you help us in any way you can.'

Mia sighed and finally looked up and held the detective's gaze. 'I saw Ben for a little while, but then we went off and did our own thing. We didn't talk about anything. We were celebrating. It wasn't a night for that and there was too many people around. I really don't have anything I can help you with. I was with my friend, Anna, for the rest of the night, before I came home around eleven. I went to bed and was on my phone until about two. Then, I went to sleep. When I left Ben, we were good. We were gonna get back together, I think, and now he's gone. And I'm just . . . I'm just empty inside. I can't believe it.'

There it was. The first lie.

And Mia knew that Detective Natalie had caught it.

7

Greg made me eat something. My body and mind protested against it for every second, but afterwards, I felt less hollow.

Slightly less.

He'd made scrambled eggs on toast.

Now, we sat opposite each other at the kitchen table. Ellie's scrambled eggs and toast having disappeared quicker than mine.

'What do we do now?'

I looked at my daughter, thought about her question and decided to answer honestly. 'I've been asking myself the same thing.'

That had been the same question rolling over and over my mind since we'd got back home the previous morning.

What do we do now?

There seemed to be no normal in sight. Maybe ever. Not unless there was a sudden commotion at the door. The police arriving to tell us a huge mistake had been made. Ben lolling in behind them, looking dishevelled and ashamed. Forgiven, before he even uttered a word.

And then, that fantasy would be replaced by the cold, dead body I'd seen earlier that day. My son.

Gone.

'We can't really do anything until the police, or the hospital release the . . . release him back to us,' Greg said, leaning against the table, cradling a mug of coffee, as if it was the most precious thing to him in the world. 'I think it'll be busy around here today, though.'

'Really?' Ellie replied, impatience in her tone. 'Does it have to be?'

'It'll be the family,' Greg said, trying to placate her, but with little of the effort he usually had. 'Gran and Grandad. Uncle Dan. Your Nan. Maybe Peter and Sarah. They'll want to be here for us.'

Ellie voiced a grunt that seemed to be acceptance. I couldn't help but echo her thoughts. The last thing I wanted was for the house to be filled with Greg's family. Or my own, for that matter.

That wouldn't be much of a problem – there was only really Val, my sister, left now.

I wanted silence.

I didn't want a permanent reminder that something out of the ordinary was happening. People with their empty stares and empty words, trying to be there for me. For us. It wasn't going to help.

Nothing was.

'I'm . . . I'm going upstairs,' I said, not waiting for a response. I heard Greg's stammering voice behind me as I left the kitchen, but I didn't turn back. Didn't try and work out what he was saying. I just hoped he wouldn't follow me.

I made my way up to the first floor and paused outside Ben's bedroom. My hand on the door. I hadn't been inside for a few days – though I knew the police had searched through it. They had taken his laptop, and some other things. They'd asked Greg about anything important that may be inside, but I knew he wouldn't know if there was.

I pushed my way inside.

The curtains were open, which wasn't usual. That was something Ben would have to be reminded to do most days.

That was if I remembered. It had been a few years since I'd stopped cleaning up after him, which was around the same time it became a teenage hovel.

It wasn't as bad as I thought it would be. Sure, the bed hadn't been made and there were a couple of glasses stained black at the bottom with the remnants of Coca-Cola. Zero sugar and cherry flavoured – the only thing he would drink. A plate with the remains of a slice or two of toast, from a couple of days before, I guessed. Something he'd made himself quietly after midnight, when he'd got home from a night with his friends. Greg and I in bed, without a worry that he would make it home safely.

The before times.

Now, I knew how precious and precarious life actually was.

The smell in there had once made me roll my eyes. Now, it was almost comforting. As if he couldn't really be gone if I could still be assailed by the scent of my son.

There were a few crumpled-up items of clothes on the floor. His desk was messy – a blank space where his laptop would have been sitting. I hadn't seen him use it in a long time. His phone was a different story. That was never far from his hand, beaming into his face.

The detectives had been back the previous evening. I didn't have many questions beyond whether they'd spoken to Mia. They would only say they'd spoken to as many of the kids that had been out with Ben that night as possible.

Greg had more questions, of course. None of them provided answers. How could they? No arrests yet – and that was the only sure sign that something was happening.

They had questions for Greg, but I wasn't around for them. They'd taken him into the kitchen at some point and I hadn't asked him when they left.

I crossed the room and lowered myself on the bed. I wasn't sure if I was supposed to pick up his clothes and bury my face into them. I'd seen enough bad TV dramas to know that was what those left behind usually did when someone had been taken from them. A chance to inhale the only thing left of a loved one.

I was sure I would throw up if I did that.

Instead, I sat there on the bed, staring at the wall in front of me. The photo grid hanging up there, filled with memories that didn't include me. Ben's friends, Ben's experiences, Ben's memories.

Faces I remembered. Faces I recognised.

Places I remembered. Places I recognised.

My son's life for the past year or two. Laid out in uniform. Pegged up on a metal grid, as if it were enough to mark a life.

I had been feeling hollowed out inside. Empty. As if something had come along in the middle of the night and taken everything inside out. Left nothing but a husk. A shell of a person.

That had been the past twenty-four hours.

Now, as I stared at my son's friends, my son's life, I began to feel something else.

Bubbling up, slowly, as if it was somehow scared to reveal itself properly. I knew I had to let it in. Open a door and welcome it.

Anger.

It had become easier more recently to feel that way.

Greg had read up about it. In one of his . . . lectures? I guessed that's how I'd categorise them. That's how they felt. He'd read all about perimenopause and its possible symptoms, when I'd dared to mention that at forty-five years of age something didn't feel right. He'd listed them off, as if he'd found the reason why I had started arguing more with him than before. Why I was suddenly finding a voice I hadn't had for the first two decades of our relationship. Why our sex life had all but disappeared entirely. As if it wasn't growing tired of being dominated by his personality and tired of not mattering to him or anyone else.

I could point to the hot flushes, the anxiety that seemed to settle in my chest and stomach and follow me around all day. The many other changes to my body. I could accept those as being the next trial of just being a woman.

The anger . . . that felt more justified. For so many reasons.

That was what I had been waiting for. An emotion that I could hang on to. That I could let consume me and take over. Embrace.

And it was those photographs and ticket stubs and printouts that were doing it. The polaroids that had suddenly become fashionable again. The tickets printed off on the dodgy HP printer downstairs, that barely worked properly. The QR codes that allowed entry into gigs and cinemas and theme parks.

Mementos that Ben had kept to place a marker on a day in his life.

Someone had stolen the possibility of any more taking their place.

No more memories to be made.

Stolen from him. From his family.

I wasn't going to sit back and wait for a police officer to arrive and tell me what was being done about it. That they were going to charge some unknown attacker, who had just wanted to steal some items from a drunk kid walking home late at night. Probably homeless. Probably desperate.

I wasn't going to wait for that.

Because I knew it was bullshit.

This wasn't random.

I had been thinking about it since the day before – when the police had been standing in my living room and I'd not told them all I'd known.

Whether it had been because I knew what I was going to do eventually. When I'd got through the initial shock.

Whether it was because I wasn't thinking straight and that once I'd started processing what happened, I would have called them back. Told them everything I knew. Helped with their *investigation*.

I knew, though. Even at the time, when it was happening. I knew I was holding something back from them, because I wanted to deal with it myself.

To discover the truth and then decide for myself what I was going to do about it.

This wasn't random.

Ben had been the target.

And he wasn't the first.

What I did know is that he would be the last one. The last person to lose their life in this small town. The last victim.

I was going to make sure of it.

I reached under the mattress and found the diary. Laid it on my lap.

I'd found it a couple of weeks earlier.

I'd not been able to help myself – I'd opened it up and read through as many pages as time had allowed. Most of it was barely legible notes that didn't make much sense. The note at the beginning had suggested that Ben had wanted to keep a diary because he'd seen some Netflix show or something. He had kept it going daily for all of four days, before it became more sporadic.

It had been one of the notes near the end that I remembered now. I found it easily enough – there wasn't much in there from the past few weeks.

Mia pretends too much. I don't think she always tells the truth. She knows she's the reason Mr Fulton and Becky are dead. I just don't know if she did it or not. I bet she does know what happened to them . . . she just can't tell anyone. Either protecting herself or someone else?

The detectives hadn't admitted to talking to Mia Johnstone, but I was sure they had. And I was sure she had pulled the wool over their eyes, with her innocent eyes and waif-like appearance.

I had never liked her. I just didn't know if the rumours about her had been true or not.

What I did know is that I wasn't going to wait around for them to let me know what she did or didn't know.

Or if they believed her.

Because I knew they shouldn't.

8

Mia knew the first person to actually show up in person would be Anna. That's just who she was. An old-fashioned girl in a modern world. Someone who knocked on your front door without prior notice. Someone who knocked on the door at all, rather than just sending a message telling you they were outside.

Someone who still called her on the phone, rather than just sending a few lines of text or a voice note.

It seemed like everyone had forgotten how to talk in person.

Mia never liked to be the one who knocked on a door or called first. Or rang someone on the phone. Or messaged first. She'd felt weird her whole life, like she was odd for wanting the same kind of friendships that had existed normally twenty years earlier.

Smartphones and the internet had changed everything.

Her mum had answered the door, just as Mia got halfway down the stairs. She heard Anna saying, 'hello Mrs Johnstone' and her mum telling her for the three millionth time to call her Jen – as if that was ever going to happen.

'Mum, we're going upstairs.'

It wasn't a question, but her mum still seemed to treat it as one.

'Do you not want to come through and talk about . . . things?'

Mia didn't answer. She motioned for Anna to follow her up and turned her back on them. She didn't see Anna's shrug of apology to her mum, but heard her feet coming up behind her.

Once inside her bedroom, Mia slumped down on her bed and waited. Anna was leaning against the closed door, staring out the window that looked out onto the back garden and then the forest that wasn't far beyond that.

The light was fading now. It was almost as if summer was already over. In some ways, Mia thought it was. First week of September and Ben Lennon was dead.

She shivered, feeling an invisible draught enter the room.

'The police have been then?'

Mia nodded, unable to look at Anna as she updated her on what had happened that afternoon. What they'd asked, what she'd told them.

'Sounds like you gave them nothing, but said enough,' Anna said, when Mia had finished. 'That's a good thing. You know people will be talking about you, so best to get ahead of it as much as possible by being as open as you can be.'

'What do you know?' Mia replied, sounding more eager than she felt. 'I can't find anything out that doesn't sound like rumours.'

'I probably don't know much more than you do.'

Mia saw through the lie. 'You wouldn't be here if you didn't have anything to say.'

'Well, it's not like I was there.'

'Neither was I.'

Anna hesitated for a brief moment, but Mia caught it. She was about to say something sharp that she would regret later, but Anna was already talking.

'My dad didn't really tell me anything,' she said, looking at the floor suddenly. 'Just a couple of things.'

Mia parked the fact she knew she was already lying. Or underplaying it. 'Do you know what happened?'

'They think it was a mugging gone wrong, I think. That's what the rumour is anyway. His phone was taken, along with cash from his wallet. Only a couple of quid, I'm guessing. It's not like we carry money these days. They left his bank cards, his ID, his keys. Some kind of weapon, maybe a bat or plank of wood. They won't know for a while.'

'Where did it happen?'

'A couple of streets away from his house. Hope Street.'

Mia knew it, of course. 'He would have been walking back from where Mark dropped him off. That's the route he took home. Who was there last night, before they left?'

'The usual crowd. They're all saying the same thing – they left him to walk home after dropping him off as normal and none of them saw anything.'

'Was *she* with them?'

Anna didn't answer.

'Mia, I don't think anything was going on you know? I think it was just rumours – nothing real. Everyone was shocked when you guys split up. They didn't believe he would do anything like that. And she denies everything.'

Mia shook her head. 'I guess it doesn't matter now anyway. I'll never know the truth.'

Only, she didn't quite believe that. She knew Ben better than anyone and he'd been acting differently for weeks. Then, there was that Snapchat she'd seen – Ben in the background of some selfie down by the front on the dips, one night she hadn't been around. 'He was close to her.'

'Doesn't mean he was cheating on you,' Anna said, always the voice of reason. Maybe he was just giving her some advice or something. You know how it is.'

'Again, it doesn't matter anymore anyway. He's gone.'

'Are you going to be okay?'

Mia almost answered, but then hesitated. Thought for a second. 'It doesn't seem real yet. I can't imagine not seeing him again, so until that happens, I'm not really thinking about it. For now, I can pretend he's still out there somewhere. Just waiting for me to forgive him.' Anna nodded, looking solemn, as if Mia had just said something profound about grief. Mia knew that wasn't the case.

Because they'd been here before.

That was the unspoken thing between them. The eight-hundred-pound elephant in the room.

This wasn't the first time.

And Mia wasn't going to mention it first, which meant that Anna wouldn't either.

'So, what will happen then?'

Anna considered the question, brushing a hand through her hair. 'There might be some people with Ring cameras round there. They'll be looking at all of that kind of thing, to see if they can catch sight of someone running off or lying in wait for him. They'll talk to everyone who was down the front last night again, now they might not be so drunk. That sort of thing. They'll make sure Ben didn't have anyone who might want to hurt him.'

Anna left that last statement dangling, giving it a few seconds before she looked up at Mia.

'I didn't want to hurt him.'

'I know, but . . .'

'But what? Because I lost my temper? That means I wanted to kill him?'

Anna sighed, only serving to make Mia even more annoyed with her.

'Just, make sure you know what you're going to say before you talk to them again,' Anna said, moving across the room and sitting down next to her. 'I know you haven't got anything to do with this, but they're going to come back. After they've spoken to everyone – and you know some people think certain things about you. You need to be prepared for that.'

'I've only just found out that Ben has been killed. Can't you wait before you start this kind of talk with me? I get that you're worried, because we've been here already, but honestly, I have nothing to hide.'

'I know, but given what's happened before, you need to think about how this all looks. To the outside, I mean.'

'I had nothing to do—'

'I know, I know,' Anna cut in, as Mia's tone switched. Became darker. 'I'm not suggesting you had anything to do with it.'

'It's just a coincidence that's all.'

'This is number three, though, Mia.'

As if she needed to know. To be told. Three people in the past two years. All of them connected to her in some way.

No good way, by the end.

'It doesn't mean anything,' Mia said, as if she believed it. It was becoming more difficult to do that now. 'Just bad luck is all. Anyway, I can't think about that right now. Ben's gone, Anna.'

'I understand. And I can't imagine what you're feeling right now.'

'Well, let me work that out in my head before you start scaring me about stuff.'

Anna reached out as if to put a hand on Mia's shoulder, then seemed to think better of it. 'Sorry, I didn't mean to scare you. I just know that you've been struggling recently and then Ben comes along and it all seems great. Until it's not.'

'And now he's dead.'

'Yeah, so that's why it's important you have someone like me to come here and get your head straight. Because people are going to start talking, you know that right?'

Mia felt a churning in her stomach at the thought of what might be about to come. The way people might talk about her. What they may accuse her of. 'I'm taking the blame for some random mugging gone wrong.'

'Well, let's hope that's all it is.'

Mia still felt like Anna was holding back on her, but guessed that she didn't want to worry her any more than she already had.

'You know the best way out of this, right?'

Mia shook her head. 'I can't think straight at all.'

'It's to find out who killed Mr Fulton and Becky. That way, people won't think you're responsible for any of it.'

Mia tried to ignore Anna's words, but they echoed around the room. The fact that Ben was the third person in their small town to die in the past eighteen months – all of them violent deaths – with no one ever found responsible . . . it was difficult to ignore the fact that her life would be easier if there was someone to be blamed.

Especially given what she knew was about to happen.

Her phone buzzed on the bed next to her – something that had been happening frequently since she'd woken up. This time, she picked it up, as Anna pretended not to look over her shoulder.

It was a tag on Instagram. From someone she didn't follow.

'Oh no . . .'

She heard Anna's words through the fog that grew around her as she looked at the picture she'd been tagged in.

It was from a night down on the dips. The promenade and sea behind that. Mia standing alone, laughing at something someone had said off camera, she guessed. Maybe it had been Ben. Or one of the girls. She didn't remember. It didn't matter. That wasn't important.

It had been scrawled over.

The word 'KILLER' crudely drawn in red across her chest.

It had started.

9

I waited until Greg and Ellie were asleep before I left the house.

I couldn't be dealing with the questions. Where I was going, what I was doing. The offer to come along, so I wasn't on my own.

I didn't want that.

It had been the worst day of my life. And it always would be. There would be a marker now – before and after.

Before Ben. After Ben.

Things would never be the same again and the weight of that was starting to feel heavy on my shoulders.

I would always be the mum of a murdered son. Someone to be pitied. Someone to be given doe eyes and a tilt of the head.

That would be my life now.

I'd seen them before on TV. The mothers of dead children. I'd always felt sorry for them and wondered how they could live with themselves afterwards. How they managed to get through each day, knowing that something was missing. Would always be missing.

Now, I was one of them.

Only, I couldn't see myself waiting around for people to do something. To give me answers. To give me some kind of justice that meant so little.

I didn't care about someone going on trial. I didn't care about someone facing a judge and being told they would get a minimum term that might – just might – be longer than Ben got on this earth.

I didn't care if everyone knew their name and what they'd done.

I'd made a decision not to wait for all that.

I knew what I was going to do to get through the first few days.

I was going to make sure the person responsible paid for what they'd done.

It didn't take too long to walk the few streets to where I needed to be. That was the good thing about small town living – everything was in walking distance and you always knew were you were going.

The roads were quiet. A few streetlights the only illumination in a clouded black sky. Most of the houses were in darkness, save a few hallway lights that had been left on to ward off potential burglars. As if that was all that was needed. A light being left on was hardly about to warn them off, I always thought. If they were determined to get inside, they didn't care. Probably made it easier, if anything.

Not that they had to worry about much of that anyway. I couldn't remember the last time anyone had talked about a break-in, or a car being taken from a driveway. Crime rates in the town were almost zero.

Apart from the three murders in the past eighteen months, of course.

Despite the fact that there was barely any crime, I knew I was being followed by the new neighbourhood watch favourite – the doorbell camera. Some people would pore over the footage the next day, see a woman walking past in a blur, before disappearing offscreen. We'd had a Ring doorbell for a few months, before I had convinced Greg it was a pointless waste of time. All it seemed to pick up was cars driving past and dog walkers using the street as a cut through. The occasional delivery. Even then, it didn't always work.

We didn't need it. It was an annoyance.

I wondered if it would have picked up someone on the night Ben was killed. Someone lurking in the shadows, that I could have recognised. Someone lying in wait for him.

Evidence.

I guessed the detectives were ahead of the game in that regard. Probably knocked on all the doors and got all that footage. Probably piecing together a timeline.

I wondered if they'd share the last moments of my son's life, as he walked down the street at two in the morning without any knowledge of what was waiting for him.

It didn't help to think of that kind of thing now, of course, but that didn't stop me. That's pretty much all I had been doing since Ben died – thinking of all the things I could have done to stop it happening or at least find the person responsible.

I couldn't go back in time. That wasn't possible. Only in fun old films or bad new novels.

That only left the option of finding out who had done this and then . . .

And then what?

I shook the thought away. I didn't need to think that far ahead yet.

I came to a stop near a lamppost, the streetlight that was supposed to be working but seemed to have flickered into nonexistence.

I stared into the darkness. Looked for any kind of movement. No hallway light left on.

I had rehearsed what I was going to say over and over if someone found me there. What I was going to divulge. What I was going to portray. The broken parent, looking to be close to him.

There was a moment when I didn't think I would be able to go through with it. That I would simply curl into a ball and wait for my life to change around me. But I couldn't do that. I wasn't going to be that person.

Once I'd begun to formulate an idea of what to do next, it felt like an incredible burden had been lifted from my shoulders. I hadn't expected to feel that way. I thought the weight of the world would have been on my shoulders for the rest of time.

Something about having a goal – a purpose – had got me moving again. Thinking clearly.

It was the worst day of my life.

It was also the best day of my life.

A dichotomy of thought, that I tried not to dwell over. I was finally doing *something*. I had spent too much time already sitting back and letting other people make decisions for me in the past day or so.

It had been going on for longer than that. Since meeting Greg, if I thought about it long enough. Life had been something that happened to me, around me. I'd got stuck in the rut of normal life, with no end in sight.

I had started hating him long before I'd realised I wanted out.

No thought of a future. No idea about what I was going to do next.

Now . . . now I had a plan.

Of sorts.

There wasn't going to be any more waiting around for something to happen. I was tired of that.

I pulled my jacket closer to me, as the cold air swirled around me and I wondered what was happening inside that house. Where she was now – what she was doing, what she was thinking.

Whether she was thinking about me as much as I was thinking about her.

I didn't think sleep would come easily for the people in that house. The police were involved – that much I knew. Whether that had any effect on Mia, that wasn't something I could know for certain.

I wanted to be close to her. To see whether there was anything that I could notice that might be different.

I knew what Mia was.

If everyone in the town was honest, they'd say the same. They already were, I knew. Ben had told me, through his own words, scribbled down in a diary he barely ever updated, but that was enough.

Mia knew what had happened to Ben. To the others too.

The light went on in the front bedroom and I thought I saw a shadow cross the window. My heartbeat began to increase, as I waited for a face to appear in the window. I could almost hear Mia's thoughts – being awakened with the feeling that someone was watching her.

I wanted to know what she was doing. What she was thinking. The panic that would be coursing through her body.

She had been able to hide for so long.

Well, she'd been found now.

This was only the beginning.

I allowed myself a small smile, as I walked towards the house and imagined knocking on the front door. Announcing my presence and telling Mia exactly what I knew.

That wouldn't be smart.

I wasn't going to let her off so easily.

She deserved so much more.

So much more hurt.

So much more pain.

So much more fear.

And I was the one who was going to deliver it to her.

There was no doubt in my mind about that.

I moved a little closer, towards the low wall that separated the pavement and their manicured front lawn. The open driveway, with two cars parked up. I could see the unmistakeable round-eyed lens of a video doorbell, next to the house number. Instinctively, I began to duck back into the shadows, but then stopped myself.

I wanted to be seen.

I wanted those inside that house to know they were being watched.

I returned my gaze up to the window above the front door. Next to the main bedroom, that was still in darkness.

I could almost see her through the curtains – no doubt that she was looking back at me.

I imagined her up there, lying on her bed. Unable to sleep, her consciousness playing tricks on her. Going over and over in her mind, what she had done.

That's what I hoped would be the case.

More likely, if she really had killed my son, then maybe she didn't care at all. Maybe she thought he'd deserved it.

That only served to increase the anger that I was feeling.

I had to control it. I knew that much. It was okay to stand there, in the early hours of the night, staring at the house. But, if I went up to the door. If I banged on it and demanded to see Mia. If I screamed "Murderer!" at the top of my lungs . . . then, that wouldn't be the best way of dealing with this.

I had to be careful.

I stared at the bedroom window, waiting.

And then, the blinds separated a little. A pale hand appearing in the slats. I peered closer, but could only see the outline of someone in the window.

Looking down at me.

I stared right back and realised I was whispering something to myself. Over and over.

'I know it was you. I know it was you. I know . . .'

10

Lying in bed, after Anna finally left to go home for dinner, Mia wondered what were the last things Ben would have been thinking about.

She wondered if he knew he was dying. Whether he had known something was happening. That it was the end. Whether his brain had a chance to let him know that he was under attack. Whether the first blow to the head had been enough to drag him from consciousness. Whether the last thought he'd had was of just mindlessly walking home and then . . . nothingness. Eternally.

There was part of her that didn't want that to be the case. The part of her that she ignored for the most part.

That part of her was telling her that she hoped he'd died painfully. That hoped he felt the same pain she had in the past few days.

It wasn't something she told anyone about – that voice in her head that would pop in from time to time. She knew it was only an aspect of her subconsciousness coming out. Not voices in her head, like some crazy person.

Still, it wasn't a voice she liked to hear all that much.

She wanted to know what his last seconds were like. Whether he knew he was about to die.

She wanted to know if he had known it was because of her. If he knew that he was just the third in what was becoming a list.

Mia felt tired. So damn tired. All the time.

And she knew it was because she wasn't sleeping. Not properly. Not like other people.

No one else knew.

Just like no one else knew that she had muddy trainers shoved under her bed. Or a fresh bruise on her shoulder that she couldn't remember getting.

Or that she was sure she'd seen a drop of something red on the socks she'd been wearing the night before – just around the top where her leggings didn't quite meet them – before she'd shoved them in the laundry basket.

The hoodie under her bed that smelled like Ben.

It had been his, after all. One of those things she'd kept when he'd been over one day and she'd thrown it on when she got cold, despite having her own. Anything to feel a part of him. She wanted to take it out now and inhale the scent left there. Only, she couldn't, because instead, she was wondering how she could get rid of it instead.

Those were things she wouldn't tell anyone. Not even Anna.

Not yet.

Mia waited a few hours before talking to her mum about what was happening online. Mainly because she knew what the response would be. One of two things.

Ignore it, it's not important, nothing can hurt you. It's not real, it's only online. They wouldn't say this to your face.

Or.

Total overreaction. Scorch the earth, go nuclear, contact everyone she possibly could to get it sorted.

Mia didn't want either of those outcomes.

She simply wanted to be listened to. To be included in the discussion of what should happen next.

That was never going to happen.

What was worse, was that her dad was sitting in the kitchen when she went down. Not sitting in front of the TV, just to add to the bad luck that she'd been facing all day.

'Mia, are you okay?' Mum was sitting across from dad, a cup of coffee in front of each of them. They had been quite clearly talking about her and now he wouldn't look at her. 'Do you need anything? Something to eat, or . . .'

Mia shook her head. 'Have you told anyone about the police being here?'

'No,' her mum said, shaking her head.

'What about Harry?' Mia said, taking a seat and placing her phone face down on the counter. 'I'm sure he already knows, but I haven't seen him leave his room all day.'

Her mum looked away. 'I've spoken to him.'

Mia nodded, wondering what her little brother would be thinking of the whole situation. Probably annoyed it might have interrupted his time playing FIFA.

'These things happen,' her dad said, speaking for the first time. He looked tired, as if he were fed up of having to deal with life and everything that came with it. 'This is why we talk so much about safety. Why you should never walk home alone at night. All you kids – you're so quick not to listen to us when we know what we're talking about. It's not always safe out there. You're not bulletproof.'

'Thanks, Dad,' Mia said, holding her head in her hands, so she didn't have to look at them. 'I really needed to hear that right now.'

'I'm just saying . . .'

'John, just let it go—'

'I can't point these things out, even when something like this happens, Jen? Isn't this a great time to drive the point home that it's not safe out there?'

'It's not the time,' Mum said, her voice raising to match and then go louder than Dad's. 'Can't you see how upset she is? She doesn't need lecturing right now. No one does. There's no point.'

Mia wanted them to stop, but they were already going back and forth. Her mum, who most of the time was softly spoken, as soon as there was a chance to argue with her dad, could rattle the plates in the cupboards with her shouting.

She missed her older sister in those moments. Emily had stayed up north after university, probably taking the opportunity to have a quiet life away from that house. At least when she'd been home they could share those looks. Those rolled eyes. Those quiet conversations. It had never been that way with Harry.

When she'd been younger, the fear of her parent's breaking up had been overwhelming. She didn't want to be like so many of her friends seemed to be. Broken homes, split lives. The idea of it frightened her. Not as much now. They seemed to exist in a continual state of almost-argument.

They seemed to finally notice that she was still sitting there after a bit more back and forth and began to calm down a little. Her mum moved from her seat and stood over her. Then, placed a tentative hand on her shoulder. Started rubbing between her shoulders.

'Sorry, we're just worried that's all darling,' her mum said, her voice returning quickly to soothing, quiet. 'When something like this happens, so close to home, it scares us, that's all.'

'Yeah,' her dad chimed in. 'I can't imagine what his parents are going through right now. It's . . . well, I can't even think about what I'd do if something happened to you or Harry. I worry every day about Emily being up there without us.'

'I know,' Mia said, sitting up straighter and lifting her head. 'But there's something I've got to show you.'

She picked up her phone, aware of her mum standing over her shoulder and already trying to get a peek. She input her passcode quickly, hoping it wasn't visible. She'd change it later anyway. 'Here, look at these.'

She'd screenshot the tagged photos and account details. She laid the phone on the counter and her mum leaned over for a closer look, before swearing under her breath. Her dad snatched up the phone and swore louder.

'Who is this from?' he said, his voice turning cold. 'Who did this?'

'I don't know . . .'

'This isn't right. I won't let this happen. I won't let people do this to you. To us.'

And for a moment, Mia believed her dad. He sounded so sure, so confident, that for a few seconds, she let herself believe that would be the case. That he would solve her problems, that he could stop everything that was going to happen next.

Seconds.

Not even a minute. A full minute. Simply a brief period of time when she had faith in the idea that it was even possible.

Then, reality hit. Life wasn't like that. It couldn't be solved as easily.

Especially not hers.

She didn't say anything. She took her phone back quietly and smiled tightly at her dad. 'Thank you,' she said, as he breathed heavily. She could almost hear his mind whirring with effort, as he tried to work out what he was going to do next. 'It'll be okay.'

Then, Mia turned and walked out of the room, ignoring the protests from her parents as she did so. They could work themselves up into a fervour of nothing without her.

They wouldn't do anything. It was always just words and nothing else.

She went upstairs, pausing on the landing as Harry popped his head round his bedroom door.

'You alright?' he said, his voice quiet. His hair had been getting even longer over the summer and it seem plastered to his forehead now. The wisps of a moustache across his upper lip, that a strong wind could blow away.

Mia shrugged. 'Wish I was anywhere else right now, if that answers your question.'

Harry smirked, which made Mia feel better for a second. More normal.

'He was a dick anyway,' Harry said, finally, as if it were profound. 'He was always pissing people off. Probably picked the wrong person in the end. And all his mates were horrible too. Could have been any of them.'

Mia found she couldn't argue with him. 'You're probably right.'

'Just don't blame yourself for it. And don't listen to any of those people around here.'

It was the most she'd talked to Harry for a while. On this level anyway. He might have been a year or so younger, but he seemed to have something about him finally.

For a moment, she didn't miss Emily as much as she usually did.

Harry turned and closed his bedroom door behind him, disappearing as quickly as he'd appeared. Mia stared at the door for a second, then moved into her own room.

Inside, she forgot quickly about her little brother's kind words.

She started to think about her luck.

Good luck didn't come in threes.

And this was the third one. The third person who had died because of her.

That made her a serial killer, by everyone else's account.

She'd looked it up. Three was the magic number.

Three people who were dead, and it had to be her fault.

All her fault.

11

The first twenty-four hours had slipped away.

I remembered watching some American reality show about true crime years earlier. How important the first forty-eight hours in an investigation were. Half of that time had passed already and nothing seemed to have happened.

It had been twenty-four hours since they'd identified Ben's body, but time wasn't moving in the same way anymore. I hadn't slept properly, of course. After I'd got back home from standing outside Mia's house, Greg had come downstairs. If he knew I'd been out, he didn't say anything. He had sat with me until the early hours, until the silence became too much for him to bear and he caught a few hours' sleep.

I didn't judge him for it. The body had a way of demanding normality. I'd even felt my eyes close. Lost a couple of hours at some point.

Ellie had been with us for the first part of the night, but had succumbed earlier than Greg.

Now, they sat opposite each other at the kitchen table. Dark circles under all our eyes. Ellie looked a decade older somehow. Overnight, she'd become a woman.

It hurt me inside.

She was eating, at least. Only a couple of rounds of toast, but it was something.

I couldn't face anything.

I wanted to scorch the earth. Go completely crazy and make sure everyone knew about it.

That wasn't the way to play it, of course. Only, it was difficult to not want to get my hands on that girl, Mia, and get her to tell me everything.

Even when I had been standing outside Mia's home the night before, there was still a part of me that hoped it was all going to be a mistake. That it was just random. A mugging gone wrong, as the police had first said. That there was no responsibility on Mia's part.

That had been smashed to smithereens at nine twenty that morning when the doorbell went.

Greg had answered the door and for a split second, I wondered if they were there because of where I'd been the night before. A spark of guilt, that was quickly diminished by righteousness. I was ready to argue with anyone.

That didn't matter, though. There was a detective in my living room and she was mapping out Ben's last movements.

'We can track him almost back to where he'd spent that evening. The dips, I think it's called?'

Detective Natalie Williams. I knew the detective constable sitting on the sofa next to her. I wouldn't have needed to be told – he looked old enough to have been in the same class as Ben. Robert Carter.

DC Carter nodded in agreement and Detective Williams continued.

'So, this is early days in the investigation, but what we can tell you is that we're treating this as a very serious murder investigation. And I really don't like telling you this, but it looks as if it wasn't as random as it first appeared.'

Greg leaned forwards, a swish of air giving me some time to breathe. 'What do you mean?'

'We can't say anything for certain right now, but early evidence suggests that someone knew your son's movements and was waiting for him. It's a bunch of quiet streets, so the idea that someone was waiting for anyone randomly doesn't quite fit.'

'You have someone then? You know who did this?'

A shared look between the detectives. Only a quick glance, but I could see that they didn't like Greg. His questions, anyway. They would have to live with him for over twenty years to get to the real hatred.

'We're at the very early stages of our investigation, Mr Lennon. This is just the beginning of finding out what happened to your son. We're keeping you up to date as much as possible with what we know.'

'So, that's a no, then.'

'Mr Lennon,' Detective Williams said, wrestling back control of the conversation. 'This means that we'll be taking a very different look at what happened to your son. It's quite clearly not a random incident. That means we can focus on other avenues of investigation. It's useful to discover this so early on.'

'I know who it was.'

I almost surprised myself at the sound of my own voice, but it was calculated. I'd been waiting to speak. Waiting for Greg to finish with his interruptions. The look of surprise on the detectives' faces wasn't calculated, though – they both turned to me in turn.

'Mrs Lennon?'

'Yes?'

A narrowed look from Detective Williams. 'Do you have something more you can tell us?'

I thought about it. Wondered if I should just let them deal with it. Not try and find out for myself.

Then I remembered all those stories I'd read over the years. All those arguments I'd had with Greg, about the justice system. How I'd always come down on one side and he another. Him, thinking that judges were soft and that murderers got out in five minutes, when life should mean life. Me, thinking that sentence lengths were usually fine, and life did mean life for the most part. You didn't just get out after twenty years and return to society like nothing had happened.

Now, I felt different. Someone had killed my son. I knew that Mia was involved in some way. Felt it in my bones. A mother's intuition, you could say. And I had a choice. I could let the police deal with it – tell them what little I knew and allow them to investigate further. That might end up with the girl being arrested. Maybe they'd link the two earlier deaths to her and she'd be charged with three counts of murder. But, I could see the future.

Young girl. Barely an adult now, never mind when two of these deaths had occurred. No real evidence linking Mia to them, otherwise she would have already been caught.

She'd be out of prison before middle-age.

And that wouldn't be right.

'No,' I said, shaking my head. 'I'm just . . . I meant I know who it'll be. Someone who wanted to get back at him in some way. Or us. I don't know. I haven't been sleeping.'

I knew instantly that Detective Williams wasn't buying it, but I didn't care. All I wanted was for them to be out of my house at that moment. Away from me.

I had work to do.

I knew Becky's parents a little. We had crossed paths a few times back in primary school, where Ben and their daughter had been in the same class. Back in first year, before friendship groups had been formed, they had been at each other's birthday parties. Then, it had been a quick smile and nod at various events held at the school. By the time they'd reached high school, I hadn't seen them at all.

It hadn't been difficult to find them. They still lived in the same house, which was only a few streets over from my own. I pulled over outside, parking outside the next-door neighbour's and clocking the red light of the Ring doorbell flashing on as I got out. Someone a little precious of their parking space, maybe checking in from work to see who was visiting. Unable to do anything about me parking outside their house, but getting angry about it anyway.

I ignored it.

The front yard was unkempt – a berry-filled bush hanging over the length of the wall that marked its separation to the pavement. It needed a trim. Hanging over the pathway. The small piece of grass that lay behind it was overgrown – tall weeds growing up the front of the house. The grey concrete that led to the front door was mossy and dirty. The white of the PVC door was yellowing.

I imagined it hadn't always looked this way.

I reached forwards and rang the old doorbell and stepped back. A small vestibule area, hardly a porch, separated the two doors. One PVC, one old wood. That opened after a few seconds and the ghost of Becky's mother appeared.

I had checked her name before leaving the house.

Lisa. Lisa Harrison.

I saw myself in a few years staring back.

If she was shocked to see me, she hid it well. She reached forwards and opened up the PVC door, making me step back as it opened towards me.

'Alison?'

Even her voice was different than I remembered. 'Yes, Ben's mum.'

'Are you . . . do you . . . are you okay?'

'I was wondering if we could talk?'

Lisa didn't seem to think about the question. Simply turned around and left the door open for me to walk in. I hesitated for a moment and then followed her inside, closing the doors behind me. Lisa was waiting a few steps inside the hallway, before motioning towards the room on her left.

'Sorry to bother you,' I said, as I followed Lisa into the living room. 'I guess you've heard what happened?'

Lisa hummed a response, motioning for me to sit down on one of the sofas. A big grey thing, that looked like it would swallow you whole. I sat down slowly, noticing instantly that the cushion sunk down into nothingness.

'Can I get you some tea? I was just about to put the kettle on.'

'That'd be nice, thank you.'

Lisa looked around the room for a second and then left me there alone. There were no other sounds in the house – which suggested Lisa was alone. The TV in the corner was paused on some Netflix show I didn't recognise. The title was in the corner.

Emily in Paris.

A vague memory came to me, of a disagreement with Greg about what to watch one night. I'd liked the look of it – he had wanted something that didn't look so 'girly'. We'd 'compromised' with some random true crime documentary he wanted to watch and that I didn't pay attention to. Played games on my phone instead.

A normal evening in the Lennon household.

I heard the click of the kettle and clatter of mugs through in the kitchen.

The fireplace was new, I thought. One of those log burner stoves that everyone seemed to have now. A big wooden beam as a mantelpiece. Another disagreement with Greg came back to me.

There seemed to be a lot more of them coming to mind than before. Usually I didn't think about all the things we disagreed about. Just silently seethed for a few hours before giving in.

'Sugar?'

I turned to Lisa in the doorway and shook my head. 'No thanks.'

She disappeared again, leaving me to look at the photographs on the wall behind me. Only three canvas prints. The one of Becky alone took up the middle space. It must have been a holiday shot – a beautiful landscape of sea and sand behind her, as she looked tanned and older than her sixteen years. Probably a few months before she'd died.

Frozen in time.

The room might have looked nice on the surface, but I could see dust on the TV stand.

A couple of stained glasses on the coffee table in the middle of the room.

Bits on the carpet, that didn't look new.

It didn't smell of anything, thankfully. I wasn't sure my stomach would have managed it.

'Here you are,' Lisa said, pausing in the doorway as she saw what I was looking at. 'I'll pop it down here.'

'Thank you,' I replied, turning back round and watching as Lisa sat down carefully on the sofa opposite me. 'I'm sorry for just dropping by like this unexpected.'

'That's okay. To tell the truth, I've been waiting for you.'

I arched an eyebrow. 'You have?'

'Yes,' Lisa said, fixing me with a stare. 'Well, maybe not absolutely certain you would actually turn up, but hoping.'

'Why?'

'Because you know who killed your son. Just like I know who killed my daughter.'

I held my breath, waiting for Lisa to confirm my worst suspicions.

'It was *her*.'

12

Mia was up early for a change.

Mainly because she hadn't slept well. Once sunlight had started creeping through the curtains, she'd given up on trying to sleep properly. She'd heard her dad going out to work. Mum pottering about, before she started working herself – in the back bedroom she called her 'office'.

Mia had spent the night thinking about what other people would be thinking about her right then.

Some people thought Mia was weird. Still, even now. Mostly it was people who had known her from primary school, when, admittedly, she had been a bit weird.

It didn't matter that she wasn't the same person now, at eighteen, as she had been when she'd been a child. When you're still finding your personality. When stepping outside of the norm a smidge was enough to be labelled weird. Abnormal. Strange.

It didn't take much at six years old, to be given that label. Eight years old. Ten years old.

It wasn't as if they lived in a big city, where it was easier to hide. To move to a different school and meet entirely different people.

The same people she'd known in primary school, had followed her to high school. No chance of escape there. Everyone recognised a face. A name.

Sometimes, it was easy to forget that they lived in a small town.

There were four options for high schools in the area. One of them was Catholic, which wasn't an option because her parents had shunned religion most of their lives. Her dad was Catholic, but wasn't about to admit it. There was an all-boys school – that was obviously not on the list. That left two. One was an absolute horror show, that no one went to by choice and seemed to be populated by kids no one had ever seen before, so that left only one choice.

It pissed her off, of course. She had made new friends in high school. Joined new friendship groups. Tried to reinvent herself. Tried to ignore the girls from primary school, who had gone to the same high school as her. For the most part, they were in the background. Every now and again, she'd hear a whisper. One of those girls, trying to make trouble.

It was okay in the end. A little rocky in the beginning, but now, she knew who she was. What she liked, what she didn't like. She felt stable. She had friends. She'd had a fair few boyfriends. She liked certain subjects. She knew what she wanted to do at university.

Everything was going well.

Yet, she knew it hadn't been under the surface. The times she'd gone home crying, wondering why no one seemed to understand her. When friends had come and gone.

What happened with Mr Fulton.

What happened with Becky.

She knew those girls from primary school liked to spread the rumours. Whisper behind her back.

She was able to ignore it, for the most part.

Now, with Ben's death, it felt different.

It felt like those whispers were growing louder.

She'd left the house, for the first time since Ben had died. Only a day had passed, but her mum said she had nothing to worry about. That Mia should go outside and live her life like normal, because she had nothing to hide.

If it had been up to her, she wouldn't have left the house until enough time had passed that people wouldn't give her the look.

The one that said so much.

She'd never been more thankful to have met Anna when she had. Someone who had been by her side for the past seven years. Ever since starting high school on the same day – from different primary schools – they'd been close. In the early years, it had been a friendship of convenience. It had grown stronger, closer, in the past couple of years, until they spent as much time talking to each other as Mia did with members of her own family. Even more, probably.

'Did you sleep last night?'

Mia shrugged her shoulders. They were walking down the side streets of town, towards the woods that separated them from the next town over. 'I'm okay.'

'That wasn't the question.'

Mia turned her head to see Anna. She was looking directly ahead, but still had that look on her face that Mia recognised so much. 'I don't need another mother, Anna.'

'Not trying to be,' Anna said, not taking offence. 'Just asking you a question, that's all. If you've not been sleeping, then that would be understandable.'

'Well, no, not much.'

'There you go.'

'I just keep seeing Ben. Every time I close my eyes. I can't stop thinking about him.'

A murmur from Anna. A 'hmm' – as if that wasn't what she'd wanted to hear.

'I know you didn't like him—'

'What was there to like?' Anna said, taking the opportunity to interrupt on her favourite topic. 'He was an arrogant piece of crap. He treated people like dirt. Why would I have liked him?'

'Not everyone,' Mia replied, her voice low, trying to mask the hurt in it. She didn't like it when Ben was badmouthed. Even less so now. It always felt like a personal attack on her. 'He had so many friends. And he was nice to me.'

'At the beginning, when he wanted something. Then what happened?'

Mia couldn't argue with that, so instead she slowed down as they reached the turning into the woods. Leaned against a low wall and puffed her cheeks out. 'Well, now he's gone, so you don't have to worry about me being hurt anymore.'

'And that's a good thing.'

Mia raised her eyebrows at Anna.

'Not that I'm saying he deserved what happened to him,' Anna said quickly, but with less conviction than she should have to be believable. 'I'm just saying, he's not worth losing sleep over. It's sad, if it was a random attack and he was just in the wrong place at the wrong time. But I'm not going to miss him. I'm not going to miss you being with him and being treated like crap.'

'It wasn't always like that.'

'Do you think the police will want to talk to you again?'

Mia shrugged again. 'I don't know why they would. I can't tell them anything else.'

'They can't find his phone,' Anna said, stopping opposite Mia and leaning back against the wall there. Only a few feet separated them, but she felt closer. 'I guess if he was robbed, then that makes sense. But they will be able to see who he called, who he texted, things like that.'

'Why would that be important?'

'Well, it'll also show things that were sent to him.'

Anna left the words hanging there in the air between them. Mia knew what she was talking about, but couldn't think about that right then. She didn't want to think about what might be on that phone. What she'd said, what she'd threatened.

It was all in the past.

'That night,' Mia said, trying to ignore Anna's stare. Unable to meet her eye. 'When I spoke to him . . . he was different. He wanted to fix things. And I think I was going to let him try.'

'I didn't know that . . .'

'I knew you wouldn't be happy about it,' Mia said, a tight smile crossing her face. 'You've been with me through the whole thing. You knew what I was going through. But, I think I was wrong. I don't think he'd been seeing anyone else. And he also hadn't been telling people about *things* we'd done.'

'That's what he told you?'

'Yeah, that, and more.'

'And you believed him?'

Mia took a second or two to answer. 'I think I did. You wait now – we'll hear all about him. He was a good guy, we thought, you know, before everything happened between us. It could have all been just a bunch of rumours. You know what it's like around here.'

'But you saw things. Messages, meetups.'

'Honestly, if you'd heard him that night, I think you could have been convinced it was all a mistake.'

Anna made a noise that sounded like she didn't quite buy that would be the case. It didn't matter to Mia. 'And now, he's gone. So I'll never know the truth.'

'It means you've got less of a reason to want him gone, though.'

'I never did in the first place.'

'That might be the case,' Anna said, lifting away from the wall and beginning to walk down the path towards the woods. She stopped a few feet away from Mia and turned to face her. 'But, when you think about Becky and Mr Fulton . . . maybe someone didn't realise that might be the case?'

'What are you saying?'

Anna cocked her head, a patronising look on her face that made Mia tense up.

'This is the third person who you've had "problems" with that has turned up dead. Don't you think that's too much of a coincidence?'

'What are you saying?'

'I'm just pointing out that it's getting more and more dangerous to be an enemy of yours. Don't you think? And I know it's not you who is doing this, so maybe someone out there is doing it for you.'

With that, Anna turned and made her way down the path, disappearing into the treeline without another glance behind towards Mia.

Mia knew she was right.

She'd known it for longer than anyone else.

As much as she'd like to believe that it was all a coincidence, there was no real doubt in her mind anymore. Ben's death had made sure of that.

It was her fault three people were dead. That was the truth.

She just wasn't aware if it was only because of her, or if she was responsible.

Because when she'd woken up that morning and gone through the clothes at the end of her bed – ones she'd worn the night Ben died – she'd also checked the hoodie under her bed.

Ben's hoodie.

Black, with a Deftones logo plastered across the front, that he'd left for her one day and she'd never returned.

There was a stain on the top right shoulder. And even against the black, she thought she knew what it was.

Blood.

13

I knew she'd be thinking the same as me.
Mother's intuition?

Absolute rubbish. It was common sense. Logical thinking.

I still wanted confirmation, though. I needed to hear her say it.

'And by her, you mean . . .?'

Lisa shook her head. 'I think you know exactly who I mean. Your son has been seeing her for months. Josh has mutual friends, so has been keeping me up to date with things. He knew why I was asking, of course.'

'He has been seeing her . . . was, I should say. They'd split up, I think. And if I'd known what she'd done I'd—'

'You'd what? Tell him not to see her? That wouldn't have worked out, you know that. These kids, they make their own choices. And he wasn't to know what she was *really* like. None of them do or she wouldn't still have friends, boyfriends, all of it. As it is, nothing has really changed for her, even after Becky was gone. I'm sure there's some whispers, but she's sailed through it all. Didn't have to move away, didn't have to change schools. Still has all the same friends, boyfriends.'

'Why do you think it was her?'

Lisa sighed, took a sip of her tea and didn't seem to like it. Set it down on the floor in front of her. 'Remember the teacher from their school who was killed? Mr Fulton?'

'Of course,' I said, deciding against picking up my own cup. 'That's why I'm here.'

'Becky knew what happened between him and *her.*'

I noticed she still hadn't said Mia's name aloud. It was no doubt on purpose. I thought it probable that it had been said many times in the house in the past couple of years. Too much.

I couldn't remember Lisa's husband's name. I noticed his pictures weren't on the wall. Or any sense of his presence in the house at all, from what little I'd seen of it. I tried to remember any whisper of them separating, but I hadn't paid much attention to local gossip in the months before. Too busy concentrating on what my own life was dealing me.

'Tell me,' I said, leaning forwards and returning Lisa's watery stare. 'From the beginning. I need to know everything you do.'

'And then what?'

I shook my head. 'I don't know yet.'

'Well, don't bother with the police. They'll not be interested. They haven't listened to me at all, even after the inquest. I think they still believe she was on her own when she died, despite all the evidence. Easier for them, I guess.'

I remembered that, at least. Becky had been murdered, but after the inquest, nothing more seemed to have happened.

'But you know better.'

It wasn't an accusation, it was an acceptance that now I knew like her. Sometimes, you just know something more than those in charge. Those with responsibility.

'Yes, I do. Just like you.'

'I haven't told them that I think it was her.'

Lisa nodded softly to herself. 'It would be pointless, probably, but I bet they're starting to think that there might be something to it. Not that it'll help anyone now.'

'So, Becky knew what happened with Mr Fulton?'

I waited for Lisa to speak, but she was looking past me, to the window and outside. I wanted to follow her gaze, but I kept my eyes on her. Waited patiently.

'Not just her.'

'There were rumours . . .'

'Of course, but no one knew the truth. We all like to bury our heads in the sand when it comes to our kids, don't we?'

I couldn't argue with that. 'Surely it was investigated?'

'Didn't matter much. The police were probably happy that he was dead. It was less work, especially when no one came forward with an actual accusation. It could all be swept under the rug. He didn't have a wife breathing hard on them. His parents were older and didn't seem all that concerned. It became just a random killing. In his own home. A burglary, they thought, given some of his things were missing. There were a spate of break-ins around that time and they thought he just tried to defend his home and it went wrong.'

'You really think she was capable of that? He was bigger than her.'

'Imagine it's three in the morning. You're fast asleep. And someone levels a claw hammer into your skull. You're not going to be able to defend yourself too well. Still, there were signs in the bedroom of a struggle, but from what I've been told, he was pretty bashed up. I think he was dead almost from the first blow. After that, it was instinct.'

I wasn't sure I followed her in believing that was possible, but I decided to leave it alone. 'So, the rumours were true?'

Lisa shrugged her shoulders. 'The only one who knows the truth is her and him, and one of them is dead. I can only tell you what Becky knew, which I think is about as close to it as we're going to get.'

I waited for her to go on, not wanting to push. Lisa glanced down at her cup of tea again, but decided against sipping from it again.

'There was a trip to Venice, for the art kids, I don't know if you remember?'

I didn't but nodded along.

'Becky was there. They weren't friends anymore – both had moved on and found new people they had more in common with in high school. I know Becky still liked her on some level – she liked everyone. Such a nice girl in that way. She wanted to be friends with everyone, but that wasn't always a good thing. She had her group of friends, and that girl had hers. That's all.'

I could feel the grief coming off Lisa in waves. Not diminished by time. It made me scared about my own future – I was looking at what I would become.

Only, the one thing Lisa didn't have was closure. She didn't have justice.

That was what I was going to get.

'When they were in Venice, Becky said a few of the other girls managed to get alcohol. A couple of bottles of Vodka, or the like, I imagine. No idea how they got it, but teenagers find a way, we all know that. Anyway, Becky told me that she didn't have any, but I'd be surprised if she didn't. I hope she did, to be honest. She was so young when she was stolen from us, that I hope that she managed to have a few experiences at least.'

I didn't have the same fear. I knew Ben had lived life as much to the full as possible. Still, there was so much he had missed out on, of course. The thoughts diametrically opposed collided into each other and gave me the beginning of a headache.

'I know what you mean,' I said softly in response. Scared of speaking too loud, too abruptly, and stopping Lisa in her tracks.

'The girls were all in and out of each other's rooms – the teachers were probably in the bar of the hotel, knowing what was going on but not really willing to get involved. One of the teachers on the trip was Mr Fulton.'

I could see what was coming a mile off.

'So, drinking happened, tongues loosened, and one of Mia's friends let slip that she'd left the bedroom in the previous two nights to go and meet him. Becky heard this, and expressed surprise, of course. It led to an argument and the teachers eventually intervened. Only a few of the girls knew what had started the argument, but I think by then enough knew about him and Mia.'

'And what part did Becky play in this?'

'She was trying to tell that girl to go to someone and tell them what Mr Fulton was doing. Trying to help her. She was only sixteen. Not only was he a teacher, but over thirty years older than her. It wasn't right and Becky knew that. She tried to help that girl and got nothing but grief for it in return. Told to mind her own business, stuff like that. But she was only looking out for a friend, that's all.'

I wanted to push back, because I had heard stories about Becky. Ben had never liked her. Said she was up herself and arrogant. One of the popular kids, that looked down on everyone else. He had been very careful about what he said after she died, but I didn't think his opinion had changed all that much.

'Did Becky tell you when she got home?'

Lisa shook her head. 'It was later. After Mr Fulton died. She said she saw Mia a few days later and she seemed so different. Like a weight had been lifted from her shoulders. She seemed happy. I told her that maybe she was. Maybe it was what she needed – her abuser being taken out of the picture must have been a good thing. Only, Becky didn't think Mia saw it that way. Up until that time, she thought that Mia was happy about what was going on. That she felt like *somebody* or something like that. She revelled in the notoriety that she had amongst some of the girls. I don't know if that could have been the case, but one thing that Becky did see was something that happened the day before Mr Fulton died.'

I held my breath, hoping this was the thing I needed. Some kind of proof, that would make it all easier.

'She was staying behind from school one day – some kind of extra help with one of her A-level subjects – and the school was practically empty. She was working away and heard shouting coming from down the corridor. Naturally, she was intrigued and went to take a look. She told me – she saw the two of them.'

I could have predicted what was coming next and it told me everything I needed to know about Mia.

'Becky saw Mia and Mr Fulton arguing. Heard them from behind a classroom door. Mr Fulton was trying to keep her quiet, but it wasn't helping. Mia was too angry. And Becky heard her say, clear as day, that he wasn't going to end it. That it wasn't over, because she wasn't going to let it be. That she'd rather die than to see it end between them. That she loved him too much.'

I knew it. It didn't change all that much in my mind – I knew this was still a teacher in his late forties taking advantage of a young girl – but it confirmed something to me.

That Mia wasn't the sweet, innocent girl that everyone else seemed to think she was.

14

The dense canopy of the woodland cast an eerie, dappled light on the forest floor, where fallen leaves crunched underfoot. It was a place they had visited countless times before, a place filled with memories of laughter and adventure. But today was different.

As they walked deeper into the woods, their shoes muddied and their breaths visible in the crisp autumn air, an unspoken tension hung between them.

In the woods, things change. The outside world becomes a stranger. The sights and sounds of life and normality fade away, until all you can hear is the stillness of nature.

That wasn't the exact thoughts of Mia, as she walked in step alongside Anna, but a rough approximation of them. Not as thoughtful, not as poetic.

'It's so quiet.'

That was about the same thing.

Mia was thinking about blood. What colour it was, when it dried on a black T-shirt. Whether it could be easily mistaken for something else. How you could get rid of it, without it ever being found again. Whether there was a chance that someone could smell it.

A dog, maybe, could do that.

She wanted to ask Anna, but it didn't seem like the sort of thing that could be asked without a million questions in response.

She didn't know why Anna had taken them there, to those woods. A suggestion she'd just gone along with, because she wasn't thinking too clearly.

If she had been, she would have said no, of course. Because there was only one thing those woods represented to her now. And it slowly dawned on her that Anna knew that too.

'Why are we coming down here?' Mia said, slowing her walk a little.

'Just a little further.'

Mia knew then that Anna was leading them to the place. She wanted to turn back and go home. Go back to bed and pull the covers over her head and wait for all this to be over.

Instead, she followed her friend deeper into the woods. Wondering what Anna was going to do when they finally reached the centre.

It didn't take long to reach it. The woods weren't exactly that big. Could barely be considered a forest, or anything of the kind. When Mia had been younger, it had seemed to stretch until forever. Now, she could see and hear the reality of life in the distance.

They reached the clearing and Mia stopped on the outskirts of it. Watched as Anna kept walking towards a tree on the other side. Stopped in front of it and bent down to see what had been left there.

Offerings. Markers. All that was left of what had been a crime scene a year earlier.

An old Netball team shirt, tacked to the tree with the name of their school on the bottom. The number four, and HARRISON emblazoned on the top. It had been signed by her teammates, but those words had been blurred in the rain that had fallen in the previous months. Mia may have been a fair distance away, but she didn't think she'd be able to make out many of the words written there if she'd been as close to it as Anna was.

'Why are we here?'

Mia could hear the nervousness in her voice. Betraying her. She wanted to sound confident. Innocent. Only, she couldn't feel that way. Because she knew Becky was dead because of her. Not how, only why.

Anna turned to her and stared back. 'I need to know. For sure. Before we go on.'

'Need to know what?'

'Whether you did this.'

Mia closed her eyes, wished there was an answer she could give that she believed in totally. That she believed in more than anything. Only, she couldn't.

'I don't know.'

Anna cocked her head in confusion. 'What does that mean?'

Mia sighed. 'It means I know I didn't actually kill her, but that doesn't mean it isn't my fault she's dead. It's not like I'm the only one who thinks that as well. I bet everyone thinks I've got something to do with it and even if I don't know for sure, she's dead because of me is what I believe.'

'That's not good enough.'

'Well, it's all I have.'

Anna sighed and came back towards Mia. 'If I'm going to help you, you're going to have to tell me everything. The truth. We've been friends for years, but I can see you're holding back on me. And I don't like it. I want to help you through this, because right now, it doesn't look good. But I don't believe you did anything bad. And I think deep down, you believe that too. I just need to know everything first, before I can help you.'

Mia took a deep breath in and decided to let go. 'I honestly don't know. I don't think I did, but sometimes things happen that I've thought about.'

'Like Mr Fulton.'

'Like him,' Mia said, her teeth grinding together at the thought of him. 'And you know what Becky did to me after he died. What she said. What she spread around. I just wanted it to stop. But she wouldn't let it. I wanted her gone, but I would never have actually done it myself.'

'She was a bitch . . .'

'She was just looking for attention,' Mia said, correcting her. 'That's all. Making herself look good to all her friends. Nothing else. She didn't care about me enough to wonder how it affected my life. She was just keeping in with her crowd. It was evil. That's all. But the kind of evil that we can do at our age and get away with.'

'So, you must have hated her.'

'Of course I did.'

'Enough to come out here and make sure she never said anything about you ever again?'

Mia shook her head. 'No.'

'You sound sure about that now.'

Mia hesitated, wondering why she could be so sure. 'I couldn't hurt her. Not like that.'

'Maybe it was an accident. You came out here, with Becky, and didn't mean for it to go that far. An argument breaks out and you hurt her. Something like that?'

Mia shook her head. 'I wasn't here. It happened at night, when I was at home. Asleep. You know that.'

'I do, but I'm trying to understand what happened here, because it doesn't make any sense. Three people dead, all with connections to you. Now, if you didn't do it, someone we know did. Has to be.'

'I guess,' Mia said, unconvinced still. She didn't want to think of someone she knew as being a killer, never mind herself. 'But I don't think so. This isn't Netflix – we live in a boring town, where everyone is boring and not potential serial killers, Anna. Mr Fulton, they said it was a burglary that he interrupted. Becky, could be anything – maybe any of the other girls she bullied, or an older boyfriend that she wanted to leave. Something like that. That's what the police thought.'

'And Ben?'

Mia shook her head. 'I don't know yet.'

'It is weird that all these people you wanted dead ended up dying, though, don't you think?'

'Yeah, don't think I haven't noticed that. Only, now with Ben, that's different. I didn't want him dead. Not anymore.'

'But you did at one point.'

'Yeah, but not in a real sense. When I thought he'd cheated on me and made me look like a fool, then maybe. But not really, just in a stupid way. I thought everyone was laughing about me behind my back again, that was all. And I didn't want that. I couldn't have that. So, yeah, at that point, maybe I didn't want him around.'

Anna shook her head. 'When something bad happens to you, why do you want them dead? Not hurt or something like that, but you just said dead.'

Mia didn't haven't an answer. Didn't even try to give one.

'But you didn't do it?' Anna said, after a few seconds of silence. 'You didn't kill any of them.'

'No. I didn't. I'm not a killer.'

'Then we have to find out what happened. To all of them.'

'How do we do that?'

Anna took a step closer to Mia. 'I don't know, but you have to promise me that everything was patched up with Ben, because that's important. It means maybe someone didn't know that and killed him, thinking that it was still the case.

'We left each other seeing a way back. I wanted to hurt him before, but that was gone. I didn't want him dead. I loved him.'

It was the first time Mia had said that out loud since he'd died and the loss suddenly hit her. It was almost a physical blow, as if someone had whacked her in the chest. She stumbled back, reaching out for something to support her weight. Her hand landed on rough bark and she leaned against the tree.

'I don't know what to do,' Mia said, her words coming out in short bursts. 'Because they'll all think I did this and I didn't. But what if I did? What if I didn't mean to, but it happened anyway?'

Anna was next to her in a flash, putting an arm around her shoulder and bringing her head closer to hers.

'It's okay,' Anna replied, shushing her as tears sprang to Mia's eyes and her breath caught in the back of her throat. 'I'm going to get you through this. I'm your friend – your best friend – and I won't let anyone make you responsible for something you didn't do. Just because they hurt you, didn't mean you did this. I know that. You're not capable of hurting anyone. You're . . . you're too nice.'

Mia let the grief overwhelm her for the first time. Thought about Ben. Thought about the time they'd lost together. All the things they wouldn't get to do. And wished it could have been another way.

Wished that she could turn back the clock and change it all.

And wished she hadn't lied to Anna about the last conversation she'd had with him.

15

I had to tread carefully. The next thing I needed to know from Lisa was why she thought Mia was the person who had killed her daughter. Why she was so convinced.

I didn't think I could just come out with it and ask for evidence. I didn't think she'd have any.

'I don't think anyone believed Mia had anything to do with Mr Fulton's death at first,' Lisa said, relaxing back into her sofa. There were no small cushions behind her for support. Just the sofa back and that was it. I looked around the room and realised it was devoid of those little touches. No ornaments, no candles, no plants. It looked bare. As if it had been stripped in preparation for a move. Only, the photographs were still on the walls.

'At first?' I replied, trying to think back to what Ben had said about Mia when he'd started seeing her. Nothing much. He didn't tend to broadcast his current girlfriend's lives around the house. 'What changed?'

'After Becky, I know there were more whispers. More rumours. Maybe because it was only a few months later. So close together. Not that the police ever linked the two together, I think. And I never understood that – two people, a student and a teacher from the same school? Dead within a few months of each other? It didn't make sense. I told them that, over and over, but they never listened to me ever.'

Lisa was going too fast for me. I wanted to know everything she did, but I don't think she got the opportunity much anymore to talk to someone who would listen.

I got the sense that people had stopped listening to Lisa a while ago.

'When I saw Ben, what had been done to him, the police said they thought it was a random mugging gone wrong. Only, I could see that he'd been beaten up. His head . . . he barely looked like my son. I don't think anyone would do that, just to take his phone and a few quid from his wallet. So, when they came round earlier and told me they didn't think it was so random anymore, I guess I wondered why it had taken them two days to realise that.'

'Who's dealing with it?'

'Detective Natalie Williams seems to be in charge. And there's some lad, who barely looked older than my son . . .'

'Detective Rob Carter,' Lisa said, cutting in. 'He was with the two who investigated Becky's murder. He's actually older than you'd think – twenty-nine, thirty, something like that – think he's one of those straight from university into being a detective. Absolutely useless, for the most part. His boss was a man, though. Don't know this Natalie.'

'She seems a bit more switched on,' I said, thinking about the detective. She seemed more determined to do her job, but I had no real sense of her at that moment. Just the air of professionalism and that she listened to everything. It wasn't enough to make me sure she would get to the truth, but I probably had a better view of the police than Lisa did at that moment. 'Not that I think they'll believe it was her.'

Lisa shook her head. 'No, probably not. When Becky was found, she'd been missing for two days. And the police didn't bother even really looking for her – they thought she'd run off with a secret boyfriend or something. They were more interested in talking to my husband, than being out there looking for her. Maybe if that random dog walker had found her a little earlier, she may have had a chance.'

'It was in the Forthlin Woods, wasn't it?'

'Yes,' Lisa said, her voice suddenly much quieter. Remembering. 'A little clearing, near the centre. It had been raining quite heavily for a couple of days, so she was out there on her own, all that time.'

'When she was found, what happened?'

'It was on the news, almost straight away. A young, bright, attractive seventeen-year-old girl? It was catnip for the press. They were here for a few days, while we tried to come to terms with what had happened. I had to go out in front of the cameras and everything, but by that point, the news moved on. I guess we couldn't compete with a Queen dying.'

I remembered the time well now. For some reason, I'd forgotten just what happened when Becky had died – how our small town was suddenly the epicentre of news. I guess I didn't want to think too much about it. Better them than us, was something Greg would say and I'd shake my head at. Maybe he was more right than I'd like to think.

'Now, it's just an unsolved murder no one can explain. They've tried to suggest she might have killed herself, but I don't think they ever really believed that was the case.'

'What did the cause of death come back as?'

'She was stabbed seven times. They weren't sure which one was the fatal one. Either the liver or lung. A few were superficial, which is what they call any wound not all that deep. That's why they tried to say she might have done it to herself, but the inquest called it intentional homicide, which made sure they couldn't get off the hook.'

I shook my head, knowing there were no words of comfort I could give that would make a difference. I knew Lisa wouldn't want to hear them anyway – she would have heard too many of them over the time since her daughter had been found.

'At first, they were all over us. They of course suspected my husband, but he was at work when she left the house, came straight home, and was with me all evening. That was all corroborated. Then, it was her younger brother, but he's eight, so that didn't exactly last long for them. Her uncle – her dad's brother – was interviewed a few times, but he had a pretty solid alibi.'

'They always look at the family,' I said, wondering how long it was going to take for them to start looking at Greg. At me. Greg might need to temper his frustration and anger. They might start mistaking that for something else.

'Once that avenue came to a dead end, they started looking into her private life. They didn't have her phone – that's been missing ever since – but she had a tablet and a laptop. There were no suspicious things on her social media. She was seeing a lad off and on for a while, but nothing came of that. And he was too sweet a boy to do anything like that anyway. After a few weeks, when they didn't get anywhere, it all just started grinding to a halt. They released her body to us and we were allowed to give her a funeral, at least. The police were there, just in case someone turned up, but it was just people in the town.'

'I remembered standing on the street when the cars went past,' I said, the memory coming back to me suddenly. The rain coming down in sheets, the wind blowing around me. I remembered just wanting to go back into my house, but feeling judged by the other people out there if I had.

'It wasn't a nice day,' Lisa said, matter-of-factly. As if it could have been any other way. 'The service was horrible. I just remember wanting to be anywhere else. The doctor wanted to put me on medication, but it was like I wanted to experience it all. Feel everything.'

'I know what you mean,' I said, wondering when I would be offered the same. Knowing I would turn it down too.

'There's something to be said about wanting to feel numb, but I need to be switched on right now.'

'Yeah, you do, before you get like me. I'm broken now. I tried for months. But no one would listen to me. I was only her mother, at the end of the day. I didn't matter. And then the detective in charge didn't return my calls anymore and suddenly it was like people would rather forget than find out what happened.'

'I'm sorry,' I said, not knowing what else to say. Scared again, that I was looking at a future version of myself. Would I be sitting somewhere, waiting for Mia's next victim to turn up? Waiting for someone to ask what I knew about her. Asking about who killed my son.

Lisa waved away my sorry. 'I've basically been waiting for someone else to come along and tell me I wasn't going mad. That I was right to think the way I have all along.'

'Have you ever spoken to her . . . to Mia?'

Lisa didn't answer for a while. Silence hanging in the air between us. It became more tense, as the seconds ticked past. I didn't know the answer – I had no idea if there had been some kind of confrontation. Ben had never mentioned anything.

'Yes,' Lisa said, finally. 'Once. It was a few months after the funeral. I bumped into her in town. I was coming out of a shop and she was just there. With some other girl, I can't remember her name. One of those that wasn't in primary school with them. They were laughing at something and I was just in front of her suddenly. It was like she didn't recognise me at first, but then something clicked and she stopped laughing in an instant. Just stopped in her tracks and seemed to freeze. I . . . I don't know. It wasn't my finest hour. But I said I knew what she'd done. I got that out, at least. That I knew she was the reason my daughter was dead. I may have raised my voice. My husband came out behind me and led me away. Told me that I was making a scene and took me back to the car. I was just shaking with anger. I wanted to do something more, but I just couldn't. Because I wasn't sure. I wasn't convinced at that moment. Now, I am.'

'Because of Ben.'

Lisa nodded, fixing me with a stare again. 'I wish it wasn't your son. I wish it wasn't anyone. But at least now, someone else thinks like me. She's done it again and I don't think she's going to stop any time soon. And I wish I could help more, but I'm just tired. I'm tired of not being listened to, I'm tired of being looked at as mad. I'm just tired of it all.'

'I'm listening,' I said, but it didn't matter. I could feel it. Lisa was shutting down again – the reliving of the worst moments of her life beginning to take hold.

I had to leave. I had to get out of there, before she dragged me down with her.

I just hoped I wouldn't be in her position in a few months' time.

16

I drove home in silence, going over in my mind what Lisa had told me. It didn't amount to much, but at least it gave me reason to think I might be right about my first instinct.

Mia was the reason my son was dead.

It made so much sense to me. Far too coincidental that he was the third person in the past couple of years to end up dead after an association with her. Far too coincidental that he was attacked after ending things with her, just like before.

It had to be her.

Mr Fulton, who it seemed had been abusing her. Dead after she threatened his life.

Becky, who knew too much. Mia didn't want her telling everyone what she'd seen before the teacher had been killed. Putting her in the frame for his murder.

Now, Ben. Who had broken up with her. Maybe she'd told him too much? Maybe he'd known something he shouldn't have?

I began to fill in the gaps of what Lisa had said. There didn't seem to be any kind of motive on the surface, but I could piece together a few things. Maybe Becky had confronted Mia about what had happened to Mr Fulton. What she'd seen in the days before his death. Mia decided she knew too much and that she needed to be silenced. It didn't seem enough, though.

I put it to the back of my mind for a while.

Something to consider later.

As I turned into my street, I noticed the police car outside my home first. Parked up, almost blocking the driveway.

I turned into it and stopped next to Greg's car. As I got out, I heard someone shout my name.

'Alison? Alison Lennon?'

I turned, still holding my car keys in my hand, feeling for the lock button on instinct. A woman I didn't recognise was standing a few feet away. A man was standing next to her. I didn't answer, taking them in.

'I'm Caroline, I just wanted to say how sorry I was about your son.'

I mumbled something that approximated a thank you and turned back towards the house.

'I was just wondering if I could speak to you for a few minutes? We would like to talk about what's happened. We can help you find out who did this terrible thing.'

I knew who she was now. Journalist. As I made a move to turn back around towards her, ready to unload some of the anger that had been building up inside me, the front door opened.

A woman stepped out of my house and came over to me quickly. 'Alison, it's okay, you don't need to speak to them right now.'

I didn't know who she was, but I could see Greg standing in the doorway behind her, beckoning me in.

I allowed myself to be led inside, but stopped as we reached the threshold and turned back to the journalist who was now standing at the bottom of the driveway.

I wanted to say something, but I couldn't find the words. An idea came to me then – I needed to build up the pressure. Make it so that there was nowhere to hide.

'You should be talking to Mia. Mia Johnstone. She lives in this town. She was the last person to talk to my son while he was alive.'

I felt the woman's hand on my back, pushing me into the house. The door closed behind me and Greg was standing in the hallway. I turned to the woman and looked her up and down.

'Who are you?'

'Louise Hale. I'm your Liaison Officer. And you really shouldn't be speaking to the press without our help. There's a possibility we'll be organising a press conference in the future and we don't want to jeopardise any of the investigation, especially by naming people possibly connected to it. Now, let's go inside and sit down. Greg, would you like to make Alison a cup of tea?'

Greg opened his mouth to argue, but seemed to think better of it. Turned towards the kitchen and disappeared inside.

I liked Louise already.

Louise had gone through her role in our house. Why she was there, why there was still a uniformed police officer sitting outside, and what was going to be happening the rest of the day.

The television had been turned off, but I had a feeling why there were suddenly more people around us.

'It's on the news,' I said. Not a question. A statement of fact that I didn't need to be verified. On some level, I'd known this would happen. Talking to Lisa had confirmed it for me – I thought back to that time and how little notice I had given it all. How little of my headspace I'd given to a story that should have been all we talked about. Instead, we'd ignored it, for the most part. Something that was happening on the periphery of our lives.

I remembered another story, from a few years before. A shooting in a town around ten or fifteen miles away. A gangland type of thing, only the person who had died had been caught in the crossfire. Simply celebrating New Year's Eve with their friends, in a pub that was so anonymous it could have been anywhere. Stepped out for a smoke and into the firing line of some horrible little twenty-year-old, with a gun that should have fallen apart it was so crudely put together.

Dead before they hit the ground.

They'd caught the guy within days. Court case in months. Life sentence, minimum term of thirty-eight years handed down before anyone had chance to celebrate the turning of another new year.

And all I could remember now about that case was people mentioning it to us. Old uni friends, family members who lived around the country.

'Hey, isn't that by you? What do you know?'

And of course, we didn't know anything. But there was something about the notoriety of the shooting that had given me a bit of a thrill.

People would be doing the same about me, I thought to myself. My family. My street.

My son.

'Yes,' Louise said, finally, leaning back as Greg re-entered the room and placed mugs of tea down on the coffee table. He hadn't asked Louise how she'd taken hers, so I assumed he'd already been dispatched to make one for her before I'd got back home.

I reached for the remote control, ignoring both of them as they told me to stop.

Sky News was already on the screen. They'd been watching before I'd come back. Ben stared back at me.

I didn't react. Didn't recoil. Didn't make a sound, as my son stared back at me from the television screen. Scant details about the case, a shot of the street where he'd been found. Crime scene tape, fluttering wildly in the wind, as some reporter stood with her back to the place where my son had died. Not the same journalist who had spoken to me outside.

'They don't have anything to really say at the moment,' Louise said, her voice lower. Warmer. 'This is just what they do. They think there's a story and go after it. We can use them to our advantage, but I need your cooperation. I understand this is the worst moment of your lives and I'm not here to force you to do anything. I'm here as the bridge between the investigation team and yourselves. I can be here for you both, your family, but I need us all working from the same page.'

I definitely liked her.

It didn't mean I was going to listen to her.

'Okay, but I'm keeping the TV on,' I said, ignoring Greg's sigh from the other side of the room. 'If people are going to talk about my family, I want to know what they're saying.'

'That's fine,' Louise replied, pulling out her phone, as it buzzed away suddenly. 'I'll be back in a moment.'

She left us in the room, as I turned the volume up on the television. The story had already moved on, to talk about other things. Wars in foreign lands, living costs crisis, and the latest culture war row that had broken out overnight.

'Where have you been this morning?'

I wanted to ignore Greg's question, but I could see he was in the kind of mood where he wasn't about to let something go.

'I went to talk to someone.'

'Who?'

I hesitated, before deciding to tell the truth. 'Lisa Harrison. Becky's mum.'

Greg thought for a moment – his mind whirring into action slower than normal. He finally placed the name. 'The girl who died in the woods? Why?'

'Because I thought she might have something she could give me. Some kind of information I could pass on to the police maybe. She's been through this so recently and Becky was the same age as Ben, so it could be . . . I don't know.'

I was only slightly lying.

'And?'

It was my turn to sigh. 'If there was anything, don't you think I would have told that liaison person or whatever she's called? She didn't really have anything that could help me.'

Greg crossed the room and slumped on the sofa next to me. 'I wish you had told me, so I could have come with you. I might have been able to help with questioning her.'

I shook my head. 'And what do you think you could have said that would have been better than what I said?'

'I don't know,' Greg said, mumbling his words now. 'I just wish you'd have told me where you were going.'

'I'm quite capable of talking to a woman about her dead child. We're on common ground for a start.'

'Oh, so being the mother is different than being the father of a . . . a dead son?'

I leaned back and began massaging my temples. The headache was coming back. 'I don't want to argue with you Greg.'

'Neither do I.'

'Well, don't then.'

Silence grew between us. Something that happened regularly, even before what happened to Ben. Now, it felt more loaded with weight. With inevitability.

'I don't want this to break us.'

I heard Greg's words, but I didn't believe them. I knew that's what he wanted to think – that we hadn't been on life support for a long time – but deep down, I knew he felt the same as me.

That this would break us. Eventually. The final nail in a coffin that had been built long ago.

I just couldn't think about it right then. I couldn't give it any headspace. I didn't care enough about it to consider what it would mean for us. Maybe I'd been waiting for something to come along and finally put us out of our misery and this was just the moment.

I didn't care.

Still, I couldn't be dealing with it right then. Not when there were so many other things to think about.

'We just have to keep going,' I said, moving to place my hand on his, before pulling it away before he noticed. His eyes wouldn't meet mine, and that was fine. 'For Ben's sake.'

'How do we do that?'

I didn't want to answer him honestly. I didn't want to tell him that it wouldn't involve him in any way.

I didn't want to answer him at all.

So, I didn't.

17

Mia made it home without giving anything away to Anna. That was an achievement, she decided, given that all she wanted to do was tell her everything.

The last conversation she had with Ben.

The truth of it.

When she walked into her house, it was silent. Her mum and dad's car wasn't parked outside, which wasn't unusual. They were back at work, after all. She had half expected them to take some time off to make sure she was okay. Make sure she wasn't left alone. Instead, life had already begun to go back to normal. Or, as normal as it usually was.

It hadn't really been proper normal for a long time.

She climbed the stairs, prepared to flop down on her bed and scrunch her eyes closed. Put some music on and drown out reality.

Only, her little brother was waiting for her.

'Where have you been?'

Mia wanted to just walk away from Harry. Leave him waiting for a response. She knew that was never going to work out well, though. He was too nosy for that.

'Out with Anna.'

'Not sure that's the best thing to be doing right now. Someone might have seen you.'

Mia regretted not at least trying to walk on by without a word. 'And? I can leave the house, can't I?'

'Do you know what people are saying about you right now?'

'Yeah, of course I do.'

Harry was only a year younger than Mia, but that didn't mean he dropped the arrogant act around her. It was worse, if anything. He carried himself with the air of someone who had never had life smack him in the face. Not that he'd had it easy – just that he'd never experienced anything difficult.

Mia couldn't remember a time it wasn't the case.

Now, he was leaning against his bedroom wall, with the most condescending look on his face. As if Mia had done something horribly wrong and only he could reprimand her for it. 'Then why are you making it worse?'

'What are you talking about?' Mia asked, unable to hide her frustration. She couldn't just walk away from him – that would just make things worse. That didn't mean she should have to deal with that. Not at home. Not where she was supposed to be safe.

'Going out with Anna, acting like everything's okay. People are going round saying you killed Ben and you make yourself look guilty doing stuff like that.'

Mia felt like she'd been slapped. She had known people were talking behind her back, but she never imagined that Harry would just so blindly say it in their own house. As if it were true. 'What?'

'It's all over Snapchat,' Harry said. 'They're saying you had a fight and it got out of hand. That you thought he was cheating on you, that you confronted him down at the dips and then you waited for him.'

Mia's heart pounded in her chest. She couldn't believe what she was hearing. 'That's not true,' she said, her voice shaking.

'I know that,' Harry said, his tone softening as much as it could for his age. His hair looked more greasy than normal – the telltale smell of a cherry flavoured vape surrounded him in a haze. 'But you need to be careful. You can't just go around pretending like nothing happened.'

'But that's not what I was doing . . .'

'That's how it looks,' Harry said, taking a step forwards, but stopping in his tracks. They never hugged, the two of them. It wasn't something they did. Never had. People might suspect it was because they didn't like each other, never mind had any love for each other. It wasn't like that, though. People didn't understand the relationship they had.

Harry wanted to be a big brother. Not the youngest. He'd been happier when they were younger and Mia showed him the world as she knew it. Then, when they'd started drifting apart in their teenage years, he'd wanted to look out for her. It had never really worked out that way, though, Mia knew.

Harry was too soft for that.

'It's not true, though,' Mia said, feeling tears springing to her eyes without warning. She blinked them away, struggling to keep a lid on her emotions. She didn't want to break down in front of Harry. She didn't want to worry him. 'I loved him.'

'They're saying it's not just him either,' Harry continued, now not looking her in the eyes. 'It's Mr Fulton and Becky. They're connecting them all now.'

'Yeah, well they're adding up two and two and getting fourteen. They don't know anything. I haven't hurt anyone.'

Harry nodded, his face softening. 'I know that, Mia. But people can be real shits. They'll say and do whatever they want to make themselves feel better, without thinking about what the end result will be. You need to be careful.'

Mia sighed, feeling the weight of the situation bearing down on her. She knew Harry was right. The town they lived in was small, and rumours spread fast. But it wasn't fair that she had to keep herself locked up just because people were gossiping about her. She missed Ben so much at that moment. He had been an oasis of calm in what had been a chaotic year.

'I hate this,' she said, her voice barely above a whisper.

Harry took another step forward, paused for a second, then seemed to make a decision. He reached out and wrapped his arms around Mia.

'I know it's bad,' he said, his words muffled as her head hit his chest. 'But we'll get through this. Don't worry. I've got your back.'

It must have been at least five years since Harry had last hugged her. Maybe closer to ten. She couldn't be sure. However, Mia felt a wave of emotion wash over her and hugged her brother back, shutting out all the negativity for a few seconds.

For the first time since Ben had died, she felt like she was safe. Protected.

Only, it couldn't last. The next time she opened her phone, it would be staring back at her. All the people who were saying nasty things about her. Who had decided she was guilty without any evidence. Who believed she was something that Harry didn't. The opposite of what her mum, her dad knew her to be. To Anna. To whatever friends she would have left by the end of all this.

She knew then that it was going to be impossible to move on this time. To live a normal life. Not after this.

Harry let go of her and cleared his throat. 'Do you want me to say something? To those people who are saying shit?'

Mia shook her head. 'It'll only make things worse.'

'Then, what are you going to do?'

There wasn't an answer for that.

'When I came home that night,' Mia said, leaning back against the wall on the landing. She still couldn't maintain eye contact with her brother, though she could still feel the warmth that Harry's arms had left behind. 'Those things I said to you . . . I shouldn't have said them. I should have kept it all to myself. I feel so bad about them now.'

'You were pissed off. And it was understandable. I know we're not supposed to talk bad about the dead, but Ben was a real dick. I never liked him.'

'I get that, but it's important Harry – you can't tell anyone about any of that. Anything I said that night – because they'll use it against me.'

'I know that, I'm not an idiot.'

'I know you're not, but you have to promise me. If any of that got out . . .'

'That was between the two of us,' Harry said, not showing any signs that he was enjoying having this power over Mia. A relief, on a day filled with tension.

'Thanks,' Mia replied, turning to go into her room. She hesitated, before facing Harry again. 'I wouldn't hurt anyone, you know that right? Not even if I thought they deserved it.'

Harry looked at her like she'd just said the most ridiculous thing ever. 'You? Of course not. You wouldn't hurt a fly.'

'Good, I was just checking. I don't want you thinking I was even capable of something like that.'

'Don't worry,' Harry said, chuckling softly to himself. 'That's the last thing I was thinking.'

Mia cocked her head, intrigued now. 'What were you thinking then?'

Harry shook his head slowly. 'It doesn't matter. I just know you would never hurt anyone – even if they completely deserved it. I know it looks bad, but as long as you tell everyone the truth, nothing bad will happen. Isn't that what mum always tells us?'

Mia nodded her head, even as she didn't quite believe the words now. It was a nice thing to think, especially when she was younger. As she'd got closer to adulthood, that sentiment had started to shift, though. Bad things could happen, no matter what you said or did.

'You were home before Ben died,' Harry said, his tone matter of fact. 'Well, at least a couple of hours beforehand. And there's enough people who know that. And it's not like we can sneak out of this house. Mum would be awake the moment we breathed in the hallway.'

Mia laughed quietly, thinking about how light a sleeper her mum was. It was the reason her and dad didn't share a bed anymore. Too many nights when she'd been shouting at him at three in the morning because he was slightly snoring.

'It'll blow over eventually,' Harry said, shrugging his shoulders. 'You'll be off to uni soon and this'll feel like a bad memory before you know it. It'll be me who has to deal with what comes next. All the talking behind our backs and that. And you know I can handle it.'

'I've got no doubts about that.'

It was weird how two kids brought up in the same house, with the same parents, same family, could be so different. Harry with his music and drama. Far too many friends. His confidence. His ability to always see the optimistic way forwards.

Mia, more in the quiet, arty role. Fewer friends, much less confidence.

Different paths. Different lives.

Harry would never be in the position that Mia was and had been.

'Don't worry about it,' Harry said finally, moving back to his room. 'Hey, have you even spoken to Ben's family? You were his girlfriend, after all. It'd be weird if you didn't even try.'

Mia thought about them – Ben's mum and dad. 'It's not like they ever really seemed to like me. I'm probably not even in their minds.'

'Still, probably makes sense to reach out to them. Maybe speak to Mum about that. Or whatever.'

Harry left Mia then, standing on the landing outside her bedroom, thinking about how she would even approach Ben's parents. How that would work.

Whether they would want her to.

What they would say.

That knot in her stomach returned with a vengeance.

18

I wanted to switch the television off, but it was impossible. My hand kept reaching for the remote control, but wouldn't quite make it. There was some kind of dreamlike quality to the whole thing, like I was asleep and unable to change what was happening to me. Only, it was very real. My son was on the TV screen. My home. My town.

It was all real.

And I wanted to turn it off and pretend it wasn't happening. Pretend that everything was normal again. That Ben could walk back into the house at any time. That my life wasn't currently being played out on the same TV where we'd watched *Brooklyn Nine Nine, The Office, The Good Place, Modern Family* . . . all of them, together, as a family. Staring at that box in the corner, not talking, but living with each other.

Now, all of that was gone.

Yet, there was something stopping me from turning over, or switching it off entirely. Some perverse part of me that couldn't tear my eyes away, in case there was a moment I needed to see.

The interviews were the worst.

Ticking round, every fifteen minutes. The same headlines, nothing changing. That didn't mean they didn't go looking for a story, though. Talking to people on the streets where I lived, asking them questions they couldn't possibly know the answer to.

'A quiet family . . . keep themselves to themselves.'

'This is a lovely place to live, nothing ever really happens here.'

'We're all just in shock. You can't believe something like this could happen on your doorstep.'

It had though. Only a year or so earlier. That's what I couldn't understand. It was as if everyone had collective amnesia. Becky's life forgotten. Her death forgotten.

It didn't make any sense.

People's memories couldn't be that bad.

I turned the volume down a little and turned to Louise, who was sitting on the other sofa opposite me. 'Why aren't they talking about the others?'

She frowned back at me, worry lines appearing in what was otherwise ridiculously smooth skin. 'What do you mean?'

'There have been two other murders around here in the past couple of years – why aren't they talking about them as well?'

'I'm sure they did at the time.'

'Aren't you interested in that, though? That two other people have been killed close to us and now Ben?'

'I'm sure the investigative team are exploring all possibilities . . .'

'Oh, don't give me that,' I said, unable to hold my tongue. 'I'm asking *you*. Don't give me a stock answer. Tell me – aren't you interested in that at all? I mean, we're not exactly in the middle of the city, right? I could understand then.'

'From what I know,' Louise began, seeming to choose her words carefully. 'There was a teacher, from the high school who died in some kind of home invasion?'

'That's right.'

'But he didn't live in this town, right? It was over in East Hilby. That's a fair distance from here.'

'Yeah, but—'

'And, the girl from the school,' Louise continued, holding her hand up to stop me talking. 'Yes, I can see how that might be concerning you. But, there were probably lots of things going on there that are different than this case. That's not to say they might not be connected, but did Ben know her at all?'

I shook my head. 'No, he didn't. Only through his connection to *her*.'

'The girlfriend?'

'They had broken up,' I said, trying to keep the anger out of my voice. 'I mean, they weren't together anymore.'

'I'm sure they're looking into all of that,' Louise replied, her attempts to dismiss me becoming more than a little annoying now. 'The best thing you can do right now is be with your family. Let them do their job. They know what's best and Detective Williams will be doing everything in her power to get you the answers you deserve.'

It was pointless talking to her. She didn't understand. She might do this for a living, but it's not as if she had lived it.

I got up and left the room, standing in the hallway trying to think of something else I could do. Something else I needed to do. I could hear Greg's voice from the kitchen, talking softly into his phone. Probably to his dad. That's who he usually went to in a crisis. Not that it ever helped – his dad wasn't exactly the best in a bad situation.

Who could I call? My mother was in her seventies now and was one of those people who thought everything bad could be solved by putting the kettle on. My dad had died a few years earlier and I don't think she'd even cried at the funeral. Wouldn't have been seemly.

I climbed the stairs and went to the only place I could feel something.

Ben's room.

It was as I'd left it a day prior. His not-quite-a-diary lying on top of his bed. Dirty clothes still scrunched in a ball in the corner of the room. I started going through his things, slowly at first, before becoming more comfortable.

I needed to find something. Anything. Just a scrap of evidence I could use.

On the wall around his desk, pictures of him at various moments over the past few years. He was the smallest in the group at first, before he'd had that growth spurt at fourteen or fifteen. Then, he suddenly shoots up. At least six or eight inches. Now, he was over six foot two – taller than his dad. Broader, too, which I knew Greg didn't like in the slightest. He was becoming a man.

Was.

He wouldn't quite make it there now, would he?

Those were the little things I would have to get used to. The fact that everything was in the past tense now. Stuck permanently, never moving forwards.

If I wasn't careful, I could get stuck there too. If I didn't have something to focus on, something to keep me going.

And finding out who did this to my son would be that thing.

I kept looking, with a renewed sense that there would be something to find.

I went through every drawer. Every hidden nook. Every piece of paper I could find. Read his homework notes, went through his drawers that were stuffed with clothes that hadn't been folded. Unpaired socks, loose change.

The room already looked like a bomb had hit it, but I didn't help matters.

There was a certain soothing quality to having a purpose. Having a goal in mind. When it was over, I could feel the abjectness of reality begin to hit me again. Slowly crawling over me, like a second skin.

One I'd be wearing forever.

I slumped down on the bed, wondering when I'd have to give up. When I'd have to accept what I was now.

I was the mother of a murdered child. That's how I'd always be looked at now. How people would refer to me.

I knew that, because it was exactly how I'd felt about Lisa Harrison for the past year. Me and the few friends I had. That's how we thought of her. Defined forever.

That was going to be me now.

There was nothing else to find in Ben's room. I knew that now. No AHA moment. No hidden object that would throw everything I already knew into a new light. No clue that would make Poirot twirl his moustache.

There was nothing there. Never would be again.

I wanted to break down. Crawl into a ball and never move again.

I wondered about all those parents I'd seen on the news over the years. Those with dead and missing children. Tear-stained press conferences, holding up photos of their frozen-in-time babies, children, teenagers.

It never leaves you. It can't.

I had to get out of that room. I had to keep moving.

Ellie was home. I heard her voice coming low from behind her bedroom door. I knocked softly and didn't hear a response. I thought about walking in anyway, but my hand didn't get as far as the handle before retreating.

I went into my bedroom instead. I could hear Greg moving around downstairs, the low mumble of his voice underneath me, which suggested he was back in the living room now. Talking to Louise. Who I still didn't understand the point of.

Why was she there, other than to get in the way?

I found my mobile phone and turned it on. I'd been studiously ignoring it, unable to wade through all the nice, heartwarming messages people had been sending me. I couldn't stomach them.

I went on Twitter or X or whatever it was called now. Saw the trending topics. Saw the name of our town. Not Ben's name, thankfully. Clicked on it and scanned through the posts. Nothing other than news stories and people wanting to lament the state of our society.

I couldn't be bothered with that right now.

I went to Instagram. Searched hashtags, like Ellie had taught me to do a couple of years before. Nothing I could see there. Facebook was pointless.

I went back to Twitter and searched something else instead. Mia's name.

I had to look for a while, but eventually I found something. It didn't have many comments – seemed to be an image that had been taken from somewhere else. Probably Snapchat or the other one I couldn't work.

It was Mia. With that friend of hers I could never the remember the name of. Hannah, or Ally. Abby, maybe. I wasn't sure.

They were down by the woods.

The tweet was talking about her being spotted going back to the scene of another crime. Lots of question marks, emojis.

It was where Becky's body had been found.

Just asking questions . . .

I had a few of my own.

19

Mia didn't think it was a good idea to google 'how to get rid of blood from clothes?'

It wouldn't take much for someone to find her previous search results and she'd be screwed.

Sometimes, watching those true crime shows on Netflix paid off. Sometimes, common sense was enough.

She thought about them coming to her small town and interviewing people for Ben's murder. Becky's and Mr Fulton's. Whether she would be asked to appear.

Of course she would.

If she wasn't in prison, of course. Then, the subject would be her.

Then, they would all be talking about her.

She didn't like that. Not one bit.

Which meant she had to get rid of the stain on her hoodie – and it didn't matter what it was. Just the idea of it being sat in her bedroom was enough.

But she couldn't google it. She couldn't ask anyone.

So, what gets rid of bloodstains from clothes, so they could never be found again?

Mia thought about it for a while. Bleach would just ruin the top, look completely obvious, and not be helpful at all.

Running it through the washing machine wouldn't be enough, she guessed. Otherwise, why would people even bother doing anything else?

She could use Harry's phone to search, but that wouldn't be fair. Plus, he kept that thing so close to him, she had no way of slipping it out of his room without him noticing.

No, that wouldn't work.

It didn't leave her many options at all.

She could burn the top. Only, they didn't have an open fire in the living room or a chimenea in the garden. Not as much as a BBQ.

Mia thought the neighbours might notice if she suddenly built a bonfire in the back garden and tried to burn her hoodie and only her hoodie.

Plus, she didn't really know how to build a fire.

She should have taken it to the woods, she thought. Destroyed it there. Only, Anna had been with her and would have wondered why they were suddenly doing that.

She had to get rid of it.

The Asda on the edge of town had charity bins for clothes, books, that kind of thing. That was a possibility, but it wouldn't take much for someone to find it, trace it back to her, what with DNA and all of that.

If she just washed it, would anyone ever make the link? Would they take all her clothes away? Would someone know what she was wearing that night? It was the only black hoodie she had, so she couldn't even pass it off as another one anyway.

She could talk to her mum and dad and explain. That might work. They wouldn't want anything to happen to their daughter, right? They would help her. They would make sure she didn't end up in prison.

They would understand.

She wasn't sure.

She didn't know why Ben's mum and dad hadn't been in touch. His sister, even. She'd spent enough time with Ben at his house for them to be on good terms. She knew Ben never spoke badly about her to them. Wouldn't they want to know if she was okay? How she was dealing with his death?

It didn't make sense that they hadn't been in touch, even with her parents.

And it was weird that she hadn't tried herself. There would be a funeral, she guessed, and she was his girlfriend. The last person he'd loved. She should be involved.

She opened her phone and ignored all of the social media icons blinking back at her with new notifications. Found Anna's name on WhatsApp and messaged her.

I need to speak to Ben's parents, right? They should know how much I loved Ben.

No reply came quickly.

She wondered how much she could trust Anna. Or anyone, for that matter.

Mia lay back on the bed, the hoodie lying underneath her on the floor below, and tried to work out if she could trust Anna enough to tell her about it.

And how she could get rid of it.

They were eating dinner in silence. The four of them. Harry having returned home from a friend's house a few seconds before the food had been plonked onto plates. At least that meant they weren't total outcasts as a family – someone wasn't put off what was surrounding them at that moment to still feel comfortable enough to invite Harry round.

The scrap of cutlery across plates, the quiet chewing, the thud as a glass landed back on the table.

There didn't seem to be anything to say.

Mia felt like they were all thinking the same thing, though.

That she was the reason there was a thick fog of tension hanging over them all. That it was her fault that people had started looking at them strangely in the street. That she was the reason why they didn't feel comfortable going down to the corner shop. The supermarket.

She was the reason why people weren't returning WhatsApp messages and phone calls.

Her brother was particularly sullen that evening. Even more so than usual.

It may have been the end of summer, but that didn't mean he wouldn't feel the weight of being under scrutiny. The few friends he had would either want to talk about what had happened or not talk to him at all.

She knew the same was true for her. She only had to look at her phone to see that was the case. On the day Ben had been found, so many had reached out, but now that had slowly trickled to a halt. No new messages, but social media was a different story.

She would save that all to read later. Her so-called friends gossiping behind her back would be what was happening instead. They'd already have groups set up, without her being involved.

Her mum and dad wouldn't get it. As usual. They'd tell her to just get on with it. Or explode with anger. They didn't really have any middle ground.

They didn't get it.

Instead, they sat in silence, as her dad's chicken fajitas lay on the plate in front of her, never looking more unappealing. Unappetising.

Old El Paso never counted on someone being under suspicion of murder.

That's what she was, after all.

'I need to speak to Ben's mum and dad,' Mia said, giving up and laying her knife and fork down on her plate. 'I think it's weird if I don't.'

She watched as her mum and dad shared a look that said so much in a single second.

'I know they're probably thinking what everyone else is thinking, but I need to do something. You know, to show that I had nothing to do with it.'

'No one thinks you did this—'

'Please, that's what everyone is thinking,' Mia said, cutting off her dad before he could start with all his endlessly positive words. It grew tiresome. 'Right, Harry? That's what everyone is saying. That your sister is some kind of killer.'

'I don't know . . .' Harry muttered under his breath, barely audible. No conviction whatsoever.

'If I can just talk to them, let them know how I feel, maybe people will stop thinking that? They'll get off my back and onto someone else.'

Mia knew she sounded desperate, but only because she bloody was. She might not be looking at what was being put out there every second, but she could still feel the weight of it on her shoulders.

It wouldn't be long until the police came back round either. And that stained hoodie was still sitting underneath her bed.

'We'll try and talk to them,' her dad said finally, his tone suggesting that was the end of the conversation.

'Yeah, okay,' Mia replied, pushing her plate back and standing up. 'While you're doing that, I'll just go upstairs and wait for the police to come for me.'

She left the table and walked out of the room, ignoring the protestations from her mum as she left. Made her way upstairs and flopped down on her bed.

Her phone was in her hand within a second. She unlocked it and clicked on to Instagram. Her inbox was showing new messages – new notifications. She clicked through a few and saw new followers. More than she'd ever had in a few hours. She navigated away from them and clicked on Snapchat. Same thing there. Stories directed at her – pictures of crying faces, asking her to reach out.

Friends that she'd added long ago, posting their feelings about Ben's death. Pretending they knew him more than they did.

WhatsApp had hundreds of new messages. It felt like a weight on her chest – being in the centre of a storm, with no escape.

And the whole time, Ben's dried blood was on a piece of her clothing underneath her bed.

Right there.

She remembered some story she'd studied in GCSE English. Someone commits a murder and then cuts the body up and hides it under the floorboards. And all he can hear is the heart still beating from beneath them.

That's what the hoodie was doing now. Underneath her. Beating away, telling her that her life was over.

Anna had finally got back to her. She opened the message, ignoring the tear that dropped from her eye and slid down her cheek. The knot of anxiety that had settled in her stomach and refused to go.

Yeah, you should. Do you want me to come with you?

She could trust Anna.

She had to.

There was no one else.

20

There's this person. Could be a man. Could be a woman. They're walking past a house, that lies empty on a dusky street. It's only early evening, but summer is well and truly over. The lights in the houses are already being turned on before eight thirty p.m.

Climate change, global warming . . . it's ruining the planet. Next thing you know, it'll be twenty odd degrees in October.

It's not returning to the scene of the crime, if no crime had been committed. It was just being in the same place as something that happened in the past.

That's the little mental gymnastics you can play on yourself. On your own mind.

The greatest thing this person has ever heard is that everyone is the hero in their own story. That every single person on the planet lives in their world. And they're the centre of it.

That's not to say you can't share the stage with others. With your family, your friends. You can care for them, love them. Still, when it comes down to it, you're the hero.

You're the star of the show.

So, you can walk down a darkening street, picking out the houses who haven't drawn the blinds yet, but have a light inside. Those people on show to the world. Sitting in their living rooms, staring at a box in the corner that tells them what the powerful want them to know. Laughing along to sitcoms with fake people laughing telling them the exact point they should echo them. Watching news channels with rolling slides of doom and gloom. War, constantly. Sometimes real war, with violence and bloodshed. Sometimes fake war, with opinions and differences. Two, three, four different sides to every argument, stoking up hatred for other people on and on.

None of it mattered. Not really.

This person comes to a stop outside a house near the end of the street. Makes as if they're checking something on their phone, but instead, they're remembering. They're remembering the last time they stopped there. Outside that house.

Stared at the lifeless windows, the door, the bricks. In silence. The only sound in the dark of the night the sound of their own heartbeat, threatening to crash out of their chest.

The butterflies in their stomach, taking flight and swirling around, crashing into each other without abandon.

It was the first time they'd ever hurt anyone. Not the first time they'd ever planned it. Not the first time they'd ever thought about it. Wanted to do it.

The first time they had ended a life.

Only, that might not be true. The rule of unintended consequences isn't one to be forgotten. So, instead of the number of lives they'd intentionally killed in the past eighteen months, there might have been more. Way more. Making a single, simple decision could end up being related to another death.

You're rushing for a train. You push past a person on the pavement. They stumble a little – not much, just a tiny misstep. You shout an apology and that person might swear under their breath, shake their head, but think nothing of it in a few seconds. They can understand, they've been in a rush before.

Only, those few seconds of interaction could mean that the moment they were to cross the road changes. They walk out a few seconds later and don't see the lorry or the bus coming. They get hit, they go down, and they die.

And all because of that tiny little interaction. A few seconds either way and that person would still be alive.

Is it your fault?

Intentionally killing someone . . . that's different. Making the decision to end a life is something else entirely.

And that's what they had done.

They had decided to kill Mr Fulton. They had broken into his house. They had taken the hammer with them. They had worn a mask, in case of DNA. Gloves, the works.

They had battered him to death. Stood over him, making sure he wasn't going to get up. They had moved things in the room, pushing things to the ground.

Done the same round the house. Made it look like there had been an effort to look for anything valuable.

Taken his phone, his laptop, his watch.

Anything they thought someone looking for a few quid would take.

Now, they were standing outside that house again. Staring at the empty windows, looking for something. An answer? A question?

Salvation?

They weren't sure.

All this person knew was that it wasn't the scene of a crime. What they had done wasn't against the law.

Because laws are made up.

They're just like everything else in the world. Things that are made up to try and make us feel better. Only, they're all fake. Everything is.

Because Mr Fulton didn't deserve to be a part of that world. That world that lives by these created norms and laws.

He deserved to be taken out of it.

Everyone is the hero of their own story. Their own life.

And sometimes, that hero has to do things other normal people wouldn't do.

No crime. Just a house, where someone had been taken out of society, like they should be.

And once you've done it once, it gets easier next time.

Until it becomes the norm.

How you deal with a problem that comes up.

You take care of it.

21

The detectives had returned. I wasn't happy about that, but it seemed like I'd have to get used to it. That would be our lives for the time being.

I didn't like the way they looked at Greg. The younger one especially. He seemed to be studying him, looking for something that wasn't there.

I guessed they'd started considering him as a suspect, given they didn't seem to have anyone else in mind. Maybe me as well. The two of us, doing it together, killing our son.

I couldn't control the thoughts that shot through my mind. Never had been able to. Greg had managed to make me stop saying them out loud, with his little comments over the years. His eyes rolling. His apologies to friends.

All those little things that I added to my mental list of reasons I disliked the man I'd married.

'That's the update,' Detective Williams said, as if she'd just delivered a sermon. 'We'll be keeping you informed as much as possible, but for now, I'm just sorry there isn't as much as we'd like right now.'

'There's bloody nothing—'

'Greg, don't,' I said, before he could make things worse. 'Thanks for coming around. And keeping us updated. We appreciate it.'

'Alison, they've told us nothing.'

I didn't want to get into an argument with Greg right then, but he wasn't exactly making it easy. 'What do you want them to say? Do you want them to make stuff up so you feel better?'

'No, I want them to find who did this to our boy and do their jobs properly. It's been days already.'

'This isn't a TV show,' I said, trying to keep a handle on the anger that was bubbling inside me. Only, I could hear my voice going up a level or three. 'It's real life and things can't just be wrapped up in an hour. It takes time. If I can see that, why can't you?'

'Stop talking to me like I'm a child . . .'

'Then don't act like one.'

I saw the young detective getting to his feet, as Detective Williams held her hands out in a placating manner. 'I understand how angry you're both feeling right now, but you can't turn on each other at this moment.'

'Tell her that,' Greg said, crossing his arms across his chest, looking for an escape out of the living room. 'I was just asking questions, that's all.'

I might not have given up before then, but I'd been close a while. I knew then, though, that it was over in my head. In my heart.

I hated this man.

It was like a silent decision made, in the back of my mind, that I could file away for the time being and not think about.

The marriage was over.

I would have felt relief, if I didn't have two detectives investigating my son's murder sitting in my living room. A liaison officer standing outside my back door, sneaking a cigarette she didn't think we could all smell as soon as she came back inside.

The young detective followed Greg as he left the room, leaving me with Detective Williams, who glanced my way, but didn't give me a warming smile. A supportive look. A tilt of the head, that suggested that she sympathised with me.

She shook her head and rolled her eyes.

'I'd like to say it wasn't expected,' Detective Williams said, sitting down next to me on the sofa. 'But, usually it's the husband who gets angry first. Women are usually just quieter about it and it lasts longer.'

'Right, he's just—'

'I know, I know,' Williams said, waving away my attempted explanation. 'Does he get like this a lot, or is this out of the ordinary?'

I didn't understand the question at that moment, so I answered honestly. 'He's got a temper. Terrible road rage. It fizzes out quickly. Usually if he realises the other driver is bigger than him and might pull up beside him. He wouldn't know what to do. Don't think he's ever formed a fist, never mind hit anyone.'

'That must be difficult to live with.'

'You get used to it.'

'He's not physically violent then?'

It was as if she were just making conversation. Something that wasn't about Ben. I was glad of the respite. 'Not at all. Slams a few doors every now and then, but we can all do that.'

'With the kids too?'

I shook my head. 'He's usually the peacemaker these days. When they were younger, they were more scared of him. When he shouts, he can rattle the furniture. Don't think he realises there's such a thing as volume control. It would scare me sometimes, even though I knew he wouldn't do anything. When they were younger, they would be frightened of him shouting. Now, they barely bat an eyelid when he's angry with them. I think they realised he wasn't ever going to actually hurt them and it's not like he ever threatened he would.'

'That must have been difficult when they were younger, though.'

I narrowed my eyes at her now. She didn't seem to be getting it. 'He never laid a finger on either of them. So he shouted . . . big deal. I was hit with a slipper on more than one occasion. My dad's handprint seemed to be a permanent fixture on my brother's legs. That was actual violence.'

'Still, it sounds like he's used to getting his own way,' Williams said, closing the notebook that had been lying open on her lap. 'And I can see you're tired of it.'

'I don't know what you mean . . .'

'I don't know if you know this,' Williams said, trying to maintain eye contact with me, as I tore my eyes away from hers. 'But, divorce rates in the police are higher than the normal population. I'm going through divorce number three, so I have some experience in the area. And I can see it on your face. You're tired.'

'I haven't been sleeping properly, as you can well imagine.'

'That's not what I'm talking about. You're tired of him. You can barely be in the same room as him, I think. He's the last person you want around. Even in this horrific situation you're in, you're not leaning on him for support.'

The way she was speaking was irritating me. 'I don't understand why you're talking about this.'

'Alison—'

'No, I don't have to sit here and take marital advice, while my son lies dead somewhere. Greg was right – this isn't helpful. Why don't you get out there and do your job properly? What about Mia? Have you even spoken to her yet? Have you looked into what she was doing that night? Because I'm not the only one who thinks she's the reason why Ben is gone.'

'Alison we're doing everything we can—'

'No, you're not, you're sitting in my living room, talking about my husband, instead of being out there and doing something to stop this happening.'

She didn't answer me, not that I was interested.

'I spoke to Becky Harrison's mum today, Lisa,' I continued, trying to maintain control and probably failing. 'She's a year on from losing her daughter and no one cares anymore. Three people have died in this town in the past eighteen months and they're all connected to Mia bloody Johnstone. And I bet you've not even met Lisa, have you? Not even bothered to look into that at all. You're just looking for a needle in a haystack that doesn't even exist. It's right in front of you and instead, you're looking at car registration plates and Ring camera footage. I wish this was a TV show – at least then everyone would know how bad a job you're doing.'

I was out of breath by the end of my little speech. I couldn't look at the detective. I didn't want to. I didn't trust that I wouldn't keep going.

'We can't act on rumours, Alison,' Williams said, matter of fact. If she had been bothered by my tirade, she didn't show any sign of it. Instead, she got to her feet. 'But, let me tell you, we're looking at every avenue of interest. Including Ben's girlfriend, his friends, anyone he might have had a falling out with in the past. And that also includes those closest to him. That's why I was talking to you about your husband.'

'Well, it's a waste of time.'

'Maybe so,' Williams said, looking down at me. Not an ounce of pity in her eyes – only a cold look that seemed impenetrable. 'But, I promise you this, I'm going to find out who did this to Ben. I'm here for you, but it's all about him. So, yes, I might ask some difficult questions, but I have to. That's my job.'

I didn't care. I wanted to snap back, but I just didn't have the energy to do it. I wanted her gone.

She wasn't going to help me.

I could see that now. They couldn't see that a teenage girl could do this, so they were dismissing it out of hand.

I wasn't going to do that. I knew the truth.

'You do what you have to do,' I said, fixing Detective Williams with a glare. I held her eyes as she stared right back at me. 'I'm going to do what I have to.'

'As long as it doesn't get in the way of what we're doing . . .'

'Of course not.'

'Alison, please, listen to me. We're doing everything we can—'

'You keep saying that,' I spoke over her, a sigh accompanying my irritation with the same line being repeated over and over.

'Because it's true,' Detective Williams said, getting to her feet. She looked down at me and shook her head. 'I know this is difficult for you. The worst moment of your life, I have no doubt about that. You've lost your son. And in a way that doesn't make sense right now. But we will find out what happened to him.'

With that, she left the room, meeting the other detective in the hallway, as I heard Greg muttering to himself in the kitchen. The front door closed and the house fell silent.

I wanted to go and find Greg. Find out what the young detective had said to him, but I knew I could probably fill in the gaps.

I knew they were looking at Greg now. Another waste of time. He might shout a lot, but it wasn't as if he could back it up.

He was a coward.

I lifted my phone from the side table where it had been lying and brought it to life. It had buzzed with a notification while we had been listening to the two detectives lay out exactly what they didn't know for the previous half hour.

It was Facebook Messenger. New message.

I don't remember when I'd added Mia's mother on Facebook, but I must have done at some point in the past. I didn't look at it that often, so it wasn't like I'd done it to keep tabs on her.

Hi Alison, I messaged the other day to say you were in my thoughts. Not sure if you got it. Anyway, Mia would like to see you and Greg. She's taken things really badly – she loved Ben and feels that spending some time with you both might be for the best. Let me know when you have time.

My first response was to want to throw the phone across the room.

How dare she . . .

The next was to swallow back the anger and bile and allow rationality to take control.

I wanted to speak to Mia. Having that happen at my house was a good start.

I began typing out a reply.

22

Mia was asleep. Dozing, more accurately. Not quite fully asleep or awake. A strange in-between feeling. Her bedroom light was on, and she'd been trying to concentrate on some YouTube video, before feeling her eyes close.

She could still hear the sound from her phone, but it was no longer in her hand. She wanted to open her eyes, but her body was refusing.

Finally succumbing to exhaustion.

It didn't stop her mind working overtime. That nervous feeling in the pit of her stomach still churning away.

'Mia?'

The voice could have been in her dreams. Might have been in her room. She wasn't really sure.

'Are you awake?'

Definitely reality. She screwed her eyes tighter, her body still trying to grasp hold of full sleep. She murmured something she wasn't sure of.

'I've spoken to Ben's mum.'

That woke her up. She opened her eyes and saw her mum standing in the doorway.

'She said you can go round. Tomorrow morning. I'll go with you.'

'Okay,' Mia said, her voice thick with sleep. She cleared her throat. 'Thanks.'

She made to turn over in the bed, but her mum hadn't moved from the doorway. Mia looked back at her, seeing her staring back. 'What?'

'Can we talk?'

She sighed. 'I guess.'

Her mum came into the room proper, closing the door softly behind her. She looked around the room, and Mia could see her holding back from telling her it needed cleaning. Tidying up. That was her go-to complaint. Her dad worked from home and spent half his time cleaning, but it was never enough. It wasn't a 'mum clean' as she'd say. And that didn't actually happen all that often anyway. Always threatened, never really happened.

It only took a couple of pairs of shoes left in the hallway and maybe a magazine on the coffee table, and her mum would start complaining about the house being an absolute pigsty.

She would only be happy if the place was empty.

Now, her mum was looking around her room for somewhere to sit. She seemed to decide on the chair by Mia's desk, but had to move the few items of clothes on top of it first, before sitting down finally.

'I didn't want to wake you,' mum said, looking around the room, as if seeing it for the first time. 'I imagine you've not been sleeping properly.'

Mia shook her head. 'It's okay, I wasn't really asleep anyway.'

'How are you feeling?'

Mia cocked her head. 'How do you think?'

'Stupid question,' her mum said, a humourless chuckle escaping her lips. 'It's going to be okay though, I promise.'

'You can't promise that . . .'

'I can. That's my job. To keep you safe. And I know it doesn't seem like it right now, but you will feel better soon. They'll find who did this to Ben and people will stop talking about you and you'll go off to university feeling better.'

'Yeah, well, that doesn't feel like it'll happen right now.'

'I know it feels like the world is falling in around you right now, but it won't always be this way.'

'I don't want to hear this right now, Mum . . .'

'Well, tough, because you need to. I know what it's like. I know what you've been through. And I know how he was really treating you.'

Mia shot her mum a look, but it didn't deter her.

'You came to me, only a couple of weeks ago, so upset by what he'd been doing behind your back. I remember your tears, just like I remember all of them. Because they always rip me apart. Your pain is my pain, Mia.'

'I haven't cried since he died.'

Her mum nodded slowly. 'Because you're not upset about losing him. I get it. He was horrible to you. Someone like that will have upset more than just you. There could be a long list of people who wanted to hurt him.'

'It doesn't mean I'm not sad he's gone though, Mum.'

'I know that,' her mum said, getting up from the chair slowly and then sitting on the bed as Mia pulled herself up. Propped against the headboard.

'I just know what people are thinking. What with the others . . .'

'And they had nothing to do with you either . . .'

Mia bit down on her lower lip. 'Think about what it looks like to everyone outside of this room though, Mum. Think about what people are saying. First that teacher, then Becky, now Ben? I would be thinking the same thing.'

'That *teacher* deserved everything that came to him. The police said it was a robbery gone wrong, so that had nothing to do with you. And Becky . . . well, we both know what she was really like.'

'I know that. But they don't. Not the people out there, who are all talking about me behind my back. Making up stories and calling me names. They think it was me. All of them.'

'Let them. You're better than all of them. You have to believe that. Believe in yourself.'

Mia drew her knees up to her chest, wrapped her arms around her legs and rested her forehead down. Closed her eyes and wished she could have just one honest conversation with her mum, when she didn't try to use platitudes and positivity to get Mia to stop being upset.

'Listen, if Ben was doing that to you, think about who else he may have treated badly.'

'What do you mean?'

'Well, if he was prepared to cheat and lie with someone like you, then think about what he's done to others. There's probably a long line of people who wished harm on him. Someone else will come out. Someone else will be the target soon enough. Don't they say it's always the family in these cases anyway?'

'I don't think so, not if it happens in the street in the middle of the night . . .'

'That's what happened to Becky, I bet. One of her mum's fancy fellas, I bet.'

That had been the rumour back at that time – that Becky's mum had affairs and one of them had either taken a shine to Becky or did it to get back at her mum.

Mia knew both of those things weren't true. Mainly because she'd been involved in those rumours starting at high school.

She wasn't aware they'd got out and become talked about amongst the parents.

'I know you're having mixed feelings right now,' her mum said, placing a cold hand on her leg. 'I can't imagine how crazy it must be to be in your head right now. I know you hated him at the end. When you came home that night, I heard you talking. I know how it went that night.'

'Then you know I lied to the police then?'

Her mum shrugged. 'It's not like it matters now. He's gone and you had nothing to do with it. Right?'

'Of course not.'

'Then, it doesn't matter. Only a couple of people know what happened that night and how things were left. I don't think Ben told anyone, otherwise his friends would already be saying stuff. Right?'

'I guess.'

Her mum slapped her knees and got up off the bed. 'So, everything is going to be okay. You'll go to see his parents tomorrow and tell them the truth – that you loved their son and miss him terribly. And then, when they catch the guy that did this, you'll be able to move on and live your life.'

It felt cold. Too calculated. As if her mum didn't care that someone she had been in a relationship with for months, who had spent time at their home so often recently, was now dead.

'This will be a memory soon enough, Mia. Just like all those times in primary school. Those early years in high school. They don't matter now, do they? You have friends, you have a future. Don't let anything bad get in your way.'

With that, her mum left the room, and Mia let out the breath she'd been holding.

She found her phone, buried in her duvet, and typed out a message to Anna. Waited for a response.

She needed to talk this out. What she was going to do, to say? Her mum didn't seem the best person to ask that.

Not the way she'd been acting when talking about Ben.

As if she were glad he was dead.

23

I slept better than I had done for a few days. I didn't know if it was because I didn't go to bed and instead opted for the sofa downstairs. A change of scenery, perhaps?

Or maybe because it was away from Greg?

No, neither of those things, I decided, as I waited that morning for the impending visit.

It was that I was feeling like something was going to happen. I was looking forward to something.

I was going to get a chance to look into that girl's eyes and know if she had killed my son.

Sky News was still on the TV and I could see they were talking about Ben again. The volume was too low and I propped myself up in order to find the remote control. That's when I noticed Ellie sitting on the other sofa, looking at her phone.

'Ellie, sorry, I didn't know you were there.'

She shrugged her shoulders at me. Didn't even look up from the screen in her hand.

I had to try and be a mum at least. 'Have you had breakfast?'

She muttered something I didn't catch, which could have been either a yes or a no. I decided that she could probably fend for herself. If she hadn't eaten, she would eventually.

I couldn't give it my full attention.

I sat up and rubbed the sleep out of my eyes. Folded the small throw I must have pulled over myself during the night and put it back over the top of the sofa. I could hear movement coming from the kitchen and thought about Greg.

Wondered if he'd make me a cup of tea and pretend like he cared about me. About how I was feeling, rather than just himself.

That felt harsh.

I realised I hadn't asked him how he was. I knew it wouldn't have gone unnoticed and I thought about how that might have made him feel. Lonely? Unwanted? Unloved?

I knew those feelings all too well.

There was a part of me that didn't think Ben's legacy should have been our divorce, but it had only given me more perspective than before.

It had made me realise the end had already come a long time before. That was all.

Or, maybe it was just a response to a major trauma? A way of distracting me from the grief that could overwhelm me. To think about my marriage failing, rather than my son being killed. To think about Ella and what she might have done, rather than let the police do their job.

To think about how all those things could be solved by me, rather than letting the guilt and grief wash over me. Drown me.

'We're all over the internet.'

I blinked as Ellie spoke. Turned to her and waited for her to say more. She was still looking at her phone. 'Maybe you shouldn't be reading about it . . .'

'Bit hard to ignore it.'

I wasn't sure I wanted to know what it was saying, but had to ask. 'What are people saying?'

'Do you really want to know?'

I sighed. 'Is it that bad?'

'Well, people think it was his girlfriend – that Mia. Only those from school and that. Most of my friends, and people who are trying to be right now, are saying that it's probably her.'

'Right. Well, the police know all about that.'

'Yeah, I bet,' Ellie said, and I realised she'd been listening to everything that had been said in the house since Ben's death. I made a mental note to try and shield her from more of my outbursts.

'What else?'

'Yeah, everyone else thinks it was one of us,' Ellie said, her tone flat, emotionless. 'There's hashtags everywhere. Apparently, it's always one of the family.'

'They don't know what they're talking about . . .'

'That's the thing isn't it? We're just news now. No one cares about him. It's just something for people to talk about.'

I couldn't disagree. 'We need to ignore all that . . . that noise. We know the truth. That we loved him and would never hurt him.'

'There's like, a ton of these true crime weirdos, who just have all these things to say. They're already putting videos out on YouTube and TikTok. They've come to the town and everything.'

I wanted to say it was going to be okay, but I remembered another death that had run on news channels for weeks. Another death that had brought these types of people out of their holes and used a devastated family for likes.

I guessed it was our turn.

'Ellie, we have to try and ignore all of that . . .'

'Bit hard when it's all out there,' Ellie said, her thumb still moving, as she scrolled through posts on her phone. 'Nothing is going to be normal ever again. Is it?'

I wanted to disagree. To tell her that wasn't the case. But I couldn't lie to her. Not then. Not at that moment. I wanted it to be over. Live our lives like nothing had happened, but that wasn't going to be how this played out.

'This is a terrible, horrible thing that has happened to us,' I said, resisting the urge to go over to Ellie and put my arms around her. She wouldn't want that. 'To Ben. We've lost someone we love and that's always bad.'

'Like when Nan died.'

'Exactly,' I said, feeling an ache in my neck. I might have slept better on the sofa, but I'd be paying for it most of the day. 'Only, this is worse. Because Ben was young. And he was stolen from us. The way it happened . . . I'm sorry you're having to deal with this. It might not be good for a while. Maybe not for a long, long time and even then, maybe never the same again. That doesn't mean I'm not going to try and make things as easy as possible for you as I can. And part of that is making sure this doesn't happen to someone else.'

'So, finding out who did this?'

I nodded. 'That's exactly what the police are doing. For now though, it's going to be crap for a while. That's just the truth. We're all going to feel like we're in a dream for some time.'

'More like a nightmare,' Ellie said, getting up slowly from the sofa and pocketing her phone. She hesitated for a second, then came towards me.

I wasn't surprised by the embrace – Ellie had always been the one who came for cuddles. Maybe less in the past couple of years, when she'd become a teenager and grown up seemingly overnight.

I felt her in my arms and tried to maintain my composure. Felt her head on my shoulder and wanted to keep hold of her forever. That's the only way I could keep her safe, after all.

That's the problem with having children.

You spend their early lives with really only one goal – keeping them safe. Then, at some point, you're expected to just send them off into the world and hope for the best.

I hadn't kept Ben safe.

That was what I would have to live with for the rest of my life. I had failed at my one job as a parent.

It didn't matter what people would say to me. What platitudes I would get. That would be the simple fact that I would have to carry with me forever.

But, I could keep Ellie safe.

And that would start with making sure Ben's killer never got the chance to do it again.

If Greg had the same thoughts as me about Mia, then he was hiding it incredibly well.

We hadn't really spoken that morning, but I sensed that he understood that something had shifted between us. That things were different and would never be the same again.

I didn't get that cup of tea, for starters.

I wasn't nervous. I'd been expecting to feel that way, given how much I'd built it up in my head. Yet, when the Ring doorbell chimed throughout the house on all the various devices, I felt calm.

Louise, the liaison officer, had arrived back at the house early in the morning. She must have been feeling like a spare part. There wasn't any real reason for her to be around, other than as to serve as a constant reminder that something bad had happened.

'I'll get it,' I heard Greg say, passing the open living room door and down the hallway. I breathed in and out slowly, as I mentally prepared myself.

I had to stay calm. That was key. If I began ranting and raving, it would be over before it had even started.

I needed information. Things I could use.

I heard the front door open and the murmurs of meeting. And then, seconds later, Mia's mum was standing in my living room.

Jenny. That was her name. If I hadn't been thinking about Mia and her family pretty much non-stop for the past few days, I probably wouldn't have remembered it. We'd only met once before. Given our oldest children had been seeing each other for months, it was weird that we could quite easily have passed by on the street and not recognised each other.

I couldn't see Mia at first. I stood up and crossed the room. Took Jenny's hand in mine and accepted her quiet statement.

'So sorry for your loss.'

Like it meant anything. I wanted to ask how sorry she was? What she could do about it? And anyway, Ben wasn't lost. He'd been found. That was the problem.

I didn't lose him. He was stolen from me.

I swallowed that all back and instead said 'thank you.'

'If there's anything you need, that we can do for you, just ask.'

I nodded, as I tried not to scream.

'Please, come in, sit down,' I said, hoping my voice didn't betray me. I sounded normal, I thought. Normal enough, anyway.

I watched as Jenny Johnstone sat down slowly on my sofa and then a young girl came into the room proper and sat down beside her quietly.

She was so small.

I don't know what I'd been expecting – I'd seen her often enough to know that she wasn't some huge figure. Some monster.

She was five foot three and a little waif of a girl.

Her eyes were bluey green, and her hair was long, dark. Black, almost. It was hanging loose down her shoulders. She came in, not making eye contact with me. I saw her stealing glances at the photographs in the room. The television on mute in the corner.

And it took everything in me not to grab her there and then. To take hold of her and do . . . do something.

Instead, I sat down, looked across the room at the girl I thought had killed my son, and gave her a comforting smile.

'How are you doing, Mia?'

24

Detective Natalie Williams had known the mother was going to be trouble from the start.

Not that she blamed her. She knew she'd be much worse in the same situation.

Sometimes, she missed the city life. These little suburban towns might be nicer on paper, but it only took one murder and the whole ideal was destroyed.

Well, three murders.

'The initial investigation thought it was suicide at first,' Carter said, sidling up to her desk and laying a thin folder down on it. 'They caught on quickly, I guess, and then the first inquest nixed that outcome. Cops agreed back then.'

'It wasn't our lot?'

Carter shook his head. 'CID down in Chesham. The woods stretch to their patch, so they took it on.'

'And you were on the team?'

'Yeah, but not for long,' Carter said, his hands interlocked with each other and dangling just below his beltline. He was still nervous around her, she realised. 'They moved me over here when the borough restructured. I was only involved a little anyway.'

'You met Becky's mother, though.'

'I did,' Carter said, quietly. 'I don't really remember it, though. I'm not sure if you know, but last summer I was working with the Matrix team on drugs. County lines stuff. The months before that are a bit of a blur.'

'Right, well maybe we should revisit her then. See if she has anything of use to us?'

Carter nodded and moved away quickly.

Natalie leaned back in her chair, regarding the slim folder Carter had left behind for her. She picked it up and considered it – not an awful amount given it contained the details about a seventeen-year-old girl's death. Suspicious as it was.

It didn't make much sense to her that it had been dropped so quickly.

She flipped through the pages, knowing there would be more to find on the system, but she preferred the written word. The penmanship, the typed-out words. All of it, in front of her in black and white.

That was where you could absorb it better. Where you could take things in properly.

She read through it and wondered how on earth they'd suspected she'd died by suicide at all.

'You've read this, right?' she said, as Carter came back into her office, hovering in the open doorway. 'What was the idea that she could have done this to herself?'

Carter cleared his throat. 'Best I can say is that there was some talk from one of her friends that she had been depressed about something. That she'd shared some violent imagery on her social media and been talking strange in the lead up to the days in which she went missing. It wasn't out of the ordinary to think she did something, I guess, but I think it was led by one particular guy—'

Natalie held up a hand. 'Say no more.'

She knew why she'd been brought into the area. The previous holder of her office had retired and not before time, it seemed. She'd heard stories – rumours, the like. It wasn't exactly a happy retirement, she'd heard.

She gathered it had long since been time for that particular guy to move on to the next part of his life.

'Problem is, that's meant we've not had the best of relationships with the victim's family since those first few days. Also doesn't help that once suicide had been ruled out, the investigation team focused on the dad.'

Natalie shook her head. 'I'm guessing it wasn't exactly a good line of enquiry?'

Carter breathed out hard. 'Not really. He was two hundred miles away for a start – working up in Northumberland. Place called Ashington. He was on a placement for three weeks, in the middle of it during the time of the murder. Staying in a hotel – a Premier Inn, with about forty cameras that confirmed his movements the entire few days that were checked. Still, it meant those all had to be checked, investigated . . . more time gone on a dead end.'

'Can't really blame the family for being against us then.'

'Probably not,' Carter replied, sheepishly, as if it were his fault. 'They made some noise about it, but then other stories came up nationally and the press died down a lot. Once we didn't find anyone within the first few weeks, it started to disappear from people's consciousness. A few local sex offenders were brought in for questioning, but nothing panned out at all. And there was no evidence of . . . that kind of thing.'

'Seems like a proper botch job.'

Carter didn't disagree.

'Well, we've got a chance to put things right now, if they're linked at all.'

Carter was distracted by his phone buzzing in his pocket. He apologised, answering it quickly. Natalie waited for him to end the call, continuing to allow her mind to tick over.

She didn't like the story that was being presented to her in the slightest. There were just enough strands to make everything much more complicated than it needed to be.

The idea that everything was linked was attractive in some ways. It would make some sort of sense. Only, it didn't fit well with what she knew so far.

Her gut was telling her something else entirely – she'd investigated more than a fair few cases in her life. More murders than she cared to count up.

Most of the time, it was someone close to the victim.

And she didn't like the way Greg Lennon was acting. She knew Carter felt the same way. There was just something about him that she couldn't work out. Some unspoken thing, that seemed to cloud the house in a fog of despair. That may be just because of Ben's death, but she'd been around enough husbands and wives going through something extraordinary to know Greg and Alison were different.

There was no love there.

If anything, she would use the word *hate*.

Carter ended his call and looked towards Natalie. 'She's gone over there.'

'Who?' Natalie asked.

'Mia Johnstone and her mother. They're at the Lennon house now. That was the LO. Said she'd asked to come over and Alison had said she wanted her to go.'

Natalie shook her head. 'Nothing good will come of this,' she said, trying to work out why people seemed to have a desire to make things more difficult for her.

Then, she started wondering if Greg and Alison had a reason to point the finger at an eighteen-year-old girl.

And maybe not at themselves.

25

You can't really recover Snapchat messages. That's the whole point of them – that self-deleting thing after twenty-four hours. That's the unique selling point of the app. A level of anonymity built into it.

That's why no one knew Becky had been speaking to someone.

Well, no one, other than the person she'd been speaking to.

It's almost as if it were designed to make it easier to build a relationship with someone that couldn't exist to an outside world.

Sure, that might change at some point. Might already have done, for all they knew. It wasn't as if the investigation had been the best. The social media posts from her family had become increasingly desperate over the year since her death. It didn't suggest that they were getting much information from the police.

That would change now, though. It wouldn't be long until they linked Becky's murder to this new one.

It would have been easier to have made it look like a proper suicide in hindsight. Only, she had fought back. Made it messy. It would have taken more planning, but at that point, panic had set in.

How had she known what had happened to that teacher?

Why hadn't she just kept her nose out of it?

Things would have been so much easier if she had just kept what she knew to herself. Didn't try and get involved.

She had to go.

It wasn't like she didn't deserve it anyway. She was a horrible child who had grown into a horrible teenager. No doubt she would have been a horrible adult too. Bullies never change. Only the targets do.

Yes, she deserved it.

As did Ben Lennon.

That's the way of the world. Or, the way it should be. Consequences for your actions. Not so much an eye for an eye, but actual real justice.

Keeping the streets clean. Keeping people safe.

No one would understand. Not outwardly, anyway. Deep down though, they would know that it made sense. Perfect sense.

Not an excuse. An explanation.

Only now, people were getting restless. The timing should have been okay. Enough time had passed since Becky's death that people wouldn't connect the two.

Yet, there was Ben's mum going to see Lisa Harrison.

That wasn't a good thing.

Lisa Harrison would be saying exactly what was expected at that point. Pointing the finger directly at the one person she thought was responsible for her daughter's death. Not understanding in the slightest that Becky was the one responsible. Not willing to accept that she had had it coming.

That the world was better without her.

She would be poisoning Ben's mum's mind. That's what would be happening behind that closed door.

That couldn't happen.

It needed to be stopped.

There might be no way of recovering those messages, but that didn't mean that links didn't still exist. Evidence, it might be called.

And it would all lead to one place.

Messy. Her death had been just that.

It was going to get worse, now Ben had joined the list.

Another problem to solve. That was okay. There was still so much that could be done.

So much that could be hidden.

And, if there wasn't a solution that was clean and easy, there was always another answer.

It was becoming easier every time. Becky's death might have been messy, but Ben had been quick and relatively painless.

The next one should be even better.

26

Greg came in with cups of tea for us all, then sat down next to me. If he was as nervous as I was feeling, he was hiding it well.

'Thank you,' Mrs Johnstone said, looking around the room. 'You have a lovely home.'

I smiled thinly, as Greg thanked her. I was trying not to stare at Mia, who was rigid on the sofa. Tense, anxious. I wanted to know what was running through her head. What thoughts she might be having.

Whether she was stressed or calm.

Whether she was enjoying this.

'I'm sorry it's taken us a couple of days to make this happen,' Jen said, looking across at the both of us. 'We wanted to give you a little time, before getting in touch. I can't begin to imagine what you've had to deal with.'

'We wouldn't want you to,' I said, risking speaking out loud. I was surprised when my voice sounded almost normal. 'It's not something anyone should have to even think about going through.'

'Of course,' Jen replied, rubbing her hands together slowly, her internal displeasure about being there coming out in the open. She must have noticed what she was doing, as she suddenly lay her hands face down on her lap. 'Mia has been absolutely distraught over it, as you can imagine. You know how much she cared for your son.'

'Yes, I know they'd been seeing each other for a while now,' Greg said, clearing his throat in a way that made me cringe inside. 'Well, a while in terms of how time works for kids their age.'

'Well, she just wanted to be here and let you know that if you need to know anything, or if there's anything she can do for the family, you know she has recent pictures that you might want . . .'

'To know anything?' I said, picking up only on the first part of the offering.

'Yeah, you know, Mia and Ben spent a lot of time together in the past few months.'

'And on the night he was murdered.'

Jen blinked back at me, as I studied them both. It was at that moment that I realised I wasn't a body language expert, so couldn't tell if someone was hiding something from me. Lying to me. It didn't stop me trying.

'Yes, I think they did see each other that night,' Jen said, choosing her words carefully it seemed. 'There were loads of the kids down at the dips, right Mia?'

Mia simply nodded. She hadn't said anything since coming into the house.

'I thought you two had split up,' I said, asking Mia a direct question I thought she couldn't ignore.

'You know what kids are like at this age—'

'Jen, I'm sure Mia can talk to me, right?'

There was a sour look that crossed Jen's face for a second, before she composed herself. She looked to her daughter, who still had her eyes cast down to the floor. 'Of course she can,' Jen said, placing a hand on Mia's knee and giving it a squeeze. 'She's just a little—'

'We were working things out,' Mia said, her voice barely above a whisper. 'We'd had some problems, but we were going to get through them. We wanted to be together.'

'What kind of problems?'

'Nothing big,' Mia replied, with a shrug of her shoulders. 'Just a couple of stupid arguments. That's all.'

'The last I heard,' I said, choosing my words carefully. I didn't want to lose her now she'd finally started talking. 'I heard that you weren't seeing each other anymore. You'd had some big fallout and it was all over. No way back. Moved on. You were both going off to separate universities and that would be that.'

'Is that what he said?'

I nodded, but she still wasn't looking at me. 'Yes, that's what he told us. Not that he volunteered the information. We just noticed you hadn't been around that often for a couple of weeks and asked him. He told us it was over and he was done with you.'

I wasn't trying to hurt her, but I could see her wince at the words. Jen was staring at her daughter now, as if this was the first she was hearing about it. I knew that wasn't the case, though – I didn't think she was as in the dark as she was portraying herself.

'What were you arguing about?' I said, softly. As softly as I could manage, anyway.

Mia shrugged her shoulders. 'Nothing big, like I said.'

'I'm sure it didn't feel like it at the time,' I replied, glancing at Greg who was simply watching the conversation unfold in front of him. He didn't seem to have any interest in it at all, which annoyed the hell out of me. I couldn't understand why he didn't see this as important. 'I remember being your age – everything feels like the biggest thing in the world at the time. If my son had hurt you, I want to know about it. We all make mistakes – especially when we're your age. So, if he did something—'

Mia shook her head, so vigorously I was worried it would fall off her shoulders. 'No, nothing like that. I . . . it was just rumours, that's all.'

'Rumours?'

'He was apparently talking to another girl, but it wasn't true. But he . . . he wouldn't just come out and tell me the honest truth. That was it. And I got angry about it, then he got angry because I was angry, and it all just blew up into a massive thing. But we were talking it through. We wanted to be together. We were talking about how we were going to see each other when we went off to uni and that.'

'You'd only been seeing each other a few months, right? How does it get this serious so quickly?'

'You remember being seventeen, eighteen,' Jen said, cutting in, an edge to her voice now that hadn't been there before. 'A week was a long-term relationship for me back then. I'm sure you were the same.'

'I guess,' I said, a thin smile appearing on my face without me thinking about it. 'Still, it seemed to distract you both, right during the time you were both supposed to be studying for exams.'

Mia shrugged her shoulders. 'Can't really control the timing, I guess.'

'It must have affected you though?'

'Not really,' Mia said, almost mumbling. 'I just tried to concentrate as much as possible. Make them two different things, or something.'

'Well you both did well in your exams, so maybe I was worried about nothing. Not that it matters now, I guess.'

'I don't even know what I'll do now,' Mia said, her voice growing quiet again. Jen shot her a look, but didn't respond. She'd probably heard it before.

I had no doubt that Mia would still be going off to university. If for nothing else than to put distance between her and this town.

I tilted my head considering her again. I wasn't sure if she was as good a liar as she thought she might be. 'That night,' I said, feeling a well of emotion building in my chest. It became a ball in the back of my throat that I couldn't swallow back down. 'How was he?'

Mia took a deep breath in, as if she were preparing herself. 'He was . . . he was just like he always was. Happy, laughing, with all his mates.'

I could see her eyes watering. I waited, watched, as a tear escaped the corner of her eye and rolled down her cheek. Jen could see it too and shifted closer to her daughter.

'How long were you with him?'

'A few hours,' Mia said, wiping away the wet on her cheek. 'Me and Anna went to meet up with everyone and he was just there. We hadn't spoken for a while. It was awkward at first, but he came over to me. Said we needed to talk.'

I held my breath, thinking about Ben's last words. Those last moments. I could see Greg tensing up and gave him a quick glare. He hadn't spoken since they'd arrived and I wanted to keep it that way. 'This was the first time you'd spoken since the rumours about him being with another girl?'

'In person? Yeah. We'd spoken loads on messages and that, but we were going round in circles. It was the first time we'd seen each other in person.'

'You must have still been angry?'

I could see her tense up.

'I guess, but we talked about it. He told me that it was all just rumours. That he loved me and not to listen to all the crap that was being said.'

Mia was choosing her words so carefully, it was difficult not to fill in the gaps she was leaving behind. There was more said, I knew that. I could see it written on her face. I made a mental note to speak to other friends of Ben's – I needed to hear more of the other side.

'What time did you leave?'

Mia glanced at her mum – the first time she'd looked at anything other than the floor since she'd arrived. 'Around midnight, I think. Me and Anna had to go home.'

'And how did things end with Ben?'

Mia sighed, quietly. 'It was . . . it was good. We were going to meet up properly the next day. On our own, so we could talk more. The last thing we said to each other . . .'

The tears started flowing now. Her shoulders were hitching up and down and a sob escaped from her mouth. I could feel myself welling up in response – there was something inside me, some kind of maternal instinct I guessed, that wanted to cross the room and take the poor girl in my arms.

Then, I thought about Becky. Mr Fulton.

There was a moment when I almost believed her. That she was quite obviously distraught, that she had nothing to do with my son's death.

Then, another part of me switched on.

It was all an act. That's all it was. A damn good one, that would fool almost everyone else.

Not me, I decided. I could see through it. I could see through the manipulation, the controlled nature of the whole thing. I could almost imagine her rehearsing this in the mirror before she came – making sure she got everything right.

I bit down on my lower lip to stop myself from saying anything.

'We said we loved each other,' Mia said, finally, between tears. 'And that was it.'

I nodded, as Jen took her daughter and held her closely. Took a deep breath, and began talking. 'You're no stranger to rumours, are you Mia?' I said, trying to control the tone of my voice and failing spectacularly. 'There's always rumours about you, right?'

'I . . . I don't know what you mean.'

'Yes, yes you do,' I said, and I could feel my hands starting to shake a little. 'I've heard all about them. I'm sure you have as well. All the things people have been saying over the past eighteen months? You can't have missed them. And everything that's being said by people who know you, who know Ben . . . what they're saying about you now, right?'

'They're not true,' Jen said firmly, as she turned back towards me. 'My daughter loved your son and wouldn't hurt him. That's why we're here—'

I waved her away, as if she was an irritant. 'It's not just Ben though, is it? That would be easily ignored. I would be able to see that. But, that's not all, is it? Because it's not just Ben they're talking about, Mia. Right? This has happened before. This isn't the first time someone who has upset you has ended up dead, isn't that right?'

'I haven't done anything—'

'Why don't you tell me what really happened between you that night, Mia?' I said, standing up and putting my shaking hands by my sides. I could feel them wanting to form into fists. 'What did he really say to you? What made you so angry that you wanted to get back at him? Tell me, tell me the truth.'

I was breathing heavily, my voice raising with every syllable I spoke, until it was bouncing off the walls around me.

I felt Greg's hand on my shoulder, but I shrugged it away. Then, I blinked and saw Mia cowering from me. Her sobbing becoming louder, as her mum moved to protect her.

'She had nothing to do with this . . .'

I wasn't listening to Jen. I was staring at her daughter, daring her to look me in the eyes. I could see it now – her standing over my son, over his battered body, and I wanted to tear her apart.

'Maybe you should go.'

It was the only time Greg spoke the entire time they were there and as I turned to protest, Jen dragged Mia up off the sofa and made for the door.

'Don't let them leave,' I said to Greg, who was staring at me like I had two heads. 'It was her, Greg. Don't you see it?'

He shook his head at me, but didn't respond. Simply pushed past me and headed out of the room following behind.

I knew he wasn't going to stop them.

He thought I was crazy.

And maybe I was, but I knew for certain now that I was right.

She was lying to me.

Ellie

She hated hearing her parents argue.

It was his voice. So condescending, as her mum tried to explain over and over her position and he didn't listen. She couldn't bear it.

There had been less of that since Ben was killed.

No, since then, it had been a lot of her mum saying she was done. Ending arguments before they even had a chance to start.

Ellie wasn't sure what to do about it. How she was supposed to act. How she was supposed to deal with it all. There was no guide for being the sister of a murdered brother. No sense of what she was supposed to do or say.

In the end, she'd just decided to keep out of the way. Set up camp in her bedroom and wondered if she'd be going back to school the week later. She hoped not. Despite it being her final year of high school, with GCSEs on the horizon, the idea of going into that place with everyone talking about what had happened to her family . . . the thought of it made her feel sick.

It was bad enough there at the best of times. She couldn't handle the looks and the talking behind her back that would happen now.

Maybe it would be a way of giving her some time off and even down the line, some kind of pass when it came to her exams.

She wasn't sure if that was even possible and she felt a little guilty for even thinking about it.

Ellie lay back, checked her phone again, and sighed. There was nothing worse than waiting for a reply. Putting yourself out there and then waiting for them to say what you wanted to hear.

There should be a timer on responding. Some sort of alarm, that goes off and won't shut down until you've got back to the person you're having a conversation with.

That'd be nice. If people could just think of others.

Not that she was worried too much. He always got back to her quickly before and this should be no different.

It was nice having someone else to talk to. Someone who didn't know what was going on in that house right then. Someone who didn't care about who she'd been in primary school. Someone who didn't know or care about anything someone else might say about her.

She missed Ben.

Not him as a person. He could be annoying as hell. Just knowing he was around was like a comfort blanket she didn't realise she needed. A buffer when it came to Mum and Dad.

Even though he was Dad's favourite.

They got on way better than she ever had with him. They liked the same stuff, had the same sense of humour, the same things in common. Not just football either – it was other stuff. She'd always been forgotten about. Or tolerated, something she'd learned about recently.

Now, Ben was gone and she knew her dad wasn't coping.

Mum didn't help. She had become different overnight. In the past few years, she'd been getting more and more quiet. Those arguments had become more one-sided, with her giving in quickly, even as Dad went on and on.

She had taken to not bringing anything up, it seemed to Ellie. Not even after she'd had a drink, which was usually the time for her to air her grievances. Up until a few years earlier, if Mum had been out for the night, her and Ben always expected there'd be an argument at two in the morning. Her mum, talking way too loud, as her dad tried to calm her down. Usually in totally the wrong way. Telling her not to shout. Trying to use logic, as if that was a magic word that would make anyone feel better. He never seemed to understand that Mum just wanted to be *heard*. To be understood.

To matter.

It must have been so damn tiring for them both.

Now, it seemed like they were just hanging on. Maybe until she herself went off to university. Then, maybe she'd get a message saying there would be two Christmases in her first year – one with Mum, one with Dad.

The idea didn't sound so bad.

Now, with Ben being murdered, she wasn't sure they would even make it that far.

Ellie felt like an afterthought.

Her phone buzzed and she picked it up, smiling despite herself.

So selfish. They shld b makin sure ur ok.

At least someone wanted to listen to her. At least someone understood what she was going through. Cared how she was feeling.

I get it. They just lost there son. But hello? Im here too.

She pressed send and waited.

It was cool that she had someone who cared. The only problem was who it was. She could never tell anyone – that was the big issue.

Not yet.

Maybe, some time in the future. When she was eighteen and it didn't matter anymore.

When she could make her own decisions and mistakes, without worrying about what her dad would say about it.

Her mum would understand, but she wouldn't get a chance to say so, without her dad getting involved.

Wanna meet soon? Just to talk?

Ellie felt something jolt inside her. Butterflies taking flight in her stomach. It had been a while since they'd seen each other – before Ben died. It had been days and she'd been desperate to see him.

She fired back quickly.

When and where?

She wondered if her mum and dad would even notice if she left the house. Whether they would notice if they didn't see her for days.

They were too wrapped up in themselves to care about her right then. She was done with her dad – had been for some time.

Her mum not caring about her in that moment hurt more.

Still, it was all going to be okay.

They were going to meet in person and just being around him would make her feel better. She just knew it, deep inside. She could imagine it, so clearly.

No one in that house seemed to be bothered about her right then and maybe that was to be expected.

It didn't matter, though.

Because *he* cared.

27

Mia had stopped crying by the time Anna arrived. Only just, and liable to start again at any moment.

She may not have shed tears for Ben before, but now they were coming in full flow. Every time she thought about him, that same emotion came to the surface. She was struggling to hold it in – wasn't even sure it was a good idea if she did.

'It couldn't have gone much worse then.'

King of the understatement, Anna was, Mia thought.

Her mum had been fuming the whole way home. Muttering to herself constantly under her breath. As if she had been of any use back there. She hadn't said a word to Ben's mum as she unleashed on Mia. She'd probably been as shocked as Mia had been, to be fair.

She hadn't expected that.

'No,' Mia said, drawing her knees to her chest as she sat on her bed. 'She thinks I'm lying. She's believing what they're all saying. She thinks I . . . I *killed* Ben.'

'She's just upset,' Anna replied, messing with something on Mia's desk. Probably an old bottle of nail varnish, or eyeliner. It needed tidying up. 'She doesn't know what to think and it's not like she's thinking clearly.'

'Doesn't help me though, does it?'

'Once they find out who did it, things will change. People will stop talking about you.'

'You believe that, really?'

Anna opened her mouth to reply, then thought better of it. Even her endless optimism was being dealt a blow it seemed.

'It is my fault anyway. So, maybe I deserve all this.'

'No . . .'

'Seriously, think about it,' Mia said, leaning forward and listing her points off on one finger at a time. 'One, people spread rumours about me and Mr Fulton. He ends up dead. Two, Becky and me have our problems, have a public argument, then a few days later she is found dead. Three, Ben. And everyone knew what was happening between us, and bang. He's dead. No one really believed I had anything to do with Mr Fulton being killed, it was just fun and I get it now. But, then Becky dies and people start really talking. It didn't take long for that to start going away though, because everyone has the attention span of a . . . of a whatever. So, Ben dying really brings it all back up. And worse, his mum *really* believes I killed him. Becky's mum probably thinks I killed her, so that's now two of them. I'm getting tagged in all kinds online, so everyone is thinking the same thing – that I'm some kind of killer. And who can blame them? Three different people have died, all of them after having problems with me. So, how can anyone think anything different. What am I supposed to do? Because I'm not even sure it isn't my fault they're all dead. What if I'm the reason three people have died? What if it's all my fault and I'm just . . . evil?'

Anna didn't answer for a while, as Mia caught her breath. When she listed it all out like that, it made things look even worse for her.

One could have been ignored. Two was unfortunate.

Three was too many.

It wasn't like they all had loads of enemies. Mr Fulton – and that's how he always would be to her . . . Mr Fulton, not Will. She didn't think he had a list of enemies.

Unless she wasn't the only one he'd been interested in like *that*.

Then, there was Becky. So many friends. So many people who disliked her. That was the price of being popular. Mia was sure there were a few people who weren't bothered too much by her dying.

And then, there was Ben.

Ben had so many friends. He was popular. Starting a relationship with Mia had been a surprise for some, but it didn't matter in the end. He still kept all his friends – they even merged with her group.

It wasn't like he was a bully or anything either. He'd never do something like that.

Not into drugs. Seemed to have no worries in the world.

So, nothing there.

No, now it all pointed towards her being responsible. And the thought of that terrified Mia.

'Two is a coincidence,' Mia said, still waiting for Anna to say something. 'Three is a pattern.'

'Have you thought about what that might mean then?'

Mia stared back at Anna, not understanding her. 'I've thought about nothing else.'

'I mean what it might mean if it is a pattern,' Anna said, slowly, as if she were explaining something to a child. 'If you haven't done this, then someone might be doing it on your behalf.'

'Someone is killing these people for me?'

'Well, yeah.'

Mia shook her head. 'That's ridiculous . . .'

'Is it?' Anna said, shifting round on the chair and facing Mia. 'Think about it. You haven't killed anyone, but you've got to admit, you haven't exactly been sorry to have them out of your life. Which means only one thing.'

'Someone is doing it for me.'

Anna pointed a finger at Mia. 'Yes. Which means you'd be in the clear.'

Mia shook her head. 'It would be worse.'

'Why?' Anna said, her face screwing up in surprise. 'It would mean people would know you didn't do this.'

'No, maybe not. But it would be worse because either people would think I made someone do it for me. Or, someone close to me did it, which means I know a killer.'

Anna nodded as if it was a great point and one she hadn't thought of, but Mia knew she had. Her mind worked much quicker than hers. She'd already be a few steps down the road, but for some reason, she always waited for her to catch up.

'If that is the case, who do you think it could be?'

Mia didn't have an answer. Not one she wanted to say out loud at that point, anyway.

'Let's not talk about that for now,' Mia said, swinging her legs round the bed, so they hung over the side. 'I want to know who's been doing this, so maybe we should try and find out.'

'And how do you think we're going to do that?'

'You said it yourself,' Mia said, a humourless smile crossing her lips. 'All three are connected to each other. Me, basically. But I'm not going to be the only one that will have been connected to them. Maybe one of the people who is currently calling me a killer is just trying to shift focus from themselves?'

Anna replicated her smile. 'It's not like they didn't have enemies.'

'Except for Ben,' Mia corrected, opening her phone and opening Instagram. 'He was liked by everyone.'

'Not everyone,' Anna said, the smile disappearing. 'No one is liked by everyone. There's always someone who is either jealous or angry. Or both. I guarantee there'll be someone at that school who wanted him gone. Same with that "teacher" and Becky.'

'I've been taking screenshots,' Mia replied, trying not to think about Ben having people who didn't like him in the world. It didn't fit in with the view she had of him now. Of herself. 'These are the accounts who have been sending me stuff on Insta. I'll do the same for any Snaps I get. I think we need to get as much as possible, so we can see if we can work out who any of these people are.'

Mia handed her phone to Anna, who took it gingerly. She started swiping across the screen, silently.

'Some of these are horrible,' Anna said, after a minute or so had passed. 'Like, properly horrible.'

Mia couldn't disagree, but she didn't want to cry again. Instead, she shrugged her shoulders in a 'what are you going to do?' motion.

She'd read through them, of course.

All of it.

Maybe it was to punish herself. For what she'd thought and felt in the past couple of years. All the times she'd thought about what she wanted to do to those people. The times she'd come home and cried in her bedroom, hoping that her life would change overnight. And perhaps it would, if certain people weren't around anymore.

There was always a part of her that had wanted them punished in some way. They deserved something to happen to them.

'I don't even know where to start,' Anna said, handing the phone back to Mia. 'But this can't go on. Maybe your mum and dad could talk to the companies – ask them to take some of this stuff down. Or to the police, at least? It's harassment.'

Mia knew that wouldn't work. Would probably make things worse, if anything. 'Yeah, maybe. There's a chance that one of these people knows more, though. If I could just talk to some of Ben's mates – the ones who were with him that night – maybe I could find out if any of them knew if something else was going on.'

'What about the girl he was supposedly seeing behind your back?'

'Keira? What would she know?'

Anna shook her head. 'Well, there's two things – one, she was seeing him behind your back and got angry that he was talking to you again. Or two, she wasn't seeing him, but was obsessed with him and started the rumours in the first place, so she could.'

Mia could see the logic. 'We need to talk to her. How do we make that happen?'

Anna thought for a second, then smiled. 'Leave it with me. I can sort that out.'

28

When Mia and her mum had left, I was still too angry to think straight. I was left standing in the living room, breathing hard, my heart beating hard enough that it was all I could hear. Blood rushing through my ears.

'I should have kept her here,' I said, as Greg came back into the room. I began pacing the floor. 'I should have made sure she didn't leave, until she told us the truth.'

'What the hell, Alison?'

I wasn't listening to him. 'I rattled her though. You saw that, right? She knows I know. And that'll mean she'll make a mistake. We need to keep the pressure on. Someone should be watching her. When that liaison officer turns back up, I should tell her that they should be following her—'

'Stop, please stop,' Greg said, coming across the room and reaching out to me. His hands landed on my shoulders, but I shrugged them off. He huffed and stepped back.

'You can't tell me you didn't see it written all over her face, Greg?'

'All I saw was a frightened young girl, who came here to show her support and had it thrown back in her face. Her mum was going mad outside, Alison. She calmed down quick enough, when she realised she was standing on the street, but you can't do things like that—'

'She killed Ben,' I said, incredulous that Greg couldn't see that. 'And we just have to get the police to apply some pressure on her and she'll crack.'

'This is ridiculous,' Greg replied, moving back and slumping on the sofa. He massaged his forehead – his telltale sign that he was stressed, or annoyed with not being able to get through to me. 'She's just a young girl. There's no way she could have hurt Ben. I know you've not been sleeping, but I can't let you start accusing everyone in the town of murder. We'll never be taken seriously. We need to let the police do their job and wait.'

'Wait? That's what you want to do? Just sit here, wallow in our misery, while someone gets away with killing our son?'

'That's not what I'm saying . . .'

'It's exactly what you're saying,' I said, letting the anger build up inside me now. Letting it take over. 'That's what you really are – you're a wait around and hope for the best guy. That's all you've ever been. Never done anything that might matter. If there's a problem, you run away. Hide until it's over.'

'That's not true.'

'Yes it is,' I said, shaking my head. I could feel myself losing it. I wanted to shake him. 'You talk a big game, but when it comes down to it, you've got nothing. No way of backing it up. That "young girl" . . . that piece of shit killed our son.'

'You have literally no evidence for that,' Greg replied, exasperated now. It wouldn't be long until he walked out of the room, muttering to himself, I thought. 'It doesn't make any sense at all. Just think of the logic. Some teenage girl is going round killing people for the past year or so and hasn't even been arrested? We didn't even hear about it before now. You've just become fixated on her, like that other girl's mum. And look at her. Do you want to become like her?'

I wanted Greg away from me, but I couldn't let him think he'd won. 'No evidence? There's literally three people dead, who dared to cross her. Lisa had to battle just to get them to say her daughter had actually been murdered and that she hadn't done it to herself. Everyone thinks just because she's this little girl that she couldn't do this? That's what isn't logical.'

'I'm not saying it's not possible, but it's hardly likely.'

'She's pretending that she was in love with our son and everything was back to normal, but none of his friends agree with that. They all say that Ben was done with her and she wasn't taking it well. She's crazy—'

'I can't take this anymore.'

'Neither can I,' I said, my voice echoing around the room. 'I'm not like you. I can't just sit around, waiting for someone else to do something. He deserves more than that.'

'So, what can we do? There's literally nothing we can do.'

'That's it then? We just accept that someone took our son's life and we do nothing?'

Greg shook his head. 'Well, no, I don't mean it like that. I mean, we don't have the ability to go out and track down our son's killer. That's just not something we can do.'

I wanted to shake him. Shake some life, some fight into him. I knew it was pointless. I was never going to change him. I didn't want to. He was who he was, simple as that. 'This is who you are. Someone who can just sit back and hope for the best. Well, there's no "best" here. It's just what it is. And we can either sit here and do nothing or we can do something.'

'What are you suggesting we do?'

'I've already spoken to Becky's mum,' I said, seeing an opening. I might not have seen a future with Greg beyond the following few months, but I could at least have someone to help me in the moment. 'She's told me a few things I didn't know before about Mia. The next obvious step is the teacher who was killed.'

'This is ridiculous—'

'We could find out if he had family,' I continued, not listening to his interruption. 'Parents, siblings, a girlfriend or whatever. We talk to them, find out more.'

'And then what? What's the endgame here? The police will already be doing this, Alison. We'll just be in the way. We could make things worse.'

'Worse? How could they be any worse than they already are?'

'I don't know,' Greg said, with a sigh of annoyance. 'I'm just saying—'

'I know what you're saying. You're pathetic. You can't even be bothered to try. Our son has been murdered and you can't be bothered to do anything.'

Greg's head shot up. 'Don't you dare.'

'Look at you,' I said, feeling unburdened by the thoughts I'd had before every other argument we'd ever had. Holding back, not just letting go. Those lines we put up so we don't go too far and say things you know can never be taken back. I realised I didn't care anymore. 'Your son has been killed and you can't even make yourself care enough to do something about it. Anything at all. You've barely shown a bit of emotion. Not just sadness, but anger. I'm angry, Greg, why aren't you?'

'It doesn't help any of us—'

'Who cares about that? You just want to sit here and just defer to the police and hope you don't have to put yourself in a little danger? Or have difficult conversations with people, so we get to the truth? Don't you want to do anything for us? For Ben?'

'I'd do anything for my family, you know that.'

I ignored the anger in his voice. Spitting words back at me. 'Are you really sure about that? Because here we are, Greg. I want to get out there and get the truth. Tell me what you'd do for us, really? Because we're at that moment right now and you're doing nothing. You're making a decision.'

'And what are you going to be able to do? Nothing, that's what, other than get in the way.'

'I don't care anymore,' I said, breathing hard. The words falling from my mouth before I even had a chance to think about them. 'You might want me to shut up and be the quiet little wife, that doesn't question anything you do or say, but I can't do that anymore. Not now. Because it's killing me. I'm not going to sit back while our son lies in a morgue somewhere.'

'He was my son too,' Greg spat back at me. 'Have you even thought about that? What I might be going through or how I'm feeling? I bet you haven't.'

'I don't care. I really don't. You didn't put your arms around me, Greg. Do you know that? When we saw him, you didn't comfort me. You only thought of yourself. I can't even imagine the level of animosity you have for me that you wouldn't even want to be near me after something like that has happened. That's our marriage now, isn't it? That's our life.'

'Please, Alison, don't do this now,' Greg said, a pleading tone to his voice now. As if I was the problem. As if I was the reason this was happening.

'You don't love me,' I replied, lowering my voice suddenly. I thought of Ellie, somewhere in the house, listening to all of this. The thought came and went quickly. 'Probably never had. I should never have forgiven you all those years ago. You only stayed with me because of the kids and now I don't even know who you are anymore.'

'Alison, please, I do love you . . .'

'I know that girl did this,' I said, ignoring him. It wasn't the time. 'And I'm going to make sure she can't wriggle out of it, like she has before.'

'You don't know anything—'

'I don't care what you think,' I said, my voice raising again. As I shouted, I heard the doorbell chime around the house and pivoted around to the living room window. I could see Louise's car parked outside and I knew I couldn't stay there. 'I'm going out. You can sit and drink tea with that woman and pretend everything is going to be okay. For me, nothing will be okay until she's made to pay for what she's done. Maybe not even then.'

'We have to think about Ellie.'

I was already moving, walking out of the room, into the hallway. I could see Louise's shadow in the doorway. I picked up my jacket and bag. Opened the door and pushed past her.

'Alison, are you okay?'

I ignored her, leaving the door open behind me. I made my way down the path, ignoring everything behind me. Around me. The window blinds being parted, to see what was happening at our home. Wanting a glimpse of the poor parents of the murdered kid.

There were reporters in cars – someone doing a live report somewhere in the town, I knew from watching the news earlier.

There was no way I was going to live in a fishbowl for the rest of my life.

I got in the car, turned it over and pulled away from the kerb.

I wasn't thinking about Greg. I wasn't thinking about Ellie. The police, the neighbours, the media. No one.

I was only focused on the road ahead and where I was going next.

29

I was a couple of miles from home, but it already felt like a foreign world. I hadn't realised how constricted I'd been feeling, being stuck in that house for hours on end. Waiting for news that would never come.

Yes, I got a few looks. A double-take here and there. I guessed that people didn't really know why they recognised my face, but it would come to them soon enough. I didn't care.

I knew some of them would have seen me on the news. Social media. That statement we'd given – on the driveway of our home – seeming more and more like a mistake.

'We could have just met at mine,' Val said, her spoon clattering to the plate as she finished stirring sweeteners into her coffee. 'I'm not sure this is where you need to be right now.'

The café was one we'd met in before – a lovely little independent, that was probably not going to last much longer since the second Costa opened a few weeks earlier. It didn't matter if the coffee, the food, everything tasted better . . . people seemed to prefer the blandness of a chain.

Val lived nearby. Probably knew everyone in the place by name. She was that type of woman. She took an interest in everything it seemed. I was the total opposite. I preferred my bubble.

'Don't you start,' I replied, staring at the large latte in front of me. I didn't want it, but I knew if I started, I'd finish the whole cup and then want another. 'I've had enough of him back there telling me what I need to be doing.'

'Okay, okay,' Val said, holding her hands up in mock surrender. 'Sorry. I just don't know what to say for the best.'

'No one does. So you're not alone in that. I don't think there's anything that can be said. I don't mind you trying though. It means you care at least. I just couldn't sit in the house again – I feel claustrophobic in my own house.'

'I know you understand, but it doesn't stop me feeling useless. I'm your big sister – I'm supposed to, you know, protect you.'

'I think that responsibility ended about twenty-five years ago, Val.'

'It never ends,' Val said, lifting her coffee and sipping at it delicately. 'Anyway, what's the latest? Have they made any headway yet?'

I shook my head. 'They keep telling us that they're working hard and they have a wealth of information and I guess "leads" to go through. Doesn't feel like they're any further than they were at the beginning, though.'

Val leaned forwards and lowered her voice. 'What about the girlfriend?'

'She wasn't his girlfriend,' I said, perhaps harsher than I intended, not that Val seemed to mind. 'She came round with her mum earlier today. I . . . I kind of lost it a little with them.'

'Unsurprising,' Val replied sitting back in her chair. 'I didn't think she'd show her face. What happened?'

I ran her through the visit and how it ended. I didn't sugarcoat it. I did mention that Greg had barely said a word, which earned an eyeroll from my sister.

She'd never liked him. Not that she'd made it obvious – I just knew in the way we know those closest to us. The words they use, the statements they make, the questions they ask.

Greg and I had been married almost twenty years and I'd known from day one that Val didn't like him. I knew she'd preferred the guy I'd been seeing for a few years before he came on the scene. It didn't matter that I'd been so bored by that poor guy's company that I still couldn't believe I managed more than a few dates with the sap, never mind two years.

Greg had been exciting in the beginning – someone with a bit of charm. He wasn't exactly good looking – he'd been a little overweight, and his nose was the most prominent feature on his face – but he'd been funny. He'd made me laugh so much those first few times we'd gone out, that I'd been more attracted to him than anyone else before.

That feeling had changed quickly.

'Well, if she didn't know before,' Val said, lowering her voice again, as we saw a couple on the next table go silent. Listening. 'She'll know now that you suspect her.'

'I don't just suspect her. I *know* she did this.'

Val opened her mouth to respond, but then closed it again. Tilted her head to the ceiling, in a way I was familiar with. She was looking for the right words to say. The right way to phrase something. Which meant she was going to say something I wouldn't like.

'I know it sounds crazy on the face of it,' I said, jumping in before she had a chance. 'But, as I've told you, he's not the first. The other girl's mum, she thinks it too. Three people who had run-ins with her all turning up dead . . . it's a pattern.'

'Don't you think there might be more to it though? It seems too obvious to be her. Like, surely if this was so easily connected to her, then she would be leaving more evidence behind her?'

I swallowed back my initial response, which would have had the couple on the next table listening even more intently. Composed myself. 'You haven't looked in this girl's eyes. She did this. I know she did.'

'I know you believe that, I just want you to be careful.'

This had always been our relationship – Val constantly thought she knew best. And maybe she did. But I didn't need to hear that kind of talk. I needed support. I knew she'd give me it no matter what, but I needed someone who believed as strongly as me that Mia was responsible.

'I know, I am being careful,' I eventually responded, through almost gritted teeth. 'It's not like I can do all that much anyway. They want me to stay at home and wait, but I can't do that. I need to be doing something.'

'I understand that,' Val said, shifting her chair closer to mine. She didn't reach out for me though. 'But you're going to drive yourself crazy if you try and do too much. Maybe you should just let them get on with things. Unless you have some kind of plan?'

'A plan,' I replied, with a humourless chuckle. 'I've not had any kind of plan since this happened. I thought having that girl in my house would help, but it didn't do a damn thing. Just made me more sure that she was lying.'

'I don't know how she could sit there and look at you both if she did do something.'

'That's evil for you.'

'Do you think this Mia's mum will make a complaint?'

I shook my head. 'I don't think she's stupid enough to do that. It would only make her look bad, right?'

'Yeah, definitely. Complaining about a grieving parent? Not going to win you many friends. Does she have many friends in town? I don't remember you talking about her much from when the kids were younger.'

'Not that I know of,' I said, giving the earwigging couple next to us a quick stare. Glare, might have been a more appropriate word. They looked away quickly. 'I don't know much about them at all.'

'Might be an idea to find out,' Val replied, following my gaze across to the other table. 'Maybe there's more to this. If they're all connected, these three . . . people who have died, then you need to learn more about this girl.'

I heard a whisper from beside us, turned to see the couple now sharing a furtive glance our way. 'Can we help you?'

The woman looked as if she wanted the ground to swallow her, but the guy seemed more confident. 'We're sorry, we just recognised you, that's all.'

'Well, why don't you mind your own business . . .'

'Alison,' Val began, but I wasn't paying her any attention now.

'No, am I not allowed to come and have a coffee because of what's happened?'

Val reached across and placed her hand on my leg. 'I'm sorry but as you can imagine this is a difficult time.'

'We understand,' the guy said, turning to Val now. 'We weren't saying anything about her, she should know that—'

'Who's she? The cat's mother?'

The guy frowned, but shifted his gaze to me. 'I . . . we just wanted to say we were sorry to hear about your son.'

So nice. So polite. So unnecessary. I waved it away. 'Come on, Val. I need to get out of here,' I said, pushing my chair back and standing up.

I walked out, leaving behind my untouched coffee. Got outside and sucked in a lungful of air. It tasted bitter. I looked out onto the street, the people passing by. I felt as though they were staring at me. Whispered conversations. The cars driving past, second looks, as they confirmed to themselves what they'd seen.

I looked back at the café – saw my sister talking to the couple and pretended I could hear their conversation. Apologising for my behaviour. Explaining I had just lost my son and wasn't in my right mind.

I hated her for that.

I felt like I had a spotlight on me. That I was marked. It was as if a beacon was flashing around me, pointing out exactly what I was.

A failure. I was someone to be looked down upon. I had failed my son. I hadn't kept my child safe – my only job.

I felt a hand on my shoulder and jumped away. I started moving, not looking back, even as I heard my sister's voice calling me.

There was no one to help me. They could pretend that they were looking out for me, but they couldn't be inside my head. They couldn't begin to imagine what thoughts I was having.

And there was only one way to stop that.

30

They were kids.

It wasn't a breakthrough thought. Original, compelling. It was a statement of fact.

They might have dates of birth that happened over eighteen years ago, but Detective Natalie Williams thought there was no chance they were the same kind of eighteen-year-old she'd been. Or anyone of her generation.

'And then, like, she said something, thinking we wouldn't hear it, but like, Rachel heard her, and like Max did too, so we knew like, she'd said it.'

Natalie tried not to roll her eyes. Tried to make out she was listening intently, as the young girl opposite her took fifteen minutes to tell her absolutely nothing.

'You were down on the dips that night,' Natalie said, trying to steer the conversation back to where it needed to be. 'And you saw Ben and Mia talking?'

'Yeah, like, they were proper intense.'

'And did you hear anything that was said?'

The girl thought for a moment, her hand still clasped to the phone in her hand, as if letting it go would be like someone drowning letting go of a life preserver. 'Not really, but like, I could guess, because we all knew what was going on.'

'And what was that?'

The girl took a breath, for what seemed the first time. Natalie glanced across at Carter, who was desperately trying to keep up with everything – still scribbling away in his notepad. She did like that he seemed to want to record everything possible. She didn't think his hand thanked him for the effort. Probably ached like a demon at the end of a shift.

'Well,' the girl began, leaning forwards as if she was going to relay the most important story they would ever hear. 'It was all over school that Ben and Keira had been hooking up. I didn't say anything, but I'd seen them a few times like, walking past my house and that together. And I know that Chris said he'd spoken to Ben and he'd been like all weird about it. So, then Ben and Mia weren't talking and weren't seeing each other anymore, which was mad, because Ben didn't even like her anyway I reckon, but he didn't seem happy about it and that, but like she turned up with that Anna girl and they just walked off together.'

'So, did you hear anything?' Natalie said, desperately trying to follow what usefulness any of this was. 'What they talked about?'

The girl thought for a moment. 'Not in like words or anything like that, but Ben told us when he came back that it was like heavy and he didn't want to talk about it and then someone said something and it was like forgotten.'

'Right,' Natalie replied, wondering if there was a bigger waste of time than trying to interview ten different eighteen-year-old's and hoping they would have something useful to add. 'So, did Mia leave after this?'

'Yeah, she just like disappeared.'

'Okay,' Natalie said, glancing at Carter and giving him a nod. 'You've been a great help, thank you.'

The girl seemed surprised that there was no follow-up, but tried to hide it. Natalie let Carter lead her out of the room and then let out a deep breath. Scrunched her eyes tight, until they ached.

'That's pretty much all of them,' Carter said, re-entering the room and forcing Natalie to open her eyes again. 'Apart from the two lads, who we spoke to on the phone the next day. And they didn't know a thing it seemed.'

'Still, we should speak to them.'

'Only one of them has mentioned anything about it being anything other than the way Mia told us.'

Natalie shook her head. 'I just don't think she has anything to do with his death and this all feels like a massive distraction.'

'Can't disagree with that.'

'Why do they all say "like" so much?'

Carter grinned. 'I wouldn't know like. It's like, a word instead of a pause like.'

Natalie wanted to throw something at him, but the grin fell from his face quickly, as he seemed to remember what exactly they were investigating. 'We're back to thinking it was some kind of robbery gone wrong then?'

'You tell me? His phone and watch were stolen. Both of those things were worth a bit of money, so that would suggest it was the case. Only, he was followed. And why would they leave his wallet? It's all a little too violent for that kind of thing. It's not like he had any kind of defensive wounds, so he didn't fight back and it all got out of hand.'

'Like he had?'

'Don't you dare,' Natalie said, shaking her head. 'That's not the same at all.'

Carter raised his eyebrows, but didn't labour the point. 'So, they took his phone and watch to make it look like a robbery, but forgot his wallet? Doesn't make much sense.'

'It does if it wasn't intentional. Sloppy?'

'Maybe.'

'Either way, we're still no closer to an answer. Which won't help us with the parents – well, the mum, anyway.'

'You asked me to look into the dad,' Carter said, leaning against the wall and scratching the stubble on his face. He didn't look tired at all, which annoyed Natalie no end.

'I did.'

'Well, he has no record, or anything of that kind, but a few searches in the past. He was the victim in a case around twenty-five years ago – ABH. Had a quick read up on it and he was attacked in broad daylight by two lads. He would have been around seventeen or eighteen years old. Was bitten on the bicep, which got the charge upgraded.'

'Not very relevant?'

'Doesn't seem to be,' Carter said, shaking his head. 'Since then, nothing at all. I've asked for people to bring the family up in the door-to-door enquiries. We did speak to the neighbours.'

'And?'

Carter shook his head again. 'They've heard arguments in the past, but nothing major. Just raised voices – they said Greg could be heard quite clearly when he was shouting, but that it happens very rarely. Nothing that sounds violent. Just normal arguments, they categorised them as.'

Natalie thought for a few seconds. 'Did they have any information on the kids? Seen them coming back late regularly, that kind of thing? Anyone hanging around they didn't recognise?'

'No, nothing out of the ordinary at all,' Carter said, snapping his notebook closed. 'They were just shocked something like this could happen in the town. Said it wasn't normal at all.'

'Apart from the other girl,' Natalie replied, thinking about Becky Harrison. How it seemed like the small town had collective amnesia about the poor girl.

It didn't make sense.

'Keep looking into the family,' Natalie said, finally, thinking about how none of the kids they'd spoken to seemed to speak about Becky either – other than to slyly suggest Ben's girlfriend may have something to do with her death. 'Also, I want to talk to Becky Harrison's mum. See what she knows.'

Carter nodded and left Natalie behind, as she contemplated the story that was unfolding. Tried to start making pieces fit.

Became annoyed when they refused to.

31

It didn't take long for Anna to arrange meeting Keira. For a start, she didn't tell her that Mia would be there, which seemed to help matters, because from the look on her face when Mia walked up with Anna, she wouldn't have come at all.

It made her want to turn back. To go back home and hide in bed again. Only, it was the first time in a few days – well, make that a year and change, to be honest – that she felt like she was in control of what was happening around her.

She was finding out what had been going on. That was the goal. She couldn't keep her head in the sand any longer. That option had gone.

She was the centre of it, after all. And if she simply sat around and waited, nothing would help her.

Mia could feel the walls closing in around her and needed to get ahead of the inevitable.

But, how do you stop them?

'What's she doing here?'

It was the greeting Mia had been expecting, but that didn't mean it wasn't still a sting.

'She needs to talk to you,' Anna said, taking the lead as she always did. Thankfully. 'And I knew you wouldn't come if you knew she'd be here.'

'No, I wouldn't,' Keira replied, folding her arms, but not walking away. 'After what happened, I can't believe you're showing your face in public.'

They were down on the waterfront – a few weeks earlier, it would have been busy with families and groups of friends.

Now, as the weather turned in early September, it was quieter. They were only a half mile or so away from where the supermarket and restaurants were, which were still bustling with life, but up there, they wouldn't be disturbed.

'Keira,' Mia said, hearing the tremble in her voice. She breathed in and out and tried again. 'I know what people are saying about me, but it's not true. I would never hurt anyone.'

Keira rolled her eyes. 'Don't play innocent now. We all know you have a different side to you. We've all seen it.'

'So do you,' Mia said, unable to control her anger. 'I know about you and Ben.'

'There was nothing going on—'

'He's gone now,' Mia said, taking a step closer to Keira. 'You don't have to lie anymore. I know the two of you were close. I loved him. I would never have hurt him. I just wanted him to be honest with me, that's all. And he was.'

Mia could feel Anna's eyes on the side of her head, but she ignored her.

'It wasn't like you think.'

'I don't really care how it was,' Mia said, waving away Keira's attempt to explain. 'I spoke to Ben all about it the night he was killed. He told me his version and that was bad enough. It doesn't matter. It's over now, for all of us. There's nothing more to be said. It didn't change anything. I knew you'd always liked him, so I wasn't surprised.'

Keira looked uncomfortable now, as Mia became calmer. 'I think what Mia is trying to say—'

Mia cut Anna off with a wave of her hand. 'Keira, I know everything. He told me. About the messaging, the meetups, what you'd talked about. I just need you to know I don't care about any of that stuff anymore. We might have got back together, maybe not. I don't know now and I'll never know. But it's important that you know I didn't hate him or you, for any of it. I loved him. But that didn't mean I was blind to it all. We're all still trying to figure all of this out, you know? What would happen next, where we'd all end up.'

'Yeah, sounds like you've got it all worked out to me.'

Mia bit down on her lower lip, so she didn't say something she shouldn't. 'I know you liked him. Maybe as much as I did. It doesn't matter now, because neither of us can have him. He's gone. But you have to know, I didn't have anything to do with it.'

Mia waited, hoping it would be enough. That her words, the confidence she felt while she was saying them, would be sufficient to get through to her.

No such luck.

'I don't know what you want from me?' Keira said, uncrossing her arms and throwing them up in the air in annoyance. 'It's not like I'm the police. Shouldn't you be saying all this to them? All we know is what we know – that you and Mr Fulton had some kind of "thing" and he turns up dead. Becky and you have an argument, and she turns up dead. And now, Ben. What do you think it all looks like? Am I next, is that it?'

If Keira was scared of what might happen to her, she was hiding it well, Mia thought. Which meant that she wasn't scared.

It was like it was all a game.

'Keira, Mia didn't have anything to do with any of this—'

'What makes you so sure, Anna? Just because she's your friend? You've said it yourself – it's weird. And now Ben's dead and everyone is talking about all of it, out in the open for a change. What do you want from me?'

'I want you to stop telling people that I killed them.'

Keira turned back to Mia, staring her down. 'Everyone's saying it.'

'Yeah, but not everyone is making fake accounts to send me stuff,' Mia said, earning a look from someone walking past as her voice went up in volume. They kept moving.

'I'm not doing that,' Keira said, looking away finally. She shifted on her feet. 'I shouldn't be here. If people saw me talking to you, then they might think I know something.'

'Listen, I know you're angry with me,' Mia replied, lowering her voice and trying to sound normal. It wasn't working. 'Maybe you should be, because I had what you wanted. But I didn't hurt him. Please, you have to believe me.'

'Why?'

'Because I know you didn't take Ben ending things well and I can prove it. So, maybe, I could tell people what *I* know. Maybe I could show them messages he sent me, calling you a weirdo who wouldn't leave him alone?'

'I don't know what you're talking about.'

Keira may have been playing dumb, but she could see her eyes shift around them, as if she was scared of who might have heard something. 'I think you do. Look, I don't think you're the one who did this, but if you keep going round saying I am, then maybe I can say the same. Right?'

Mia wasn't sure if it was something in the tone of her voice, or if she just wasn't as good a liar as she hoped, but something shifted in Keira's expression.

Keira shook her head and started to move away. 'I've got no idea what you're talking about, but I have to go . . .'

Mia stepped forward, blocking Keira's path. She flinched at the movement, as Mia held her hands up. 'I'm being serious, I didn't do anything.'

'Mia . . .'

She ignored Anna's voice. 'You just have to stop doing this to me, that's it. That's all I want.'

'I'm not doing anything,' Keira said, but it was written all over her face. 'Leave me alone.'

'I loved him,' Mia replied, wanting to reach out and grab Keira by the shoulders. Shake her until she believed her. 'We were going to be okay. We were getting back together. He loved me.'

'Why are you lying?' Keira said, unable to help herself it seemed. She was shaking her head, as if she was annoyed at herself for saying it. 'It was over. It was done. Even after your last little chat with him. He told you about us?'

'Yes,' Mia replied, her voice almost not there. 'He told me everything, but it was going to be okay. We were going to get past it. We were going to get back together and that was it. I left that night thinking it was all going to be fine. And then . . . and then he's gone.'

Mia could feel tears creeping into the corners of her eyes. A drop falling out and disappearing on her cheek. Her throat closed up.

She thought she saw Keira smirk back at her.

It was as if time stopped.

She wanted to do something to wipe it off her face. She wanted to hurt her.

She could feel her fists clenching by her sides.

Her heart rate increased, her breathing becoming faster.

She wasn't seeing red. Anger wasn't really like that. It was a feeling like burning inside her. This unremitting bubbling, that couldn't be stopped. Her skin was on fire. Her mind racing, thoughts of what to do next hurtling through.

Mia felt Anna's hand on her arm, but she shook it off.

Keira knew.

She wasn't sure how. It must have happened after she'd left Ben that night, but she knew.

She hadn't told anyone, otherwise the police would have mentioned it, she thought.

'I'm going,' Keira said, fixing Mia with a stare now. The previous fear she had been feeling from Mia's presence seemed to have disappeared. 'Are you going to stop me?'

Mia shook her head. Stepped aside and let Keira walk past. She glanced towards Anna, who hesitated and then followed Keira.

The low wall of the promenade was rough as Mia placed her hands on it and looked out to the sea. The waves looked calm, as they hit the wall below her.

She thought about climbing over. About the feel of the water, as it would crash into her.

Keira knew.

It wouldn't be long before she told everyone else. Probably had messages from Ben. Calling Mia all kinds of names. Crazy, weird, strange.

The same names she'd been called for years.

It was nothing new.

She wasn't sure how long she had been standing there, staring at the water below, before Anna returned. Time didn't matter.

'Mia?'

She didn't turn around to look at Anna. Didn't answer her. Because she knew what was coming next.

'Why didn't you tell me the truth?'

32

I had to start at the beginning. That was the only way of doing it right. Of following everything in order, so I could make sense of it.

That meant finding out what happened to Mr Fulton.

I knew he didn't have a wife, or children. That had been one of the things people had mentioned when he'd died – as if it was a good thing. As if not leaving behind a grieving family was somehow a blessing.

Maybe it was. I think it would be easier to be alone the way I was feeling at that moment. To not have loved or been loved.

After I'd left Val at the café in town, I'd got back to my car and called Lisa Harrison. She'd known how to get in touch with Fulton's sister. Passed me a number, which I'd called instantly.

She was only a half-hour drive away and was happy to meet me. I didn't think that was odd, until I was pulling into the car park of a retail park I'd thought about visiting a few times but never made the effort.

I walked into Costa Coffee, seeing a woman staring back at me as I walked in. She was seated facing the door, taking far too much interest in anyone walking in not to be waiting for someone.

I didn't need an introduction. I didn't need for her to be wearing a red carnation. It was obvious.

Mainly because the poor woman looked the image of her brother.

'Hayley?' I said, as I got closer to the table. She was already holding out a hand and smiling stiffly. 'Sorry if you've been waiting.'

'It's fine,' Hayley replied, standing up a little, before getting her legs stuck between the table and chair and dropping back down. 'No problem at all. Can I get you something?'

I shook my head. 'I've just had one,' I lied, thinking about the untouched latte back in that café. 'Thanks for meeting me so quickly. I wasn't sure if you would.'

Lines appeared on her forehead, as she frowned back at me. They disappeared quickly. 'Of course, Lisa told me who you were and I didn't think it would be appropriate if I didn't make the time.'

'Do you work close by?'

Hayley nodded. 'A few minutes away. Sorry for making you travel, but this is technically the end of my lunch hour.'

'I won't waste your time,' I said, sitting back in the chair and giving a quick glance at the other tables around us. It wasn't busy but there were a few people dotted around. Mostly dressed for office work – men in shirts and ties, women in smart blouses, trousers or skirts. They all seemed far too engrossed in their own conversations to pay any attention to ours, but I still lowered my voice. 'It's about your brother.'

'I gathered as much,' Hayley replied, picking up a sweetener packet from the saucer holding a tall mug of coffee. She waggled it back and forth, before opening it and pouring the contents in. She stirred it in as she continued to talk. 'I haven't spoken to Lisa in a while, but she caught me up when she called. I'm sorry to hear about your son.'

'Thank you,' I said, accepting the lament in a way that surprised me. Whenever anyone else had said those words to me, I felt irritation, but with Hayley, I felt it was genuine for some reason. Probably for the same reason I'd been able to talk so freely with Lisa – at least they understood.

That's if Hayley felt the same way about her brother, of course. It wasn't a child.

The irritation began to creep in, as my mind began to whir.

'Lisa said you wanted to talk about Will?'

I blanked out for a second, before I realised who she was talking about. 'Sorry, I never knew his first name. We always heard of him as Mr Fulton. Even after he died, the kids would refer to him as that. I probably heard his first name at some point, but I guess it never stuck.'

I could hear myself babbling, but Hayley didn't seem to care.

'That's how it is for teachers,' Hayley said with a sad smile, that didn't reach her eyes. 'I guess it's nice in a way. A form of respect.'

'I still think of my teachers that way,' I said, thinking of the few I still remembered. Or cared to. 'Almost thirty years later, I think if I bumped into one of them, I'd still call them sir or miss.'

I watched as Hayley brought her cup to her lips, her hand showing a little tremble as she did so. I frowned a little at the sight, but thought it was just the fact that she was meeting someone for the first time, to talk about something she probably didn't want to talk about.

'My son didn't have him as a teacher, as far as I can remember,' I said, tucking a strand of hair behind my ear, as it came loose from my ponytail. 'They were all shocked when it happened of course. It was pretty much all he talked about around that Christmas.'

'I can't imagine how tough it was on his students. He . . . Will was always really close with his students.'

I caught something in the way she'd said the last part. I wasn't sure what it was, but there was a slight hesitation. As if she were choosing her words carefully. 'The school had a memorial evening for him. I don't remember seeing you there for that. Raised money for charity, that kind of thing. It was a nice event.'

'I couldn't face it.'

'I'm not sure I could have either,' I said, wondering what the school's plans would be for Ben. If they were already in motion. Whether it mattered that he had officially left only a few weeks earlier. A-Level results day had been the final act. Maybe that would mean they wouldn't do anything.

I wasn't sure if I wanted them to do anything or not. I couldn't bear the idea of being asked to go. To stand up and have the spotlight on me. On Ellie.

'My daughter – she had your brother as her teacher for a year,' I said, remembering now. 'It was during Covid though, so we only met him on screen for Parents' Evening. It was all broken up into four-minute slots, then the screen would go blank. Didn't really give much of a chance to get to know him.'

Hayley stiffened, her gaze fixed on the table between us. 'Oh, that's . . . that's interesting.'

I could see it written on her face – something she was trying to hold on to. Something she wanted to say, but was doing everything in her power not to blurt out. It was becoming a physical battle. I searched for the right thing to say, in order to get her to open up, but I didn't need to wait long to realise what it was.

'How old is your daughter?'

Hayley may have tried to ask it in a way that sounded casual. As if she were just making conversation. Only, she wasn't very good at hiding. Maybe it was because she'd been doing it for too long. Or now that her brother was dead, she didn't feel the need to do it anymore.

'It was during her first year, so she'd have been eleven. She's fifteen now.'

I watched as her shoulders relaxed a little. She mumbled something that sounded like 'great age', which was a lie known to any parent in the world.

She didn't have children then.

I had to tread carefully, but I knew I was going to get something from her. Maybe not the whole story right then, but part of it.

'You loved your brother,' I said, not asking. I knew the answer. It wasn't going to be one she gave me, but I could see it.

'Of course,' Hayley replied, not indignantly, like I'd expected. 'He was . . . he was a good guy. He was always there for people, when they needed him. We used to talk all the time. That's the thing I miss most, to be honest. Just having someone out there that cared enough to keep in touch without being prompted, you know? Just knowing there's someone out there who thinks about you. I haven't really had that.'

It was her turn to babble, I realised. Because she didn't want to tell the truth.

I leaned forwards, laying my hand down on the table closer to her. 'Is there something you think is important to tell me? About your brother?'

She shook her head no. 'I don't know what you mean . . .'

'They never found out who killed him,' I said, lowering my voice as a couple left the nearest table and walked past us. 'Or why. It was an absolute tragedy. I know, because I'm living my own right now. It's the not knowing – that's been the hardest thing to deal with right now. Not knowing why, who, all those things. And you've had that for almost two years.'

'Right,' Hayley replied, taking another sip of her coffee. Occupying her hands. 'It's been hard.'

I tilted my head, looking across at her. She was still staring down at the table. 'What aren't you telling me, Hayley. There's something, right?'

'No, there's nothing . . .'

'I know what you're going through. I'm willing to listen to whatever you have to say. I'm not going anywhere.'

Hayley took a deep breath and finally lifted her head. 'I never said anything to Lisa, because I was scared.'

'Scared of what?' I said, feeling my heart begin to beat harder. My stomach lurched, as I started to work out what was coming next.

'That her daughter may have been one of . . . one of *his*.'

33

It was as if the outside world had stopped existing. That it was just the two of us sitting there, in an empty Costa Coffee, on some anonymous retail park, at the side of a busy A road.

It wasn't where I'd thought I'd learn something I think I'd always suspected.

It didn't make sense otherwise. Fulton's death. It had to be for something.

Something bad.

'I shouldn't be talking about this,' Hayley said, shifting in her seat, as if she wanted to squirm away. Slink away from the table unseen, going back to her quiet life. Unseen, unheard. 'It's not like I know anything.'

I had to tread carefully, but I needed to hear it. 'There's nothing you can tell me that'll be the worst thing I'll hear this week. This year. My entire life. I just need to know as much as I can, because my son is gone. I want to know the truth, everything.'

'It's not going to help in any way, though,' Hayley said, shaking her head. 'It's just pointless. They're never going to find out who hurt him. It's been too long.'

'What if it's the same person? Who killed your brother, Becky Harrison, and now my son? Doesn't that make sense?'

'You said it yourself – there was no link between them at all.'

'Your brother,' I said, seeing she needed a little prompting now. And losing my patience. 'He was a good teacher, that's what they all said, but you knew something else, right?'

She didn't say anything for a while and I was about to speak again, when she sighed and finally spoke.

'Do you know how you can love a monster?'

I frowned, shaking my head in confusion.

'Be related to one,' Hayley said, answering her own question, as she avoided my gaze across the table. 'Remember when you were in school and there was always a male teacher who the girls would talk about? Who was always a bit more attentive, a bit more interested than was sometimes comfortable?'

I nodded, but didn't interrupt.

'They were always the easiest ones to avoid,' Hayley continued, lowering her gaze again. 'The obvious ones, you know? But then, there are those men out there who are a bit more careful about it.'

I knew where she was going, but sat back and let her tell the story herself. I needed to hear it, process it, and see where it fit. Even though I could already begin to see it for myself.

'I don't know what you know about Will. About his background. He always wanted to be a teacher – left school and went to university, a few years before me. Got a placement, and was always in high schools. He was always well liked, but I noticed he never really stuck around one place for very long. I used to tease him about it – saying that he was always looking for the perfect school, the perfect life. Never finding it, because it didn't exist. It wasn't just that though – he never had girlfriends. Never brought anyone back to meet me, or the family. That had always been the way though. He didn't date when he was a teenager. Never went to parties, or clubbing when he was at university. He always preferred his own company. I asked him once, if there was something he wanted to tell me, maybe. That he might be scared to reveal his . . . his *sexuality*. He laughed it off. Said there was nothing to tell. He just didn't want to discuss his sex life with his sister.'

'I never had a brother, only a sister, but I understand that,' I said, risking an interjection. 'It's probably some quintessential British thing inside all of us.'

Hayley let out a humourless chuckle. 'Maybe. Yeah. That's what I thought anyway. Then, I bumped into him a few years ago, by chance. This was when he was working down near Crewe. I had been visiting a client at the weekend, something I never do, but sometimes you just have to work around their schedule. Anyway, I just happened to be passing Nantwich and remembering there was a nice place to sit by the river there. We'd been there when we were kids. I parked up, walked down to this river, and he was just . . . there. It was a complete accident, but I've never seen him look more scared.'

I waited, as Hayley drained the last of her coffee in one long swig. Her hands were trembling more now. She was glancing back and forth around her, as if she were preparing for an attack. I could barely hear her as she continued in an even lower voice.

'He was with a young girl,' she said, almost stumbling over her words. She swallowed something back. 'A teenager. She was blonde, so slim. He towered over her. At first glance, she looked about eighteen, but I could see it – the way we used to try and make ourselves look older than we were, right? Makeup a little overdone, clothes a little uncomfortable. I was so shocked, I didn't know what to say. Will just looked at me, like he wanted the ground to swallow him up. He told me she was a friend, didn't even tell me her name. It was so awkward, I just made my excuses and left.'

'Did you talk to him about it later?'

Hayley nodded. 'I left it a few days, which only made things worse in my head. I knew what she was.'

'A student.'

'Yes,' Hayley said, almost inaudible now. I thought I saw the glimmer of a tear in her eye. 'I didn't know what to do. What to say. It wasn't like I caught him doing anything physical with her – they were just sitting there, on the grass, talking. It could have been innocent. I wasn't to know. When I spoke to him a few days later, he told me this story about his student having problems at home – abusive parents, etc etc. He was just trying to help her. But, I knew my brother. I knew when he was lying. And it sounded too rehearsed. Like he'd spent a few days honing his story, so that's when I knew he was hiding something. That he was ashamed of what he was doing.'

I felt revulsion, physically, my stomach churning as I began to process what she was telling me.

'I started putting things together,' Hayley continued, her embarrassment about what she was saying beginning to come through. 'The fact he never seemed to stay at one school for long. That he never settled down, or showed any sign of doing so. I never had any evidence, other than what I'd seen that day, and I don't know . . . I guess I didn't think he could be doing something like that.'

'You never want to think about someone you love doing something that bad,' I said, swallowing back the bile forming at the back of my throat, as I knew I couldn't lose her at that moment.

I wanted to shout. I wanted to scream.

I thought about Ellie. About the idea of a teacher at her school, someone in a position of power, doing something as sick and twisted as this.

And his sister could have done something to stop it.

'Maybe it was as he said,' Hayley said, wiping away a tear from her cheek, looking past me and towards the exit. 'I don't know. But then I spoke to Lisa Harrison and she told me that there were rumours going around the school. She told me like they were stupid and ridiculous. That no one believed them, but I knew. I knew and I did nothing.'

'Why are you telling me?'

Hayley hesitated, unsure of herself suddenly. 'I . . . I've just been holding on to this for so long. I didn't think I'd ever tell anyone, but when I found out about your son – another kid from the school, who was connected to my brother in a way . . . I couldn't take it anymore. I couldn't handle the idea that maybe this all started with what he might have done. I just want it to stop. Will is gone now and yeah, maybe I'll be hated if it all comes out, but I promise you – I didn't know for sure. I had suspicions, but that's the way life is now, isn't it? It feels like everyone is suspected of that type of thing now and I didn't want to add to it.'

'You don't have kids, do you?'

Hayley shook her head no. 'I was married, until recently. It never happened for us. We didn't even really try.'

I could see something under the surface there. Something she didn't want to say. Probably some kind of trauma from her childhood, I guessed. It would make sense – probably something her brother used to justify himself and his behaviour.

I didn't care.

I took a deep breath in and let it out slowly. Tried to focus. 'Lisa told you about this girl – Mia?'

'Yeah, she mentioned her a few times,' Hayley replied, crossing her arms across her body. A type of self-comfort, it seemed. 'She was convinced that she had something to do with her daughter's murder.'

I nodded. 'And I think the same about my son. They had been . . . seeing each other for a few months. Broken up recently and I don't think she'd taken it well. Given what happened to Lisa's daughter, and your brother . . .'

'You're thinking now, after what I've said, he might have been . . .'

She didn't finish her sentence, instead casting her eyes to the table in front of her and shaking her head.

'Do you think it's possible? That the rumours were true?'

Hayley sighed and checked her phone. 'I've got to get back—'

'Just tell me,' I said, shifting my own chair back as she rose to her feet. 'Do you really think your brother may have done something to her?'

'I think you know the answer to that question. I'm really sorry, I've got to go. I'm sorry for your loss. I'm sorry I can't be any more help.'

And then, she was gone, leaving me standing in the coffee shop. Watching her leave. More sure than ever that Ben's killer was Mia.

34

Mia and Anna were walking off the waterfront and back towards town. The silence had grown heavy between them, as Mia tried to find the right words.

It wasn't until they reached the bombed out church, on the outskirts of the town centre, before she started talking. They slowed down, knowing they weren't going any further.

At least not together.

'It wasn't a lie,' Mia said, coming to a stop on the old stone wall which surrounded the church. She leaned her back against it and wrapped her arms around her body. 'I didn't lie to you.'

'What happened between you and Ben that night?'

Mia breathed in, let it out with a sigh. 'It was pretty much as I told you. Only, it didn't quite end with us deciding to get back together.'

'That's literally what you told me though,' Anna said, shaking her head. She was still standing away from Mia, putting space between them. 'So, I think it is a lie.'

'No, I don't know what Keira told you—'

'She didn't just tell me,' Anna said, waving a hand towards Mia to stop her in her tracks. 'She showed me the messages she swapped with Ben after you spoke to him that night. He was pretty adamant that it was all over. That you'd gone mad and he was done.'

'It wasn't like that.'

'Well, why don't you just tell me what it was like then? Why not tell me exactly what happened?'

Mia didn't answer, casting her eyes to the ground, trying to find the right words. The right way to tell Anna and not have her leave her there instantly.

'Mia, you've got to start talking,' Anna said, when Mia took too long. 'I don't know if you've noticed, but there isn't really anyone else who has believed in you since day one. Who has been telling people they're wrong about you. Who has been by your side since all this began. I'm fast becoming your last friend. You know this – no one is reaching out to you anymore. After those first few hours when Ben was found . . . it's all gone quiet hasn't it? All those groups on Whatsapp with nothing in them for over a day now? Nothing from anyone other than me, right? It's because everyone thinks you had something to do with this, and I don't know how to tell them they're wrong anymore. Not if you're not telling me everything.'

'I know this,' Mia replied, her voice faltering a little. 'But it's not that easy.'

'Just start with the truth. That's all I'm asking.'

'We weren't supposed to see each other that night,' Mia began, deciding it was time. Anna was right – she didn't have any choice. And it came down to trust. She really only had one person left that she could trust. Her. There was no way she was going to get through this without her. 'I knew he was going to be there – I knew everyone was going to be there. It had been planned for weeks. I thought it would be the last chance I'd have to see him, before uni started. So, I decided to go and speak to him. See if anything had changed in his story.'

'And had it?'

'We didn't even get into it. I went down the dips with the other girls and it took an hour before he came up to me. He'd been drinking, as everyone had been, but he was talking clear, right? And we were just talking rubbish, you know? About other stuff, what we'd been doing, what other people had been doing. Like we always did. It was just like it had always been. And then, we started talking about us. Me and him. How he missed me, that he wished that things hadn't spiralled out of control and got to where they had, all that kind of thing.'

'And that's what you told me. But it didn't end that way.'

Mia shook her head no. 'It was going so well, we had plans to meet up the next day, because I had to get back home. We stepped further away from the group and were saying goodbye, and then he leaned in for a kiss. That's when things changed. I don't know why, but I just got this feeling. It came over me and I just backed off. He looked at me like he was confused and asked me what was wrong.'

'What was it?'

Mia looked off down the street, towards the centre of town. It would be busy down there, but at the church, it was quiet. The trees weren't making a sound, no passing traffic. It was as if they were the only people around.

'I knew he was lying,' Mia said finally, looking back at Anna now, staring into her eyes that were unblinking and trained on hers. 'I just knew it, he had been lying to me since the Keira stuff had all come out. And then, when I felt his breath on my lips, I just got this feeling inside that I couldn't ignore. I imagined his same breath on hers and I couldn't take it anymore. I just . . . I just lost it. I didn't shout. I knew people would hear if I did. I just told him exactly what I thought. That I knew what had happened and just pushed and pushed him to tell me exactly what had been going on.'

'And he did.'

'Yeah,' Mia said, remembering his face, as it finally crumpled and he accepted there was no way out. And the feeling she'd had as her worst fears had been confirmed. 'He told me they'd been sleeping together. Pretty much off and on since we'd been seeing each other. Then, he went straight into telling me that it was no big deal – that he and me weren't that serious in the beginning and it would only happen when they'd been at parties and drinking and I wasn't there, or we were having an argument . . . all the bullshit you can imagine.'

'I'm sorry,' Anna replied, taking a step towards Mia. She made as if to reach out, but stopped herself. 'What happened next?'

Mia thought about what to say. Whether she should keep going. What Anna would say in response.

She decided she'd already gone so far. She should tell her story.

'I told him it was over,' Mia said, quietly now. 'That he had made me look like an idiot and I wasn't going to take it anymore. I told him he was nothing – that he was scum, every name I could think of. And he just laughed at me.'

Mia closed her eyes, back in that moment. Hearing that laugh, as he took in what she'd said. She could feel her hands tremble, as she remembered them forming into fists that night. The feeling inside her, as she listened to him mock her. Disregarding what she was feeling.

She had felt tears welling up in her eyes that night, but not now. It was only the red raw fire in her stomach, as it built up inside her. It had been worse when he'd been in front of her, but she could still feel it now – lingering still, only a few days on.

'He called me names,' Mia said, blinking away the wetness in her eyes. 'He said everyone knew I'd slept with Mr Fulton and who knows who else. That the only thing he was worried about was having caught something from someone like me.

That he had only been with me, because he knew how easy I was.'

Anna's hand found her mouth, as Mia looked away again. Unable to see what was going on behind her expression. How she was reacting.

Mia closed her eyes again, wishing she was somewhere else. Anywhere, other than in that town. In that place.

'He said he should have listened to everyone who told him that I'd killed them both – Mr Fulton and Becky. He said he'd make sure everyone knew the truth about me.'

'It doesn't sound like him at all,' Anna said, her voice coming through the darkness behind Mia's closed eyes. 'I guess you never really know someone. Did you leave then?'

'I told him,' Mia began, opening her eyes, finding reality again. 'I told him that I was going to make him pay. That if he thought what happened to Mr Fulton and Becky was bad, he had to wait until he saw what I did to him.'

Mia saw Anna wince and felt instant regret at saying that final line out loud. 'I didn't mean it, of course,' Mia said, trying desperately not to lose her now. 'I was . . . I was just angry, that's all. I wanted to hurt him. As much as he'd hurt me.'

Mia watched, as the cogs began to whir in Anna's mind. She wasn't sure how she was going to react, what she was going to do.

She didn't expect her response.

'He deserved it,' Anna said, after what seemed an eternity for Mia. 'He was an arsehole. I told you that from the beginning.'

Mia let out a sigh of what she thought might be relief. 'It doesn't mean I did anything to him—'

'That doesn't matter now,' Anna cut in, with a wave of her hand. 'What's important is that obviously Ben told people you said this to him. At least Keira that we know of. Although she wouldn't tell me exactly what you said, she hinted around it. Which means it was probably by Snapchat and the messages are gone. So she can't prove it. Neither can anyone else, or the police would have already pulled you in. It means you can get ahead of this. We need to come up with a plan if they do come knocking. So, run me through the rest of the night and we can work out if there's a hole, or a gap, we need to fill. Am I the only one who knows you said this to him?'

Mia thought for a second and then lied again. 'Yes.'

'That's good,' Anna said, pulling out her phone and checking the time. 'We should go back to your house. Work out what we do next.'

Mia nodded, peeling herself away from the crumbling wall and followed Anna as she started walking.

Thinking about who else knew about Ben and that night.

And what that might mean.

35

Becky Harrison's mum refused to see them. Wasn't willing to talk to the police again. And Detective Natalie Williams couldn't really blame her.

She was surprised there wasn't a formal complaint made about the investigation that had been carried out into Becky's death. It seemed as if incompetence had been the number one rule once she'd been found.

'They really thought this wasn't a murder?' Natalie said, as Carter gathered up the file on Becky's death. 'How long did they run with that?'

'Couldn't have been more than a week,' Carter replied, stepping back and hovering in the doorway. 'Still, must have felt like an eternity to her family.'

'Doesn't make much sense at all,' Natalie said, running a hand through her hair. She was constantly worried that it was feeling thinner by the day. She'd even started taking some weird supplements a friend had recommended. Red jelly things. She didn't think they were doing anything.

Getting older was no fun at all.

'So, we can't search Mia Johnstone's house, which means no access to anything electronic that might help,' Natalie said, shaking the morose thoughts from her head. 'Have you got anything from any of the other friends that were in the group? Any screenshots, conversations Mia was part of, anything that we could use at all?'

Carter hesitated, then shook his head. 'There's nothing from Mia directly. Just some random conversations, that don't put her in a good light, but are just gossip more than anything.'

'The girl Ben was supposedly cheating on Mia with,' Natalie said, doodling on a pad on her desk. She was writing names and drawing lines between them. It sometimes helped to keep her mind straight. Most of the time, they looked more like shopping lists, only for people. 'She doesn't have anything from Ben that night saved at all? None of the conversation whatsoever?'

Carter grimaced. 'It's that Snapchat thing. Deletes all the messages after twenty-four hours, unless you choose to save them. She didn't think it was important in time and without Ben's phone, we can't see anything from that.'

Natalie shook her head. 'Honestly, just when we start getting to grips with new technology, it just gets more difficult. So, right now, we don't have anything at all. Is that right?'

Carter's silence seemed to suggest that was the case, which put Natalie on edge. The outside pressure was only going to increase, as time went on. If Becky Harrison's death hadn't kept the public outside the town intrigued and interested, she guessed Ben Lennon's only a year later would. And even if it was just some kind of scare story in a tabloid, it would be enough for it to make her life more difficult than it needed to be.

'We have two very similar families,' Natalie said, thinking out loud. Carter might as well have not been in the room, as she wasn't even talking to him anymore. She just needed to hear herself speak. 'Both the old two point four standard – two couples, married twenty years or more. Two kids – a boy and a girl – of very similar ages. Not a single one of them with a dealing with the police at all in the past twenty years. All of them work, in different jobs, in different parts of the city. All of them have lived here for almost all their lives. Yet, they never met each other.'

Carter frowned, then began flipping through his notepad. He seemed to have a photographic memory of everything he'd written down and it was only a few seconds before he was agreeing. 'Yes, that's right. They've never met. Didn't even seem to know each other at all.'

'Despite their two oldest children being in classes together.'

'Only in high school,' Carter said, reading over his notes. 'They went to different primary schools. And the two younger siblings, there's a couple of years between them. So, they're not in the same classes or friendship groups at all.'

'So, nothing that links the two, other than Mia and Ben.'

'Right.'

Carter sounded unsure what Natalie was driving at, which was good, as neither did she. 'From what we know about Mia, I think she's a victim of bullying as a younger kid, gets new friends, but that can't stop her from finding herself as a victim of rumours and stories again. I just don't buy into the idea that she's going round killing all these people. And there's no evidence to suggest that she has someone else doing it for her – her dad may be a bit angry, but nothing out of the ordinary. I think we need to start looking at other factors here. We're being sidetracked by all of this local gossip, about a teenage girl, who's five foot nothing and weighs eight stone wet through it seems to me. We have a six-foot-two young man, attacked and killed in the street. This may not even have been targeted. It could be as we thought at the start – a robbery gone badly wrong. That's the truth of it. And we're now getting bogged down in all this mess.'

'Could be,' Carter replied, not sounding convinced himself. Natalie waited for him to say more, but he had closed up shop and wasn't willing to contradict her.

That wasn't a good sign.

'Listen,' Natalie said, standing up and getting ready to move. For what, or to where, she wasn't sure, but she knew she couldn't sit around there anymore. 'If you think I'm missing something here, then by all means—'

'It's not that,' Carter interjected, before she could finish the thought. 'I just don't want us moving on from the idea that we're overlooking the possibility that there's some fire to all this smoke we can see. And we're not even considering the teacher in all of this – back when Lisa Harrison was still talking to us, she mentioned the teacher a number of times.'

'Have any of the kids we've spoken to said anything outside of rumours they'd heard about him?'

Carter shrugged his shoulders. 'Makes sense though, because it's not like they would know, unless they had been approached by him in the same way.'

'But we don't have a single shred of evidence that this Fulton guy has ever been suspected of sleeping with his students.'

'We don't.'

'Then maybe we should push that idea with Mia Johnstone then,' Natalie said, making a decision. 'See if we can get a reaction. Because, outside of that, there's no real evidence of anything being linked to her whatsoever.'

Natalie followed Carter out of the door, decision made.

It didn't make her feel any better. The idea that the girl they'd spent only a little time with those past couple of days could be capable of anything like she was being accused of, was ridiculous to her.

But then, she'd heard stranger stories. Been a part of them, come to that.

Still, that wasn't what her gut was telling her and she'd come to learn that sometimes she didn't put enough stock in what it would tell her.

Maybe it should be one of those times, when she stopped being distracted by other things and actually listen to it for once.

36

I wasn't sure what to do next. I knew I had more evidence against Mia, but it didn't matter unless Mr Fulton's sister would tell the police about it.

And I didn't think that was going to happen. I wasn't sure that the fact she thought her own brother was possibly sleeping with his students was enough to do something now. Even more so that he was dead.

I wished I had someone to discuss all of this with, but I couldn't think of anyone I could trust. Val would think I was crazy now, after the scene in the café. Or, maybe not crazy, but close enough. Enough to think I was stupid for looking into this myself.

Greg was useless. Had been since Ben died.

I felt a wave of guilt wash over me, as I thought about Greg. I wasn't sure what was going on in his head. I hadn't asked.

I hadn't cared.

It was pointless anyway. He never listened to me before, why would he suddenly do so now?

I had friends, but no one I could go to with this.

There really was only one person I could go to.

I pulled the car to a stop outside Lisa Harrison's house, checking there wasn't anyone lurking around. I had started doing that in the town now – my son's death was on all the news channels, so it would make sense if they were wandering about the place, looking for a story. Me being with the mother of another murdered teen in the area would probably be enough.

I didn't see anyone, but then, I wasn't sure I'd know what to look for anyway.

Lisa answered more quickly this time round, ushering me in without a word. I followed her into the living room, just as she switched off the TV.

'I don't mind,' I said, motioning towards the television as I sat down in the same place I had the previous day. 'I'd be more shocked if you weren't watching it. Everyone is.'

Lisa shook her head. 'You don't need to see it. I know I didn't.'

I glanced to the arm of the sofa where Lisa was sitting and saw her phone screen glaring back. I couldn't read anything on it, but I knew it was Facebook. 'What are they saying?'

Lisa looked back at me with a confused expression. 'Who?'

'The local gossip pages,' I said, shaking off my jacket. It felt like Lisa had the heating on, which, given it was early September and the cost of gas was ridiculous, seemed a mistake. 'I know they're all talking about it.'

'Nothing interesting,' Lisa replied, pressing a button on the side of her phone, the screen going black in an instant. 'The usual call for National Service to come back, the town has gone to shit, won't someone do something about all this violence etc. I think they forget we had the same things when we were younger.'

'You didn't grow up round here though,' I said with a frown. 'Not that I did myself, but I think Greg would have mentioned knowing you from school or something?'

Lisa shook her head. 'Only a couple of miles down the road, though. The other side of the city. It's weird round here – you come to a town close by and no one knows who you are. I've lived here for probably the same amount of time you have. So, you know what it's like.'

I did, of course. I'd never felt more like a stranger than in the past few days. I had friends, but none I could really rely on it turned out. They were fine when organising a lunch date, or the occasional night out, but when your son is killed, people didn't really know what to say or do.

'I spoke to Hayley,' I said, settling back on the sofa. It didn't seem like I was going to be offered tea this time and I was glad of it. My stomach didn't want anything. 'Mr Fulton's sister. She had some interesting information.'

'Was it about her brother sleeping with his students?'

I wasn't surprised that Lisa knew. 'She said she hadn't told anyone—'

'I read between the lines,' Lisa cut in, with a dismissive wave of her hand. 'What else could it have been, really? I wasn't sure, of course, so didn't say anything. But I think that's what Becky knew about Mia. That's probably what got her killed.'

'But why would Mia do that? It's not like she wouldn't know that she would be considered the victim in this type of situation?'

'I don't know. That's what I've been trying to work out for the past year. It must have been more. Becky would have tried to help her, I know that at least.'

I stored that information in the back of my head. I was getting one version of Becky from her mum, but that might not be the real version.

That made me think of Ben. And whether I knew everything about him I thought I did. Not that it mattered – there wasn't anything he could have done that would deserve being murdered for.

'If Mia had been abused by this teacher and tried to end it . . . you're saying Mia killed him because of it?'

Lisa ran hands through her hair. It looked more scraggly and tired than the day before. It matched her. She didn't look to have slept since I'd turned up on her doorstep a day earlier. 'Maybe, I'm not sure. It gives her a motive though, doesn't it? And if Becky knew about it, so did others. There's no doubt about that. You hear rumours all the time. If we had some kind of evidence, maybe it would make the police look at it more. Did Hayley say she'd tell them? About her brother?'

I shook my head. 'She ran out before I could convince her. I will try again. Won't stop me telling them, of course. Not that they'll listen to me.'

'I know all about that.'

'I'm just trying to work out what to do next,' I said, fighting the urge to yawn. I was tired, but I couldn't do anything about that right then. I had to keep going. Sitting down was a mistake. 'She was in my living room and I did nothing. I should have done something then, when she was right in front of me. Lying.'

'She came over?'

I realised I hadn't told Lisa about the visit from Mia and her mum. I quickly updated her on what had happened that morning, waiting for Lisa's response. It didn't take long.

'I don't know how you did that.'

I shook my head. 'It wasn't like I had much choice. If I'd just attacked her, who would look like the crazy, violent one then? She knew I was on to her though. That I wasn't believing her little act.'

'How did her mum react?'

I tried to remember, but failed. 'I wasn't paying her any attention. I was focused on Mia. Probably as shocked as Mia was that I knew what she'd done. She probably thinks her daughter is completely innocent. She'll never believe she raised a killer.'

'Or she does know and is currently trying to work out how to keep her out of prison. Or . . . whatever happens to her.'

'Right,' I said, not really listening anymore. I was trying to recall Mia's mum's face, her reaction, her expression, but was coming up with nothing in my memory.

'So, what *are* you going to do next?'

I tuned back in, as Lisa asked the question. 'Well, I have something about the teacher and how that might relate to her. She'd probably deny it, but maybe I could speak to some of the other kids and see if there were rumours about the two of them. That's a direct link between the two of them then. There's already a link between her and Ben. That would just leave Becky . . .'

I searched Lisa's face for any sign that she was holding something back, but I had no idea what I would be looking for. A slight hesitation, or looking away from me?

There didn't seem to be any sign of anything.

'I think she killed my daughter because she could,' Lisa said, without pausing. 'Maybe because she knew about her and Mr Fulton, or some other ridiculous falling out, but I know it wasn't anything Becky did that would cause a reaction like that. It was . . . it was vicious. Hateful. And then we had to endure a wait for it to even be considered murder? What kind of monster does that?'

I listened, as Lisa continued, realising quickly that I wasn't going to get anywhere with her. She was so filled with darkness when thinking about Mia, about her daughter's murder, that she couldn't think straight. She couldn't be helpful, because logic and reason had long since been replaced by helplessness and pain.

I needed to stop Mia, before anyone else went down the same road.

Before *I* did.

37

When I finally arrived back home, I walked into what felt like an ambush.

The two detectives from the previous day were back. Williams and the young guy, whose name I couldn't remember. Greg helpfully reminded me, as he waited in the hallway for me to take off my jacket.

Carter.

Far too young to be there. Far too young to help them. Far too young to realise how serious this was.

I didn't want them there, but I had to speak to them. I had to do something.

'We understand you had Ben's girlfriend over this morning,' Detective Williams said, her voice flat, emotionless. I couldn't get a read on her thoughts in the slightest. 'We'd like to know what she said, what she told you.'

'Nothing helpful, like a confession,' I replied, unable to control myself. I didn't sit down this time, moving across the room to stand in front of the window. It was getting late in the afternoon now – and despite it being only early September, the light was growing darker outside. 'Probably about the same as she told you. That she and Ben were together, young and in love, and that she is desperate to find out what happened to him.'

Only, that hadn't been what she'd said in my house. She'd said pretty much nothing.

Greg took over, this time he sat down on the opposite sofa to the two detectives, as Carter made notes as he spoke. He detailed the visit, stopping before he reached the end, when I'd started making accusations.

He was useful for a change.

Not that it mattered.

'Thank you,' Detective Williams said, sharing a quick glance with Carter. 'We have spoken to Jenny Johnstone who gave us her . . . account of what happened this morning. I don't think she wanted to make a complaint or anything of that sort . . .'

I heard a noise emanate from within me, that could only be described as a 'scoff'. Something I'd never associated with me before, but it was the only accurate way of saying what it was.

Detective Williams didn't even blink.

'She seems very aware of what your current situation is and is empathetic to it, so doesn't want to make things worse. She agrees it was a bad idea for her to come here with her daughter and that won't be happening again in the future.'

'Empathetic?'

Williams glanced at Greg, then back at me. 'Yes, as in she has compassion and understanding about what you and your family are going through right now. However, she doesn't want her daughter being accused of murder by the mother of her boyfriend.'

'Ex-boyfriend,' I muttered under my breath. 'This wouldn't be a problem if you just talked to her again. Questioned her about a few things. And her friends too. Ben's friends . . . they'll tell you the truth.'

'We have spoken to them,' Williams said, not a hint of exasperation in her voice. She seemed calm. Too calm. 'I can assure you that your son's murder is being investigated to its fullest extent.'

She took a breath, as I waited for her to actually give me something useful to grasp on to. That they were in fact getting close to an answer. To justice.

'The thing is,' Williams continued, as Detective Carter laid his notebook back on his lap. 'What makes things more difficult in cases like this is when the family isn't behind us. Isn't allowing us to carry out our work unencumbered by distractions.'

'I'm a distraction now?'

'No, I'm not suggesting that,' Williams said, seemingly choosing her words carefully. 'However, your actions in the past couple of days haven't exactly been helpful to our investigation, as much as they might be unintentional. We understand the depth of feeling, that you want to do as much as possible to find out what happened to your son, but your actions are having an effect on our investigation.'

I took a breath, tried not to lose my temper. 'Me talking to people is "affecting" you finding my son's murderer?'

Williams shook her head. 'Not exactly. But you must understand – the more pressure you put on people who may or may not be connected to this situation, the more difficult it becomes to get a clearer picture of what happened that night. We want to speak to them while they have clear minds, clear heads. We don't want to give them the opportunity to be on the backfoot instantly as soon as we arrive on their doorstep, if that makes sense?'

It didn't. 'So far, you've been told who has the greatest motive to hurt my son and spoken to that person once. In her home. For a few minutes. That doesn't exactly fill me full of confidence. So, yes, I'm going to do what I can to move this along a little quicker, because you don't seem to understand what you have on your hands here.'

'We understand your feelings . . .'

'Alison, please,' Greg said, suddenly from the sofa. He was rubbing his forehead – the action he always did when I was annoying him. Meant to convey stress, it only annoyed me further. 'Can't you just let them do their job? They're trying to find out what happened to Ben and you going off and doing stuff is only making things worse.'

I stared at my husband, wishing he'd look at me. He refused.

He would wait.

I turned back to the detectives. 'When I do something wrong, let me know. But, I think I'm going to carry on doing whatever it takes for you to realise, finally, that you have someone out there killing anyone who has a problem with her. Three so far – maybe more, I'm not sure. And you're not even willing to listen to me.'

'Of course we are willing, Alison,' Detective Williams began to say, before I cut her off.

'No, you're not,' I said, peeling away from the windowsill and moving to the middle of the room. 'You're here, instead, to tell me to back off. As if that's something you should have any right to say to the mother of a murdered child. As if that's not something you would do yourself. You've got kids, right?'

Williams didn't answer, but I knew it was the case anyway. I could see it in her face.

'You're telling me that if something happened to them, you wouldn't be out there trying to find out for yourself what happened to them? That you wouldn't be making every single one of your colleagues' lives a living misery until you got answers?'

Williams stared back at me and I expected her to disagree.

'I'd be doing what you're doing and more,' Williams said, finally, with a shrug of her shoulders. 'But what I'd hope is that there was someone to tell me that I wasn't helping in the slightest. That, in fact, I was making things worse.'

'And would you listen?'

It was the first time I saw her hesitate over an answer. 'I don't know.'

'I think you do,' I said, crossing my arms across my chest. 'Let me tell you what I've found out, while you've been more concerned about me talking to people. I've spoken to Becky Harrison's mum – Lisa – who was in my position a little over a year ago. For far too long, your "colleagues" tried to suggest Becky killed herself, when it was obvious that wasn't the case to anyone with a pair of working eyes. She told me that her daughter and Mia had a falling out before she died. That it was bad – everyone was talking about it. Then, a few days later, she turns up dead. And this is only a few months after the teacher, Mr Fulton, is found dead. I'm betting you don't know what links Mia to him, do you?'

The two detectives shared a glance, but didn't respond.

'I'll tell you,' I said, getting some small amount of enjoyment out of knowing more than them. 'He had a reputation for moving around schools a lot. Almost fifty, never married, looked younger than his age. Good looking, you might say. Always got on well with his students. Probably got good reports from the higher-ups at these schools, because the students were too scared or indoctrinated by him to come forward and tell them what he'd been doing.'

I saw Williams shift in her seat and could sense she already knew what was coming.

'I spoke to his sister,' I said, not caring that I was throwing her under the bus. 'I bet you didn't even think to do that. She told me everything. How long she'd suspected he might be sleeping with his students, that she'd even caught him outside of school with a young girl once. No reason for them to be together. He got scared when she saw them together. Tried to come up with some bullshit explanation, but she knew what was going on. He never had girlfriends, or anything like that. She didn't see him after that. Then, she hears about him dying and the circumstances. Speaks to another mother and starts putting things together.'

There was a silence as I paused that I enjoyed. 'He must have been seeing Mia. Tried to end it or wouldn't come out in the open about the "relationship" and she took her revenge. If she'd have stopped with him, everything would have been fine with me – one less paedophile to worry about. Only, she didn't stop there. She carried on. She killed Becky Harrison because she knew about it and was probably going to start talking about it. Then, she killed my son.'

'Alison, there's no evidence for any of this . . .'

I turned on Greg, as he opened his mouth and spouted his ridiculous words. 'If you say one more thing to me, while you sit around and do nothing, I swear—'

'What? What will you do?'

I knew what I wanted to do, but the two detectives had already got to their feet. I wasn't sure if it was because they had decided it was time to leave, or if they had noticed how quickly Greg had changed the tone of his voice.

'Why don't we go outside, Alison,' Detective Williams said, not phrasing it as a question. More an order. 'We need to talk – just you and me.'

I followed her, feeling Greg's eyes on my back as I went.

There was a moment when I thought about dropping the whole Mia thing with the police. Letting them go where it was obvious they wanted to. The easier answer.

Someone closer to home.

I could have thrown Greg under the bus in a heartbeat. Let them think he killed his son. And maybe that would have been nice – to watch him sink under his own hubris. And then deal with Mia myself.

The idea was tempting.

38

We stood on the patio out the back of my house. And it was *my* house. Not Greg's. He wouldn't be here much longer and it would be properly mine. It had been bought based on the inheritance I'd got from my mum dying. That had covered the majority of the purchase. And it was in my name.

He didn't have good credit. So, some machinations had been done, and the house was mine.

I'm sure he'd try and fight it, but would give up easily. Just like with anything else that took too much work.

'I understand your frustration,' Detective Williams was saying, as I tuned back into her speech. 'But I can't have you going around making these kinds of accusations, without any evidence. You're going to affect the case we're building, so I'm asking – I'm *telling* you – to stand back. I know you're not going to want to, but if we arrest someone, the last thing I need is a lawyer making any prosecution difficult because the victim's mother has been accusing the wrong person. Or, if it does lead to this Mia, that you've poisoned the well, so to speak, with any witnesses. So, please, spend time with your daughter. Maybe try and mend some fences with your husband and realise you're in this together.'

I'd been expecting another version of this speech, but hadn't expected her to try and bring my relationship with Greg into it. 'With respect, I think you should concentrate on listening to what I have to say, rather than what me and my husband's relationship might have to do with anything.'

'Alison—'

'Listen to me,' I said, stopping myself from prodding a finger in her chest. 'I've given you more information in the past twenty minutes than you've probably got in the past few days. Go and speak to that teacher's sister. Go and speak to Becky's mum – if she'll let you in the house, after what you lot did to her last year. Actually go and question Mia properly. Then, you can come back and tell me what I should be doing. Until then, I'm going to do whatever it takes.'

Detective Williams sighed, looked off into the distance, down the bottom of the back garden. In the distance, I could see the sun disappearing behind grey clouds.

'I can't tell you what to do, but I can tell you you're not helping your son here. You need to let us do our job and find out the truth. Otherwise, you could end up with no justice whatsoever. I really don't want this to end up with you being arrested for doing something that I could stop you doing here and now. I know how frustrated and enraged you're feeling, but that's not going to end anywhere good for you. Please, just take some time, breathe, and mourn your son. Let yourself think about him and what he'd want you to do right now. He wouldn't want you to get yourself into trouble, would he? He wouldn't want you putting yourself in danger?'

For a moment, I thought about just letting them get on with it. Maybe Ben would be the voice of reason. Maybe he would be telling me to let other people put themselves in danger.

Maybe he would be telling me that I didn't know the whole story yet.

And then I remembered the rebellious streak in him. The one he got from me. Yes, it may have been long since buried, but when I'd been a teenager, I'd been just like that. I'd been the one to take drugs and have sex and get drunk, before

I'd even celebrated my sixteenth birthday, never mind my eighteenth.

That's what I'd passed on to him. And something I'd forgotten about myself. That I was never satisfied to just let someone else take the lead. That I would always think for myself. That I was stronger than I realised.

All the things I'd suppressed for the past twenty years. Thought of it as 'settling down', but instead, now I realised, I'd instead been pretending to be someone I wasn't.

It had taken a major trauma to reveal that. Which is why my marriage had been faltering and was now broken beyond repair.

I wasn't being who I really was.

I wasn't going to say that to Detective Williams though. 'Okay, I'll step back.'

Detective Williams seemed to visibly relax. 'That's great to hear. And I promise, we'll keep you updated with everything we do, what we find out.'

'I just want to ask you for a favour,' I said, making an attempt to sound calm now. *Relaxed*. 'Please, speak to Mia again. Really push her on the things I've told you. I just think if she's backed into a corner, she might react in a way that reveals the truth.'

Detective Williams hesitated, then finally nodded. 'We planned to speak to her again, so you have my word that we'll do so strongly. We'll look into everything you've told us and use it as we need to.'

'Thank you,' I said, turning my back on her and going back inside the house. I waited in the kitchen, listening to Greg talk to the two detectives quietly in the living room, then in the hallway, then on the front doorstep.

I knew what he'd be saying. He'd be minimising what I'd said – he'd be trying to make out that I was stressed out and not thinking straight. Making excuses for my 'behaviour', as if it were some kind of problem he had to put up with.

All the things he'd always done, that had only led me to being quiet. Being silent. Years of being told you're silly for thinking something. Stupid, an idiot, for not being in lock-step with his thinking.

He came into the kitchen, standing in the doorway, staring into space. Just *being there*. Not engaging. Not talking to me.

Ellie was upstairs, as she always was. I wondered what she was thinking the whole time this was going on just feet away. She'd hear everything, as the kids always did.

'I'm not interested in being told how I'm wrong,' I said, taking the lead for once. 'I'm not interested in you telling me what I should be doing, or thinking.'

'The woman said she'd had a good chat with you,' Greg replied, rubbing his forehead – again. It was almost like he did it on purpose, every time I said something he didn't like. Every time I said *anything*. 'That you were going to wait for them to do their job. Because that's what they're trying to do, without you getting in the way.'

'I'm not getting in the way,' I said, unable to hide my frustration. 'I'm just doing what they should be.'

'There's no need to shout—'

'I'm not shouting,' I said, shaking my head, letting out a chuckle. Then, I raised my voice. 'This would be shouting.'

I saw Greg flinch a little, as my voice echoed around the kitchen.

'You don't get to just say something that isn't true,' I said, leaning against the island and trying to work out what I saw in this man twenty years earlier. 'Not anymore.'

'I'm not saying anything.'

'You've spent years telling me that I wasn't right,' I said, more calmly than I was feeling. I was surprised just how calm

I sounded. 'In all your little, underhanded ways. Making fun of my mistakes with the family, with friends. Making out I never knew anything. Putting me down at every opportunity you could, just to make yourself feel good. Look good. Well, this is it Greg. This was your chance to show just how good you are. And look at what you've done.'

'Don't you think I want to be out there, Alison? Don't you think I want to be finding the person who did this to our son and killing them myself?'

I shook my head. 'You're not fooling anyone anymore, Greg. You've never so much as looked at another guy wrong in all the years we've known each other. You like to talk a big game, but when it comes down to it, you're just scared. You haven't got it in you at all.'

'You don't know what you're talking about . . .'

'Oh, I've heard the stories,' I said, enjoying myself now. Saying all the things I'd been thinking for years, but never wanted to say, because I was afraid of where it would lead. Now, I didn't care. 'Your brother talking about these supposed fights you've been in, but I've seen no evidence of any of it. Remember all the problems we had with the neighbours in our old house and you did what? Nothing, that's what. You pissed and moaned to me, talked about going round and sorting that meathead of a bloke out, but you never said a word to him. And now, your son has been murdered, and you haven't so much as left the house. I know who did this to him. Have you spoken to her family? Gone round and taken her dad outside for a "chat"? No. You've done nothing, as always. You want to wait for the police to do something? Well, you go ahead. I'm done with waiting for you to do anything. I'm done waiting for you to act like the man you've always pretended to be. I don't need you anymore.'

'Oh, so you're going to tell me you're leaving me again?' Greg said, as I grabbed my jacket and walked down the hallway. He was shouting after me, but I knew what was missing.

Protest.

He knew I was right.

'You're doing nothing for him,' Greg said, as he entered the hallway behind me. 'Or Ellie, or me. Your family needs you here and you can't even give us that.'

I turned back to him, as I opened the front door. 'I'm doing *something*. That's the difference between us.'

I slammed the door behind me, walking up the path and unlocking the car. I turned back to the house and glanced up at the window.

Saw Ellie in the gap in the blinds in her window. The small box room at the front.

I looked away quickly, so she couldn't see my face.

39

Anna had left five minutes before the police arrived on the doorstep again. Mia heard them talking to her parents for a little while, before they called her downstairs. She had been standing at the top of the stairs, but hadn't been able to hear what they'd been saying.

She had no doubt it would have been her dad saying that she didn't want to be bothered and why had they come back and a million other reasons why they shouldn't be in the house. Her mum would be trying to keep everything calm, but inside would be seething at the intrusion.

Neither of them would blame her for bringing this all to their doorstep. It would be everyone else's fault.

She needed that to be the case for a long time to come, because this wasn't going to go away easily.

'Mia, the two detectives would like to speak to you again,' her mum said, in a sing-song voice . 'Are you okay with that?'

'And you don't have to be,' her dad interjected, just to make his point.

'It's fine,' Mia said, coming into the living room proper and seeing the man and woman from a few days previously. Natalie and Rob. She remembered their names, easily it turned out. 'I've got no problem with it.'

She sounded calm. Willing to talk. That was one of the things she'd discussed with Anna earlier.

They'd planned for a couple of hours for this. She hadn't expected it to happen a few minutes after she'd left, but it wasn't a problem.

None of it was.

That was key – Anna had said. That she act like she was an open book. Not hiding anything. They'd be looking for that kind of thing.

'We'll just be in the kitchen,' her mum said, this time, her voice faltering a little. 'If you need anything, just give us a shout.'

Now she knew what the discussion had been about. They wanted to talk to her on her own.

Again, no problem at all.

She felt butterflies taking flight in the pit of her stomach. She glanced at her dad as he was leaving the room – he didn't look happy about the situation in the slightest. She saw her mum pull on his arm, making sure he left.

This was it.

This was the last time she'd be speaking to the two detectives in her own home. The next time . . . she didn't want to think about the next time, because she knew where that would be.

In a police station. An interview room.

Anna had told her that. She'd been right about everything so far.

'We just wanted to go over a few things, Mia,' the woman was saying. Natalie. Or was it Natasha? She wasn't as sure now. 'Rob will take some notes while we talk, but it'll be me and you talking, okay?'

It was Natalie, Mia decided. Natalie Williams and Rob Carter. It would have bugged her for a while if she hadn't remembered. 'Yeah, that's fine.'

'Right, so if we could just go over the events of the night when you last saw Ben again.'

Mia recounted the same story she had the last time they had been there. This time round, she added a few details, just to add flavour, as Anna had said. Nothing huge, just enough to make it seem truthful. Which it was, of course.

'And then I left them at the dips and came home,' Mia finished, unable to look the detective in the eye yet. 'It was around midnight, I think. I spoke to my mum and I think my dad was already asleep, as he was on an early shift. My brother probably heard us.'

'So, the last conversation you had with Ben ended amicably?'

Mia breathed in, before she gave a response. Something Anna had told her to do.

Just breathe.

'Amicably might be pushing it a little, but it certainly didn't end like really bad or anything,' Mia said, concentrating on keeping her voice steady and calm. Succeeding. 'We'd been up and down the past few weeks, because of some rumours that had been going around about him and another girl. I've been hurt before, so I'm highly tuned to look for anything like that. He seemed sincere, so I believed him. But I was still feeling a bit off about the whole situation, so it wasn't like we were before. I could see us working things out. Although, he'd been drinking that night and I hadn't, so I'm not sure how he felt about the conversation. We did make a plan to meet again this week.'

'I can remember what it was like at your age,' Detective Williams said, leaning forwards, almost as if she was trying to block off the other detective from hearing her. 'Lads at that age too. They were always a pain in the arse, am I right?'

Mia almost took the bait, but absorbed the words well. She wasn't going to be led down that particular path easily. 'They can be, but Ben was different. He's always been honest with me. Which is why it was partly my fault that we were on the outs a bit. I should have trusted him more and we spoke about that.'

'So, you came away from seeing him that night thinking you two were back together and everything was going to be okay?'

'Something like that,' Mia said, not liking the phrasing of the question. She could tell that she wasn't being totally believed and that annoyed her. 'We were going to see each other again and talk more.'

'When he hadn't been drinking?'

'He wasn't drunk—'

'No, but he had been drinking,' Williams said, cutting across her. 'That must have made the conversation more difficult than it might have been?'

Mia held back a sigh of annoyance. 'No, it wasn't like that. He was fine. He listened, he talked . . . he'd only had a few, I think. He wasn't falling over pissed or anything like that. We had a good conversation.'

'When you talk about honesty – is that something you've had a problem with in the past?'

Mia heard Anna's voice in her head. *Careful*. 'Just with other lads I've seen in the past. Nothing major, just the usual stuff.'

'So, nothing that would make you have a big reaction if you felt like your current partner wasn't being totally honest with you?'

'Nothing bigger than any other person might.'

Williams seemed to think about her answer for a few moments. Or her next question, maybe. Whichever it was, it gave Mia some time to compose herself.

She didn't like where the line of questioning was going.

'We've spoken to a number of Ben's friends,' Detective Williams said, breaking the silence suddenly. 'And other people in the area, just to get as full a picture as we can about the situation. Some of them gave a very different perspective on your relationship. And your history.'

'Yeah, well, there's just some people round here who don't like me and never have. So I wouldn't listen to a word they said. It's all just rumours and things they make up about me.'

'Rumours like what, Mia?'

'All kinds of stuff,' Mia said, forgetting what her and Anna had spoken about now. She was trying to work out who had said things about her. Who had been telling the police stuff about her. Keira, probably, despite Anna talking to her. It had probably been too late. She guessed the police had been talking to his mates since it happened – poking and prodding them into saying whatever it took to make her look like a liar. Like someone she wasn't. 'Loads of them hate me, because they think I killed Becky Harrison and got away with it.'

Williams's eyebrows raised up, but Mia missed it. She wasn't looking at the two detectives now.

'It's not my fault she was seeing someone she shouldn't have been and got herself killed, but because we had a massive fallout before she died, I'm suddenly the one to blame? That's not fair. None of them ever wanted to hear my side of the story at all. They just made their minds up about it.'

'You and Becky Harrison had an argument?'

Mia wasn't listening. 'It's not my fault if people talk about me behind my back and then make stories up. And the one time I stand up for myself, she gets herself killed and I'm suddenly the one to blame? That's not fair. I had nothing to do with it. Doesn't stop them all talking about it though. Calling me names and stuff.'

'What was the argument about, Mia?'

Mia took a breath and realised she'd been speaking without thinking – something Anna had repeatedly told her would be a mistake.

She'd been right.

Now she was in a corner and she wasn't sure how to get out.

'I can't really remember—'

'Oh, I'm sure that's not the case,' Detective Williams said, as the other detective scribbled notes down in his pad. 'Think about it. Just for a few moments. I'm sure it'll come back to you.'

Mia's mind ran through the possible answers. She couldn't remember what she'd thought up earlier, if it ever came up.

She was failing.

'I . . . I don't want to talk about it,' Mia managed to stammer out, but it wasn't enough. She knew it wasn't.

'Was it about the teacher?' Detective Williams asked, leaning forwards so she could catch Mia's eyes. 'Mr Fulton, was it? The one who died a few months before Becky did?'

Mia's mouth opened, but nothing came out. Something inside her protected her from her initial desire to shout and scream and hurl abuse at the mention of *his* name.

'We know this might be difficult, Mia, but we're here to help. If there's something you need to tell us, we're just here to listen.'

Mia could feel the walls closing in around her. Becky, Mr Fulton . . . now Ben. She had two detectives in her house, talking about all three.

And she felt small. Alone.

Just like before.

'Please, don't . . .' Mia said, feeling the tears springing to her eyes easily. Far too easily. 'I can't.'

'Mia, we just want to get to the truth here,' Detective Williams said, her voice like silk. 'It's important we know what's happened. If there's something you want to tell us . . .'

'It's got nothing to do with any of you!'

Whatever had been protecting Mia suddenly disappeared. She watched the detective recoil from her scream, then the door being pushed open and her dad storming into the room, closely followed by her mum.

'What's going on here?'

'Mia, are you okay?'

Her mum and dad were talking over each other, as her mum reached her side and draped a hand over her shoulders. She could feel tears rolling down her cheeks, as she buried her face into her mum's chest.

'I think it's time you left,' Mia heard her dad say, muffled against the softness of her mum's sweater.

She heard them leave, making no apologies for what they'd done to her.

It got them out though. And, maybe that was the best outcome she could have wished for.

They knew about him.

They knew about Becky.

They were putting it all together. A couple of hours talking things over with Anna had been pointless. Childish, she thought now. That they could even begin to come up with a plan that would get her out of the trouble she was in.

And she was in deep now.

40

I left with no particular place to go.
Ended up on the street where Mia lived with no memory of how I'd got there. I was parked up, a little further down than her house, just watching it.

Staring into the growing darkness – thinking about the people inside. The parents. The brother.

Her.

Wondering what was going on behind their eyes. Inside their minds. Whether they all knew what was living under the same roof as them.

Whether they had begun to suspect.

Whether they had no idea at all and just thought it was all a coincidence.

Was anyone that stupid?

I thought about Ben and Ellie. What they hid from me, what they kept to themselves. I had met Mia a few times in the previous months, but had no idea about the whole story she brought along with her. I'd heard the rumours, of course, but that hadn't been enough.

I'd been too wrapped up in my own thoughts and feelings. The anxiety and low moments, I focused on over and over. My rapidly disintegrating marriage and what it would mean for me moving forwards.

The idea of meeting someone else at my age . . . I'd spent months thinking about that single thing.

So, I'd not paid much attention to what Ben and Ellie had going on in their young lives, and that made me feel more guilty than I thought possible.

I'd always wonder if I'd spent time thinking about Ben and his life a little more, maybe I could have made a difference.

I'd never know now.

I saw the two detectives pulling up outside Mia's house and almost ducked back inside my seat. Watched them get out, having a soundless conversation, before knocking on the door.

Saw them go inside and almost followed them. Almost snatched the car door open and ran to the house. Banged on the door and demanded to be let in, so I could hear what they said to each other.

I resisted the urge, but only barely.

Around thirty minutes later, I saw movement, as I watched the front door, barely blinking. My neck strained from the tension and fixation.

The door opened and I saw who I assumed was Mia's dad, saying something to the two detectives as they left.

Why hadn't they arrested her?

I saw Mia's dad standing in the doorway, watching them as they left, before scanning the street left and right, before closing the door behind him.

The detectives left, leaving the road silent again.

I wanted to know what had been said. I willed my phone to begin to buzz on the dashboard, where I'd kept it in sight. Wanted to hear Detective Williams's voice, telling me they had spoken to her and decided she was lying.

Nothing came.

Seconds ticking by. Became minutes. Became hours.

I was tired. Hungry. Thirsty.

Still, I couldn't move.

I felt as if I were on guard. A stakeout. Sentry. Keeping a watchful eye on the house, as if I could just wait and catch her for myself.

The eighteen-year-old girl living in that house had killed my son and all I could do was sit outside and wait for . . . what? For her to come out, wearing a big sign, saying she killed him and there was nothing I could do about it?

Or, to come out holding a hammer, that had been used to kill Ben, Becky, the teacher . . . who knew how many more?

Because there would be more. There always were. And would be, in the future if she wasn't stopped.

I glanced at my phone as another message came through from Greg. He'd sent three in the previous hours. All pleading for me to come home, to talk things out, that he wanted to listen to me. I knew that wouldn't be the case – instead, I'd have to listen to him, as he told me what my problems were and how to solve them. That's how it had always been between us.

I didn't have the capacity to go through that right then. It wasn't going to help me, or anyone else.

The lights started to go out in the houses around me. I wondered if anyone had spotted me sitting in the car outside. Not from Mia's house, but I thought she might have neighbours that would take notice. There was a split-second where I was worried that her mum and dad might suddenly come out and approach, but I realised I didn't care.

Let them.

I had every right to be there. And maybe I'd be able to learn something more from them if they did. What they did and didn't know about their daughter, perhaps?

They might all be in on it. The thought hadn't occurred to me before then, but I wondered what I really knew about that family. I'd not paid enough attention to her mum, which I could have kicked myself for. I knew she had a younger brother, but I didn't know anything about him.

It was her I was focused on. The rest could be swept along if need be.

It was close to eleven p.m. when I got the message. It was a text message, which wasn't what I'd been expecting. Usually, it was all WhatsApp and Facebook for me.

The only text messages I received were from O2 and various companies that had my phone number somehow.

This was from a number I didn't recognise. Wasn't saved in my contacts.

If you want to know what happened, go to the bombed out church. Half past midnight. I won't wait.

I realised my hands were shaking as I read the message again. And again.

I knew where they meant, but I suddenly didn't want to be alone.

Then, I thought of Ben. About Ellie.

This wouldn't be Mia. She wouldn't be this out in the open. It didn't stop me replying to ask.

Who is this? Is it you?

I waited for a few minutes, but didn't get a response. I navigated through my phone and called the number. It went straight to a message.

This number is unavailable . . .

No ability to leave a message. I googled the number, but nothing came back.

It was almost a couple of hours until I had to be there, but I had no reason to stay where I was and wait. I turned the engine on, then turned it back off again.

If it was Mia, then it made sense that she would leave the house before midnight, in order to make it there in time. Maybe I could have filmed her on my phone as proof? I checked my phone had a voice recorder and found it easily enough. At least I could have something that could be used as evidence.

I waited.

I checked Google Maps – it would only take a few minutes to drive out to the outskirts of town and to the bombed out church – a ridiculous name for a place. I remembered finding out that's what locals called it and asking Greg about it. It was the place of legend in the town amongst kids and teenagers, he'd told me. Every local ghost story seemed to involve it in some way, with numerous tales told about its origins and what happened there now. He had told me the true story. Apparently it had been bombed in World War Two – a stray that was supposed to have dropped in the port area of the city. Destroyed the church, but killed no one miraculously. It was left to rack and ruin instead, becoming the subject of scary stories for children and a place for teenagers to hang around at night.

He had taken great delight in trying to scare me with the stories he'd heard as a kid – that the bells still rang out at night. A warning for anyone coming too close, when there was no one around. The church had been derelict for years. Various plans had been made to reconstruct it, but instead, it had been left as a monument to a time that had long since passed.

An hour went by. Somewhere in the distance, I thought I heard bells clang midnight.

There was no movement from the house.

I had to take a chance. Leave and make my way to the church.

I drove there carefully, the streets quiet, still. I didn't see another person on the journey there. Apparently, I was the only person stupid enough to be driving out to the edge of town at gone midnight.

I parked up and got out of the car, before I gave myself the chance to change my mind. The air was colder now – early September breeze rippling through the trees. The church was only accessible by crossing a field, that was bordered by a few houses. I didn't need to walk very far, before they were out of sight though.

It could have been the middle of nowhere. It was difficult to see where I was going, so I switched on the torch light on my phone and pointed it towards the ground.

A few minutes later, I finally saw the stone of the walls that surrounded the broken-down building appear. Up ahead, raised up on the hill where it sat in ruins. The sky had turned misty at some point, as if it had been raining all day and was struggling to clear. I couldn't see the top of the building, as it crept towards the darkness above.

I could hear my heart beating wildly in my chest.

It felt like a mistake.

It *was* a mistake.

I had come out there, with no method of defending myself, and no one knew I was there.

I wanted to turn back. Find my car and drive home. Or, I could have called the police right then, so at least someone knew where I was.

I didn't do any of those things.

Instead, I waited, in the darkness, for her to arrive. Because, I thought it had to be *her*.

I felt the brick beneath my hand as I reached the old building, turned and looked out in the darkness. Listened carefully, for any noise, but could only hear my own breathing.

Minutes passed, as I periodically checked the time on my phone. Every time, the glare of the screen was blinding in the blackness of the night.

Every time, I thought about the fact that I was illuminating myself. Painting the target clearly.

I was alone.

I was going to give up, as it got closer to one a.m., but I hung on, hoping that I was going to finally get what I needed.

She may have a hammer on her. She may have been sneaking up on me, as I stood there waiting.

It wouldn't matter.

I wasn't going to go down without a fight.

Still, I thought I had been played with – that no one was coming and that maybe this had all been a ploy to make me move from near her house.

I shook my head at the possibility that I had fallen for it hook, line, and sinker . . . whatever that meant.

Then, I thought about Ellie. And Greg.

Maybe that was why I had been brought here – so they would be in more danger. My stomach lurched at the thought and I started to move.

That was when the hand came around my neck and across my throat.

41

Mia didn't want to speak to her parents, but she didn't have much choice. Her mum was sitting far too close to her – now she wanted her space again. Her dad was quietly fuming, pacing the living room, muttering under his breath.

'I'm okay now,' Mia said, pulling away from her mum and finding her phone on the sofa next to her. She picked it up, but didn't bring the screen to life. 'I just got upset when they were asking me all those questions.'

'We shouldn't have let them talk to you on your own,' her dad said, coming to a stop finally. 'They lied to us – said they just wanted to make sure you were okay and that you were eighteen and that you could talk to them alone without us worrying . . .'

He kept going, as her mum reached out and stroked a hand against the top of her arm. Mia wanted to shrug it away, but knew that would just hurt her more.

'I'm okay, really,' Mia said, as her dad paused for breath as he ranted on. 'They just started talking about things I didn't want to talk about, and I didn't know what to say.'

She heard her dad mutter something under his breath again, that sounded a lot like '*that teacher . . .*' but decided to ignore it. 'I'm going upstairs to call Anna.'

Mia didn't wait for her parents to say anything more – standing up quickly and going out of the room. She made her way upstairs, seeing her brother's bedroom door close as she made her way onto the landing. She thought about knocking and seeing how much he'd heard, but decided against it.

She wondered how he was dealing with all of this. He was so quiet, so withdrawn, that she didn't think it would be very well.

Mia closed her bedroom door behind her and flopped on the bed. Found Anna's number and video called her.

'They came round,' Mia said, not waiting for Anna to say hello. She could see her bed posts behind her, so knew she was alone.

'That didn't take long,' Anna replied, sitting up, the view changing slightly. 'What happened?'

Mia recounted the visit from the police – not leaving out anything. Anna didn't react at all, as she quietly ran through all the questions, and the answers she'd given them.

Mia made sure to let her know that she'd taken her advice all along . . . right up until they'd mentioned Mr Fulton.

'They *have* been doing their research on you,' Anna said, almost to herself. 'I guess people have been talking to them.'

'Did we expect anything else?' Mia replied, shaking her head. 'They're starting to think I had something to do with this . . . all of this. And there's nothing I can do about it.'

She talked with Anna for another thirty minutes or so, before ending the call. She felt better afterwards, after Anna talked her through her options – what she could do next and how she could approach things when they came back round.

Because they would come back round. They both knew it.

Mia didn't think it would be for a cosy chat again. Next time, she thought they'd be asking her to go down to the police station. And she was eighteen now – she wouldn't have her parents in the next room, able to jump in and bring an end to any questioning if she needed them to.

She knew it would be Ben's mother who was directing all of this towards her. She'd seen the way his mum had been looking at her, the whole time she'd been at their home. And then, all of the things she'd said to her, at the end.

Ben's mum thought she'd killed her son. She was convinced of it.

Just like Becky's mum before her.

If that teacher had any close family, Mia had no doubt they'd be thinking the same thing.

If she could just present them with the actual killer, it would make things all go away. If she could just tell them who had done it, then she would be free of it all. Free to move up north, go to university, leave all of it behind her.

Mia got out of bed and listened at the door for a moment. No one out there. She opened the door quietly and heard murmurs of conversation going on downstairs – her mum and dad, no doubt working out what they were going to do about all of this.

She slipped into their bedroom, not turning the light on. Made her way to the window – the blinds closed, which meant she had to part them a little to see outside.

Mia looked out into the street and saw that Anna had been right.

'She's probably watching you. She'll know we saw Keira earlier and that's why the police came round. She's keeping an eye on us, to see what she can make up and tell them.'

Down the street, she saw a car that didn't belong to any of the neighbours, parked up – George from number thirty-eight had been forced to park over the small entryway that wasn't big enough to park a car up really, that ran between his house and number forty. He wouldn't be happy about that.

That wasn't the only tell.

Every minute or so, a light came on inside the car, briefly illuminating a figure sitting in the driver's seat. Not enough to see anything like facial features, or even if it was a man or a woman, but just enough so Mia could tell that someone was sitting in the car.

They were watching the house.

It had to be her. Ben's mum.

She let the blinds go, before she could be spotted staring out into the street. Stepped back and tried to work out what to do next.

She didn't need to wait long.

Her phone buzzed with a message only a few minutes later and she had her answer.

Mia knew what she was going to do next.

End it, before it went too far.

Mia heard her dad follow her mum to bed around eleven thirty p.m. stumbling on the stairs as he moved up them slowly. Muttering and grumbling to himself, as he always did after too many drinks. He would pass out in minutes, she thought.

Maybe, he hadn't been drinking. Maybe he was just angry, after what happened earlier. Yet, she knew he'd have started on the bottle of wine that was on the top shelf of the fridge. Then, it would have been a few beers. It used to only happen at the weekend, but had started creeping into the week now.

No one spoke about it. Mia only knew because she'd seen the empty bottles and cans in the recycling bin in the kitchen and wondered how long until it was daily.

She envied him in a way. At least he had a way of escaping the real world, even if it was only for a night or three.

Mia waited another twenty minutes or so, then lifted herself out of bed. She was still fully clothed – her mum had popped her head round the door around eleven, but she'd pretended to be asleep. Breathed slowly, as she sensed her mum staring at her in the darkness.

She wondered what had been going through her head. Wondered what her mum really thought about her.

Whether she was starting to think there was something wrong in that house.

Mia moved slowly across her room, opening the door just wide enough to slip out. Avoided the creaky stair as she made her way down and slipped her shoes on.

There was no way she was going out the front door, that would have been noticed instantly by her mum, who seemed to sleep with one eye and ear open.

That said, it was easier to get out than she'd thought it would be. Out the back door, with the back gate keys left in the lock – she hoped no one tried it, as it would mean they'd be in the back garden within seconds, but what then? Wasn't like she hadn't locked the back door behind her.

It was colder than she'd been expecting – summer well and truly over then, Mia thought. The hoodie she was wearing over a thin T-shirt suddenly felt inadequate. She shivered, but kept moving forwards. Hoped that by the time she made it to where she was going, she would have warmed up.

She needn't have worried. Nervous energy was coursing through her veins now, which put all thoughts about the coolness of the air around her from her mind.

It was dark. Pitch black, in most places. She knew the streets, the roads, by heart. She'd made the journey countless times, so it was almost on autopilot. Her eyes adjusted quickly, but it didn't matter all that much. There were still shadows all around her.

The only sound was the soft thump, as her trainers hit the tarmac. Her own breathing.

It was a half-hour walk she did in less than that. She was out of breath by the time she reached the place. Resisted the urge to pull out her phone and turn on the torch – she didn't want to announce her presence.

Her heart was a jack hammer in her chest. Hands shaking. Body shivering without warning.

She tried to ignore it all. Ignore all the signs that said it was a bad idea to be there. Ignored the reasons she should have turned back around and gone home.

The crunch of the grass under her feet made her wince. She crept more softly, walking across the field, and only seeing the black shadow of the place up ahead.

The bombed out church.

A memory came to her – around six or seven years earlier, she remembered being on some kind of camping trip. Brownies, or Girl Guides, one of the two. Someone in the group was trying to tell a ghost story and scare the rest of the girls, but it wasn't working.

Something about the bells ringing at night, when there was no way they were still working.

Mia had never been there at night and the reality of it began to take hold. She wasn't sure anymore that it was a good idea to go there, late at night. Alone.

In those final few yards walk, she couldn't work out what she expected to find. To see.

To feel.

Mia wondered if it was simply a way of trying to find something, or someone, that couldn't be found. It reminded her of that book she'd pestered her dad to let her read for years. She'd been far too young for it, but he'd relented one day, in the summer between primary school and high school. She'd just turned eleven years old, and already devoured all the Harry Potter books. Had gone through her Enid Blyton phase, that she couldn't talk about anymore, as she was 'problematic' according to TikTok.

In some ways, this midnight adventure reminded her of those old dusty paperbacks she'd read at seven or eight years old. This was something the Secret Seven or the Famous Five would do. A mysterious relic of an old church, late at night.

She wished she'd had a dog to bring along with her.

The book she'd *really* wanted to read now was seemingly the only book her dad owned. *The Stand* by Stephen King. It was huge. Over a thousand pages. That was basically the only reason she'd wanted to read it – because it was so big. It presented a challenge and that's what she'd wanted.

Her dad kept saying no, though. Said it was too adult for her. Then, she must have caught him on a good day, or he hadn't been listening, because one day, he'd finally said yes.

Yes, she could have just downloaded it or got it from the library, but there was something about being given permission to read it that felt important. Made her feel grown-up.

Mia had read that book and couldn't believe this was the sort of story that could be told. That this was the type of story she could be reading. That stories could have that kind of power.

Walking across that field, up the small hill, in the almost pitch black darkness, the bombed out church looming over her . . . it felt like it would have fit into that book very well. The journey to it might have been shorter, but she felt like a character from *The Stand* – looking for answers that she could never find.

And she suddenly felt very small and alone. And afraid.

Scared out of her mind.

It had only been a few hours since she'd been there, but it was different at night. Not just in look, but feel as well. It was more menacing, more foreboding somehow. It had no real form, other than as a great monument plonked on the hill. The sense of danger had only increased, as she had moved quietly towards it. Listening out for any sound of someone guarding the place.

There was no sound. There was no one there but her, she thought. That should have been the signal to her that something wasn't right, but absence of something doesn't mean that there's anything missing.

She'd read that somewhere.

Mia wasn't alone.

She realised that too late.

She'd obviously approached from a different route, rocking from side to side.

Mia stopped in her tracks, as her eyes squinting in the darkness realised who was standing only a few feet away.

Ben's mum.

She'd come to the bombed out church.

Mia breathed in, just like Anna had told her to long ago. How breathing in and out – something as simple as that – could make everything feel calmer. Make everything okay.

She took one step forwards and was ready for whatever was about to happen.

Another step, then the ground suddenly started lurching towards her. She didn't feel the impact, the grass under her face. She didn't hear the sound of anyone behind her. Another breath in the night. She didn't see them come up behind her.

She didn't see them step over her breathless body and move towards Ben's mum.

One moment, she had been walking, the next she was in the dark.

She embraced it.

42

Getting away with murder is difficult.

No one ever tells you that. Not enough, anyway. There's so much to think about. To consider. You have to get so many things right, that it almost makes it impossible. Almost makes it not worth doing.

Almost.

If it's necessary though, you just have to.

It's really simple. Murder is always bad, you'll hear, but then, what about all the murders that are fine?

In war. We hear that all the time – casualties, they're called. Not murder victims. They're justified as the cost of whatever the war might be about – and that seems to be an elastic thing right now.

Then, what about self-defence? Someone attacks you, you defend yourself, and the attacker dies instead of you... that's not murder, apparently.

There's a question – someone breaks into your home, your family asleep upstairs in their beds. This person creeps up and opens the door to your kid's bedroom. Your kid wakes up and sees the person.

This burglar doesn't want to be caught.

He has to silence this child.

Only, when he grabs the kid, it screams out. You hear it and burst into the room – this stranger has a pillow over your kid's face, trying to kill him.

Is it murder if you kill that person?

Of course it isn't, people say. They're just defending and saving their kid.

That murder is fine.

Accidental murder – a driver who doesn't see someone crossing the road ahead. They're unsighted by something or other. Or, someone runs out in front of the car.

Complete accident.

That driver still killed that person, but that's okay. It was an accident.

You can justify killing someone if you want to.

Getting away with it . . . that's more difficult. And possible, with the right amount of planning and careful execution.

Until people start poking their noses into things. That's the problem. When people who don't need to worry about evidence, or anything like that, start getting involved. Hiding from the cops is easy, but normal people, who don't have to concern themselves with making sure everything is done by the book . . . that's where the problems arise.

Ben's mother – Alison. She was one of them. There was a chance she could have been just another one, like Becky's mum, Lisa, who would have gone quietly.

Only, now, Lisa had been all riled up by Alison's nose poking. Come out of it again.

And now Alison had got too close. Started adding two and two and making five.

That was a problem.

So, she had to be dealt with. Unfortunate, but it was all part of the justification – three murders, that could all be explained, to a rational person.

There weren't many rational people left, though.

Sure, it was sad for the families left behind. Of course it was. No doubt about that at all. Didn't make any difference, though. What's done is done.

They wouldn't know the real person behind each supposed 'murder victim'. The paedo teacher, the bully, the cheat.

They could never be those things to the family that grieved them.

Silence was the only way to get away with murder. Making sure no one could talk. Distraction and silence. Look over there, at that bigger thing, that doesn't make sense. And no one knows anything. No one can say anything anymore.

Silence.

That was the way to get away with murder.

Silence all those with big mouths, with things to say. All those that couldn't just let it lie.

The only way.

43

I felt my heart stop.
I felt my breathing shut down.

There was no other way to describe it – I felt like a statue, as if I'd been turned to stone. As if I'd looked into the face of Medusa in the darkness and not even known.

I couldn't move.

The hand gripped me round the throat, slipping round then, until the crook of an elbow tightened its grip and I was in a headlock.

For a moment, I didn't do anything. I couldn't breathe, couldn't see. The shock had taken over my body and there was nothing I could do.

I felt breath on the top of my head, as my legs began to give way beneath me. Felt something wet drop on the side of my face. I closed my eyes for a brief second and it was almost as if my body and mind reset itself.

I had to fight.

I began to struggle, but I had already been locked in place. I'd given them the upper hand without knowing, making things more difficult. A few seconds, that's all it had taken. That didn't mean I was going to go easily.

It didn't feel like an eighteen-year-old girl's arm around my throat.

The thought came quickly, disappearing just as fast, as my mind focused on what was happening to me.

Everything I had within me, I put into trying to break away from the grasp – the chokehold that I was under. Every ounce of strength and might.

It felt useless.

I was trapped. I couldn't move, couldn't speak. The grip only grew tighter, and a low groan escaped from my throat. I was moving on instinct now, as I realised I couldn't take in a breath and the world around me began to blur.

I could still move my legs. I began to try and move, but I was locked in place. Whoever had their arm around my throat was bigger than me, that much I could work out.

I had seconds.

Then, it would be too late. I would slip into unconsciousness, and it would be over.

There was a shift in their weight and I used the opportunity. I kicked back, finding something solid behind me with my foot. It was the wall behind me, but it gave me the goal in mind. I was struggling more now, as I lifted my hands and grasped the arm that was around my neck. I found flesh and began clawing at it. I knew I'd broken skin, as I heard an exhalation come from behind me.

I still couldn't take a breath.

I started kicking behind me, trying to find a target. After four or five attempts, I finally connected with what I thought was the knee of whoever was holding me.

I caught it good.

The chokehold wilted a little and it was enough for me to take a breath. I pitched forwards, trying to take the person off balance and it worked too well.

The ground was rushing towards me. I thrust my hands out to break my fall and realised too late that I was taking whoever was holding on to me with me.

I hit the floor and it didn't matter that it was only grass and soil. It felt like hitting concrete. The little air I had been able to take in was suddenly sucked out of me, as my chest took the brunt of the impact. Then, the weight on top of me.

None of it mattered in my head. I was still fighting for my life. I didn't care that I couldn't see anything, wasn't breathing properly. Adrenaline had taken control of me now and I was moving constantly. Twisting and turning my body, so I could get away.

It was too dark to see what was around me and I wanted to see their face.

It was never going to happen.

I began breathing a little, taking in air, as the body on top of mine tried to shift and take control once more. I was already moving. I felt hands on my body, but I was already moving away and trying to get back to my feet. Crawling on my knees, as unseen hands grabbed at my waist.

The hands dug into my skin, sending a shockwave of pain through my body. Trying to pull me back down to the ground, as I desperately tried to move away. There was a slam, as something that felt like a brick crashed into the top of my leg. And again. I realised it was a fist, pounding against me.

I screamed and the world span into a cacophony of noise.

I didn't even know it was me at first. My ears rang with heat and my throat burned with effort, but it wasn't until I felt the grasp on my body slacken a little, that I realised I could wriggle free and get to my feet.

There was no pause. I ran. Hard. I heard a shout from behind me, but I didn't turn around. I didn't care what it was – a warning, a threat, just pure unbridled anger. I was only concentrating on my legs pumping ten to the dozen beneath me. Desperately trying to keep my balance, as the ground grew soft and more muddy around my feet. It was as if it was trying to grab and pull me down. Pull me under.

Keep me there.

I wasn't going to let it.

I couldn't see the car, where I'd parked it earlier, but I knew it was out there, in the darkness. I just had to keep running.

I thought I heard footsteps behind me – pounding into the soft earth. Imagined a hand reaching out, grabbing the collar of my jacket and pulling me down. The thought kept me going. Too scared to look over my shoulder and lose a single second I could be using to escape.

The earth beneath my feet suddenly changed and my feet went from under me. I had hit the pavement that bordered the field and the mud on my shoes hadn't caught up.

I was falling.

It happened so quickly, that I didn't even have a chance to throw my hands out to break my fall. I hit the tarmac, my left shoulder taking the brunt of the impact. My head snapping back and my legs twisting at an awkward angle. I heard the cry of surprise escape my throat and hated the way it sounded.

When I hit the ground all the air in my body disappeared. I couldn't move for a second, then I remembered that hand reaching out in the darkness and I could feel my body moving again.

I blinked against the dark night and placed my hands down for support. Lifted my body up and started walking.

Then, the black night was suddenly on fire.

Red and blue, crisscrossing the air around me. Flashing across my face, making me close my eyes, lifting up a hand to shield them from the sudden intrusion.

Confusion was all I could feel. I didn't know what was happening. I heard a shout, the echo of a car door slam, and I turned to run again.

'Don't move!'

I heard the words, but I didn't take note. I was shuffling forwards, still trying to find my feet under me, so I could run again.

There were footsteps behind me, growing closer. I tried to move quicker, but it was as if I was walking through harsh waves of water, crashing into me, as my confusion grew and I couldn't work out what was happening around me.

I felt a hand on my shoulder and I cried out. Pulled away, but it was on me again. It grabbed hold of me and I screamed.

'It's okay love, calm down . . .'

The words didn't make sense. Nor did the deep, gruff voice it came from. I could see the flashes of light all around me now and it was as if something clicked in my head suddenly.

It was police car lights.

I turned finally and was almost knocked to the ground again, by a bloke a foot taller than me, wearing a yellow hi-vis jacket. I could feel the roughness of his hands on mine, as he took hold of me.

'Are you okay?'

I couldn't focus, falling into his arms as my legs finally gave way.

A few minutes later, I was sitting in the back of a police car, an extra coat around me as my entire body continued to shiver uncontrollably.

The adrenaline had left my body without warning and I couldn't stop it moving. Nervous energy taking over and trying to find an escape.

I'd managed to croak out a few words to the police officer who had finally stopped me trying to run. Told him I'd been attacked and that my son's murderer was out by the church.

He'd recognised me then. I saw it flash across his eyes, then his mind try to make sense of why I was there and what I'd been doing.

I think he'd decided it was above his paygrade and instead left me with his partner who was currently leaning against the car to the side of me. I had my legs out the side of the car, trying to piece together my thinking, so I could make sense of what was happening around me.

I didn't get the chance.

The copper came back on the scene, beckoning his partner over, while keeping his eyes on me. I couldn't hear what they were saying, but it didn't look good.

I hoped they'd found whoever had tried to attack me – actually *did* attack me – and that they were currently working out how to arrest them or something. But wouldn't the copper have come back with them? In handcuffs? Surely . . .

It was Mia, only it wasn't. It couldn't have been. Because a girl that small, that young, couldn't have been strong enough to take hold of me like that and not be overpowered quickly.

Only, it had to be her.

The copper who had managed to get me under control, as I had been losing my mind running away, came back over. Looked down at me and hesitated.

'Did you find her? Them? Whoever it was?'

'Can you stand up for me?'

I frowned, then slowly got up, getting out of the car gingerly. 'What's happening?'

'I'm arresting you on suspicion of assault . . .'

Those were the last words I heard, before they became a blur of unreality. Didn't hear him finish the sentence. The caution. Didn't feel the handcuffs slipping over my wrists. Didn't see anything around me.

I could only think of Ellie and Greg, back at home, wondering where I was. Wondering if I was going to be okay.

I could only think of Ben and how I'd failed him.

44

It was late at night when Natalie Williams got the call. She would have ignored it usually – but she was awake anyway.

It was Rob Carter calling, which couldn't have been a good thing. Not at any time of the day.

'Boss, it's me,' Carter said, sounding far too excited for a call at two in the morning. 'Sorry to call you late, but you're going to want to know about this right now.'

'What is it?' Natalie replied, hearing a grunt from her husband, as he turned over in bed and made sure she knew he'd been disturbed.

'Alison Lennon has just been nicked,' Carter said, almost stumbling over his words, 'Down by the bombed out church—'

'The what?'

'And Mia Johnstone has been taken to hospital, unconscious.'

Natalie sat up in bed, trying to blink the sleep away from her eyes. 'Start over. Slowly.'

She was already moving by the time he got his first sentence out. Pulled on clothes she couldn't see in the darkness of the bedroom. Not caring. Padded down the stairs and pulled on her shoes and thought about running a brush through her hair and deciding she didn't have enough time.

Ending the call, just as she found her car keys, she turned back to see her husband at the top of the stairs.

'I've got to go in,' she whispered up towards him. 'Sorry, but there's been a—'

He waved away her explanation. 'Don't worry, you go do what you've got to do. I can handle it.'

'Thank you,' Natalie said, then turned around and made her way out of the house, found some chewing gum in the centre console of the car and popped two in her mouth as she pulled out of her driveway.

Within fifteen minutes, she was parked up at the station and entering the building.

Carter looked like he hadn't left the place. In fact, he looked far too good to have been on shift only a few hours earlier. His suit looked immaculate – as if he had just picked it up from the dry cleaners and slipped it on.

She hated him in that moment.

The HQ was almost silent at that time of the morning – only a few people dotted around, doing what she assumed was important work, or unnecessary overtime.

She wasn't too concerned.

'They're holding her down at Shore Lane, so we should get down there, before some uniformed copper makes a mess of things.'

Natalie nodded in agreement and let Carter take the lead. Slipped into the passenger seat and tried to stay awake, as they drove out of the city and towards the town.

'What's the bombed out church?' Natalie asked, as they got closer to their destination. 'Never heard of it before.'

'Oh, it's just some old church that got hit during the war. Never repaired, so people just started calling it that. Made for some good ghost stories when we were kids, but nothing special. It's on the edge of town, so usually it's a place that younger teenagers will congregate to drink or whatever, but even that's stopped now. They're usually down on the front at the dips. Or the park, up near the centre.'

'Right, and do we know how Mia is doing?'

'No update at the moment,' Carter said, indicating right and turning into the small car park outside the local police station.

It possibly could have waited until morning, but Natalie wasn't exactly thinking straight. It was less than an hour since Carter's phone call had woken her up and there were already other members of the team who were being called back in.

For what? She wasn't sure.

'I'm thinking Alison Lennon has gone full vigilante,' Carter said, as they got out of the car, speaking to her over the top of it. 'Attacked this young girl and then got picked up for it.'

'I'm guessing that won't be her story.'

She was right, as she invariably turned out to be.

Alison was sitting in a holding cell, waiting for their arrival. Natalie wasn't sure they got many arrests at that time of night in the small station and didn't seem set up to take them in. From the simultaneously confused and wired faces of the two uniformed coppers who were standing next to the closed door, she felt her instinct was right.

'Run me through what happened?'

The bigger of the pair took the lead, saying they had been called out by an unknown caller, who said they were watching a fight next to the bombed out church, that there was a lot of screaming and shouting. They had been only a minute or so away, and made their way over quickly.

What had confronted them was a woman crying and shouting, running across the field. They managed to contain her.

'She said someone attacked her,' the copper said, his thumbs tucked into his vest. 'Started babbling about some girl who had killed her son, that she came to meet someone at midnight and was then attacked from behind. Barely got away. Very scared, shivering, the works. I went up to have a look around and found the girl.'

'Did you manage to speak to her?'

'Who, the girl or the dead lad's mum?'

Natalie ignored the categorisation of Alison Lennon. 'The teenager. Mia, wasn't it?'

He shook his head. 'She was unconscious when I got there. I stabilised her, secured the scene with the help of the other crew that came onto the scene. They called another paramedic in and I went down and made the arrest.'

'How did you know it was Mia?'

'Her provisional licence was in her pocket,' he said, confidently, as if he'd cracked a big case that had flummoxed everyone around, rather than simply finding something that had been dropped. 'These kids use it for ID these days. I remembered a bit of intelligence about the murders and put two and two together. Got them to call you guys in.'

'Thanks,' Natalie replied, turning to Carter and giving him a look.

He took it for what it meant and began to usher the two uniforms away from the door. Natalie bent over, looked through the plexiglass that was separating them from Alison inside.

She was sitting up on a plastic chair, that looked bolted to the floor. Rigid, unmoving, and staring straight ahead.

Natalie shook her head sadly and glanced to her side as Carter returned. 'We need an update on the condition of Mia. See if she's awake and talking.'

'That's what I asked your man back there to do. And to make sure her family is aware of what's happened to her and all of that.'

Natalie turned to Carter, nodded her head. 'Nice. Good to see you taking initiative.'

'Got to do something before those two cans of Monster wear off,' Carter said, a boyish grin across his face. It slid away slowly as he turned back to the closed door in front of them. 'What are we going to do about this?'

Natalie thought for a moment, trying to make her own mind up. 'I guess we're best going in and listening to her story. I think we know what it's going to be though.'

'Same old, young girl killed my son and you lot won't listen to me?'

'I guess so,' Natalie said, but it didn't mean that she didn't exactly disbelieve what Alison had been saying. The more this case went on, the more she felt that all wasn't as was usual. 'Is it ridiculous though? Some of the stuff that's out there right now, would it really be a stretch to think that a teenager could do something like this?'

Carter seemed to think about it for a few minutes, before shaking his head. 'This has been going on for over a year if that was the case and I just don't think anyone could keep themselves out of trouble that long. Or go so long between killing. Once you kill one person for crossing you, doesn't everyone suddenly become a target?'

'Maybe,' Natalie said, not really buying it. 'Anyway, let's go and talk to her. See if there's anything new she can tell us.'

Natalie took the lead, opening the door and walking into the room. She waited as Carter came in and stood beside her. Alison lifted her head slowly, blinking as the harsh light above them shone in her eyes.

'Alison,' Natalie said, her voice soft, purposeful. 'How are you doing?'

Alison looked between the two of them, then lowered her head again. Her shoulders began to move up and down, and a noise came from her.

Natalie was confused for a moment, before she realised what she was doing.

She was laughing.

45

I didn't mean to laugh.

It just sort of came out. Like I wasn't under control of myself anymore – and to be fair, that's exactly what was going on.

Nothing was going as I'd planned. Before Ben's murder and more so since.

I realised it had only been a couple of days since we'd been woken in the early hours of the morning and thrown into this nightmare. It felt like an eternity instead. I couldn't remember sleeping since, but knew I had. A few hours here and there.

Sitting and waiting in that police station, I had almost fallen asleep a few times. Then, I'd suddenly remembered where I was and snapped awake again.

I had heard who they had found in that field.

Mia.

Only, she had been attacked, they'd said. Assault. That's what I'd been arrested for. I definitely hadn't hurt whoever had attacked me. Maybe a couple of bruises, would that be enough? Probably. My first thought was that she'd hurt herself, but that didn't make much sense. Surely they would know the difference?

She'd been ahead of me the entire time.

Still, it hadn't been her who had attacked me. I couldn't make myself believe that. It was dark though. I had been scared.

I didn't know what to think anymore.

Maybe it was all a big mistake, bringing me there. Arresting me.

Even so, I could tell I was being treated with kid gloves. Given who I was. What I'd been through that week.

I wondered how long that would last.

'Alison, do you want to tell us what's happened tonight?'

The detective looked tired, I thought. Her eyes were a little more glassy than usual. Hair looked less in place. And it looked like she'd got dressed in the dark – one of the buttons on the white blouse she was wearing hadn't been done properly. A gap appearing at her navel. She hadn't seemed to notice.

'I was hoping someone could tell me,' I said, glancing across the room at the younger guy, who was standing over by the door still. Detective Williams was standing opposite me and took the opportunity to lower herself onto the bench that ran across that side of the wall.

'It seems you didn't really take our little talk to heart,' Williams replied, her voice betraying her a little. I could hear the weariness in it. 'Why were you out there, that late at night?'

She seemed to be skirting around the main issue, but I decided to let her for now. 'Because I was told to go there.'

Williams arched an eyebrow. 'Really? By who?'

I shook my head. 'I don't know. I got a message from an unknown number, saying that I would find out what happened to Ben if I went there. Alone. I tried to call it back, but it had been switched off. I went, because what else was I supposed to do?'

'Maybe call us and let us in on what's happening?'

Both Williams and I looked across at Detective Carter, who seemed a little perturbed himself that he'd voiced the thought that he hadn't meant to.

We both ignored the interruption.

'Tell me exactly what happened this evening and leading up to reaching that church.'

I breathed in and told the truth. Told the detectives exactly what I'd been doing – sitting in my car outside Mia's house when the message had come through. Waited until the last minute, to see if she walked out first, but then couldn't wait any longer.

Told them what the message had said.

And then, when I'd reached the bombed out church, walking up to it alone and standing waiting.

I sensed that she was impressed, but was trying to hide it. I wasn't sure why she would be – I knew she'd do the same.

I knew so many people would do the same exact things I'd done.

'So, you're standing there, waiting for what, you don't know,' Williams said, leaning forwards on the bench, her hands dangling in the space between her long legs. 'And then, you say someone grabbed you from behind?'

I nodded slowly. 'I just felt an arm come around my neck. You can probably see the marks.'

Detective Williams glanced, as I craned my neck for her to see. I wasn't sure if there was anything there, but it certainly felt like it. She didn't give any indication that she'd seen anything.

'You didn't hear anyone approach?'

'No, not a sound,' I said, trying to sound like I was telling the truth. Which I was, of course, but there was something in the way she asked the question that made me more keen to have her believe me. 'It was out of the blue. I was just standing there, looking out across the field, when I was just suddenly unable to breathe.'

'How long were you standing there?'

I wasn't expecting the question, so hesitated a moment or two. 'I don't know . . . about half an hour, maybe?'

'Are you asking me or telling me?'

I narrowed my eyes. 'Telling you. About thirty minutes.'

'So, you started fighting back?'

I was struggling to keep up with her line of questioning. Probably something she was doing on purpose, but it was no less effective for knowing that. 'Yes, when I realised what was happening. I managed to go to the ground and then when there was an opportunity, I managed to break free.'

'Then what happened?'

I told them about finally getting free, running for my life, before reaching the end of the field. Being confused when I saw the red and blue lights, and then not realising it was a police officer who tried to grab me.

'I must have looked like a crazy person,' I said, sighing and shaking my head. 'I should apologise to that poor guy.'

'Were you making any noise as this was going on?'

I thought for a second. 'I think I was. Shouting, screaming, making noise without even realising.'

Detective Williams shared a glance with the other detective and then leaned back on the bench against the wall behind her. 'So, you reached the field, were there for a short while, grabbed from behind and you managed to extricate yourself from that position quickly, you'd say?'

'It felt like a long time.'

'But, in reality, what would you say it was?'

'I don't know,' I said, trying to work out what exactly she was trying to discover. 'Maybe a minute, or two.'

'And then, you're at the edge of the field within what, ten, twenty seconds?'

'About that, yes.'

Detective Williams nodded to herself. 'See, that presents us with a problem. Because the call about an incident occurring in that location came in about the time you made it to the church. That's how the two officers managed to actually be on the scene when you reached the edge of the field.'

I opened my mouth to respond, but Detective Williams was already continuing.

'So, you understand why that presents us with a problem, because if what you tell us is true, who made the call before you even arrived at the location?'

'I don't know,' I said, trying to work out an answer to an impossible question. Because how *could* I know? 'Maybe whoever attacked me?'

'And then, that's before we even get to the fact that when officers searched for the person you say attacked you, they find Mia Johnstone unconscious instead. You think she attacked you?'

'Yes,' I said, too quickly. 'It has to be. She killed my son. And the two others, and knew I was getting close to proving it. So, she made me go out there in order to silence me.'

Only, that didn't make any sense, now I thought about it. The arm that had been around my neck didn't feel like it had belonged to that skinny eighteen-year-old girl.

It felt stronger than that.

'So, how does she then end up unconscious, having been attacked herself?'

'Maybe she did it to herself,' I mumbled in response, which earned a look from Detective Williams that screamed *'come off it'*.

'I don't think that's exactly what happened,' Detective Williams said, her voice lower now. More ice to it. 'I think the order of events is – you meet Mia at the church, you get into a long, protracted argument, which is noticed by someone in the vicinity. You do something that you regret – you hurt the girl – and then you run off. Right into the waiting arms of our officer out there. Does that sound closer to the truth?'

I couldn't shake my head hard enough. 'No, that's not what happened—'

'Alison, no one would blame you if you lost it,' Detective Williams said, reaching across and placing a hand on my knee. 'If you did something you regret. The stress you're under, it's unimaginable.'

'Believe me, it's imaginable from over here,' I replied, moving my leg, so Detective Williams's hand slipped away from it. 'But that's not what happened.'

'Alison, it's the only way any of this makes any kind of sense.'

'That might be, but it's not the truth. Someone made me go out there tonight and when I arrived, I was attacked.'

'And you say you received a message on your phone?'

My eyes brightened suddenly. 'Yes, you can check it. Find out where the number is from and who sent it to me. You'll see then that it came from either Mia or someone connected to her. Right?'

Detective Williams glanced at the other detective. I followed her gaze and saw the younger guy shake his head slowly.

'I had it,' I said, realising what the head shake meant. 'But I must have dropped it during the whole thing. It'll be on the field somewhere, I bet. Just call it.'

'We'll do that,' Detective Williams said, no conviction in her voice. 'For now, you sit tight and we'll let your husband know where you are, okay?'

I nodded in response, feeling the fight leave my body. I could almost feel the walls around me growing closer and closer.

I was trapped.

And I was absolutely certain that Mia had something to do with that. The only issue I had now was that it wasn't just her.

She had someone helping her.

46

Mia had woken in the ambulance, but was told later that she'd been conscious for longer than that. She just didn't remember.

She slept most of the night. Lying uncomfortably in a hospital bed, while her mum and dad kept vigil by her side.

She felt taken care of, looked after. Like a child for the first time in ages.

Not that she would ever tell her parents that. They had been talking about her becoming an adult for a lot longer than she'd ever considered the idea.

Now, she was lying in bed, trying to work out what had happened to her.

A doctor had been by, but had spoken to her mum and dad more than they had her.

Age is just a number.

'Babe, the police want to speak to you,' her mum said, rubbing her hand over the horrible sheet that was covering the bottom half of her body. When she'd woken up, she realised just how itchy and disgusting it was and wanted rid of it. She'd not complained out loud, but internally, she felt like she needed a shower just being in the place.

'Do I have to?' Mia replied, wincing as she sat up a little. There was a pain in her shoulder that hadn't been touched by whatever painkillers they'd given her. Probably paracetamol. They wouldn't have given her anything stronger, given she hadn't complained.

'I think it's important, so that . . . that *whoever* did this gets what's coming to them,' her dad said, on his feet, pacing on the other side of the bed. He stopped for a moment, shaped as if to say something, then stared at her mum instead. Indicated with his head that she should be the one and continued to pace.

'I know this week has been hard on you,' her mum said, using a voice Mia hadn't heard in a number of years.

'Hard isn't the word . . .'

'Listen, it's all going to be okay,' her mum continued. 'You need to tell them everything that happened, so that they can find whoever did this to you. And . . . well, why you were out there and things like that.'

Her mum mumbled the last part, knowing that it was something they hadn't spoken about yet. Why on earth she'd been out there after midnight, without anyone knowing. Mia was more sure about the answer to that than she probably had a reason to be.

'Okay,' Mia said, finally, accepting that she wasn't going to be able to get away from speaking to the cops. 'I'll do it now. Get it over with.'

Her mum patted her hand, giving her a smile that didn't reach her eyes. Stood up and left the room, leaving her alone with her dad.

Mia waited a few seconds, before looking over at her dad. He was looking out the window, having stopped pacing the floor. Slowly, he turned around and looked back at her.

'You okay?' her dad said, which in his language meant more than a simple two words. He had never been the best at displaying his emotions, but all it meant was that a simple hand on the shoulder, or a two-word question represented so much more than it seemed on the surface.

Mia felt tears spring to her eyes, but she made no effort to wipe them away. 'I'll be fine, Dad.'

He seemed to consider her for a few moments, then nodded to himself. 'Whoever did this to you . . .'

Whatever he was going to say next was cut off by the door opening and her mum coming inside, closely followed by the two detectives from the previous evening.

This hadn't been what Mia had expected. From the look on her parents' faces, they hadn't either. She'd thought it would be some uniformed officers, like the ones who had found her at the bombed out church. Instead, this was more serious.

'Mia, how are you?' Detective Williams said, not a hint of something hiding behind the concern she was voicing.

'I'm okay,' Mia replied, glancing at her for a second, before looking away.

'Have you found whoever did this to my daughter?' her dad said, before the detective had a chance to speak again. 'They told us they'd arrested someone at the church, but no one has told us anything.'

'Mia, we've just got a few questions for you, okay?' Detective Williams said, seeming to have not heard Mia's dad at all. She hadn't even looked in his direction since they'd entered the room. 'We're just going to run through the events of the night, as best you remember them, and then we'll let you get some more rest, okay?'

Mia wanted her to stop saying the word 'okay'. It was beginning to grate on her. 'That's fine,' she said, turning her body a little so she could face them. 'I don't really remember much, though . . .'

'Don't worry about that,' Detective Williams replied, sounding very different than she had the night before. Or was simply a good actress. Probably a bit of both. 'Let's start at the beginning, okay?'

That word again. Mia felt her toes clench. She breathed in and started talking. 'After you left, I spoke to my friend Anna for an hour or so. Then, later in the evening, I got a message on my phone. It's gone though. So, I can't show you it.'

Mia saw the young guy behind Natalie taking notes behind her. He arched an eyebrow when she said her phone was gone, but she ignored it and continued.

'It said that I should go to the bombed out church at one a.m. That I should come alone. I ignored it, because obviously I wasn't going to just do something like that. But then, they sent me a picture. It was of Ben's mum parked outside our house.'

Mia heard her mum mumble something under her breath and her dad started pacing again.

'Another message came through then that said that they had proof that I wasn't involved with Ben's murder. Or Becky's or Mr Fulton's and that they were a friend. That they were going to a lot of trouble to help me and that I should meet them. But it had to be out of sight and late at night.'

'Mia, why didn't you tell us?' her mum said suddenly, the pleading in her voice almost a dagger in Mia's heart. 'We could have helped you. We could have gone with you, kept you safe.'

'Because I was scared, Mum,' Mia said, turning to her mum now. 'I didn't know who to trust anymore, because everyone seems to think I did this and I wasn't sure if you were one of them.'

'I would never—'

'I wouldn't blame you,' Mia said, letting the tears fall now. They were welcome to the party. 'It looks so bad. But I swear, I didn't do anything.'

'Mia, if we could get back to the messages,' Detective Williams cut in, not a hint of emotion in her voice. No indication she believed Mia at all. 'You didn't recognise the number?'

Mia shook her head. 'They were text messages, which I never get. And I've not seen the number before at all.'

'You decided to go.'

It wasn't a question, but Mia nodded anyway. 'It was a longer conversation. I said no, of course, because I didn't trust them. I thought it might be someone from school or something like that. But they knew things.'

That made Detective Williams perk up a little. 'Things like what?'

Mia hesitated, then continued. 'They knew what happened between me and Mr Fulton. And me and Becky. And me and Ben. Things only we'd known about, that I hadn't told anyone else. They knew I hadn't hurt anyone and that I needed to trust them as they were the only one who could prove it for me.'

Detective Williams shared a look with the young guy behind her. 'You decided to go.'

'Yes, but only because they weren't going to help me if I didn't. I didn't want anyone thinking I wasn't prepared to do whatever it takes to clear my name. I didn't want Ben's mum thinking that I had anything to do with this anymore. It was a chance for me to prove I'm innocent.'

'So, you go to the church alone?'

Mia nodded. 'I didn't think I had a choice.'

'Then what happened?'

Mia took a breath, found the back of her head with her hand and slowly stroked the bandage that was stuck there. 'I waited a few minutes, listening and looking out for someone who was coming. I took out my phone, to put the torch on, so they could find me. That's when I saw her in the distance.'

Mia saw Detective Williams tense up for a moment.

'Ben's mum,' Mia said, even though she knew the detective knew who she was going to say. 'I switched my torch off quickly and tried to work out what she was doing there.'

'Did you say anything to her?'

Mia shook her head. 'It gets a bit hazy then,' she said, looking away from the detectives. 'I can't really remember much.

I just remember panicking and thinking about leaving. Then, I heard a shout or something. It's all a bit blurry. Then, I was falling and it all went black.'

'You didn't see who attacked you?'

'No, but there wasn't anyone else out there,' Mia said, sure of herself. 'I would have heard them. It was pitch black and dead silent. If anyone had come across that field, I would have heard them. And I was there long enough for someone to be hiding to come out. I saw Ben's mum, then in no time at all, I was hit from behind. I think. As I said, it all gets really blurry from then. I don't remember even coming here.'

'That bitch . . .'

Everyone snapped towards Mia's dad, who had stopped pacing and was now facing the rest of them. His hands were fists, clenched at his sides. 'Well, what are you going to do about this? This woman has been harassing my daughter for days now and look what's happened. She's now attacked her. She could have killed her. I hope you've arrested her.'

Detective Williams sighed almost soundlessly. 'We'll be carrying out a full investigation,' she said, looking back at Mia. 'You said you don't have your phone?'

Mia shook her head. 'I must have dropped it or something. It'll be on the field, near where I was found. Or someone took it.'

Detective Williams stared at her for a few seconds, as if weighing up what she'd said. Then, seemed to accept it and turned to her mum. 'Can we speak outside?'

Her mum nodded and as Detective Williams turned to leave she looked back over her shoulder. 'Take care of yourself, Mia. Feel better.'

Mia didn't respond, instead laid her head back and stared up at the ceiling.

Things were worse now. She could tell that instantly.

The detective hadn't believed her.

47

At least it wasn't a proper cell. It didn't make it any more comfortable, but I'd seen documentaries on TV, that made it look like hell. This could have been any small office in a normal building.

I guess they didn't really know what to do with me.

There was no clock in the room. Or window. So, I wasn't sure how long I was sitting in there. I had pretty regular visits – the officers who had brought me in had been replaced. A new one had been in to check on me for the past few hours. Or minutes. I couldn't be sure.

Offered me food, drink. Magazines. As if I was waiting for an appointment and not to see what the hell had been going on out there.

I started counting. Mainly because reading *OK!* magazine had taken me about thirty seconds, before I threw it on the floor. The tea I'd been given had tasted like dishwater. The frozen ready meal I'd been given was still sitting in its tray next to the magazine. Plastic fork sticking out of it. I'd taken one whiff of it and my stomach had lurched.

I counted to a hundred once. Then three more times. The officer came in, made sure I was okay, and then went back on his way.

What the hell *had* happened the night before?

I started piecing it together, from what little I knew. Someone had obviously called the police before I'd even got out of my car when I'd arrived – probably watching me, making sure I got there. Made me wait a few minutes, then attacked me.

It hadn't been Mia, so who could it have been?

I had my thoughts, of course. Her dad, for one. That made the most sense. He would have been powerful enough to match the arm that had gone round her neck. That hadn't been Mia. Or her mum, for that matter. When I thought about grabbing hold of it now, I remembered it being thick.

So, the dad. Had to be.

But why would Mia have been attacked in that instance? I couldn't see her own parents doing something like that. Too many things could have gone wrong. I'd heard them talking about her being unconscious, which means she must have been hit hard enough to take her out, which could have been hard enough to kill her.

A parent couldn't have done that.

And what would have been the point – to frame me? Why try and kill me at all in that instance, because that's what had happened to me the night before. I'd escaped death.

He wasn't going to let go of me. That had been clear and obvious. He'd tried to choke me to death.

I thought back to the teacher, Mr Fulton, and Becky. Both had been attacked with a weapon, just like Ben. There had been no weapon the night before – I wouldn't have been sitting there if there had been, I realised. A crack to the back of my head and I would have been down and gone within seconds. That's how quick and simple it would have been.

The image of Ben flashed in my mind. I sucked in a breath, when I realised that's what he would have felt. One moment, walking home late at night, invincible. The next, a crack to the back of his head, without warning. And the ground hitting him, while someone holding a hammer cracked him with it over and over.

I couldn't think about that right now. I would fall into a hole of despair and never get out.

No.

I had to think.

So, a different method this time. That's all.

But it hadn't been Mia. And there was only one person who would want my son dead. And that was her.

Right?

I suddenly wasn't sure anymore.

Someone who wanted to protect Mia enough to want to frame me for her assault, wouldn't have done that to her, surely?

I realised I wasn't dealing with logical people then. These were people who thought killing people was justified.

The officer came back in again. I glanced up, ready to say I'm okay and didn't need anything, but he was already talking.

'Detectives Williams and Carter have asked me to bring you down to the main station. We'll be leaving now.'

He was standing holding the door open for me, so I got up. Followed him out, glad he hadn't handcuffed me.

I was in the police car within a minute or so, sitting in the back while he drove. The crackle of his radio was intermittent and the only sound inside the car.

I looked out the window, as the town I'd grown to know passed by me. I wondered if I'd ever get to come back. Whether I'd be charged within the next hour, and maybe not get bailed. And even if I was, would I be allowed home? I didn't know how any of it worked.

Greg would know. Or think he did, anyway. He'd quickly google it and tell me a rough approximation of what would happen.

I'd probably not be allowed to speak to him, though. Not properly.

I was in trouble.

I knew that much at least, even if I couldn't work out what really happened the night before, I knew I was up shit creek with no boat, never mind a paddle.

'I'm sorry about your lad,' the officer in front said, breaking the silence. 'Should never happen, that.'

'Thank you,' I replied, my voice barely above a whisper. I don't think he heard me, but he carried on anyway. 'What's your name?'

'David Penny,' he said, glancing over his shoulder at me. 'Call me Dave.'

'I'm Alison,' I said, but knew it wasn't needed. He knew who I was. It just felt like the only thing I could say.

'No one should have to bury their child. I'm just sorry that they couldn't stop it.'

I frowned, confused as to what he was saying. 'Who's "they"?'

'You know. The detectives who have been working on this thing. That's three in the past year and I've been telling everyone that they're all linked. We've not had a single murder in this town for twenty-odd years and then three all at the same time – doesn't make any sense to me. Has to be linked.'

I swallowed, wanting to make sure I was hearing him right. 'Do you know the girl who they found last night, where I was attacked?'

The copper nodded, indicating as he reached the roundabout that led onto the A road that took them towards the city. 'Yeah, I know her dad well. We were in school together. Nice guy. Not sure about the wife – we haven't really kept in touch all that much. Just here and there, you know? That's how it is these days. I don't have that social media stuff either, so makes it more difficult. My missus, she's got everyone on Facebook. Don't even speak to each other anymore – but they know everything that's going on in their lives alright.'

'What was he like?' I asked, treading carefully. I wanted him to keep talking and not clam up. I didn't think I'd have to worry about that, though – he seemed like the type of man who enjoyed the sound of his own voice.

That accounted for a large proportion of them, to be fair.

'Good lad,' he said, glancing over his shoulder as another car approached from the right, before pulling away. 'Could be relied on, if you know what I mean. If there was a problem with his mates or whatever, he was always there. Ready for anything. Not that he was violent or anything like that, but you could tell he could handle himself. Everyone gets in fights when they're in school, but he was a bit different. Always wanted to try and work it out with talking first. I like that. I respect that. More now, than I did then, obviously. The amount of men who act first without thinking . . . that's half my job.'

'How come you didn't keep in touch then?'

'Well, we weren't close mates or anything like that. Just had a few of the same classes in high school. Seen him around town a few times, when I'm out and about, but I don't even live in town anymore. Just work here. Met a girl over the water, didn't I. Had a choice of living here, or in a nice posh estate over there and it wasn't even a question.'

He chuckled to himself and I decided I liked this man. Despite him reminding me of Greg a little too much. He was around our age, maybe a few years older. He had what my mum would have called a 'friendly face'. I had a memory of Greg giving me the same feeling and wondering how it had disappeared and I hadn't noticed.

'What do you think happened to my son? To the others?'

He sucked in a breath and shook his head. 'Bit above my paygrade that . . .'

'Indulge me,' I said, leaning forwards, so my head was between the two headrests in front. I could smell his aftershave

– I thought it might be Armani Code, one I'd bought for Greg a few years earlier, but he never used. I loved the scent. Maybe he knew that and that's why he never wore it.

'From what I know and I've heard, I think logically it has to be something connected to that family. Nothing else makes much sense. All three have a connection to the daughter, I know. Thing is, I know Steve, or I did anyway. I've been doing this job long enough that I feel like I'd know a bad guy from a good one and I wouldn't think he was bad at all.'

'What about Mia's mum, Jen?'

'Quiet as a mouse. Don't even remember her from schooldays. She was a year or two below, I think, so that's probably why. Still, it's not like we're in a big town, or city, I know most people.'

I sat back, trying to work out how any of this helped me. I didn't think it did.

'Thing is,' Dave said, slowing as we approached the exit on the A road and the city came up in the distance. 'What I do know is that there's not a lot someone wouldn't do for their kids. I'm sure you're the same, which is why you're sitting in the back of this car right now. They might be out the home, off to university, or old enough to deal with things themselves. I'll tell you, that's what it's like. I still get told to be careful by my dad and I'm twenty years older than he was when I was born. It never leaves you, that need to keep them safe. Make them happy. Maybe that can lead to all kinds of bad things, that kind of thinking.'

I realised quickly what he was suggesting, but it didn't quite ring true. It couldn't be. Mia was the one behind all of this – killing Ben was personal. As was Becky and the teacher. And messy. Someone of my age would have taken more care. They would have been less likely to leave a trail.

Her parents would have been more careful, I thought.

No, it had to be her.

Yet, I could already feel how wrong I had been. How I didn't really know anything, when it came down to it, because I wasn't there.

I hadn't been there for Ben.

I let Dave continue driving, going silent. Lost in my own grief.

48

I knew I was being treated differently because of who I was. What I represented.

I imagined they were petrified of what the media would do to them. What social media would do to them.

Arresting the mother of a murdered child, while they were still looking for his killer . . . it didn't look good.

Unless, they started thinking a little differently about things. I could feel that anxiety crashing over me again, as my mind whirred into action.

I was tired. My bones ached with exhaustion. I could almost feel it over me like a wet blanket.

And now, I had a bigger worry.

I knew the questions would be coming. That they would be different now.

The two detectives were waiting for me, when I arrived. I was ushered into a room, quickly and without stopping – as if I was being shielded from prying eyes.

I knew it was so as few people as possible would know I was there.

'I think it'll be too late for that,' I said, as we sat down in a room that was hidden away down a corridor. Away from the main office space – containing only a small sofa and a couple of chairs. The walls had been painted a soft blue – a small coffee table separating the sofa and chairs. A box of tissues, left open and half empty.

'Too late for what?' Detective Williams asked, motioning towards the sofa for me to sit down and taking a seat opposite me.

'I imagine everyone will know I'm here within a few minutes.'

Detective Williams cocked an eyebrow, then pursed her lips. 'I imagine you're right about that.'

'Then, you know how this'll look, right?'

'Of course,' Detective Williams said, holding her hands up. 'But, it's not like we can ignore this kind of thing, you agree?'

'Do I need a solicitor?'

'We just want to talk things over,' Detective Carter said, interjecting for the first time. Detective Williams seemed okay with the interruption, which I noticed as being unusual. 'You have been arrested for assault, but we're obviously treating this a bit different than we usually would. Because of the . . . the circumstances.'

'The circumstances being that my son was killed a couple of days ago and you don't seem to have any clue who did it, despite me telling you over and over.'

Detective Williams leaned back in her chair, fixing me with a stare. 'Do you have a problem with anger, Alison?'

The question seemed to come out of nowhere and I didn't have an answer ready. I paused, thinking it over. 'No.'

'Okay,' Williams said, considering the answer. 'Only, we've both witnessed you becoming increasingly exasperated in the past few days, and understandably so. I was just wondering if that was something you had an issue with lately?'

I shook my head. 'Not at all. I'm just trying to find out what happened to my son. That's all.'

'And your relationship with your husband – is how you interact with him usually so combative, as we've witnessed ourselves?'

'I don't understand what any of this has to do with what's happened . . .'

'Oh, I can answer that for you,' Detective Williams said, suddenly leaning forwards, still not tearing her eyes off me. 'Think about how all this looks right now. We have your son murdered earlier this week and now his girlfriend attacked in the middle of the night. And you are found running away from the scene. What would you think in this situation?'

I could feel my self-control waning. 'I hope you're not accusing me of doing something to my son?'

Detective Williams didn't respond. Didn't so much as blink. 'I'm going to ask the question again – do you have a problem with anger?'

'No.'

The detective blinked finally. 'We really want to help you and your family, Alison, but you're not making this easy. Please, help us out here, as we're unsure what you think you were doing out there last night. So, tell us. What happened?'

I ran them through the sequence of events again, this time labouring over some of the points. How the arm felt across my neck, the weight of it, how scared I was. That I was convinced I was going to die there.

The two detectives listened dispassionately, the younger guy making notes constantly. It seemed to be all he ever did.

'I never saw Mia,' I finished, sitting back on the sofa. 'But it doesn't surprise me that she was there. I was told to be somewhere, I went because I have to find out what happened to Ben, and while I was there I was almost killed.'

'So, you never saw anyone at all?'

I shook my head. 'Didn't even hear someone come up behind me.'

'How did you lose your phone? Did you know it had been taken from you?'

I looked up towards the ceiling trying to remember. 'I think it was in my hand when I was attacked. I probably dropped it at that point. Has anyone been out to look over the place and see if they can find it?'

'We haven't been able to find anything,' Detective Williams said, shooting a quick glance towards Carter who shook his head a couple of times. 'Were you wearing any kind of jewellery? A necklace, bracelet? I know your rings have already been taken from you, but that's all you were wearing.'

'No, just my rings,' I said, suddenly aware of how empty my finger was. I couldn't remember the last time I hadn't been wearing my engagement ring, my wedding ring . . . I quite liked the feeling.

There was another shared look between the detectives. I didn't like it. 'Look, what is it? What aren't you telling me, because I think I have the right to know. I'm the one who was attacked and now I'm being questioned like I've done something wrong.'

'You don't think you did anything wrong?'

'No, of course not,' I said, wondering if I was losing my mind. I couldn't believe I was being asked these questions at all. 'Maybe, if I felt you were doing everything you were supposed to be, then I wouldn't feel the need to be going out there. Tell me, did you even talk to her last night? At her house? After you left me? Because I know you were there for under thirty minutes and it doesn't seem to have stopped any of this. It doesn't seem to have had any effect at all.'

'We did speak to her,' Detective Williams replied, speaking quickly then running a hand through her hair. 'These things aren't like they are on TV, Alison. She wasn't about to start confessing if she was involved. It takes time, like I told you. And the worst thing we can have right now is anything muddying the waters. And your actions last night are the epitome of that.'

'Well, I'm sorry for making your job more difficult, but maybe spend a few minutes in my shoes and you'll realise it's not all that hard after all.'

'Alison—'

I was too tired to listen to her anymore. 'Please, just decide what you're going to do without my input. I've told you everything that happened and unless you're going to charge me with something, or actually come up with a reason I'm here, just let me be. I'm done talking now. I just want to leave and go back home.'

Detective Williams glanced across at the younger guy, who had finally stopped scribbling in his notepad. Turned back to me and stared me down for a few seconds. Slapped her knees and got to her feet.

'Okay, that'll do for now.'

'Next time we have a conversation,' I said, as they made for the door. 'I want my solicitor here. And I'll make sure he lets certain people know what you're doing to me.'

I saw Detective Williams's shoulders sag a little, but she didn't turn around. Simply left the room and closed the door behind her, leaving me alone in there.

I wasn't sure what I was supposed to do, other than wait, but it turned out it wouldn't be that long anyway.

In the meantime, I continued to go over everything again. Tried to make it into some sort of sense.

There was only one way the story fit – and that was if Mia was involved, but had help. And despite what the kindly officer who had brought me to the city had said, I didn't think it could be anyone other than her father.

Which gave me more than one target.

The situation couldn't have been worse, in Natalie Williams's mind.

'Do you think she's bluffing?'

Natalie looked over at Carter and shrugged. 'Who knows what's going on in her mind right now? Maybe she attacked the girl, maybe she didn't. What we do know is that if this gets out, we're not going to look good.'

'So we're going to let her go?'

'Do you think there's anything else we can do here?'

Carter didn't respond, which Natalie took to mean he agreed. She leaned back in her chair and tried not to think about how tired she was feeling. 'We're going to call the husband and tell him the situation, and have him come and get her. We'll talk to her again, before he gets here.'

'Okay,' Carter said, already looking through his notes and finding the number. A dialling tone filled Natalie's office, once he'd keyed in the number and put it on speaker. Greg didn't take long to answer.

'We're not sure we can protect her from herself anymore,' Natalie said, once she'd spent a few minutes bringing him up to date. In all that time, Greg had listened in complete silence – so silent, she'd actually asked a few times if he was still on the other end of the phone. 'This isn't going to work out well for her if she continues down this road, Greg.'

'I understand,' Greg replied, his voice tight, low. 'She's just not thinking straight right now. That's all. She's too emotional.'

'Which is understandable—'

Greg continued, as if he hadn't heard Natalie. 'She gets this way now. Especially in the past few years. You can't talk to her, if she's like this. I try and try to keep her on a straight path, but she never listens to me. Even when she knows I'm right. All I can do is apologise for her actions, whatever they might be. I find myself doing that more and more these days.'

'Greg, Alison has been through a lot this week, just like you have—'

'It doesn't mean you shouldn't listen to me . . . listen to *reason* though, does it?'

Greg's voice filled the room so suddenly, that Natalie almost took a step back from the phone speaker.

'That's what happens all the time – no one ever listens to me, when I know what I'm talking about.' Greg was on a roll now and Natalie held a hand up towards Carter, as he opened his mouth to interrupt. She leaned closer to the phone, listening to every word.

'The kids, they got older and started thinking that they knew everything and look what happens? Alison . . . she used to pretend to listen to me, to understand that I was just trying to make everything okay, but I've seen it in her face now. She doesn't care what I have to say. She doesn't care that I'm just trying to do the best for my family. They're all the same. If she'd just listened to me in the first place, none of this would have happened.'

Natalie looked across at Carter, who was making a note of everything Greg was saying now. She raised her eyebrows, but he didn't look up, continuing to write as Greg continued to talk.

She could hear the frustration in his voice, the hurt, the grief. Yet, there was something else she could detect underneath the surface and it gave her pause.

It was anger.

I'd asked for a solicitor within seconds of the two detectives coming back into the room, which earned a look from Detective Williams. She'd shaken her head.

'That won't be necessary,' she'd said, reaching out and placing a hand on my shoulder. 'We're just going to have a quick chat.'

'A chat?'

'Did you attack Mia Johnstone?'

I shook my head. 'I've already told you, I had no idea she was there.'

'For some reason, I believe you,' Detective Williams said, as Carter bit down on his lower lip, probably to stop himself from talking. 'The problem I have, is that when you look at the facts as we know them, it doesn't look good for you.'

'Which is why I asked for a solicitor,' I replied, with a shrug of my shoulders. 'What did she tell you? Is she blaming me for what happened to her?'

'The victim doesn't know what happened, other than placing you there,' Detective Williams said, choosing her words carefully it seemed. Not willing to say Mia's name. 'But, we already know you were there. She can't identify you as her attacker, but suggests you were the only person she saw. What she doesn't say, is that there was any kind of physical altercation with you, which means we can't account for your injuries.'

I was surprised at that. I'd expected her to have concocted a whole story about what happened. That seemed like she'd made a mistake.

'I can see your injuries more now,' Detective Williams continued, indicating my neck. 'It looks much worse now than it did last night. Fresh, as well. Which I think corroborates your story, that there was possibly someone else out there last night.'

I didn't think that would be the reason they would let me go. I think I'd hit a nerve by suggesting I'd happily tell people outside what was happening. 'You don't think she was lying then?'

Again, Detective Williams hesitated before answering. 'I can't say yes or no to that. I'm not sure what the truth is about what happened last night. What I can say is that we don't have any evidence yet to say one way or another and I'm mindful of the fact that we currently have under arrest the mother of a murdered child.'

I knew that was the problem they had. It was the reason I hadn't been locked up properly, or been put in an interview room.

They were scared of how it looked.

It made me more sure than ever that they were never going to see this through.

They didn't know what they were doing. It was too much for them.

I wanted to start ranting and raving, as I realised that they weren't cut out for their job. That they weren't good enough to find my son's killer. That they had three deaths on their hands and no idea how to stop it from happening again.

Instead, I kept quiet, because I knew what was coming.

'We're going to release you on bail, but keep this very quiet,' Williams said, as if she was doing me a favour. 'Greg is on his way to pick you up and the Liaison Officer is going to be staying at your house. I'm not going to lie to you – she's there to keep an eye on you now. I don't want you leaving that house. You need to sit with your family and get through this with them and let us get on with working out a resolution to your son's death. We're the ones in charge here. You have made too many mistakes and made things more difficult for us and I understand why you've done those things, but it's over now. I don't want the press finding out about any of this. I don't want the armchair detectives on social media making all of this worse. It's already got out of hand, but it's over. We'll come to you with any information we need to and you'll just have to sit and wait. That's what the situation is right now, because of what's happened in the past few days.'

I sat there and took it all. Didn't argue, didn't answer back. Just absorbed her words and nodded along.

'Look,' Williams said, leaning closer. 'I understand. We all do. This isn't the first time we've been through something like this, but it is for you. Everyone reacts differently and I'm not suggesting you've reacted in the wrong way. The problem is, you're severely limiting our ability to do our job for you and your family right now. This is why we're here. We're not here to do anything, but find out what happened to Ben and give you justice. I know it probably feels right now like it's you against the world, but I promise you, it's not. We're here, in you and your family's corner. But most importantly – I'm here for Ben. He's my only concern now. I want to find out what happened to him and we're going to do that.'

I almost went with her on her little tour of platitudes. I almost believed that if I just went home and waited, eventually they'd knock on my door and tell me they'd arrested Mia and she was going to be charged with Ben's murder.

That I would walk into court one day and hear her found guilty.

And then what?

What would I do then?

No one could tell me the answer to that.

I almost went along with it all. I knew that wasn't going to be the ending here, though.

'Thank you,' I said, once I realised that she was waiting for me to say something. 'I'll go home and wait.'

Detective Williams considered me for a few seconds, then seemed to accept my lie. 'Okay, that's a good thing, Alison. And I promise you, we'll keep in constant contact with you. Your LO will be able to keep you updated on everything that is happening. I promise you that. There'll be no more times when you don't know exactly what we're doing. We haven't been good enough at doing that for you and I apologise.'

'Can you tell me how far you've got up to now?' I said, hoping the question was okay. That it would still lead to them getting me out of there. 'Just, I mean, I don't even know who you've spoken to, whether you have any possible suspects...'

Williams glanced at Carter and seemed to sit back. I realised I hadn't really ever heard him talk.

'We've followed up on a number of lines of enquiry,' Carter said, stepping forwards and reading from the pad he was holding. 'Your son was well liked, but also there was talk that there were maybe a few people who didn't like him and his friends all that much. He had some issues with other lads his age, from other schools, but nothing suggests that there was any kind of gang mentality going on, or even fighting.'

I knew all that. Of course. I'd read news stories about young lads being stabbed in the city, but it felt so far away from our lives, that I didn't suspect Ben might have got caught up in that.

'There was, of course, some discussion about his relationship with Mia Johnstone. And how that was going. We had varying stories about it, with some friends saying they seemed very much in love and that they were happy. Others saying the complete opposite. We've had trouble wading through the usual teenage stories.'

I almost chuckled at that, thinking he couldn't have been that far away from being a teenager himself, but I kept myself under control.

'There's no history of any complaints made by or against anyone close to Ben. Or Mia, his girlfriend—'

'That's not true,' I said, speaking before I had chance to control myself this time.

Carter looked up slowly. 'That wasn't the end of my sentence. Mia has had accusations in the past from the mother of another murder victim. These were fully investigated at the time by the team and no evidence whatsoever was found to connect Mia to that victim and the crime that was committed.'

I closed my mouth and clenched my jaw. Ground my teeth together, to stop any further outbursts.

'Various interviews have a wide range of possible avenues of investigation, that we're carrying out as we speak,' Carter said, finally looking up from his notebook. He may have looked barely over sixteen, but he was starting to impress me. 'However, at the moment, we haven't formulated a suspect—'

'That'll do,' Detective Williams cut in, before Carter could continue. I suspected he had gone too far, but I knew where he was going anyway.

'Okay,' I said, easing the tension before it had a chance to grow. 'Please keep me updated.'

'Good,' Detective Williams replied, slapping her knees and getting to her feet. 'You've already been processed, as has the victim from last night. If anything comes back from the lab, we'll be having a different conversation. For now, I know exactly where you'll be if anything changes. Right?'

I nodded silently, itching to get out of there. I knew I was lucky – if this had been any other time, there wasn't a chance this would be going the way it was.

They were scared. Scared that Greg or my sister would be talking to the media. Posting on Facebook and Twitter and wherever else that they had arrested the murdered kid's mum, for something unconnected.

They were scared that I couldn't be controlled.

I was happy to let them think they could wrestle it back.

Because, they couldn't hear what was going on in my head. They didn't know anything.

That was the problem.

They had no idea.

And I wasn't going to sit around and wait for them to work that out for themselves.

50

Greg arrived in no time at all and it was as if I was in a daze as he drove me back home.

He didn't speak for the first ten minutes. Just sighed quietly to himself, shooting me occasional glances that I felt on the side of my face.

Then, when he decided he'd had enough of waiting for me to talk, he finally opened his mouth.

'What the hell were you thinking?'

I turned slowly, saw him staring ahead, as the traffic on the A road back towards town began to grow a little. 'What?'

'What? That's all you have to say?'

'What do you want me to say?'

'I want you to talk to me,' Greg said, gripping the steering wheel a little tighter. I could see his knuckles turn white against the black leather. 'That's what I want you to say. I want you to tell me what the hell is going on and how it's come to this.'

'Do you care?'

'Of course I do.'

I thought for a second, then gave a shrug. Told him everything that had happened the previous night. Even when I reached the part where someone had their arm around my neck, trying to choke the life out of me, he didn't react.

When I was finished, there was silence in the car. We'd reached the outskirts of town and he seemed to have gone the long way round, so as to avoid the church. I wondered how much he'd been told by the detectives. I didn't care all that much.

'Well, do you see what happens when you try and take things into your own hands? You almost get yourself killed.'

'Get myself killed?'

'You know what I mean . . .'

'Yeah, I do,' I said, a snort of derision escaping from me. 'That's the problem. You think everything I do is wrong.'

'I don't—'

'Why are you lying?' I said, cutting across him before he had a chance to start in on his usual speech. I couldn't hear it right then. 'You're perfect, you're always right, that's what you think. That's always been our problem – every argument, you can't deal with the idea that you might be wrong.'

'Why would I argue a point if I thought I was wrong?'

'That's not what I'm . . . for God's sake, you never listen to me. And then, our son is killed, and you expect everything to just happen around you and when I'm not prepared to accept that, I'm wrong. I'm not doing grief right, I should just be sat at home, waiting for them to knock on the front door and let me know who killed my son.'

'So, instead, I should be out there accusing everyone and anyone of killing my son?'

'That's not what I'm saying,' I said, running tired hands through tired hair and over tired skin. I wanted to close my eyes and have Greg magically disappear. 'I couldn't do what you've done since we saw Ben in that hospital morgue. I'm not saying you're wrong, but what I don't need is you lecturing me on what I *should* be doing. Just let me do what I need to do.'

'But, now you've gone and got yourself arrested. And that affects me and Ellie. Don't you realise that?'

He had me there. That annoyed the hell out of me. I wasn't about to tell him that, though. 'I'm just trying to do what's right so we can sleep at night knowing the person who hurt our son can never do it again.'

'Why do you care, though?'

My head snapped towards his, but he was already babbling on. 'I don't mean about Ben and what happened – I mean about stopping it from happening again? We've already had it happen to us. We're already going through it. It's not like whoever it was could kill our son again. So, why do we care about someone else's son or daughter, or whatever? I don't. I just want to think about Ben, and Ellie. And you. And how the hell we get through this.'

I thought about what he was saying for all of two seconds and dismissed it. 'They don't know what they're doing back there, Greg. They're still talking to teenagers and marrying up stories, and ignoring the idea that one of them might have done all of this. They don't even act like anything is linked – what happened to that teacher, to Becky Harrison . . . it's like it's too big for them to handle or think about, so best just to ignore it. Meanwhile, a few minutes from our house, a potential serial killer is living without any fear. Who might be next? Maybe it'll be me – they tried last night. What about you? What about . . . ?'

I didn't finish, unwilling to say Ellie's name, but Greg knew who I meant. He didn't respond – as we turned the corner at the top of our street.

I needed some rest. My eyes were burning. The pain in my forehead was getting worse by the second. I thought about what I was going to do as soon as I got in the house – go upstairs, check on Ellie. Then, I'd lie down in my bed and let myself sleep for a few hours.

Just a few hours. That's all I would need.

Then, I would do something. Anything. I didn't think that the Liaison Officer would be in our house all day and night. She'd leave at some point.

There were more cars than usual parked on the street. I could see tired eyes reflected back at my own, as people in the driver's seat popped up as we drove past.

Journalists. Possibly.

I knew it was more likely to be those armchair detectives. Scavengers of real-life crime.

I saw a couple holding up phones, as Greg swore quietly under his breath.

'What's going on?' I asked, as I saw a group of two or three odd looking people standing outside next door but one.

'They think we killed Ben,' Greg said, unable to hide the hate in his voice. 'Well, not so much you, as me. I guess people always think it has something to do with the close family. Remember that woman who went missing and ended up being found dead in the river? There's still a bunch of people online dedicating their lives to trying to prove the husband did it. I've been expecting it really. Some of them think it was you, but nowhere near as many. That might change if what happened last night comes out.'

Now I knew why I'd been treated with kid gloves by the detectives – they knew this was coming. And I wasn't sure if they weren't thinking the same thing anyway.

I knew Natalie Williams didn't like Greg. That wasn't difficult to work out.

There was a chance they'd let me go so easily just to see what I did next. They didn't have any evidence right then, so maybe they thought letting me go, all worried and panicked, might lead them to something.

'Ellie told me all about it,' Greg said, pulling the car onto the driveway and switching the engine off. 'She's . . . she's really upset, Alison. I think you should try and talk to her. She doesn't really like talking to me about her feelings, you know that. I always got on better with Ben.'

'I will,' I replied, taking off my seatbelt, aware that Greg hadn't moved. I looked over at him and realised how sad he looked.

Just . . . broken.

Beaten.

What little fight he'd had in him had disappeared. I could see that suddenly. He looked his age and beyond it, for the first time. I'd never noticed how old he'd started to look. How his skin was starting to sag a little. The grey hairs poking through the dark brown. The bags under his eyes.

It wasn't those things, though.

It was his body. It didn't look as solid as it once had. Even compared to a week earlier. It was drooping, empty.

I couldn't look into his eyes. I knew what I'd find there.

I turned away and got out of the car, walking quickly to the front door and going inside. Louise was holding it open for us, thankfully, but I didn't say anything to her.

I went straight upstairs and found Ellie. She was lying on her bed – the US version of *The Office* playing on her small TV attached to the wall at the end of her bed. Her window looked out onto the street – the joy of having the box room at the front of the house. Her wall was attached to the main bedroom, which was probably why Greg and I hadn't had sex in months. Difficult to let yourself go when your teenage daughter was only a few feet away.

'You okay?' I said, leaning against the wall for support. I felt like I could drop at any moment. 'I know, a stupid thing to ask . . .'

Ellie grunted a response, which may have been yes or no. I don't think she was sure herself.

'Listen, I know it's been hard the past few days . . .'

'It's okay, mum,' Ellie said, still not looking over at me. 'I understand.'

'It's just . . . I don't want you to believe I'm not thinking about you and what you might be going through after what happened to Ben. I am. And I'm sorry I haven't been here enough for you.'

'Honestly Mum, it's fine. Don't worry about me.'

'Are you sure you're okay?' I said, taking in my youngest. She had seemed to grow up overnight. One day, she was this tiny thing, that fit in the crook of my arm. Now, she was a few inches taller than me and seemed so switched on to the world around her. I'd blink again and she would be an adult. Maybe with her own family. Her own home to look after.

I hoped.

Because, now, everything felt so fragile. The things that only happened to other people had somehow managed to happen to us. And that wasn't supposed to happen.

Ellie finally looked over at me and I could see tears in her eyes. 'I just wish he was still here.'

I crossed the room in a single movement, dropped to her side and drew her to my chest. She buried her head and I held her as she sobbed. Tried to keep control, but struggled. My body burned from the effort, as I held my daughter in my arms. Wished I could take away all the hurt she was feeling.

Her phone had dropped to the bed, as she held onto me and I focused on that, rather than lose control.

A notification flashed up on the screen – some kind of message. It came and went in a second or two, but I'd seen something.

I shook my head, worried that I was now seeing things. I knew I hadn't been.

I pulled away from Ellie a little, as she wiped at her face and looked her directly in the eyes. 'Ellie, this is really important. I need you to tell me something and I really need you to tell me the truth.'

Ellie's face scrunched up in confusion. 'Yeah?'

'Who have you been talking to on Snapchat? Is it her?'

Ellie's eyes snapped towards her phone and then down. 'No.'

'Who is it then?'

It came to me then. Where we were sitting. 'Ellie, you're talking to him, aren't you?'

Not Mia.

We were at the front of the house – where the box rooms were all situated in the houses in these streets. Just like Mia's house.

'It's not what you think . . .'

I wasn't listening to Ellie anymore. I was already pulling away and moving.

Not before I grabbed her phone.

51

I grabbed Greg's car keys from the hook on the wall by the front door. Didn't think to grab my jacket, as I was already opening the door and leaving.

I heard my name being shouted from inside the house, but I wasn't listening. I was only moving forwards, before my body and mind tried to stop me by collapsing.

If I just kept going, then that wouldn't happen.

Somewhere in the back of my mind, as I reversed off the driveway and saw Greg and the Liaison Officer Louise emerging from the house, I knew what I was doing was wrong.

I should have been telling the two detectives what I was thinking. What I was doing. I should be letting them work it all out. Sort everything and I could just wait at home for the conclusion.

That wasn't going to happen.

I peeled away quickly, reaching the end of the street in a second or three, ignoring the faces of those reaching for their mobile phones, in order to film themselves and me.

I'd seen it all before. I wasn't going to wait around and let them make me something I wasn't. Something Greg wasn't.

He might have been prepared to accept the idea that they should just wait for the police to do something. I wasn't in the slightest.

This was my job.

Within a few minutes, I was out of the town and down on the seafront. I pulled over and parked up away from the few motorhomes that were down there. They were fewer in number than ever, now they were charged for overnight parking.

I found Ellie's phone and held it in my hand. It was locked.

The phone flashed with an incoming call from DAD and I swiped it unanswered. I knew it would be coming. It wouldn't be the last one.

A few years earlier – back when we had first allowed the two kids to have their own phones, one of the rules had been that Greg and I knew the passcodes to get into it at any time. Not that we ever did. No fingerprint or face recognition access alone. There had to be an unlock pattern to open it.

It turned out that they were more excited about having our hand-me-down phones than any worry about privacy. I guessed Ben had changed his a number of years ago, but wouldn't know.

Everyone in the house used the same pattern – even Greg and I. Not that I ever felt the need to check.

Maybe everyone had changed it and not let me know.

I held my breath and tried it on Ellie's phone.

The screen came to life and I traced my finger over the screen. In less than a heartbeat, her home screen was there.

I may have violated any sense of privacy. I may have completely upset her by taking her phone away with me. I didn't care. I needed to confirm what I'd seen, see if there was anything else there to see, and I needed time and space to do those things.

Another call from Greg. I swore under my breath, and swiped it away again. I had to concentrate, didn't he realise that?

First, the message I'd seen flash up on the screen.

It was a Snapchat one. I pulled down the top of the screen and found it.

Harry J.

That's all I'd needed to see.

Mia's brother. Talking to Ellie. I opened it, feeling my breath starting to shorten, as I waited for it to come up. It felt like an eternity, but it was only a second or two.

I wasn't all that familiar with Snapchat, but it looked fairly basic. There was a small avatar in the top left-hand corner, the name of the person next to it.

Then, the messages.

It was him.

I couldn't scroll back all that far – it looked like messages were being deleted regularly. Not surprisingly.

I didn't want to think what Ellie's motivation might have been. I couldn't think about that right then.

All I needed to know was what they were talking about. How far this went.

Ellie had told him about me being arrested. He'd told her that Mia was getting out of the hospital at some point that day, so how bad could it have been. It looked like there was some missing parts to the conversation, it was impossible to work out everything.

I got the jist.

That wasn't the reason I had run from the house so quickly though. Not the *only* reason, anyway.

It was because I realised something.

The oldest kids in any household ninety-nine times out of a hundred, would get the bigger room than the siblings. And in all of these three-bedroomed houses we seemed to live in around our part of town, they all had the same layout.

The main bedroom at the front. Next to it, the small box room.

I didn't think Mia's family would be any different.

That meant, a few nights earlier, when I'd been standing outside their home and saw that face appear in the window, it hadn't been Mia cast in shadow.

It had been her brother.

I'd assumed it was her room, but I had been wrong.

I lifted the phone, wondering what the relationship between Ellie and Harry Johnstone was. I didn't want to scroll back too far, so I checked something else instead.

Their streak.

I remembered Ben telling me about it – a kind of competition of sorts, is how I understood it. How many days consecutively you could talk to someone.

I checked Ellie and Harry's and almost dropped the phone in shock.

They'd been talking for over a year. Without me knowing.

I didn't have time for maybes, but I knew I would look back at this moment for the rest of my life. This moment, when I learned I had failed at the one thing you cannot fail at and get away with it.

It didn't matter right then. I had to keep going.

I managed to navigate back to the chat and opened up the keyboard to send a message.

There was a moment when I thought about stopping. About not doing what I was about to do.

Then, I thought of Ben. And Ellie, and what all this meant for her. What she was doing and the trouble she might be in. I had to stop it.

If I couldn't save Ben, I could save her.

I typed out a message.

Need to see you. Meet at the dips?

I waited, staring at the screen, hoping that he didn't immediately suspect it was someone other than Ellie.

I tore my gaze away from the phone screen and looked out towards the sea. The sky above looked dark and angry. As if it was making a comment on what I was doing.

And what *was* I doing.

What was my plan? I had got so far without one, that I hadn't considered that. When I got Mia's brother to meet me, what would I do then?

It was getting later in the day – the sky not only dark from approaching bad weather. That time before day and evening, when everything becomes a little blurrier. A little more tinged. When someone put the light on and you wondered how on earth you'd been able to read something or function at all in the seconds before.

It didn't take long for the message to come through.

It popped up on screen and I read it greedily.

Not dips. Too busy. Down by the river like last time. In a hr ok? Bout 8

The river. I wasn't sure what part that would mean. I knew there was access through the woods, but that would mean traipsing through and trying to work out where exactly he meant by 'last time'. I had no idea Ellie had ever been into those woods alone, never mind by the river.

Could he mean somewhere else, I thought. The river wound its way through the outskirts of town and through others. That wouldn't be right, though. It's not like either of them drove and why would they get on public transport, just to go near a river that was only a ten- or fifteen-minute walk from their home?

It had to be in the woods.

Where Becky was killed.

I took a moment, then replied.

Yeh np.

That seemed like something Ellie would type in response. I wasn't sure. Harry had replied so quickly, that I was convinced he had no idea it wasn't her.

I had to move. If I stayed in one place too long, I started to feel the lack of sleep and food catching up with me. And I needed to get to the woods before Harry did.

I wasn't sure if the police would be looking for me. Probably, I guessed. They wouldn't be too happy to know I'd listened to them for all of five minutes.

A pang of guilt came and went. Ellie had been crying into my shoulder only half an hour earlier, and I'd just pushed her away. Run out of the house.

I thought about what she must be thinking right then and whether I would ever be her favourite parent again.

Maybe in time.

When she realised what I was saving her from.

I couldn't think about those things right then. I had to go. I had to move.

I hoped I came up with some kind of plan on the way.

52

I parked Greg's car up on a street a minute or so away from the west side entrance into the woods. Got out, pocketed Ellie's phone, and made my way towards it.

I wished I'd picked up my jacket. The early September breeze was cooler than I'd been expecting. I ignored the chill that ran through my body and kept moving.

By the time I made it into the woods, I was sweating. Something I knew would happen. Hitting my mid-forties and all that came with it, was sometimes a blessing.

Sometimes.

Other times, it was a pain in the arse.

Most times, would be more true. All times, absolutely on the money.

Still, being hot at that moment was at least something. And it took my mind off what in the hell I was thinking of doing right then.

I knew where I was.

I hadn't been into those woods for a long time. We'd had a dog, years earlier. A mad border collie, that never seemed to switch off. Barney. We'd got him around the time Ben had been born – not a decision that I'd been a massive part of, I remembered well. Greg had decided he wanted a dog, to go along with his new son, and as with everything in those first ten years together, he got his own way.

That had changed over the years and about the time we'd started arguing more, until I had started shutting down.

Sadly, it didn't make it past its twelfth year and we'd decided not to replace it. Still, I remembered we'd brought it for walks out this way on occasions. Mainly, it had been down the front. That's why I'd loved living near the sea – the smell of it, the infinity to look out over.

I didn't go to the sea all that often anymore.

Work and home. That's all I knew now.

The occasional visit to the GP, retail park on a Saturday.

I couldn't control my thought process, as I walked through the woods. I wasn't alone – I passed a fair few dog walkers and joggers on the way. Even despite it getting darker by the minute, there were still some people prepared to be out there at that time of night.

My mum would have asked them if they didn't have homes to go to.

I missed her so much.

She would have been right there with me, I liked to think. Ready to go to war for her child. Her grandchild.

The ground was soft – not muddy, not yet, but well on its way. In a few weeks, it would be treacherous going.

The wind whistled through tall trees above me, as I tried to get my bearings. I listened, but didn't hear the river nearby. I knew it was close though. I'd been walking long enough to know that.

My heart was beating so hard that I thought I might pass out. That it would crash out of my chest and lie on the floor in front of me. Still, I kept going.

I should have called the police. Told them where I was going. I thought about messaging Greg and at least telling him. I had Ellie's phone in my hand before I decided against it.

I had to do this. I had to be the one who found our son's killer.

Harry.

I didn't know the boy – I'd heard about him, from Ben. I only knew his name because one of the detectives had mentioned it a day or two earlier. Ben had only mentioned him in passing as Mia's little brother.

If she had just turned eighteen, that meant he could be any age. I imagined it was around sixteen.

I wondered what his motivation could be. What his reasoning could be. Obviously it was to seemingly protect his sister in some way.

I thought about where I was. What had happened to Becky in these woods, a little over a year earlier. The violence that had been carried out.

I was forty-four years old. I might not have been that tall, but I was an adult at least. I could deal with a fifteen, sixteen, seventeen-year-old boy, right?

There was no way I should have been there.

I realised that now. The right thing to do was to turn around and get away. Make sure there was no way he could get away with it. Only, I needed to hear him tell me he killed my son.

I needed to hear him tell me *why*.

I turned right at a fork in the pathway, instinctively knowing that was the right way to go. I wished I knew where Becky had been killed, so I knew if it was the same place. I didn't remember the river being mentioned, but then, I hadn't paid much attention to it all back then.

Not my circus.

Another of my mum's sayings.

The treeline seemed to grow closer around me and it became more difficult to see more than a few yards in front of me. It was almost paralysing, but I had come so far.

These were the final steps. I had gone through enough. I deserved this.

The trees broke suddenly, the path extending out and the space opening up in front of me. I could see down to the river's edge, as my eyes became more accustomed to the lack of light from above.

I pushed through, as I left the treeline hanging over me, as the path I was on became more malformed. It didn't quite lead down to the river itself, and the ground underneath my feet became softer and my walk became more of a trudge.

I imagined lights bouncing from these trees in the hours to come – once they found Greg's car, and came looking for me. Shouting my name out, desperately trying to track me down.

They would think I'd gone crazy. Probably already did.

The closer I got, the more I could hear the water at the river. The only sound in the silence of the woods.

The riverbank stretched a few feet, before the river opened up in front of me. The water flowed slower here, but would eventually quicken over to my right, until it became a fast-moving stream that if you got caught in, would swallow you whole.

It flowed through the town, through the neighbouring ones, then back towards the Irish sea. An infinite loop, that didn't make much sense to me. I remembered years earlier, my mum and dad bringing us down to the river in happier times – when they weren't arguing constantly or not speaking at all.

The memory was a happy one. Well, it had been, until that moment, when I realised I'd managed to replicate my parent's relationship almost immaculately. Not that Greg was my dad, or I was my mum – I guess it just happens.

That day, down the river a good few miles, we had sat in the sunshine, eating sandwiches and cakes mum had baked. Val had smiled at me and we'd both known in that moment that we should savour it. Because there wouldn't be many more of those moments left.

We'd been right.

What would mum think of me now?

Would she be proud?

It didn't matter.

I turned around, looking back into the fading treeline. I couldn't see much anymore, the light even out in the open rapidly disappearing as the evening took hold.

There were no sounds of twigs snapping underfoot. No leaves rustling on the ground, bushes being pushed aside.

It was dead silent.

I could hear my own breathing. My own heartbeat.

'You came.'

I almost fell over in shock, as the voice came out of the darkness. At first, it was as if the voice of God was talking to me, coming from above me.

Only, this voice was human.

I swallowed back bile, as my body began to shake. I was shivering again – the menopausal sweating becoming a distant memory. Now I was there, I wasn't sure what I was going to do next.

Because that wasn't the voice of a teenage boy.

I'd got it wrong. Again.

'Stay right there,' the voice said, a little closer to me now. 'Don't make a single move.'

It wasn't like I was thinking about moving anyway. I was stuck in place – fear coursing through my body and freezing me in place. Flight or fight – it was neither. I couldn't move even if I'd wanted to.

I heard movement coming towards me and the sound of bootsteps on the ground. Then, I heard the voice clearer than

I had and that made my heart stop for a beat or three. And my mind to splinter and crack.

It was Ellie.

It was her voice.

Only a single word. That's all I needed to recognise it. It came across the space between the river and the trees and broke me in two.

'Mum.'

A word that looks so insignificant written down, but means everything and more.

And as the sound of someone approaching became louder and louder, as I was still frozen in place, I realised that I *had* failed. That everything I had tried to be, tried to do, had been for nothing.

I hadn't lost one child.

'Don't move.'

As Ellie came into view, walking side by side with Mia's brother – a boy I didn't know and didn't even consider before that day.

When I'd been focused on Mia and Ben and Becky and that damn teacher . . . I hadn't been thinking about Ellie. I hadn't been thinking about her at all.

No, I hadn't lost one child.

I'd lost two.

53

Natalie Williams was trying to calm Greg Lennon down and failing spectacularly. Carter was even more useless. It was as if something had snapped inside him and he couldn't control himself anymore.

'What are you doing? What are you *actually* doing about all this?'

Williams stayed calm. It was important that she did so, because everything else was getting out of control. 'We have units out looking for the both of them now.'

'She's crazy,' Greg said, pacing up and down his kitchen. Which was no mean feat, given it wasn't exactly that big and the island took up most of the space. 'She could be doing anything.'

'I'm sure they're both going to be fine.'

'Yeah, that makes me feel better.'

Williams shot Carter a glance and then left the kitchen and moved into the living room. Louise was still in there, sitting on the sofa, rigid as if sitting to attention.

There was a part of Williams that felt sorry for her, but only a small part. 'You should have stopped her.'

'I know,' Louise said, as if she'd already accepted her screw up and everyone else should just get over it. 'What was I supposed to do though? She was out like a whippet. I wasn't about to start chasing her down the street. Especially with all those people out there.'

Williams glanced at the living room window, as if they were all standing out there now. And when she thought 'all', she realised it was about six people. With phones. And followers on social media that barely reached double figures.

Pointless ever worrying about them, she'd thought to herself on more than one occasion. That didn't seem to be the case for everyone else though.

'And she didn't say anything before leaving?'

Louise shook her head. 'We didn't even realise she'd gone before we heard the door slam behind her.'

'Have you been upstairs? Looked over her things, see if there's anything that would suggest why she might go?'

Louise hesitated and then shook her head again. 'I was on the phone to you guys, sorry. Maybe I should have done that.'

'Yeah, maybe you should have,' Williams said, turning around and leaving the room again. She had never felt more out of place than then. It might have been better for her family that they had moved to the other side of the country, to what was ostensibly a quieter life, but it hadn't helped things in the slightest.

Because when something major had come along, no one seemed prepared for it in the slightest. Not even prepared – more about being able to actually do their jobs.

As she reached the hallway, she almost ran into Carter. He muttered an apology that barely came out of his mouth.

'What?' Williams said, as he blocked the way. 'I was just about to go upstairs and check over her bedroom, see if there's anything useful that might suggest where she might be going . . .'

'He's just said something weird,' Carter replied, his voice quiet, indicating with a nod of his head over his shoulder towards the kitchen. 'I don't know, I thought you should know.'

'What is it?' Williams said, growing impatient at the fact this young bloke never seemed to just spit things out.

'Well, maybe not weird, just . . . I don't know, I can't work him out.'

Williams waited, a hand on one hip, the other on the wall beside them.

'He said she's been talking to someone,' Carter said, finally. 'He wasn't sure who it was, but he knew it was a guy. Said he caught her out one day. If she hasn't got her phone, then maybe that's where she's gone?'

'Why is it weird?'

Carter hesitated, then stood up to his full height. 'I just think surely it's something that should have been mentioned earlier? Don't you think? Like, why is it only coming up now, when she's left the house the way she has?'

He had her there. It was weird. 'Okay, go up and search the bedroom. See if there's anything there. I'll speak to him and see what else they've not told us. And tell that Louise to wait outside and make sure none of those TikTok idiots get anywhere near the house, until uniforms show up.'

Carter gave her a nod, and Williams stepped aside as he moved into the living room. She moved back into the kitchen, to find Greg sitting at the kitchen island with his head in his hands. She felt simultaneously sorry for him and also wondered if her own husband would cut a more pathetic figure if they ever went through something like this.

It made her feel guilty.

'She has been speaking to someone?'

Greg hummed a response.

'Do you have any idea who it might be?'

Greg shook his head. Obviously he'd talked himself out now, but Williams pressed on anyway.

'Is there anything else you think might be important to tell us? Because now would be the time. Anything at all, that might not even feel remotely important, but I need to hear it. Because I'm getting a little impatient right now and if all of this is silly family drama, that is stopping me from finding out who killed your son, then you best be damn sure I'll let you know over and over.'

Greg lifted his head, unable to meet her eye. 'I can't think of anything. I just want all this to be over.'

'Well, it will be soon, I hope.'

'See, that's what you all keep saying. That you hope, that you can't promise, all that kind of stuff. I just want my family back together.'

The feeling that Williams had of him being pathetic gave her a pang of guilt now, as she realised what Greg really was.

A man without a clue.

'Look, we're going to do the best we can to find out where she is,' Williams said, trying to take a nicer tone with him. 'And to give you some sense of closure—'

'There'll never be any closure.'

She couldn't argue with him there. 'Okay, maybe not that, but at least you'll know what happened and where you're going. Right now though, we just have to find her and bring her home. We can deal with everything else after that.'

Williams wasn't sure if he accepted what she was saying, but at least he was quiet now.

That was something at least. Even as everything else unravelled out of control.

54

I couldn't make sense of what was happening in front of me. There was Harry – Mia's brother – standing a few yards away from me. He was holding something in his hand, but I wasn't sure what it was. I could guess that it was nothing good.

And there was Ellie. Right beside him.

I couldn't see the expression on her face, but my first thought that she was in danger felt wrong.

'Why couldn't you just leave it, like everything else, Mum?'

She sounded like the fifteen-year-old kid she was. Like they weren't standing in the middle of the woods, next to the river, in the ever-darkening evening.

Alone.

With the boy who had killed Ben.

'What's going on, Ellie?' I said, knowing instinctively the answer. Knowing I needed to hear it from her. 'Why are you with him?'

'Mum, you could have just done nothing, that was what was supposed to happen.'

I wanted to close the distance between us, but Harry's presence stopped me. He didn't seem interested in getting involved, but I needed him to.

I needed Ellie to understand what was going to happen here.

'He hated me,' Ellie said, sounding closer suddenly. As if I could reach out and touch her. I couldn't. She hadn't moved. 'You didn't get it – I tried to tell you and you didn't listen. And he was going to tell you . . .'

'Tell me what?'

'About me and Harry,' Ellie said, her voice a whine that didn't quit. 'He found out and was going to tell you and Dad and I knew what Dad was going to do. He was going to tell me I couldn't see him anymore and that he was no good and all that rubbish.'

'Ellie, what are you saying?'

'I'm saying that he brought it on himself.'

I wanted to be shocked. Rocked. Astonished. Instead, it made sense to me. In a way that Mia killing Ben never had really. I may have believed it with everything inside my body, but there was just something about it that never felt quite right.

It didn't explain so many things, but Ben's death . . . it felt more personal than that teacher and Becky Harrison.

It felt like there had to be a reason for it.

'So . . . so you what?' I said, needing to hear it from her own mouth. Her own words. 'What did you do, Ellie?'

'I didn't do it, Mum, I swear,' Ellie replied, her hands coming up in front of her. 'But it had to happen. And if you and Dad had done what you were supposed to do, then none of this would be happening now.'

'It was you,' I said, looking at the silent boy standing next to Ellie. Only, he didn't look like a boy in the fading light – he looked all of his seventeen years. Almost a foot taller than me and stocky with it. He was a man, for all intents and purposes.

I was no match.

'Mum, you have to understand, we didn't want this.'

I was ignoring Ellie now. I couldn't even begin to understand anything she was saying right then. I faced this boy-man instead.

'You killed Ben. And Becky. And that teacher.'

'Mum . . .'

'Be quiet, Ellie,' I said, stunning myself with how forceful I sounded. How like her mum I still was. 'I'm talking to him.'

'It's okay,' Harry said, placing a protective hand on Ellie's shoulder. The sight of it made me shudder. 'I can explain it.'

'Don't touch my daughter,' I said, taking a step towards him. I saw his head shoot towards me and it stopped me in my tracks.

'Mrs Lennon, I know you're angry, but maybe if you just listen, then you'll understand why we've had to do what we've done.'

I couldn't believe he was being polite in this situation. It made the whole thing absurd. I almost laughed out loud, but managed to control myself. 'You killed them before Ben. Before Ellie. Unless this has been going on for longer than I think?'

'No, the teacher was before I met Ellie,' Harry said, his voice gruff, deeper, as if he were still getting used to it. 'But Becky was because of Ellie. Well, not because of her, but *for* her. It's difficult to explain, but that's how she knew I'd do anything for her.'

'Aw,' Ellie replied, reaching out and rubbing his arm lovingly. 'That's so sweet, but she was so bad, someone was eventually going to do that.'

'What are you even talking about?' I said, interrupting the love fest. 'Ellie and Ben didn't know Becky.'

'Oh, Mum, everyone knew her. She was the school bitch. She was horrible to everyone. And then, one day, it was my turn. Only, Harry came to the rescue.'

'See, Mrs Lennon, she was probably going to have to go, after what happened with Mr Fulton, because she knew too much. But I didn't have the same motivation as I did with that paedo. This was different – it was someone our age and she hadn't really done anything wrong to me. Then, she went after Ellie.'

'She was a bully,' Ellie said, a pleading tone coming to her voice. 'And she was after Mia – had been for a long time. And I saw that and just lost it one day. Told her that it wasn't on and embarrassed her in front of her friends.'

'And you were two years below . . .' I said, rubbing my forehead in frustration, that I didn't know any of this had happened. 'So, she lost face.'

'Exactly,' Harry said, as if I was understanding. 'And she couldn't handle that. First, it was just the usual bullying stuff – she'd call Ellie names and try to intimidate her, but that didn't work. Ellie is too strong for that.'

'Then, she came for me, and I didn't know what to do. She cornered me after school one day – near these woods as it happens – and if it hadn't been for Harry, she might have really hurt me. She was just screwed in the head, Mum. Honestly.'

I turned back to Harry now. Listening, but not really taking any of this in. 'So, you killed her?'

'If I hadn't, things would have got worse.'

He was saying it like he'd had to put down a dog who had attacked a baby. Rather than a human being, who was just being a teenager.

'Why didn't you just come to me and your dad and tell us what's going on?'

Ellie laughed. 'Like you would have listened? I've told you both so many things that's happened to me over the years and you've done nothing about any of it. Those girls in primary school, who wouldn't be my friend anymore, and were horrible to me. You went to the school and they did nothing, just like you. And you just forgot about it. Then, in year seven, when those new girls were bullying me every day, and I'd come home crying, and you'd just tell me it would all be okay and that one day I'd look back and it would be a memory. And that lad, in year nine, who kept barging into me, and really hurt me. Then he was being horrible to me, do you remember what Dad did about it? Nothing, that's what. So, I stopped talking to you both about it. I just tried to get on with things, and then when Becky started doing it to Mia, I just snapped.'

I couldn't believe that was her memory of those events – I remembered well all the meetings we'd had with the school over the years. The time Greg spoke to another girl's dad and sorted that situation out. The times I'd spent with Ellie, as she cried, and I listened and made her feel better.

I really had failed.

'So, when Harry comes along, and saves me, things changed,' Ellie continued, kicking at the soft ground with her trainer. 'But I knew you and Dad wouldn't accept him – he was older than me. Almost the same age as Ben. You would have gone mad. So, we kept it quiet. Then, Ben finds out, and he was always horrible to me. And Mia.'

'He wasn't horrible to her—'

'Yes, he was,' Harry said, quickly, interrupting me before I had a chance to say any more. 'He cheated on her, treated her like crap, and was nasty with it. I wouldn't have done anything though, but then he turned on Ellie. I was doing the right thing.'

'Yeah, he was, Mum,' Ellie said, backing him up. 'He was everything you told me a boy shouldn't be. Anyway, Harry didn't mean to kill him. It was an accident. It was supposed to be just something to cut him down a peg or two, that's all. Make him feel less invincible and that I had someone on my side. A message, if that makes sense?'

'None of this makes sense,' I said, shaking my head. 'I'm sorry you were going through this Ellie, but it ends now. It's gone too far. We're going to go home and speak to the police and sort all of this out. Harry can go home to his parents and explain what he's done and they can work out how they're going to approach this, but he killed your brother. My son. And he'll have to pay for that.'

I took a step forwards, ready to take hold of Ellie's hand and lead her out of the woods. Another step and then I saw what Harry was holding.

A hammer.

The hammer.

I wasn't sure if it was the same one that he used on Ben, but I had a good idea. I stopped moving and realised why I was there.

I looked towards Ellie, who couldn't meet my gaze.

'Ellie, you need to stop this.'

She buried her head into Harry's shoulder. I could barely hear her speak, but just enough to know I wasn't going to walk away without a fight.

'Do it quick,' Ellie said, pulling away from Harry and stepping away. She turned her back on us and had her face in her hands. 'Just, do it quick. Like Ben.'

And Harry started walking towards me.

55

Harry was walking towards me, and I realised I was cornered. I had the river behind me and no other way to escape. I took a step backwards and felt my foot slip on the ground beneath me.

'I'm sorry Mrs Lennon,' Harry said, getting closer to me. 'I wish I didn't have to do this.'

I still couldn't get past the fact he kept calling me that. 'Harry, listen, it doesn't have to be this way. We can get you help – both of you. It doesn't have to end here like this. She'll never forgive herself if you do this.'

'We've spoken about it a lot,' Harry said, taking another step towards me. 'We know why this has to happen. We can't have a future together if we don't. I know you're not going to let us. We love each other.'

I thought back quickly to being a teenager, hoping there was something I could say that would make sense to him. To both of them.

'Harry, think about it,' I said, hearing the panic in my voice. 'They're going to know it was you. People know where I am. They could be here already. They're going to see you going out of here and put it all together. If I can do it, so can they.'

He laughed at that. 'They have no idea. They probably think it's Mia, or my dad or something. Once this happens, with Mia being in the hospital with them, they'll know it was someone else. And they'll never think it was Ellie. I'll protect her, don't worry. My parents will tell them that I was with them and they won't think Ellie would kill her own mother. Everything is going to be okay, I promise.'

I took another step backwards and almost lost my balance. My eyes wouldn't leave his and he was still coming towards me, the hammer hanging loosely in his hand.

'Listen' I said, holding my hands out in surrender. 'I won't tell anyone about this. It sounds like the teacher and Becky had it coming and I can forgive you for Ben. I swear. Just, don't do this. You know she won't be able to live with herself.'

'You'll never forgive me for Ben. Or Ellie.'

'I will,' I said, quickly, almost tripping over my words. 'I swear I will. I just can't let you do this. Ellie, please, you won't be able to live with yourself if you do this. Dad will be broken. And you'll know forever that you killed your own mother.'

I saw a hint of hesitation in Harry's features, as he got closer to me, and I could see him a little more clearly.

I didn't wait for another opportunity.

There were two options – diving into the river, the unknown, and trying to get away. Only, I knew how quickly that could make things worse. That I could be dragged away and under, before I even had chance to make it to safety.

The other option . . .

Fight.

I started moving, quicker than I thought I was capable of doing. In the blink of an eye, I was on him, and wished I'd thought about the plan a little longer.

I grabbed his arm, the one holding the hammer, and tried to make him drop it. With the other hand, I was clawing at his face. I saw Ben in my mind and felt more anger than I thought possible course through me.

This boy had killed my son.

I was screaming, but it was as if the sound was coming from far away. I was only concentrating on him. I felt his fist crash into the side of my head, but I wouldn't let go, even as he tried to swing his hand.

I didn't feel anything connect. I was still holding on to his arm holding the hammer and making sure he couldn't use it.

'Stop it, let go of him!'

I heard Ellie shout, but I took no notice of it.

Harry was as strong as I'd expected him to be, but he didn't have the same fight as I did right then. I felt us starting to slip on the ground, gravity trying to take us down. I kept pushing him back, as he swung his free hand towards me. I felt blows on my shoulder, my arm, my jaw.

It was the jaw that did it.

It was as if someone turned out the lights for a second. One moment, I was fighting him, the next, I was falling into the black.

He fell too. Landing on me. I wasn't aware of that in the moment – I hit the ground and was still for a second. My head spinning, a feeling of wanting to throw up suddenly coming over me, as the world blurred into nothing around me.

It was only the sound of Ellie's voice that stopped me slipping away entirely.

'Is it over?'

I couldn't let her walk out of those woods with this boy. I couldn't fail again.

I felt Harry scrabbling to the side of us, as he leaned his weight on me. He smelled like a teenage boy – sweat and hopelessness assailed me. I could hear him grunting with effort, blood dripping from his cheek. I had done that, I thought. I had broken his skin.

He was looking for the hammer, which he had lost contact with in the fall. My thoughts were becoming cleaner, clearer. I knew I didn't have more than a few seconds.

He reached across my head and I raised my knee, driving it directly into his groin.

I felt him exhale, then slump over me. His weight fell on me and he started groaning in pain.

'Stop please, I don't want this anymore.'

I didn't take any notice of Ellie. I wasn't listening.

I didn't think twice about doing what I had to.

I made a choice.

I dragged myself from underneath him, towards the edge of the river bed, where the water was shallow, and stepped forwards. I didn't feel the cold of it at first. Not until I had moved even further in and the water came up around my calf.

The water stayed around my knee for a few steps, then, in the next step it seemed, I dropped what felt like the length of a building.

I went under the water, the cold hitting me like a train. It shocked the breath out of me and I swallowed water as I tried to fight my way back to the surface. I thrashed my arms around, until they hit the air and then my head followed. I spat water out and gasped in lungfuls of air.

'Mum!'

It was Ellie's voice, but it may as well have been a stranger's. I wasn't listening. I was trying to gain purchase on the river bed below. I wasn't tall enough. I wasn't finding anything underneath my feet and the more I moved, the more I went back under the water.

It was moving fast now.

Harry and Ellie were at the riverbank, behind me now, but they may as well have been in a different country for all it was worth. Now I was in the water, there was no escape. I struggled against the current, as it rose and crashed against me.

I gulped more air into my lungs and tried to keep moving forwards. I was spun around and I saw torch light bouncing off the water and the screams and shouts of my daughter. Both for me and for *him*.

I was in trouble.

The thought hit me and made me panic. I thrashed my arms against the water and went under again. Came up and was facing the other way again. The darkness, only slightly illuminated by the lights being flashed my way. I heard a splash behind me, but I was moving again. Doggy paddling my way against the strong current of the river, as I drifted further away.

'No!'

The scream cut through the night, but it made barely a dint in my mind. I was too busy trying to control my body from giving into the panic and adrenaline coursing through it. I had to get to the other side now.

It was a losing battle.

My body was still in shock from the cold, moving slowly against what was becoming a more forceful current the further I moved. And that wasn't far. I was furiously waving my arms through the water, but seemed to be stuck in place. I could feel myself wanting to give up. To simply let the river take me.

Then, I caught sight of the other side of the river ahead of me and it gave me a renewed purpose. I doubled my effort, desperately wading through the water, which felt like moving my arms through quick-drying cement. I swallowed more of the water, my head going under and under, but I kept going. Kept moving. Unwilling to allow myself to be beaten.

Something slapped me across the face, but I couldn't see what it was in the dark. It scraped against the skin and I could feel the sharp biting pain that sprung from it.

I ignored it.

I continued to move my arms, kick my legs, as the growing tide tried to steal me away from my goal.

I could feel the energy drain from me, being sucked into the water and disappearing.

I went under again, but kicked my legs back to the surface and when I looked again, I was only a few yards away from the other bank of the river. My feet hit something and I scrambled for purchase. Underneath the water, I found the river bed, as the ground finally came back to me and I was able to stand on something solid.

There was a moment when the water tried to claim me back for itself, but I stood firm and heard myself cry out and my throat felt hoarse. It was almost a croak of effort, but it was all I needed. I grabbed hold of something in front of me – branches, a bush, something – and pulled myself onto dry land.

I had somehow made it across.

I crawled out of the water and lay on the ground for a few seconds, trying desperately to get my breath back. I turned and got onto my knees and faced the other side of the river. I couldn't see all the way across – only a pinpoint of light, that seemed to sweep across me, but couldn't reach far enough to put me in a spotlight.

I shivered as the cold air hit my wet body. My clothes hugged me too tight, making it difficult to move. I crawled on my knees, before I lifted myself up onto my feet. I was drenched through and moved my arms to hug them around my body. The cold was making it hard to breathe.

I looked back across the river and there was a crash of water.

I realised it was Harry's voice I'd heard shout out. I saw him desperately swimming against the water, before he disappeared from view.

I looked out, hoping to see Ellie's face staring back at me.

There was no one over there anymore.

I knew it hadn't been Ellie who had been screaming after me, as I'd swam across the river.

It had been Harry. And now, he was in the water.

Going after Ellie, who had come to try and get me.

I stood on the edge of the riverbank and my first instinct was to jump in. To find my daughter, drag her back, and to safety.

My second instinct was to do nothing.

I stood there for a moment.

Then, another.

I stood there for a long time.

After

The sun dipped below the horizon, casting long shadows across the tranquil park. It was a place where laughter and joy usually echoed through the air, but tonight, it was different. Silent. As if it had known I was coming.

I sat on a weathered bench, my eyes fixed on the distant horizon, lost in memories. Of past days, that seemed to have not existed anymore.

How could I trust my memory?

There was solace to be found in some of them – the idea that there had been good times – but they were all tainted now.

As the wind whispered through the trees, a figure approached, her steps hesitant and slow.

I felt the presence before I saw her. I turned my head and locked eyes with the woman, who seemed to be carrying the weight of the world on her shoulders. I could feel my eyes mirroring her own – burnt black with pain and despair.

We understood each other more than we cared to.

I knew people would talk about her meeting me there. It didn't matter – here, there, everywhere . . . wherever it was, no one would understand.

We understood each other.

Without breaking the silence, Lisa moved closer and took a seat beside me, both of us gazing at the same distant point in the horizon. The world around us faded into insignificance as our shared grief united us.

Finally, Lisa spoke softly, her voice trembling with emotion. 'I lost her two years ago today,' she said, her words carrying the weight of an eternity of pain. 'But you knew that, right?'

I turned my head, my eyes meeting Lisa's. 'Of course.'

'It feels like both a lifetime and like no time at all.'

I knew that feeling well. It was how I always felt now.

A moment of silence passed between us, broken only by the occasional rustling of leaves in the breeze. Then Lisa continued, her voice barely audible, 'Do you ever feel like the world has moved on, but you're stuck in this, like, never-ending darkness?'

I nodded, the prickle of tears coming to the corners of my eyes. 'Every single day. It's as if time has stopped, but life just keeps going on for everyone else.'

'I can't laugh anymore,' Lisa said, shifting back on the bench. 'It feels like I'm betraying her.'

'I don't think anything will ever feel right again.'

We were like two shipwrecked souls clinging to a piece of driftwood in a vast, turbulent sea.

'What's the latest?'

I took a breath, realising it had taken less time to get to it than I'd thought it would.

That's why she'd come.

Not to share her grief with another grieving mother. Not to lean on me, and I in turn lean on her, for support and comfort.

It was because I could tell her things she wouldn't know.

'He's blaming her, she's blaming him,' I said, choosing my words carefully. I didn't want to upset her any more than I already had. Just by dint of being a parent. 'We've got her a good defence solicitor, according to Greg. His parents have paid for it. He won't talk to me about it really. He left the day Ellie got out of hospital.'

I still remembered standing at that riverbank, making that choice.

No one other than Lisa knew that part.

I had confessed it, when I had gone to see her and told her everything. She knew two arrests had been made and that was it. That was before Harry was charged with three counts of murder and attempted murder on me.

His name had been on social media within minutes. His link to Mia being the reason, I guessed.

I needed to be the one that told her that Ellie was the unnamed teenager who had been arrested alongside him.

Word would have got out quickly enough, I knew that. I just wanted her to hear it from me.

That had been four months earlier. I had expected the opposite reaction when I told her what had happened – especially when we got to the part about Becky.

About the kind of girl she had been.

I had chosen my words carefully and caveated everything with 'so they say' and all that jazz. I needn't have bothered.

I think Lisa already knew what kind of girl her daughter had been. Had probably been called into school and been spoken to about her behaviour.

It didn't mean she deserved to die.

'Once the trial starts,' Lisa said, pushing a few dark strands of hair away from her face and gripping the edge of the bench. 'We can't see each other anymore.'

I nodded, knowing that would be the case.

Knowing that would be the end.

'I haven't told anyone we've been meeting,' Lisa continued, turning towards me. 'They wouldn't understand. They don't know what it's like. I remember those first few days, when we both still thought it was Mia. I remember that you were feeling the same as me. Still are. And you've lost two kids now. Not that it's a competition.'

I couldn't speak. There were no words. I had no one else now. Val could barely look at me, without tearing up. She didn't know what to say, what to do. Greg had left me alone in the house that held nothing but sadness and memories of a better life.

I had nothing, other than my poor, broken daughter, who was starting to understand what she'd done.

I hoped.

'When they ask me for my statement, when it comes to sentencing,' Lisa said, standing up, and facing me. 'I'm not going to hold back. On both of them. I hope you know that and understand.'

'I do.'

'Okay,' Lisa said, turning back towards the park. In the distance, I could see the playground, where I'd pushed first Ben, then Ellie, on the swings. I could almost hear their laughter, their squeals of delight.

I knew Lisa was thinking the same thing.

'I will forgive you,' Lisa said, still looking away towards the playground. 'Just not yet. I understand at least – there's no rulebook when it comes to being a parent. It's not really your fault that your daughter grew up to be what she was. It's not even their fault with that boy. There's no one to blame really. That's what makes it so much harder.'

She left me sitting there then, as I thought about the words she'd said. The fact that we're all just trying our best to do what we can.

And that sometimes, it's just not good enough.

It gave me some clarity. I wanted to turn my back on Ellie, back on that night at the riverbank. I wanted to let her go.

I hadn't made that choice in the end. And I wasn't making it now. I was going to be by her side, to the bitter end. I knew what that would make my life – it had already started. I couldn't stay in that town anymore. Too many people knew what had happened. I'd have to move away. Greg and I would become strangers. I'd be alone, forever. I couldn't face the idea of dragging someone else into this mess that was my life now.

It didn't make any difference.

I'd lost one child.

I couldn't lose another.

Want to know how you love a monster?

Give birth to one.

Mia

She wasn't sure what happened to it.

She'd looked for it as soon as she'd been released from the hospital and gone back home. It had been ransacked it seemed – as if someone had broken in and everything had been tossed and turned.

It had been the police, searching their home after Harry had been arrested.

They should have found it then. And then maybe things would have been different.

Only, someone had taken it before then.

Mia wasn't sure how she'd known, or why she hadn't mentioned it, but it hadn't been her parents who had moved it – they hadn't moved from her side.

They were moving. She wasn't going to university that year now. Maybe never. Everything had changed.

She was going to be in a new place, away from all the people who knew what had been brought up under their roof.

A killer.

Mia had shut down all her social media accounts as soon as she'd been able to. They found her phone in Harry's room, but it was now evidence. She didn't think she'd ever see it again.

They would have read everything on there. The thought of it made her heart beat a little quicker, but she knew it was all going to be okay.

There was nothing on there that would link her to the murders.

There was nothing at all that would now.

Because Anna had saved her.

She wasn't sure why she'd done it. They hadn't talked about it yet. But she must have known what it meant. Mia wasn't even sure when she'd found it – probably on one of those days in the aftermath of Ben's death. Spotting it on the floor and picking it up. Seeing what was on the shoulder and knowing what it was.

And she'd still tried to help Mia.

She wasn't sure why.

That meant there was one person out there that knew there was more to the story. One more person who knew that her brother and Ben's sister weren't the only ones involved.

Mia wondered if her brother would ever tell.

It wouldn't help him.

No one would believe him now.

She still remembered coming home that day, after the argument with Mr Fulton. No one else at home, other than her and Harry. She'd not been able to hold it all back anymore. He'd asked if she was okay, for the first time ever it seemed, and she'd collapsed on the stairs.

She'd told her brother everything.

There was only a year between them. They'd been close forever, but at that time, it had felt like they had been drifting apart. It was normal, of course, but they'd always been as thick as thieves. There was part of her that thought Harry didn't like her anymore. That she represented everything he hated. Trying to be popular, trying to be with the in-crowd and failing spectacularly. She had friends, when he had none, though. Maybe that's all he'd seen.

That day, she realised how much he loved his sister.

What he'd been prepared to do for her.

Mia knew that they thought Becky died because of Ellie, but she knew better. She knew that coming home and it just being them, she could push him again.

He didn't need much.

That's what she'd learned. He just needed pointing in the right direction and things happened.

When he'd told her that Mr Fulton had been taken care of – that he wouldn't be hurting her anymore – she should have felt bad about it. Especially when she read the details about his death. What had happened to him.

Instead, she'd felt good about it.

And she'd wanted to feel it again.

That's why Becky had died.

And that's why Ben had died.

She'd come home that night, after they'd argued, and Harry had still been awake. He must have sensed something, because he came into her room. Heard her crying softly in the night, as their parents slept unaware.

He'd just needed a little push.

Only, this time, Mia had wanted to be there. Wanted to see it happen.

And as she'd cradled Ben's head in her lap, watching him die, she'd known that it would have gone on and on.

That unless someone had stopped Harry, he would have continued to be her protector. That he would have done anything for her.

It wasn't Ellie's fault. She might have put the ideas in his head, but he never would have done those things if it wasn't for Mia.

He'd even hurt her, in order to throw Ben's mum off the scent. It hadn't been enough, of course, but it might have worked. They weren't exactly professionals at this type of thing. Harry had been caught, with Ellie, and it was all over it seemed.

Mia was free.

And now, only Anna knew that Mia had been there.

'I knew you'd still come round,' Mia said, as they walked towards the woods. She hadn't left the house much in the previous few months – she was so aware that people knew her face. Knew what her family was now involved in. She had a big coat on, her face almost entirely covered. Still, she thought people would recognise her. Say things. She felt safe with Anna by her side. 'I can always count on you.'

'Of course,' Anna replied, slipping her arm in Mia's as they walked. 'I'd do anything for you, you know that.'

Mia held back tears, as they entered the woods. She didn't know what she'd done to deserve a friend like this.

Why Anna would help her.

'What did you do with it?' Mia asked, having waited months to finally talk about it.

'It's gone,' Anna said, with a finality that could be trusted. 'Burnt to a crisp. No one will ever know it existed.'

Mia took a breath, as they trudged through the woodland. She thought about the marks she was leaving. The boot prints, the fibres falling from her leggings. 'Do you not want to know how it happened?'

Anna stopped, turning towards her. Mia couldn't catch her eye. 'I think you were angry and tried to stop your brother when he took that to mean he should do something about it. Right?'

'Right,' Mia replied, but she caught something in Anna's expression. A knowing smile. 'That's about the jist of it.'

'That's what I thought.'

They walked a little further, until they were completely alone, in the middle of the woods. There was no sound.

If Anna was scared to be alone with her, she showed no sign of it.

'You know,' Mia said, unlinking her arm from Anna's and moving away a little. 'You never told me you thought it was Harry. Why?'

Anna shrugged her shoulders. 'Didn't think it was my place.'

'Why do you want to help me so much?'

Mia watched, as Anna thought for a few seconds. 'You're my friend. Probably my only real friend. And I take that seriously. Now, we're linked forever. There's no way we won't be in each other's lives until we're grey and old now.'

She followed that up with a small chuckle that ran ice cold through Mia's veins.

It was the wrong thing to say.

Anna knew all her little secrets. And she couldn't sleep another night with that knowledge out there.

She'd learned from Becky's death – how to make sure this wasn't treated like a murder. How to get away with it properly.

To not have these middle-aged mums running around, saying her name to everyone. Saying she was a killer.

She knew how to make sure no one knew the truth.

Harry was gone. There was no one to give that little push to anymore.

Only herself.

And as she slipped the blade down her sleeve, she wondered if this was how he'd felt.

Whether he'd known just how powerful he was.

Mia smiled.

She knew he had.

Acknowledgements

Without so many people, this book (and this career I have) wouldn't be possible. Here are just a few names I'd like to mention.

Jo Dickinson, who changed my life over a decade ago. I'll never be able to express my appreciation for what you've done for me over the years. I wouldn't want anyone else in my corner. Thank you for always believing in me.

The entire Hodder team, including Alainna Hadjigeorgiou, Alice Morley, Jake Carr, and so many, many more. Thank you so much for all your work.

My agent, Kate Burke, who continues to be a champion and guiding star. Thank you for all you do. Everyone at Blake Friedmann for their continued support and excellent work.

The QC's, Mark, Craig, Susi, Cally, and Mark – a better group of degenerate quizzers I'd be unlikely to ever meet and be able to spend time with. You're good people.

The Fun Lovin' Crime Writers – Val, Mark, Doug, Chris, and Stuart. Sharing a stage with you is one of the greatest joys in my life.

My aunty Joanne. Your resilience in the face of utter despair has been nothing short of life-altering. You're an inspiration to us all and I hope you feel the love we all have for you. We'll be here at any time, whatever you need.

The Veste family, who take a crisis and turn it into an opportunity.

Val McDermid, for being my mum. Jo Sharp for the same reason. I love you both.

Andy Veste, for being all the awesomes.

My extended family, the Woodland's, the Hale's, and the Robertson's.

All the parents, Alan, Tracy, Sue, John, Carole, and Al.

Jurgen Klopp, for the last eight years.

Marie Ennis, for being the best cousin anyone could ask for (and the only one who reads these things).

And saving the best for last, Emma, Abigail, and Megan. Bryan Adams said it best, so I won't even try to top that. I love you all and think of myself as the luckiest dad and husband there could possibly be.

THRILLINGLY GOOD BOOKS FROM CRIMINALLY GOOD WRITERS

CRIME FILES

CRIME FILES BRINGS YOU THE LATEST RELEASES FROM TOP CRIME AND THRILLER AUTHORS.

SIGN UP ONLINE FOR OUR MONTHLY NEWSLETTER AND BE THE FIRST TO KNOW ABOUT OUR COMPETITIONS, NEW BOOKS AND MORE.

VISIT OUR WEBSITE: WWW.CRIMEFILES.CO.UK
LIKE US ON FACEBOOK: FACEBOOK.COM/CRIMEFILES
FOLLOW US ON TWITTER: @CRIMEFILESBOOKS